CU00703861

Main Character hides his Strength
Book 2: Demon Realm

Main Character hides his Strength series

In reading order-

Enemy of the World
Demon Realm

Main Character hides his Strength
Book 2: Demon Realm

Roadwarrior

Oppatranslations

Oppatranslations, LLC.
5110 Ravenna PL NE #201
Seattle WA 98105, USA

oppatranslations.com

Translated from the Korean by Edward Ro and Minsoo Kang.
Edited by – Sahil Bansal, Luke Thompson, Ideal_Editor

First published by Oppatranslations, LLC 2020

© Roadwarrior 2016
English translation © Oppatranslations, LLC 2017

The moral right of the author and illustrator has been asserted.

All rights reserved. No part of this publication may be reproduced,
distributed, or transmitted in any form or by any means, including photocopying,
recording, or other electronic or mechanical methods, without the prior written
permission of the publisher, except in the case of brief quotations embodied in
critical reviews and certain other noncommercial uses permitted by copyright law.

Print ISBN: ISBN- 978-0-9992957-3-1

Send us feedback regarding any problems at oppatranslations@gmail.com

Our website for more novels by us https://www.oppatranslations.com/

This is a work of fiction. Names, characters, businesses, places, events and incidents are either the products of the author's imagination or used in a fictitious manner. Any resemblance to actual persons, living or dead, or actual events is purely coincidental.

Contents

Chapter 1   1
Frontlines of the Demon Realm

Chapter 2   19
Penal Unit

Chapter 3   47
Underground Kingdom

Chapter 4   70
Those who swallowed the Nahak

Chapter 5   93
Tomb of the Avian King

Chapter 6   117
The Last King

Chapter 7   144
Echoes

Chapter 8   167
The King's Request

Chapter 9   184
Crusaders of Salvation

Chapter 10   208
Invasion of the Demon Realm

Chapter 11   233
Tomb of the High Devils

Chapter 12　　　　　256
Lords of the Tower

Chapter 13　　　　　280
The Abandoned

Chapter 14　　　　　306
Order of the Iron Blood Knights

Chapter 15　　　　　330
Facing Them Alone

Chapter 16　　　　　372
Followers of Calamity

Chapter 17　　　　　394
Bid for Redemption

Chapter 18　　　　　418
Debt of Punishment

Chapter 19　　　　　440
Heading to the Demon Palace

Chapter 20　　　　　457
Hesthnius Max

Afterword　　　　　474

Chapter 1 – Frontlines of the Demon Realm

The far northern territory of the continent, the Demon Realm, was a place where fire and ice coexisted. The demons were inherently evil creatures that worshipped strength and considered deception a virtue. They were normally preoccupied in their own lands with territorial disputes, but once an undisputed champion rose among them, they would gather en masse and launch an organized invasion into the continent.

Hesthnius Max was the first true king of the demonkind in over several centuries. Known to be a hero chosen by the demon god himself, he unified the demons under his rule with overwhelming might and malicious wit, becoming the first calamity itself as prophesized by the Scripture of Calamities. However, it was not as though humans and the other races of the Other World were watching idly as the demons stirred.

The Order of the Iron Blood Knights, a body of powerful military might that was based in the Storm battlefront, stood steadfast at the northernmost border of the continent that contained the entrance to the Demon Realm. Fortifications were made along these borders like a web of chains to prevent the invasion of the demons.

The areas where the demon world and the human world met were called the Battlefronts of the Demon Realm.

"..."

Sungchul now stood upon that very place. He had stepped into the land of death, where fire and ice danced side-by-side, after having slaughtered countless demons.

So, I ended up coming back to this place. Sungchul looked at the familiar sunset with cold eyes. The expanse of land was an eyesore filled with a desolate gloom that hung in the air. There was a thunderous roar to the north followed by a slight trembling of the earth. The stench of sulphur carried by the wind tickled his nose.

Sungchul climbed the slope of a mountain and headed toward human territory.

"What are you going to do now?" Bertelgia tossed the question into the air from her place in his pocket.

Sungchul walked in strides as he answered, "After a break, I'll go back to the Demon Realm to fight against the devils."

There were a lot of options, but Sungchul wanted to personally test the magic he had obtained from Airfruit. He wanted to know how effective he was against the devils as a mage. His policy was to determine his limits and weaknesses to properly gauge his growth.

Sungchul climbed midway up a rocky mountain facing a frozen sea. From a distance, it had looked like just one of the many rocky mountains, but it had blackened traces and firewood hidden underneath an ashen cloth along with several pieces of iron scraps of indeterminable purpose, all indicating that someone had been here.

He began to grab some firewood along with the iron scraps lying around, as though it was his own home, to fashion himself a decent cooking pot. This place had been one of his campsites in the past. Sungchul, who was welcomed by neither humans nor demons, had created several hideouts along the various Demon Realm Battlefronts to rotate and find some rest. Of course, he created his favourite dishes here too.

He approached a massive boulder blocking a cave beyond the camp. It had no sign of intrusion. Only some small bugs called Demon Lice ran off in surprise. Sungchul took a deep breath and gripped the massive boulder with both hands. He didn't need things like handles.

CRUMBLE!

Anywhere his fingers sunk became handles. Sungchul waited briefly with his fingers embedded directly into the boulder until he suddenly lifted it.

"...It's not even that shocking anymore." Bertelgia flapped in the vicinity while staring blankly at the scene.

THUD!

The boulder blocking the cave was moved slightly to the side. The blunt shock that had enough force to cause a slight tremor on the ground could be felt beneath Sungchul's feet.

He brought out a piece of wood that had been burning underneath the pot and used it as a torch to enter the newly opened cave. The cave was filled with various pieces of pottery made of clay; fermentation pots made by Sungchul's own hands.

Sungchul found a pot among several pots that had been left to the side with a large stone pressing down on top. He tossed the stone to the side and opened the container. Within the pot was a plant root about the size of a human child that had been pickled bright red. Sungchul's mouth began to water.

"T-That is the Mandragora?!" Bertelgia, who had eventually followed him into the cave, saw the mysterious plant within the pot and shouted in surprise.

Sungchul nodded. "There is no better delicacy than Kimchi made of this little guy."

He pulled off a leaf of the pickled Mandragora kimchi and savoured the flavour in his mouth.

[The Score of this Recipe is… 12 points!]

The score was rubbish, but the taste within Sungchul's mouth was grander than any delicacy.

"Mm." He closed his eyes and savoured the taste for a bit while Bertelgia hurried out of the cave muttering to herself, "My god… to make some weird food out of that precious thing…"

Sungchul cooked some soaked rice in the cooking pot. There was no need for any other side dish. He ate his bowl of rice and the pickled Mandragora with the scenery of the Demon Realm before him.

After eating his fill, he sat on a flat piece of rock and closed his eyes. The sulphur-infused breeze that flowed through the Demon Realm lightly brushed his hair. He opened his eyes after a bit of rest, rose from his seat, and made his way deeper into the land of the demons.

***

The lower ranking demons blocked Sungchul's path as he approached the corridor connected to the Demon realm. These were a lower species known as imps that looked like hairless monkeys, and all they had in their thick skulls were gluttony and evil.

"Kyiiii!"

The imps made a threatening gesture with their pitchfork by feigning a stabbing motion in the air.

"Uuu...I hate those things." Bertelgia, who had returned to her normal size, flew off to some high perch where the imps could not reach her. Sungchul scowled at the approaching imps and extended his finger.

Glare

Out of his fingertip, a beam of light burst forth toward the body of one of the imps.

"Kyiiii!" The imp who had been hit thrashed about wildly before his body became charred. The imps who had been making empty threats suddenly rushed toward Sungchul together.

SWISH! SWISH!

The rusted pitchforks flew toward Sungchul's body. He dodged the spears with little effort and repeatedly fired off Glare multiple times.

SIZZLE~ SIZZLE~

The imps who had been pierced by the light hobbled about before dying. After he had consecutively killed ten imps, the imps who had been full of spirit began to hesitate. Sungchul knew the reason why. *It is finally making an appearance.*

THUD!

The earth began to crack, and something came forth from below. With a height of about five meters till its revealed torso, it was a large demon with the odd appearance of a fish head and the body of a man.

"Kyaaaa!"

A Deep Sea Demon. They were one of the gatekeepers guarding the entrance to the Demon Realm. The only reason why Sungchul had bothered to kill the worthless imps was to call out this fellow.

This demon race from the depths below had the intelligence of a fish, but they were infamous for their powerful strength and dexterity along with their incredible vitality. If he could kill one of these monsters that even the mages of the Royal Court could not overcome, Sungchul judged that he would be able to do meaningful damage to Hesthnius Max.

"Kyaaaaaa!!"

The still half-buried Deep Sea Demon let out an earth shattering roar. The bellow of the beast scattered the remaining imps who ran amok and disappeared into the narrow caves, leaving Sungchul alone with the Deep Sea Demon.

Its empty fish eyes glared at Sungchul until it suddenly raised its arm into the air to strike him down.

SLAM!

As the fist covered in scales struck the ground, the earth shook with the impact as it shattered the surface, launching rubble in the air.

Bertelgia, who had suddenly attached herself to Sungchul's back, spoke in a meek voice. "Hey, shouldn't we escape?"

"..."

However, Sungchul wasn't going to heed her advice; he took another step forward.

"Uuuh... it might not even be enough to have ten lives if you're with this person." Bertelgia resigned to being in the safest place, Sungchul's pocket, and shrunk down to a compact size as though she was throwing up her hands.

How long will this work? thought Sungchul. He didn't have great expectations. He realised that his Magic Power didn't exceed 200, and the magic he was truly in command of was only of the third circle. The reason he was battling with this demon anyway was to witness his limits with his own two eyes. Sungchul then began to move.

The fish's eyes continued to track his path. Sungchul dashed beside it and extended a finger toward the Sea Demon.

Glare

A beam of light akin to a spear stretched out from the tip of his finger and targeted the demon's arm.

SIZZLE-

A dark smoke rose from the Sea Demon's flesh, but that was it.

"Gyaaaa!!" the Deep Sea Demon let out a roar before swinging its arm in a frenzy to attack Sungchul.

SLAM! SLAM! SLAM!

The ground shook, and the earth exploded like a fountain. But such an attack from the Deep Sea Demon was meaningless to Sungchul. He continued to evade lazily, as though he was on a picnic, and dodged all of its attacks while continuing to experiment with his only offensive magic on various body parts of the Deep Sea Demon: arms, legs, torso, face, then eyes.

SIZZLE-

The Deep Sea Demon's eyes were seared with a beam of light, but as the fish's eyelids blinked from the bottom-up, Sungchul's attack was easily negated.

It is still too early.

He knew this, but the fact that he couldn't even manage to scratch the creature was a depressing thought. He needed a stronger magic. He retreated for now.

The Deep Sea Demon roared in the distance and continued to pound the earth. Whether that was a roar of victory or a threatening gesture born of instinct, Sungchul didn't know.

"Hey, Bertelgia." Sungchul forcefully dragged Bertelgia from his pocket.

"Hear not! See not!" Bertelgia appeared as though she had clenched her eyes and shut her ears, although it was questionable whether a book could do such things.

"Pay attention." When Sungchul shook her a few times, she regained her senses and looked at her surroundings.

"Huh? What about the fish-face?"

"Over there," said Sungchul as he pointed toward the Deep Sea Demon howling in the distance.

Bertelgia slid down Sungchul's hand as though she was melting in relief and let out a sigh. "I wish you'd stop with the dangerous games."

"It's not dangerous at all. More than that, I have something to ask you."

"About what?"

"Is there any Alchemy quest that you're aware of that can raise Magic Power by a large margin?"

"Alchemy quest?" Bertelgia, who had been drooping against his palm, suddenly perked up and exploded into her original size. She also fluttered before Sungchul with vigour and spoke in a different voice. "Are you saying that you're prepared to walk the path of the Creationist?"

"Creationist or whatever is fine. I just need a quest that can bump up my Magic Power."

It wasn't the time for beggars to be choosers. Sungchul was prepared to do anything it took for him to accomplish his goal, even if it were the Alchemy-related quests that don't appear to have any direct connection to the objective.

Bertelgia floated in the air in thought, then spoke without much confidence. "Mmm... There aren't many that you can do in your state."

"Is that right?"

"You're too inexperienced, even if you've created a 5th level Alchemic item. I'd recommend making every Alchemic item below the 4th level at least once."

"How many are there in total that qualify?"

"82 items."

It was a bleak number.

"Mm. I'll take back my previous request." Sungchul gave up on it without any hesitation, but the one who jumped up was Bertelgia.

"Hey! Wait a minute! You've made 12 items below 4th level so far. You just need to synthesise about 70 more!"

"That's still too many."

"It's not that many! Not that many at all! It can be easily accomplished if you make a habit of practicing Alchemy in your daily life!"

"Mmm…" Sungchul didn't look convinced, but he decided it might not be bad to follow Bertelgia's advice.

If I synthesize successfully, my Magic Power and Intuition will naturally rise by a small amount. It might not be bad to try one or two on a daily basis as a change of pace.

Sungchul thought to use every method possible. However, anything relating to Alchemy was more of a secondary objective. He decided to seek out a certain man after his fight with the Deep Sea Demon: Sarasa's father. The man going by the alias Deckard. It wasn't clear what level of mage he truly was, but what was clear was that he was not someone average, as he was the son of the mighty Altugius. It was said that he was looking for a method to stop the Calamity. He had to have been desperate to seek out ways to hone his own strength. That is… if he was anything like Sungchul was eight years ago.

I think Altugius said that he was active as a mercenary mage along the Storm Battlefront?

The Storm Battlefront. It was a shaky alliance created out of desperation that formed one of the three major factions of the northern continent. Unlike other factions, the Storm Battlefront was mainly comprised of dwarves who used their peerless dwarven architecture to create a powerful network of fortifications to block any possible demon invasion. They also have been known to have surpassed the withered Order of the Iron Blood Knights as the most powerful faction in the north.

The problem was that Sungchul had poor relations with the dwarves, because he had stolen Fal Garaz, an item revered as a divine artifact, from their temple.

At the very least, this isn't somewhere I can use my real name, thought Sungchul.

Dwarves had a historic tradition of recording those that sinned against them in a book of grudges. The name that took the first line of this book of grudges was none other than Sungchul Kim.

***

"What kind of alias would suit me?" Even Sungchul had moments where he couldn't help but worry. He began to think deeply about the alias he would use when he arrived on the frontline. It seemed like a childish concern, but it meant something to him. He believed that a name held power.

For instance, the name "Sungchul" was possibly the most widely-known name in this world. It had a weight of its own. But if he were to use other names, such as Ahram Park or Krill Regall? He would be considered nothing more than Generic Minion A.

"How about Eckheart?" Bertelgia had been watching Sungchul's deliberation from the side and offered her opinion.

"I refuse." He flatly rejected it, and Bertelgia's color briefly turned red. He narrowed his options down to three, then etched them into a rock with his fingertip: Esper Kim, Chulin Kim, and Fabre Kim.

"Oooo…." Bertelgia let out a taunt.

"Something wrong?"

"Something's very wrong. What the heck is Fabre? You sound like someone that never had any friends!"

"It's the name of a scholar more famous than your father."

"Don't say such things. Anyways, all three options are bad."

Sungchul's eyes lit up. "What's the issue?"

"Why do all the names have Kim? Can't you just forget the Kim? What do you think you're using an alias for? Isn't it to hide your identity?" Bertelgia said everything she wanted to say despite fluttering about wildly.

"…"

Sungchul grew quiet. He knew that Bertelgia wasn't full of nonsense.

"If you got nothing, then pick something mage-like. I thought you were going to go to the Storm Battlefront or something as a mage anyways?"

"More accurately an alchemist first and mage second," responded Sungchul.

"Then a name with an S or T at the end would work! I don't know why, but famous mage names usually end with S or T."

After hearing her suggestion, Sungchul immediately added an S and removed the Kim. He added three more names for a total of six names in the rock: Espers, Chulins, Fabres, Espert, Chulint, and Fabret. Sungchul rubbed his chin as he muttered the names to himself to check how they sounded.

On the other end, Bertelgia was fuming. "Why are you so attached to those three names? All three are awful!"

"In the end, I think they all sound better than Eckheart?"

"Ugh. Good for you. Really. Why not just use a name from the Seven Heroes at this point?"

"The Seven Heroes?" A strange light flashed in his eyes. The names of the Seven Heroes weren't that well known, but their names had significant weight since the past. Sungchul began to recall their names in his head.

Desfort, the leader of the Seven Heroes. Dragoman, one who reached the peak with swords. Daltanius, pursuer of endless strength. Sajators, the mage of multicast. White Shadow, the assassin without a record. Vestiare, the Echo Mage. Ga Xi Ong, the Devourer of Souls. Which name among these should be chosen?

"I choose White Shadow," said Sungchul after briefly giving it a thought.

"White Shadow? That weirdo who wraps himself with that white cloth thing?"

"You've seen White Shadow?"

"Yea, but only from a distance. I haven't even heard him speak. He's a lunatic like the other Seven Heroes and writes instead of using his perfectly good tongue to communicate."

"I see. How did you manage to meet him though?"

He knew that Bertelgia and Eckheart were from the same era as the Seven Heroes. However, there was no guarantee that these people would ever meet just because they lived in the same period. Especially since the Seven Heroes were top of the elite during their era. But Bertelgia immediately replied without hesitation.

"The Seven Heroes were regulars at Dad's shop. They always ordered a bunch of stuff before they left for battle."

"Hoh... is that right?"

"Yep. That's why my dad called himself the Eighth Hero."

"What did the Seven Heroes usually buy?"

"Well, I was really young, so I don't remember much, but it was mostly potions like Elixir and high firepower Alchemic Bomb. The bratty kid mage and the bitchy woman bought Mana Essence and Dark Crystal."

"Could I make those with my ability right now?"

"You could make some, but not others."

Sungchul nodded at her assessment. He felt amused by Alchemy, but he was getting fed up with making useless alchemy items. But if the items were good enough to be regularly used by even the Seven Heroes, then from a manufacturing standpoint, Sungchul might be able to tackle the creation process with a sense of ambition.

I think it might help if I synthesise things every now and then to raise my alchemy technique and knowledge as she suggested. They might be good for me.

He chose the name and his goal and descended from the wild rocky mountain moving toward the stronghold.

***

The Battlefront of the Demon Realm was largely divided into four regions. The first region was the flat plain to the west that was mostly a wasteland. This region contained the most conflicts out of the four regions and was occupied by the Order of the Iron Blood Knights. They utilized the high mobility of their mighty Mobile Fortresses and the strength of their powerful knights to defend their territory.

The second region was a mountainous area with rugged mountain ranges that had the appearance of folding screens. This territory was a part of Storm Battlefront. The Dwarves, who call themselves children of the mountains, built impregnable fortresses all over the mountainside, squashing any desire for the demons to try and invade them.

The next region was a sea of trees underneath the mountain range. This region was occupied by an alliance of Elves called the Varan-Aran. Antagonising these people was like making an enemy of the forest itself. There were no records of hostile demons surviving the forest.

The final region was located behind the other three, called the Backline. This region that can't exactly be called the frontlines was occupied by the allied air fleet of the Human Empire, mercenaries of the Allied Merchant's Guild, the Sword Masters of the Ancient Kingdom, and a reserve force composed of various units sent by supporting factions. Marquis Martin Breggas, a former Sixth Champion of the Continent, was assigned to lead and manage the combined forces gathered there. Sungchul picked Trowyn, a city within the Backline, as his destination.

The reason he didn't head directly to the Storm Battlefront was simple. The Backline was where most people congregated, and it was known that all information regarding the frontlines flowed through here. More than anything, the recruitment of mercenaries occurred here too. The free city of Trowyn was the busiest area of the Backline and was most apt for Sungchul's needs.

"..."

Sungchul arrived at the walls of Trowyn at early morning. However, the city guards were unusually grim. The city borders were ceaselessly patrolled by packs of werewolf soldiers and knights on gryphons were looking down from the skies.

Sungchul could force his entry, but he didn't wish to attract such attention to himself at this place. He would go through proper channels if he could manage it. After coming to this decision, he hid within a field of reeds and observed the situation. He overheard conversations from merchants, housewives, and soldiers until midday and got a grasp of the situation within the city.

There was only one reason the city was on full alert: It was the Enemy of the World. It was known that the Enemy of the World had left for the Demon Realm, so notices requesting high alert with the authority of each ruler had been spread throughout the frontlines as it couldn't be predicted when the Enemy of the World will appear again.

"Really. What did you do that made everyone hate you so much?" Bertelgia asked, exasperated.

"I did cause some problems. I emptied a vault, stole a hammer, destroyed a Royal Palace, and killed a rotten prince..."

"Wait, now that I'm listening to all this, it doesn't really sound like a little?"

When Bertelgia retorted, Sungchul shook his head and continued, "Those things were inconsequential. First and foremost, the real reason why they resent me is because I am powerful. Next, it is because I disagree with their ideas. A good mixture of the two created this level of fear and resentment."

Sungchul pulled out an outfit from the Soul Storage. It was a worn-out brown coat and military pants that had become grey as its colours faded away. Sungchul pulled off the clothes he had been wearing without thought and changed into his new outfit.

Bertelgia made a serious request while he changed. "Ugh. Even if I am a book, I am a maiden at heart so I'd appreciate it if you didn't just strip naked without warning."

Of course, Sungchul didn't give her plea a second thought. "Isn't it enough to just close your eyes?"

Sungchul put on a snap-buttoned plaid shirt over his muscled body.

"Mmm…" No matter how you look at it, the plaid shirt looked bad. It must have turned out like this because he had been stealing the clothes of the Summoned at the Golden City before entering the Summoning Palace without checking them. Sungchul ripped the shirt off and buried it before pulling out another shirt of a similar style.

"Mmm." He had been trying to put in some effort behind it, but his outfit hadn't progressed an inch from his hobo appearance.

"Wouldn't the clothes of a Summoned stand out?" Bertelgia flew around Sungchul once and judged his outfit.

Sungchul shook his head. "There are several groups of Summoned that purposely try to wear styles of clothes similar to their original world's."

"Why?"

"It is to avoid losing their distinct identity even after coming to this world. Well, a lot of the people that choose to keep the clothes from their original world often choose the path of a Returnee."

A bitter memory passed by Sungchul's eyes. *If only she had chosen to return, all of this could have been avoided.*

The past was the past. Sungchul brushed the memory aside and looked onto the main road.

"Anyway, how will you get into the city? I don't think they'll just let you in."

"How many people do you think come in and out of Trowyn? It's thousands, if not tens of thousands, of people. It's not easy for a couple of guards to inspect all of them."

Sungchul stood on the side of the main road and waited for a wagon en-route to the city. It didn't take long for such a wagon to appear.

It was a transport wagon with a forgettable old man, pulled by a pair of old and skinny horses. Sungchul carefully looked at the wagon before he let it pass.

"Why did you let that one go? I think you'd be safe if you hid in the stuff at the back."

Bertelgia spoke from his pocket, but Sungchul just shook his head.

"The worse the cart and its driver look, the stricter the inspection."

Sungchul let several more wagons pass until a massive stagecoach pulled by a team of eight angelic horses, the Pegasi, approached from the distance. Seeing that the stagecoach was pulled by pegasi and it had a floatation stone instead of wheels meant that it was a high-class stagecoach capable of flight.

"Hmm. That one looks like someone with some money would be riding it?"

Sungchul nodded at Bertelgia's words and blocked its path.

"Could I get a ride? It is quite bothersome to walk all that distance," said Sungchul as he handed out a single silver coin to the driver.

The driver let out a laugh and shot Sungchul a cold glare. "Do you think you can ride this stagecoach with just a single silver coin? Get out of the way!"

He raised the whip in order to move the carriage, but Sungchul pulled out something different. The driver's eyes changed. It was because a shiny gold coin was held in front of him.

"I don't quite know the value of goods very well yet, is this enough?" said Sungchul.

The driver looked at him once again.

Sungchul looked like a typical Summoned on the outside. He looked pitiful, but his appearance was that of a young man in his twenties or thirties. The driver had recently heard of the existence of the Preselected among the Summoned who received privileged treatment upon their arrival to the Other World. *Is he one of those idiots? Whatever, I can just earn some coin.*

Finally, he received the coin and carefully examined its surface. Where there was supposed to be a mark for the mint, it was etched with the marking of the Human Empire foundry.

It's clean, thought the driver.

There was an order trickling down from above: *Report anyone with an unmarked coin to a superior officer.* It was a task not even a horse driver of the transportation company affiliated with the Allied Merchant's Guild could forgo. Also, the coin was confirmed to be without problems. There was no reason for the driver to reject Sungchul.

"Open the second door and get on. Don't bother the other guests."

Sungchul excused himself before entering the cabin. When Sungchul opened the door to the cabin, Bertelgia whispered in a quiet voice, "It looks like you've done this before?"

"..."

Sungchul didn't confirm nor deny it. The cabin was more or less empty. The only guests were a middle-aged noblewoman with a fan made of the tail feathers of a rare bird, a man of sophisticated airs reading a book with a monocle, and a stubborn-looking male dwarf whose feet didn't quite reach the wagon floor. It was just these three. They glanced over at Sungchul as he stepped onto the coach, but didn't make much of it. However, Sungchul could see a hint of revulsion on their faces, especially the noblewoman.

"We're departing." The coach left on a relatively light note. Green farmlands could be seen outside the window as they passed the rural villages of the border on their way to the castle gates.

There was a formation of five guards examining the coaches as they entered.

Due to the slight angling of the road, Sungchul was just barely able to watch a wagon undergo the inspection through the window. The one currently being searched was the rickety load-bearing wagon ridden by the old horseman that he had just allowed to pass. Four guards surrounded him as they stood beside the wagon's load with their tridents in hand. Bertelgia squirmed at the sight as though she was on the wagon herself.

Soon, the head gatekeeper's commanding voice roared, "Commence Special Search!"

As soon as his order fell, the four guards began to stab away at the bale of hay with their tridents with fearsome vigor.

"Hundred Spear Thrust!"

It was an inspection that would not only make a pincushion of anyone inside, but shred them to pieces as well. Sungchul stroked Bertelgia in his pocket and quietly whispered to her. "Do you get it now?"

Bertelgia shook her body lightly. Soon, the turn for the coach that Sungchul was riding came. Unlike the previous search, the guards and the gatekeeper had a completely different attitude. They didn't even dare to open up the coach door, and only spoke to the coach driver. After a few words from the driver, the gatekeeper nodded and gestured to let them through.

"Pass!"

The noblewoman's face grew ugly, but she didn't make any further actions. She had decided that exercising her patience a bit longer was less effort than reporting the repulsive man. Thankfully, this allowed Sungchul safe entry into the town center of Trowyn. It was an economic result at the expense of some time and a gold coin.

Sungchul, after arriving at the town center, entered into the back alleys to seek out an information broker. He inquired between several information brokers to find the one who had his finger on the pulse of the battlefield. The one who met the qualifications was a disabled veteran missing an eye and a leg. Sungchul held out several silver coins and asked a question.

"I am seeking a mercenary mage by the name of Deckard."

"Deckard?" The former soldier looked up at him with his remaining eye. When Sungchul nodded, the man let out a sigh before speaking again. "If the Deckard you speak of is the mercenary mage affiliated with the Storm Battlefront, he is probably... well... he's most likely dead by now."

"What does that mean?"

"He committed a crime and got assigned to the Penal Unit."

Chapter 2 – Penal Unit

It was a common occurrence for soldiers of both private and state armies who have committed a crime to be assigned to dangerous missions to absolve themselves. However, the Demon Realm Battlefront was unlike other battlefields in the sense that the repercussions were significant and the enemies were existences to be feared. The ratio of deserters was significantly higher than other battlefields which made strict military discipline a requirement. The Penal Unit was one of the measures set forth to maintain the frontlines of the Demon Realm.

The soldiers of the Demon Realm Battlefront treated being assigned to the Penal Unit as a death sentence. It was because the casualty rate was at 90%, but as far as anyone could tell, the 90% was only a statistic, and most Penal Units resolved such mistakes with a wipeout. As someone who had served on the frontlines of the Demon Realm the longest, there was no way that Sungchul didn't know this.

"What is the Penal Unit?"

Sungchul responded to Bertelgia's question with a brief answer. "A fish on a chopping block."

Sungchul followed the road to the recruitment centre to put in a request as a mercenary. As the battlefront always had a need for soldiers, their background check was considerably loose. The mercenaries that came to the frontlines were almost always criminals or debtors escaping their debts. Being stringent with the check would only reduce the amount of soldiers that were willing to fight on the frontlines.

"What will be your branch of service?" a recruitment officer with a grotesque scar in the shape of a devil's claw across his face asked the question with a grave voice.

"Mage," answered Sungchul.

"There are more than a few type of mages… do you specialise in Dimensional magic? Supporting magic? Combat specialist?"

"Combat." Sungchul then added one more thing. "Alchemy."

"What good is Alchemy… Just forget about that one unless you want to be stuck in a factory pumping out potions."

"…"

When the military branch was selected, the recruitment officer asked regarding his preferred frontline. Of course, the battlefront the officer suggested was the most dangerous one.

"How about the battlefront supervised by the Varan-Aran Tribal Alliance? It's a good opportunity to get close to some pretty elf women."

"I'm sorry, but I can't get it up."

"Oh… that's quite awful."

"I want to go to the Storm Battlefront."

"Storm Battlefront… well, it might be better for a man with a condition such as yours to end up in a place full of dwarves."

The matter got wrapped up at a rapid pace. Sungchul got dispatched to the Storm Battlefront as a mercenary mage. The location that he was dispatched to was a small fortress known as the Black Hills, but that didn't matter because he caused trouble from the very first day he arrived.

"White Shadow! I hereby transfer you to the Penal Unit for violence toward a superior officer, insubordination, and destruction of property!"

After the order was passed down, Sungchul had a cloth with the number 34 written on it forcibly attached to his ragged coat.

"What's this?"

At Sungchul's question, the soldier who was sewing it onto him answered curtly, "What do you mean what's this? It's your prisoner number."

Sungchul was swiftly sent to the Penal Unit at the forefront. It was even decided that he was to be transported by a gryphon.

The rider of the gryphon laughed loudly as he dropped Sungchul off. "This will be your burial grounds. Recruit, it is suitable for idiots like you that fuck up on day 1!"

"…"

"I might be back in about two weeks. Let's see if you're still alive by then!" said the rider as the gryphon blew up a storm as it ascended into the sky and headed north. Sungchul looked around his surroundings. There were several tents that appeared to belong to the Penal Unit visible in the sunken portion of a high elevation basin. Sungchul compared the number of tents with the number of wood-burning stoves to estimate their headcount.

Approximately 300 people?

However, the number was revealed to be closer to a hundred members. They told him that they had suffered heavy casualties that cost them half of their members in a major battle recently.

The vice-captain of the Penal Unit, Genghis Aaron, was a middle-aged man that looked as ferocious and agile as a panther. He appeared as though he could hold his own in a fight, and it reflected his ability. He was a former Sword Master of the Ancient Kingdom in the ranks of Superhuman who had over 300 points each in Strength, Dexterity, and Endurance. However, his nickname within the Penal Unit was Rockhead. He was a pure idiot who didn't even know simple addition and subtraction.

"Welcome, number 34. To the Penal Unit that is."

"…"

Genghis quickly scanned through the documents that Sungchul brought with his eyes before speaking in what sounded like a mutter.

"Now let's see here… Assault of a superior officer and insubordination… with a bit of property damage for fun? Let me just have you know one thing." Rockhead smirked and pulled out his blade part-way.

SRRRNG.

The unusual blade wrapped in a violet light revealed itself.

"Insubordination before me means beheading."

"…"

When he was done reporting in, a stumpy dwarf approached Sungchul. "Are you done reporting in, number 34?"

On the chest plate of the dwarf who was wearing full plate armor despite not being in the middle of battle was attached a cloth with the number 0 written.

"Who might you be?"

"I am the oldest veteran of the Penal Unit, 'Hell Fist' Arkaard." Arkaard showed Sungchul the fist that he was so proud of. The steel gauntlet wrapped around his fingers sparkled with the engraved words 'Hell Fist'. "However, just call me number 0. That's the Penal Unit tradition!"

"..."

"Anyways… there are no officers here, commissioned or not. There were both in the past, but they all ate shit during our last battle."

"I'm looking for a mercenary mage by the name of Deckard," said Sungchul.

"Deckard? Ah, are you talking about number 22?" Arkaard's face lost composure for a moment.

"Does he happen to be dead?" Sungchul immediately followed up with another question, but Arkaard shook his head.

"He's alive."

It was a relief. Bertelgia shook her body with joy in Sungchul's stead.

"But, that friend will not live much longer."

"Did he receive a critical wound?"

Arkaard shook his head once again.

"No, he continues to volunteer himself to the most dangerous missions. It's as though he came to this place to die."

"I wish to meet him at least once. Where can I find him?"

Arkaard pointed toward a particular tent. It was a cosy tent placed next to a pointed rock that looked like the blade of a spear. Sungchul displayed the appropriate amount of formality before excusing himself and headed toward the tent that Deckard was supposedly residing in.

He could hear the sound of blades clashing and ragged breaths being drawn near the tent. It was the sound of two men sparring. One was wielding a sword while the other wielded a staff, and they were sparring with such intensity as if they were fighting on the battlefield itself.

The one wielding the sword ended in victory, and the one with the staff dropped his weapon and fell onto his butt while sighing loudly.

"Isn't this enough, Deckard?" asked the sword wielder.

Sungchul's sights turned toward the man referred to as Deckard. He was well past middle age, but his face still had remnants of youth. He looked more like Sarasa than Altugius.

The man looked too tired to even lift his own body, yet he called out for another challenge. The one wielding the sword firmly declined. "I'd rather not exhaust myself before a battle. We never know when we're going to be sent in, so let's just call it quits here."

After the spar ended, the onlookers scattered. Sungchul waited for the onlookers to disappear before he approached Deckard who was standing by himself.

"Are you Deckard?"

Deckard, who was still breathing quite heavily, looked up toward Sungchul. "Who are you? I don't think I've seen you before?"

Sungchul handed him the item he had received from Altugius. Deckard's face lit up in surprise.

"How did you get a hold of this?"

"Professor Altugius sends me to you. He told me to seek you if I sought to raise my Magic Power substantially within the shortest amount of time."

"Ah, you've voluntarily come to the Penal Unit for such a purpose?"

"There is no time to be picky about the method."

"Could I take a look at your stats then?"

Sungchul agreed to Deckard's request. Deckard pulled out a scroll, which he ripped apart, then he looked at Sungchul's stats. Laughter soon exploded from his mouth.

"What a reckless man. It's probably not my place to say this on our first meeting, but isn't it excessive to come to the frontlines of the Demon Realm with only that level of stats? With your current stats, forget getting stronger; you'd only get in the way." Deckard harshly criticised Sungchul.

"Since I am already here, isn't going back no longer an option?" replied Sungchul.

Sungchul had received the order to complete five missions under the Penal Unit. If he left the Penal Unit before completing this order, he would be considered as a deserter. Sungchul was referring to this fact.

Deckard simply looked indifferent. He put on the shirt dangling under the tent and spoke again. "The only reason I have come here is to push myself to my limits. It was for the express purpose of cultivating fast growth that I have constantly placed myself in dangerous and difficult-to-overcome situations. Such as the man now called the Enemy of the World had done."

Deckard would never know, even in his wildest dreams, that the man he spoke of as the Enemy of the World was standing right before him. He continued speaking, "It's not really a boast, but I have built this body through considerable training to be a powerful mage and warrior. Thanks to this, I was able to preserve at least my life through many dire situations during my missions. How about you? I would imagine it'd be difficult to survive."

"If I do survive?" Sungchul retorted in a calm voice. "If I do survive, will you impart what you know to me?"

Deckard looked deep into Sungchul's face, then spoke curtly. "Rockhead is planning something stupid for tomorrow right at this moment. Try and survive that. If you do, I shall share with you a quest you might be able to complete."

***

The next day.

As Deckard had said, Rockhead gathered all the members of the unit. Eighty lifers had gathered, excluding the injured. He stood on a podium and spoke in a uselessly heroic voice.

"As you all know, the demon scouts have taken over a particular guard post affiliated with our Storm Battlefront. That guard post itself doesn't have much importance, but what matters is its location. Headquarters says that we must recapture that guard post regardless of cost."

He then spoke of his plan next.

"Currently, our numbers are at eighty-three members. Twenty in the north, twenty in the east, twenty in the west, and the remaining members will come with me and attack the fortification from the south."

Surprisingly, that was the entire plan. Rockhead didn't impart any idea on how each designated unit will coordinate with each other or move at all. He only had an attack from every side on his mind. "If we attack from every side, the demons will not be able to endure it!"

It was truly a thoughtless plan, but no one dared to say another word. The fact that Rockhead was feared for his strength was one thing, but they also knew that he wasn't a man to be reasoned with.

Rockhead soon divided all of the troops into four, and veteran soldiers were designated as the leaders for each group. Each group, composed of a unit of twenty, was given a magic scroll for signalling, and their march toward death began.

Sungchul entered the unit designated as the third group. The strategy went along relatively smoothly, and the Penal Unit arrived at the guard post with no major issues. They then encircled the guard post containing the demons.

"Let us go, my fellow brethren of sin!" shouted Rockhead with his blade held high.

UWOOONG–

A bluish aura emanated from the violet-tinted blade. It was the speciality of a Sword Master: Sword Aura. He stood at the front to lead the attack.

"Follow me! Let us all be atoned!"

The demons stationed on the guard post were mostly weaklings, and their numbers were few. Rockhead scaled the post wall and climbed onto the watch tower. The demons could do nothing but be helplessly slain by his blade. The guard post was recaptured quite easily with no casualties. It was all over before the eastern and northern groups could even begin their attack.

"Isn't this too easy?"

The veteran soldiers felt a terrible premonition. The all-important strategic point had been hollowed out with nothing but bait. If the demons intended to defend the guard post, there would be a Balroq at the very least or a Baal-grade demon or two, but only feeble goblins and imps were stationed at the guard post.

The soldiers felt a sense of Deja Vu. The situation unfolding in the current moment seemed extremely similar to the last battle, one where half of the Penal Unit had fallen in a tragic combat.

Finally, the most veteran soldier among them, Arkaard, advised Rockhead, "Commander, I think the demons gave up the guard post a bit too easily. It reeks of a trap. It might be good to fall back for now and watch their movements."

This head of rock wasn't one to listen to reason. He instead raged at Arkaard and criticised him. "What kind of pussy talk is that? Number 0! Can you call yourself a Penal Unit member after such talk?"

"But… it just doesn't feel right. Didn't we lose half of our unit in a similar fashion during the last battle?"

Normal people would feel discouraged after experiencing such utter defeat, but Rockhead wasn't as such. He spoke boldly without a hint of shame on his face. "Even if this was the trap of those demons, we must hold our ground!"

He went a step further and gathered all forces, and gave a rousing speech with a voice filled with determination.

"Our mission is to secure the guard post until the main forces arrive. The first stage has been completed successfully. All that is left is to hold this guard post until our lives are spent. Hold your grounds, my brothers!"

Deckard, who heard the speech, let out a frosty retort. "I don't recall having such a brother."

Sungchul was in agreement, and soon the gut feeling became a reality. Five soldiers deserted. One of the deserters was caught by Rockhead and hung as an example, but that was only the beginning. When the sun fell, signs of demons began to appear from all over. The scouts continuously brought ill news.

"Objects suspected to be Hell Siege Engines detected! Approaching from the north!"

"A swarm of imps suspected to be in the hundreds climbing the mountain ridge and approaching from the west."

"One Balroq confirmed! More than two Baal-grades approaching as well."

When darkness fell, the Penal Unit, composed of about eighty members, was surrounded by devils and demonfolk in the thousands.

"Didn't I tell you? It's not so easy surviving in this place." Deckard spoke in a silence appropriate for the Storm Battlefront after approaching Sungchul. He handed Sungchul a single scroll. It was a long-distance teleportation scroll.

"If you rip this scroll, you'll be teleported to the orange-tinted mountaintop that is the Penal Unit headquarters."

"Why are you giving this to me?" Sungchul bluntly threw out his question.

Deckard simply scratched his head. "You seem to have Alchemist within your classes. If the situation seems disadvantageous, just rip the scroll, bow down to the Storm Battlefront liaison, and beg for forgiveness. An alchemist can be pardoned for his crime and be pulled out of the Penal Unit in exchange for forced labor at a potion factory. Isn't it better working to the bone for two years than dying?"

It appeared as though Deckard had been giving Sungchul a lot of consideration. However, his concerns were misplaced. Sungchul returned the scroll and asked another question in a calm voice, "The promise from before. Is it still valid?"

Deckard only smiled bitterly. "It's valid."

Deckard let out a sigh before leaving Sungchul. Not long after he left, the sound of drumming could be heard. It was the drums of the demonfolk. The shrill sound of a bone horn followed soon after that, sharply tearing through the air. The demonic forces soon began their attack.

***

The war machine made of steel in the shape of a gigantic scorpion spat out green flames from the tip of its tail. Hell Siege Engines were frequently used by Demon forces during large-scale sieges. The cackling of demons echoed in the dry air as the Hell Siege Engines spat out flames. The magic cannon of the devils installed on the portion of the Siege Engine which resembled the mouth of a scorpion shot out green fireballs that drew an arc in the night sky as they struck the walls of the guard post.

BOOM!

The entire guard post shook as the inextinguishable green flame roared ferociously at the point of impact, causing tiny demons made of fire to scatter about like ants.

"Kikikiki!"

They were from a lower class of demons called the Minor Ember Spirit. All they knew was sticking to nearby people and causing them to ignite, but even these demons were a danger on a chaotic battlefield.

Genghis Aaron, the Rockhead, stepped on a Minor Ember Spirit with his steel boots and extinguished it. "Stomp on those tiny shits and get rid of 'em unless you want to catch on fire later!"

The soldiers followed his order and quickly began to stomp out the Minor Ember Spirits. However, the siege engines continued to unleash their payload, leaving dozens of new Minor Ember Spirits to run amok within the walls as the vanguards of the Demon army began their advance while beating their war drums.

"Humans! Kill 'em all!"

Monsters reaching five meters in height began to reveal their forms in the darkness. They were Depraved Trolls. Steel blinders were tightly attached to their flesh and skull so as to obstruct their vision and vile demonic magic was cast upon them to further empower their brute strength in order to use them as a vanguard in large scale battles.

"Mages and archers to the front! Focus fire onto the big ones!" commanded Genghis.

An elven soldier holding a bow pulled out an arrow shining in a silvery light from his quiver and pulled his string. He would have aimed for its eyes if they were normal trolls, but due to its steel blinders, it didn't have any particular weaknesses. The elven soldier aimed for the imp riding on a palanquin tightly strapped to the back of the troll's neck instead.

The imp was a sort of a driver, which controlled the troll's movement by manipulating a wooden peg buried deep enough into the troll's neck that it touched the spine.

FWIIK~

The elf's arrow sailed through the air and accurately pierced through the imp's throat.

"Kyeeek!" The arrow had punched through the imp's neck. It fell leftward while still holding onto the reins, and the Depraved Troll followed the dead imp's lead turning toward the left.

"Gwuuuuh~" The troll continued turning left until it was on a collision course with another troll.

"Grab it! Grab that thing!"

Other imps frantically pulled off the dead imp from the driver's seat and tried to regain control, but another arrow from the elf struck the replacement imp's body, causing the blind troll to complete its collision with the other troll.

"Gwuuuuuh!!!" The troll that had been tortured continuously throughout its life and stressed to the absolute limit began to swing its fists in a mad frenzy at the thing it had collided with. The other troll didn't hesitate and swung back in response.

BOOM! BOOM!

As the two massive trolls began to fight to the death in the middle of the vanguard units, the enemy's assault devolved into chaos. Dozens of imps marching around the trolls' feet were crushed to death, causing the following procession to stop momentarily.

"Good job, Fagan!" Deckard tossed a compliment towards the elven man, then headed to the front of the guard post with his staff in hand. Two bulky men grabbed their shields and protected him. Soon, Deckard's eyes became dyed in a shimmering light.

"You shall feel the might of the Heavens!"

A complex magical formation appeared around his staff. Sungchul could not decipher the concepts behind the magical formation, but he could make a guess towards what magic he was trying to use.

Is he using Meteor?

The dark clouds covering the sky suddenly cleared and something fell from above.

"It's M-Meteor!!!"

The demons pointed toward the sky and screamed out in alarm, but no salvation awaited them. Stuck in between the rear guards and the brawling trolls, they could do nothing but watch as the blue comet flew down onto their heads.

BOOOOOMM!!!

A massive explosion occurred in the middle of the enemy's battle formation, and everything surrounding it was swept away. When the dust settled, countless corpses of demons were revealed in a concentric circle. This was the might of Meteor, the spell widely considered the raison d'être of the School of Cosmomancy.

Genghis looked at the scene with smug eyes while stroking his sideburns. "As expected of Number 23. The ace of the Penal Unit!"

However, the assault of the demons was just beginning. The Balroqs and Baals, along with other upper-class demons, didn't budge while looking over the battlefield with an oppressive atmosphere from beyond the Hell Siege Engines. To the upper-class demons, the death of a couple of insignificant demons didn't matter.

"Keep sending in the insects."

It was a tried-and-tested tactic to exhaust the enemy with inferior demons, then obliterate the enemy with the devils afterwards. They still had plenty of fodder and the night was long. On the other side of the hill hidden from view were hundreds of low-class demons marching towards them even now.

The impressive talent of the Penal Unit allowed them to repel the approaching enemy, but they eventually lost their edge and became exhausted.

"There is no end to them, sir!"

The battle line moved up to where his subordinates were. The elf who had been making the trolls stumble with his impressive archery was now fighting with his blade as he ran out of arrows, and the mages were being driven to exhaustion as they squeezed out the last of their mana.

"Fuck…" Deckard let out a heavy sigh as he continued to gulp down water from his waterskin, whilst thinking that if he had been drinking mana essence instead, he could have landed another meteor on top of their heads.

"When is the main force coming? We're defending this spot to our last breath here!" Genghis was yelling into the bright blue magic formation on the palm of a mage wearing a blue wizard's hat. Sungchul knew what the magic formation was for. It was a communication formation. It was a convenient magic that mages of the school of Empathomancy boasted, which allowed people to transmit voices over long distances like mobile phones. An uncertain and hesitant voice could be heard from the other side of the magic formation.

"I'm sorry, but we weren't notified in advance regarding the status of the attack strategy. If we were told ahead of time regarding this plan, we would have sent out…"

"Fuck! The order to capture the guard post came from your end!!" Genghis shouted at the top of his lungs. It was so loud that the chaos of the battlefield seemed to grow silent for a moment afterwards. "Those fucking bastards. They tell us to capture the guard post, and now they say this? A strategy report? Tell them to go fuck themselves. Fucking bastards! All of my men are about to die! What are they going to do about it? Who's going to be responsible for this?"

There was only a sound of gulping as if the person on the other end of the magic formation was suppressed by Genghis' rage. Genghis clenched his eyes and gritted his teeth.

"Okay, I understand for now. First off, we have taken over the guard post, and we are still guarding it. However, you have not sent over the backup forces that were promised, and we are going to lose both the guard post and my men. Do you admit to this?"

"No, Mr. Aaron. That isn't the case at all. If only you had submitted the status report, we would have promptly…"

"Can't you shut the fuck up?!"

"…I'll call over the chief commander." The voice of the speaker on the other end of the magic formation sounded like he had already reached the end of his patience. Even Genghis who was bellowing until a moment ago stopped and cooled his head.

"It's fine. I'll bring up this incident another time. The situation is urgent at the moment. Over and out," said Genghis and gripped the shoulder of the mage wearing the blue hat.

"Sir Genghis!" A voice could be heard from the magic formation, but he had waved the formation away.

"Bastards. It's always like this! This is why they're losing all the major points!" Genghis spat onto the ground and turned his eyes again toward the battlefield. The battle was taking a turn for the worse. The trolls were all killed, but the gaps created by the Hell Siege Engines allowed the imps to flood in like the tide and the lower demons to climb the watchtower with ladders.

The casualties of soldiers were minimal, but the conclusion of the battle was becoming clearer as time passed.

Arkaard spoke with urgency. "Commander! We must pull back!"

It wouldn't be a retreat in reality, but rather a final attack to create an escape route. Genghis nodded. "Okay! We'll just have to give up the guard post at this point. I'll lead the way, so, everyone, follow me!"

Genghis held his violet-tinted magic sword and stood at the front. It was timed right after they had repelled another wave of assault from the enemy. The imps and demonkind soldiers climbed up ladders to reach the watchtower while eighty or so soldiers fought with their lives on the line to defend against the attack. Sungchul was also in the centre of it all.

"…"

Two imps with steel tridents rushed toward Sungchul, but he burned them away with Glare. Next was the Demon soldier. The plum-skinned lower demons with horns played a pivotal role in the demon army as they had little magic power, but had decent abilities and greater physical prowess and stamina than the average human.

"Kwaaa!" The demon soldier swung a scythe weighing several dozen kilogrammes toward Sungchul. Sungchul dodged the blade with minimal movements, then placed a beam of light within its open mouth.

"Kwaaaaaaak!"

Glare's beam pierced through the roof of the demon's mouth and seared its brain. It couldn't penetrate the helmet, but the demon's crimson eyes turned white, and it fell at Sungchul's feet.

"Quite impressive." Deckard approached Sungchul and covered his back.

"It was nothing."

Another demon soldier leaped at that moment. This time, it was an assault from the skies.

"Die! Human!" A winged demihuman with the skull of a bird dove in from the sky with a shout. It held a long spear in its hands covered in steel gauntlets and aimed toward Sungchul's head.

"Watch out!" Deckard extended his staff in an effort to cast a spell, but his mana was already exhausted. Glare didn't materialize. Deckard could only watch with eyes filled with horror as the aerial soldier ambushed Sungchul. Sungchul only continued to look forward and it wasn't clear whether he was aware of the ambush.

However, Sungchul's body moved fluidly like water right before the spear could have pierced his skull. His figure appeared like a mirage to the flying demon. There was no impact behind the demon's spear, and its prey was standing off in the distance.

CLANG!

The trusted spear made sparks as it hit the floor of the watchtower, and the demon flopped onto the floor with all of its momentum.

"Guuuuh…" The aerial soldier flapped its large wings and tried to fly, but Sungchul's Glare blew away both of its wings.

"Kwaaa!" The wingless demon rolled about on the floor. Sungchul grabbed an iron mace on the ground and executed the demon.

POP!

The demon's skull splattered along with its beak.

"Amazing." Deckard looked at Sungchul with disbelief. "You. You don't look like a beginner? Who are you?"

Sungchul was about to turn around to reply, but Genghis' powerful voice swept through like a typhoon.

"Now! Soldiers! I will open us an escape route. Follow my lead!"

Genghis swung his violet-tinted magic sword and jumped from the watchtower. Demon soldiers wielding long spears tried to fend him off, but they fell away like leaves from a tree as Genghis' blade flashed about in the air.

"Let's go!" Genghis kicked away the demonic dogs and imps with his feet as he opened up a path.

"Looks like story time is over. It'll truly become dangerous from this point on, so take care of yourself," Deckard advised Sungchul.

It was now the soldiers' turn. They followed Genghis' lead down the watchtower onto the opened path. The unlucky few were skewered by the raised spears of the demons, while the injured were left to their gruesome fates against the assault of imps and demonic dogs. The survivors fended off the constant assault of the demons as they followed at Genghis' rear with the violet flashes of his sword's aura guiding their desperate escape.

Deckard was fighting with a sword and shield instead of his staff. STAB!

A demon soldier fell as it bled out green blood. To the right, Arkaard was slaughtering imps with his axe swinging it like a windmill, and Fagan the elf was decapitating demonic dogs in a dance. Deckard looked toward the rear. There was a single black-haired man wearing the number 34 on a ragged coat following silently. There was no fear or confusion on his face. It was completely neutral.

That man... just who is he?

He was definitely not any new recruit. That level of leisure and skill ingrained into every fibre of his being was not something that happened overnight.

"Let's go! I see the end! Keep at it 'til the end!" Genghis, who was leading the charge, shouted noisily. Shrill laughter and shouts of mockery could be heard from the rear. The guard post fell back into the hands of demons, and Balroqs and Baals arrogantly flapped their wings in the moonlight while descending on the top of the watchtower. The heads of the dead were propped onto skewers, and their flesh became food for imps and demonic dogs. Of more than eighty men of the Penal Unit, there were only twenty-five survivors.

"Gasp... Gasp..." Deckard, who was among the survivors, was heaving for breath, trying to relax. It was a frantic escape against impossible odds.

Once he had a moment to catch his breath, he sought out the man who was following behind them. But the man himself, number 34, already stood before Deckard.

"I have survived the battle as promised. It is time to keep your end of the deal." He spoke casually without a single hair nor breath out of place.

***

Even the veterans were in a state of panic after the massacre that led to the death of over half of their unit. However, Number 34 was indifferent despite how recently he had been recruited.

"Just what are you?" Deckard asked the question with honest curiosity in his eyes. Sungchul figured out his intentions.

Was I too hurried?

It looked as though he earned himself some undue attention, so there was now a need to make up some explanation. A brilliant idea formed in that instant. Sungchul spoke in a low voice. "I am a Former Returnee."

Among those who returned to their original world, there were those who had chosen to come back to the Other World. These were people that had tasted bitter failure after being unable to re-adapt into the modern world. Unable to forget the overwhelming power they once wielded, they made the choice to return.

Whatever the reason was, that brought them back here, they were widely regarded as being much more powerful than their status points would otherwise suggest, and a good majority of them actually were.

"A Former Returnee…" Deckard couldn't hide his surprise at the news.

"I was at the Demon Realm Battlefront before I returned. I fought at the Forest of the Lichen Fog of the Varan-Aran alliance."

"It has been long since that forest got taken over by demons."

"In any case, the battle just now was just one of countless that I've already experienced on a daily basis. It also looked like the demons were keener on recapturing the guard post than our annihilation."

In reality, the Balroq and Baal that led the demons never stepped forth nor did they release their elite troops. It was nothing more than expending their easily replenishable pawns to chase out the meagre humans, although it would have taken at least the Balroq himself to take out the frenzied Genghis Aaron.

"Mmm…" Deckard didn't appear to be completely convinced, but there was some logic to follow in what Sungchul was saying.

Sungchul spoke further. "The reason I want to find a way to get stronger quickly is to survive."

"If you wanted to survive, this is the wrong place," Deckard said curtly.

"I am being chased by a nemesis. If I don't quickly gain strength, I'll lose my life."

As Sungchul pressed on, Deckard let out a sigh as he formed a shining orb and handed it to Sungchul. It was an Orb of Knowledge. Those that placed their hands on it would gain the information within.

"Take it. These are all the quests that are appropriate for you."

Sungchul touched the orb to acquire the information within. A quest soon appeared before him in shining letters.

[No Title]

Grave Cleaning – Clean out the swarm of imps that are disrupting the grave of Elven Warriors. / Reward – 5 Magic Power, 1 Mid-Grade Magic Power Essence.

Deckard pointed toward a rocky mountain off to the distance with his staff. "The graves of Elven archers of the Aran tribe are in that direction. The quest itself might be possible if you really try your best, but the problem lies in getting there."

"Is it demon territory?"

Deckard nodded at Sungchul's question then turned his back to walk away.

"Get some shut-eye. Something might suddenly happen at any moment."

Despite the warning, Sungchul headed off toward the rocky mountain by noon. Despite it being labelled as demon territory, the opposition was mostly small patrols. Sungchul lightly evaded their efforts and arrived at the grave of the Aran tribe, then proceeded to clean out the imps that had built their nest there.

Once the imps were cleared away, the spirits lingering within the gravesite rewarded Sungchul 5 Magic Power and a mid-grade mana drink. It wasn't anything impressive, but Sungchul knew the advantage of stacking up these unimpressive rewards. He leisurely returned to base and proceeded to start another job past his sleeping comrades. It was Alchemy.

Sungchul pulled out Eckheart's portable alchemic cauldron behind the barracks and began gathering ingredients from his surroundings as indicated by Bertelgia. He then proceeded to synthesise everything. Genghis Aaron approached him as he finished his third Alchemic item.

The well-built man stretched out his arms with a lazy yawn as he walked over to Sungchul and spoke with a look of wonder on his face. "Recruit? What is it that you are doing?"

"As you can see, I am in the middle of synthesising."

"I can see that, but I'm asking why you're doing it." Rockhead's response was unusual. It looked as though it bothered him that Sungchul was synthesising alchemic items.

"I wanted to create some useful items for battle. I learned a lot from the previous battle."

Rockhead didn't press the issue any further after listening to such a model response, but instead, he made a gentle expression and gave a word of advice before leaving. "If you want to survive, I suggest you keep up your physical strength. Anyways, it looks like we'll have plenty to eat today? Seeing as we've cut down on the number of mouths to feed."

Seeing him spit out such tactless remarks, it was obvious how he earned his nickname. However, Sungchul got the impression that Genghis Aaron wasn't as simple as he appeared. He was especially cunning when making his report to headquarters. He was fully aware of the organizational problems long plaguing the front lines of the Demon Realm, and even seemed to be actively taking advantage of them. It wasn't something he could do if he were truly an idiot.

It soon became evening. Genghis had started up a raucous party. The portions of food and alcohol allocated for the dead were given out to soldiers. The mourning for the dead lasted a full ten seconds.

Sungchul chewed on the tasteless but overly abundant food while sipping his drinks by himself. The night sky of the Demon Realm Battlefront had a reddish tint. It was because of the light emitted from the flames of hell that never went out.

"Status Window."

He pulled up his status window, which he hadn't seen in a while. The unadjusted screen of the full status window overwhelmed his vision.

[Current Status of Sungchul Kim, "The Destroyer"]

[Blessings]

1. Covenant
   (Unknown)
2. Unshakeable
   (Immune to Mental Attacks)
3. Blessing from God of Chaos
   (10% Bonus to Strength, Dexterity, Vitality)
4. Heir of Heracles
   (+100 Strength)
5. Bloodline of Zealot
   (Major Bonus to Regeneration when Below 10% Vitality)
6. Champion of Humanity
   (+ 50 Resilience)
7. Rapid-Bow of the High Elven Kingdom
   (+ 30 Dexterity)
8. Heart of an Ancient Warrior
   (+5 Strength, Resilience, Vitality / Resilience)

[Curses]

1. Covenant
   (Unknown)
2. Final Declaration of Grand Mage Balzark
   (-10 Intuition)
3. Blessing of Blademaster Karakardra
   (+ 1 Dexterity, -1 Strength)
4. Ancient God's Champion, Arrak – Garr's Criticism
   (-3 Strength)
5. Dark Dragon Groteus's Karmic Curse
   (- 20 Strength, -20 Vitality)
6. Adelwight of the Haunted Forest's Common Curse
   (- 5 Strength, Erectile Dysfunction)
7. Enemy of the Kingdom

(Faction: Nemesis of Human Kingdom, Blank Check Reward)

8. Destroyer of Hora Mountain Sect
   (Faction: Nemesis of Hora Mountain Sect, Destroyed)
9. Destroyer of Mewra Sect
   (Faction: Nemesis of Mewra Sect, Destroyed)
10. Enemy of the Allied Mage's Guild
    (Faction: Nemesis of Allied Mage's Guild and Sub guilds)
11. Steel Fist Curse of Crimson Orc Chief, Drakuul
    (Race: -30 Orc Favor)
12. Recorded on Dwarven Book of Grudges
    (Race: -200 Dwarf Favor)
13. Recorded on Allied Merchant's Guild's Blacklist
    (Faction: Trade impossible with Allied Merchant's Guild and their affiliated factions)

...

[Class]
Main Class – Primordial Warrior (Mythic)
Sub Class – Echo Mage (Legendary)
Sub Class – High Class Chef (Rare)
Sub Class – Alchemist (Rare)

[Stats]

Strength	999+	Dexterity	853
Vitality	801	Magic Power	183
Intuition	173	Magic Resist	621
Resilience	502	Charisma	18
	Luck	18	

[Soul Contract – 6 Slots]

1. Soul Harvester
   ([Legend] Vitality Leech 15%, Vitality restored from fallen enemies)

2. Thunder Shield

([Legend] All Magic Damage reduced by 50% / Negate all mental attacks below legend rank)

3. Eye of Truth

([Legend] Negate all blessings below Epic rank / Identify all items, consumables, and skill details)

4. Soul Storage

([Epic] Can store 1500 different items)

5. Deceiver's Veil

([Rare – High Tier] Conceals status window)

– Blank –

[Weapon Proficiency]

Blunt Weapons – Max Proficiency

Sword – Master (85% until next level)

Axe – Expert (22% until next level)

Spear – Expert (18% until next level)

Bow – Master (82% until next level)

Polearm – Expert (11% until next level)

Staff – Veteran (44% until next level)

Unarmed – Grand Master

[Achievements – 592 in Total]

Member of the Original 500

First Warrior

Killer of Kobold Chief Garlagu

Veteran of the Battle of Avaron

588 more…

The status window was a type of epic; a memoir of the path an individual had taken during their life in the Other World. How many conflicts had he been involved in before now? Every single day he had experienced battles that would be called "a battle of a lifetime" for anyone else. He received countless blessings, but also terrible curses. He was also hiding power that he could not yet reveal to the world.

I am a tool for my purpose. Sungchul's eyes flashed a single time within the darkness.

Deckard approached him in that instant. He plopped down onto the dirt beside Sungchul and spoke while staring off into the sky. "Is Sarasa doing well?"

Sungchul nodded.

"That kid… how is she? Pretty?"

Sungchul was about to shake his head but nodded instead. Deckard, who hadn't seen Sungchul's hesitation, continued to look toward the sky while speaking with a voice wet with emotions.

"That kid… she was so much more beautiful before she took on that form. The entire school made a fuss whenever she was around, and her power was so strong that she broke the Soul Absorption Stone. That kid… she did something not even I could."

Deckard looked happy as he spoke of his daughter, but he would undoubtedly grieve if he saw the current state of her changed face. Sungchul didn't say anything.

"Anyways, you said you were a Former Returnee?" Deckard reinitiated the conversation. Once Sungchul looked in his direction, Deckard took a sip of alcohol and spoke again. "You're in quite the rush. Seeing as you've come here of your own volition to harden yourself."

"I could even go places rougher than this."

"That's quite the resolve."

"Didn't you also come here to grow stronger?"

Deckard nodded. "That's right. I came here seeking strength."

"Because of the demon tribes?"

"That too, but there is also another reason." A meaningful smile formed on Deckard's lips. He looked up into the rosy night sky and continued, "According to a rumor, there is a dungeon around here created by an ancient mage. A dungeon filled with an unbelievable amount of magic power."

"Who made this dungeon? The Seven Heroes perhaps?" asked Sungchul.

Deckard shook his head. "They are beings that existed before the Seven Heroes. In the era of a calamity before the calamity resolved by the Seven Heroes. A forgotten age lost to time."

"Quite interesting."

The era of the Seven Heroes was even considered ancient, and barely any records remained. Their names were not being recorded properly, and only a handful of people remained with the correct knowledge of it. He was talking about something from a time before this. In other words, an individual from an unfathomably ancient and bygone era.

"I came to this place following its clues. It was one of the reasons I got sent to the Penal Unit too. The Penal Unit always operates on the front lines, so it makes it easier to approach the dungeon. But there is another benefit; it is a good place to cultivate your skills."

"I agree."

The demons were strong, and their numbers were endless. That meant that as long as you could survive, it was possible to drive yourself into life-or-death battles that tested your limits. The warrior class was meant to bloom with combat.

Sungchul had also cultivated his abilities on his own by slaughtering countless devils, and he continued to challenge himself with danger; trusting his stats as a foundation to steadily gain power that exceeded the limits of humanity. Deckard must have come to the same conclusion.

"Thanks to it, I think I have reached a point where I can confidently say I am quite strong. It's probably about time for me to challenge that place."

"Where is that place?"

Deckard pointed to his feet in reply to Sungchul's question with a smile on his face.

"It's somewhere below here. It is a place called the Underground Kingdom from a forgotten era. Even I don't know where the entrance is. I only have few clues to go on."

"The Underground Kingdom…"

It sounded familiar. At a distant past, there was a story of a group of people of the forgotten era that attempted to escape the calamity by digging underground and eventually forming their own kingdom. It was a story that was treated as folklore or children's bedtime story, but Deckard must have learned something about it.

"Now that winter is approaching, the demons will be attacking less frequently. Since you and I are both people constantly thirsting for strength, why not go together to check it out sometime?"

He was a good person. He was good-natured but also very considerate. Sungchul judged him as such, but good people didn't last long in the Other World. The demons ambushed the base within the cover of the night.

The demon's attack was easily repelled mostly due to Aaron's efforts, but he couldn't prevent casualties from occurring.

"…"

Deckard had received a critical wound and had fallen unconscious. It was such a sudden event that not even Sungchul could intervene in time.

Chapter 3 – Underground Kingdom

Deckard's condition was serious. He overcame a critical point through emergency procedures performed with herbs that an elven man named Fagan had on him, but he still did not regain consciousness.

"He constantly pushed himself too far. Adequate rest is also necessary. He ran out of mana at a critical juncture again," said Arkaard who was beside Deckard when he was injured. It had been something Deckard would have been able to take care of easily had he been able to use Glare, but his magic failed at a critical moment, and he was pushed into a corner which allowed him to be mortally wounded.

"The problem is the poison. The imp's weapons are coated with some dirty poison made by fermenting troll shit. We washed away all the poison, but some of it already made its way into Mr Deckard's body and is chipping away his vitality." Fagan, who was known to have fought the demons from a young age, accurately diagnosed Deckard's current condition. Sungchul also agreed with his assessment.

Sungchul immediately headed out to start sifting through dirt in search of something. He found a plant that was growing along some rocks that appeared like a plantago and grabbed a handful. The plant was named the Solitary Plant and was sometimes seen in this area. If the plant was ground and applied to the afflicted area, the imp's poison could be neutralised to a certain extent. It was one of many useful things he picked while living on the Demon Realm Battlefront. The effect was mediocre at best, but in a place like this with no doctors or priests, such herbs were worth its weight in gold.

As he was preparing to pound it with a pestle, Bertelgia suddenly popped out to speak. "You're just going to use it like that?"

Sungchul nodded in response, and Bertelgia rebuked him.

"You're going to reduce its efficacy like that, and you don't even know what kind of side effects it might have. Why not act like an Alchemist and apply your skills to solve the problem?"

Bertelgia was giving luxurious advice in such dire times when every second counted, but as he thought on her words a bit more, it did have some rationality to it. As they say, "When you're in a rush, take a step back." Sungchul checked on Deckard's condition once again. It looked like he could hold on for a moment longer.

He left the barracks again and took a whiff of the Solitary Plant. Alchemic information relating to the plant appeared before him.

< Thousand Year Solitary Plant >

Level: 3

Grade: B

Attribute: Wood

Effect: Detoxification, Poison Damage

Note: A perennial plant found on rocky mountains near the Demon Realm. It has a neutralisation effect due to the influence from the Demon Realm. However, it is also poisonous itself, so take care during usage.

"There is also poison in the Solitary Plant." Sungchul had used the Solitary Plant many times, but he wasn't aware that the plant itself contained poison. It was because the plant was not only rare; it was incredibly bitter and its distinct smell prevented it from being used as anything else other than medicine.

"Of course. It is a plant growing off the radiating demonic energy from the Demon Realm. It wouldn't be able to survive without producing toxins to protect itself. It's a characteristic shared by all the flora growing in this region next to the Demon Realm," said Bertelgia.

This meant that there was a need to neutralise the poison. Sungchul brought out the Soul Storage and began to lay out the alchemic ingredients he had gathered over time as he contemplated a solution.

He was most confident with using what he had always used: Blind Man's Grass. It felt as though the Blind Man's Grass, with its similar wood attribute, would be most suitable when used with the Solitary Plant. However, Bertelgia landed on his hand as he reached for the Blind Man's Grass and spun side to side. "Nu-uh!"

"… what are you doing?"

"Don't look for the easiest path; think a bit harder."

"Think about what?"

"Don't just think about extracting the poison, but look at the situation in its entirety. The characteristics of the poison inside Mr Deckard for example."

"You mean the troll shit poison?"

"Yep. Isn't that ultimately what you're trying to detoxify?"

Pitchforks with troll shit smeared on them were lying all over the ground. Sungchul grabbed one and took a whiff to check. He then began heaving from the atrocious stench, but he could see the alchemic information regarding the shit poison appearing before his eyes.

[Troll's Faeces (Northern)]
Level: 3
Grade: A
Attribute: Metal
Effects: None
Note: According to Legend, these Northern Trolls were raised like cattle by a now extinct kingdom of an avian race. This avian race used the faeces for several different uses, but one of them was gathering it to form metal. Keep in mind that the sense of smell of this avian race was not well developed!

Reading the note, something clicked in Sungchul's mind. "The troll shit has the same properties of rusted metal."

Bertelgia's body shook up and down. "Mm-hmm. That's exactly it!"

Solitary Plant. Blind Man's Grass. Troll shit. He looked at these conflicting ingredients, then turned his attention to his other ingredients.

Alchemic items had one of five attributes: Fire, Water, Wood, Metal, and Null. Other than the null attribute that only exists in theory, it would not be an exaggeration to claim that everything in alchemy can be broken down to these four attribute categories. Each of the attributes also has a beneficial or detrimental relationship with each of the others. It was a complex system where fire overpowered wood and metal, and water overpowered fire and metal. However, water was weak to wood. Even so, the system doesn't have too strict of a rule; thus, the strength of each attribute could change by its concentration.

Sungchul focused on the fact that the troll shit had metal attribute. The suppression of metal element required a superior fire element type alchemic item. However, he didn't have any fire attribute item that could easily subdue the metal attribute. The only alchemic item in his possession with enough impact to overpower the metal attribute contained the wood attribute. It was the porous seeds of the Firework Tree that he used to create the Alchemic Bomb (Darkness) at Airfruit.

"Mmm…" Sungchul let out a groan as he continued to brush the fuzzy seeds.

Bertelgia who was watching him from the side thought to herself. *This guy… he has talent. To find the answer among all those ingredients… Is it intuition or is it luck?*

Bertelgia wanted to let him think on it a bit longer, but she also knew that there wasn't much time. She threw out another piece of advice. "Attributes can change for certain items if you process them."

"So that was the case." Sungchul's eyes lit up. It was a refreshing feeling as though a fog had lifted as soon as he heard her advice. His movements were quick, but he carefully trimmed each seed with great care and attention. That aspect was also a plus in Bertelgia's eyes. *As expected. He definitely has talent.*

The ability to exercise this level of leisure, even in the middle of a crisis, was considered a part of someone's gift in alchemy. It wasn't just an insult to say that the lazy and half-assed could never be an Alchemist. Sungchul, who was pruning each seed, began to pound the seeds with a pestle and synthesised a bright red powder from his alchemic cauldron with a couple of additional ingredients.

< Essence of Porous Seed >
Level: 3
Grade: B
Attribute: Fire
Type: Explosive
Effect: Ingredient for Explosives. Handle with Care.

He succeeded in converting the wood attribute into fire attribute. Sungchul looked at the ingredients in his possession once again: Solitary Plant, Blind Man's Grass, Essence of Porous Seed.

The recipe hadn't been given to him, but the vague idea of how the alchemic item would form appeared in his mind. The experience he had gathered and the knowledge he accumulated were applied to his creativity, which led to a creation of his own.

He immediately began working with controlled haste. He added the concentrate he gathered from the crushed Solitude Plant to distilled water. He then boiled the mixture to evaporate the water. Finally, he filtered the mixture through a filter leaving only the concentrate on it. It wasn't something anyone had taught him. He applied the process of synthesising wood attribute items directly to this item. This was meant to remove the impurities and retain only the concentrate with the desired components.

Sungchul added the Blind Man's Grass to the cauldron and boiled it to create a separate counteragent, then added the Solitude

Plant concentrate and the Essence of Porous Seed to the mixture. He hesitated regarding the amount of Porous Seed Essence to add…

"For that, it's fine to just add a little bit." Bertelgia gave her input at the critical moment, and Sungchul began to add a minute amount as though he was flavouring a dish with salt with a faint smile on his face. Finally came the synthesis. He stirred his mixture within the alchemic cauldron and obtained a result after a considerable time had passed.

[Synthesis Success!]

It was a reward befitting the effort. However, there was more to his reward than he thought.

[You have successfully produced an Alchemic Item without anyone's teaching, using personal experience and knowledge as your foundation.]
[Great Alchemists have no use for recipes.]
Reward: +10 Magic Power, +15 Intuition

Unexpected words along with a strange light that burst forth from Bertelgia's body were drawn to Sungchul's body like steel to a magnet.

"Bertelgia, what is this?" Sungchul looked directly at her as he asked his question.

"That is one of the trials of the Creationist. I did help out a bit though…"

"…"

It wasn't a simple trial. Sungchul recognised that the new strength that entered his body did indeed come from Bertelgia. It was similar to the instance in the basement of House of Recollections with the Baal. He felt uncomfortable about it, but there was a more important matter at hand. He checked the item produced within the cauldron.

< Antidote >
Level: 3
Grade: A
Attribute: Fire
Type: Medicine
Effect: Cures poison. Specialises in poisons with the Metal attribute.

It was the appropriate item. It had even received an A grade.

"Wow! It's even an A grade?! Even though it was the first recipe you created." Bertelgia shook her body within his pocket. Sungchul immediately grabbed the antidote and entered the barracks. Arkaard and Fagan were caring for Deckard inside.

"Could I have a moment?" Sungchul excused himself and approached Deckard.

Arkaard saw that Sungchul held something in his hand, and asked bluntly, "What is that?"

"It is the medicine that will save this man."

Sungchul popped open the antidote and poured the antidote over the wound on Deckard's neck. Deckard let out a loud moan in pain. "Mmm...."

Arkaard's eyes were no longer friendly, but Fagan held him back from the side. Instead, he shot out a question in a frosty tone.

"What is this made of?"

Sungchul didn't give him a glance as he answered the question. "1000 years old Solitude Plant."

Fagan nodded. Arkaard also nodded but made another rebuke.

"If you use the Solitude Plant now, Deckard won't be able to hold on for much longer. Did you know that Solitude Plant has poison?"

"This is made after removing that poison." Sungchul opened Deckard's mouth and had him drink the antidote. He spat out most of it, but a few drops had been swallowed. After a few moments, the fever finally subsided. Another critical moment had been passed safely.

—

The demon race goes into seclusion during the winter because demons are weak against the cold. Of course, the high-ranking demons would not suffer from a slight chill, but their minions were affected. The low-ranking demons that formed the bulk of the demon army could not endure the cold, and so they had to remain in their posts. A brief peace took place on the Demon Realm Battlefront during the long winters as the demons were not a race known for taking the initiative.

The Penal Unit was no exception. They received no further attacks from the demons after receiving significant damage from the ambush last week. Even the patrols that made the rounds reported back that the demons had returned to their fire and ice-covered homeland.

Sungchul took this peaceful moment to roam about the rocky mountains of the Demon Realm Battlefront on his own. He was seeking the entrance to the Underground Kingdom that was supposed to exist around these parts. Deckard, who was sent to the rear, gave him a bit of information. Deckard told him that the entrance to the Underground Kingdom existed on the rugged rocky mountains where the realm of demons and humans met.

He had said that the location would reveal itself during an eclipse, but there were still two months to go until the next one. Sungchul didn't have the luxury of waiting that long. This was the reason that he was turning the rocky mountain upside down by himself. He continued spending his days eliminating the disparate mobs of demons he met with magic as he roamed until he saw an unusual scene. A ship that navigated the skies, an airship, leisurely travelled across the skies of the Demon Realm Battlefront.

It's not a ship from the Human Empire. Is that the flag of the Ancient Kingdom?

The Ancient Kingdom. It was a militaristic nation steeped in rich history that was known to be the longest living human nation on the continent. They view the usage of magic as unjust, and thus strictly forbid its usage. Instead, they systematically developed people to the peak of sword mastery and used them as their main force. Such people were existences known as Sword Masters. These Sword Masters, all with skills on par with Aaron Genghis, were what allowed the Ancient Kingdom to retain their place as a powerful nation even in the centre of the continent. However, Sungchul knew that they secretly utilised mages despite their outward taboo of magic.

A small party of thirteen people descended from the Ancient Kingdom's Airship. Sungchul noticed that half of them were mages with a single glance.

What is an Ancient Kingdom Airship doing in a place like this?

The mystery was resolved before long. A female mage in command of five homunculi beneath her feet stood over a fissure in the rocks and recited a spell. The fissure opened, and a cave that opened downward like a well revealed itself.

***

A foreboding region opened up beneath the entrance that was facing the sky. There was an airship in the air, and Ancient Kingdom soldiers were guarding the entrance. And if that wasn't enough, a portion of the mages had set up a barrier there as well.

Sungchul patiently watched their movements. Once it was sundown, several people emerged from the hole riding the lift and returned to the surface. There were thirteen people when they descended, but only seven came out, and one of them had severe injuries that required him to lean on his companions.

"Shit. There are too many monsters. We'll need an army and not an exploratory team at this rate." An extremely tall and well-built youth spoke as he wiped his blade soaked in blood.

The gloomy female mage next to him stood beside him like a shadow. "Didn't I say it before? We'll need at least five Sword Masters before we can break through the area."

There were five homunculi around her skirt that reached down to her feet, wearing metal masks and armed to the teeth.

"Our strength isn't enough, see-yeyo?"

"Bring more Sword Masters-yeyo!"

"Lady Mimi's assessments are absolute-yeyo!"

The five homunculi began to shout as they hopped about distractingly. At that moment, a man jumped off from the airship above.

There were several dozens of meters of distance between the airship and the ground, but he had jumped off with no hesitation. The ground tremored lightly with a BOOM! Sound, which caused all heads to turn toward him.

"Scout Leader. Mimi Azrael! Report the status of your progress."

It was a gray-haired Swordsman with a mane and a full beard that was similar to that of a lion's. The full plate armor that covered his entire body was adorned with white gold, and the man appeared to be of great status. Sungchul instantly recognized the man.

It's Willie Gilford.

The man held a spot among the Thirteen Champions of the Continent. He was the Seventh Champion: Willie Gilford. He was the very first Sword Master among the summoned and had gained great renown throughout the continent through his overwhelming mastery over the sword and his fighting spirit of a lion's.

Of course, he was Sungchul's acquaintance. They were together in the battle against the Demon King on the Demon Realm frontlines. They never shared many words with each other, but Sungchul knew that he was a meticulous and detail-oriented strategist despite his clumsy appearance.

The gloomy woman called Mimi looked at him with depressed eyes and answered him calmly. "As you can see, we lost half of the exploratory squad."

"Cause?" Willie spoke as he stroked his sideburns.

"There were too many enemies. Your Majesty added a Sword Master and 5 Sword Adepts to our unit, but their strength was lacking."

Willie raised his hand, interrupting Mimi, then turned toward the young man and spoke in a growl. "Mikhael Gilford. Is what she says true?"

The young swordsman named Mikhael looked blankly with a dark expression, then nodded. "A lot was omitted, but what the witch says is overall the truth."

The youth's voice and appearance were similar to William's. Sungchul could now recognize Mikhael as Willie's son. A fire lit in his eyes. *That's right. You fuckers must have called it quits because your own damned children weren't affected by the curse.*

He could still recall the scene clearly. People believed that the Thirteen Champions of the Continent did nothing, and recorded history reflected the fact that the gathering of the Thirteen Champions had remained idle. However, the truth was different.

The Thirteen Champions of the Continent had at one point invaded the Demon Realm. They had also managed to force their way through the Demon King Hesthnius Max's Palace reaching his chamber. If they had torn the door open and entered at that time, the first Calamity would have ended right then. But a conflict of interest occurred at that moment.

Someone spoke up. "After we kill the Demon King, the Seven Heroes will appear once again. Can we handle the Seven Heroes? What about the next Calamity after we manage to kill them?"

That one line of questioning ruined everything. Sungchul still remembered the face of the woman that had asked the question.

The Second Hero of the Continent and the Master of the Floating Isles, Executor Aquiroa.

Above all else, he had tried to kill the old woman himself, but her Floating Isles was a hidden location under a veil of secrets. It was not possible to know where it was nor could he find it, despite all of his efforts. He had tried many times to determine its location, but it was all for naught. Time passed by as Sungchul was deep in thought.

"Have your men set up camp and remain on standby. I'll gather all the skilled ones near me and add them to the unit." Willie spoke in a booming voice. Mimi didn't show much of a reaction, but Mikhael rose up in protest.

"Father, wasn't this plan supposed to progress in secret? There is a concern that the secret might leak if we bring in outsiders carelessly."

"There is no concern. Dead men tell no tales." Willie pulled his blade from its sheath. A blade enveloped in faint shining blue ghostly aura was illuminating the surroundings.

Sungchul who saw this scene thought to himself, *I see that he refuses to do it himself no matter what.*

At Willie's strength, it would be possible to clean up whatever was underground with ease. However, the reason why he refused to go himself was due to his natural cautiousness. Willie only fought battles that were assured of being a victory; he never permitted even a bit of uncertainty. It was this mentality that had lost him countless opportunities, but allowed him to never fall into dire straits.

"I'll return after a week. Set up camp here and defend this location." Willie left most of the guards with the camp at the entrance of the cave and took the airship heading southwards. Whether from whim or with intent, he peeked towards the ridge that Sungchul was hiding in. However, it would have been impossible to find Sungchul who had completely suppressed his presence. "Did I mistake it? I thought I just felt something very ominous."

The airship disappeared from his sight, and Sungchul returned to observing the camp.

The female mage named Mimi entered her own barracks with her homunculi and Mikhael took a rest sharing conversation with his subordinates. The airship had left, but the barrier was still formidable, and there were Empathomancy mages stationed that could make contact with the outside at any time.

Sungchul felt tempted to step out personally, but he resisted the temptation. There was still plenty of time left. There was no need to overexert himself. Also, the second of the two roll calls of the day was fast approaching. Missing a roll call was considered desertion. Aaron, who everyone feared, was no real match for Sungchul, but Sungchul wanted to stay active within the Penal Unit for a while. He left the scene with a slight regret.

***

When Sungchul returned, there was a commotion in the camp. Three soldiers were tied down to a rack and were being flogged by Aaron. Sungchul recognized them as some of the five that had deserted during the battle. It wasn't a wise choice to desert in the frontlines of the Demon Realm. Different from the regions of the rear, deserting the Penal Unit who were at the forefront of the Demon Realm frontline would mean surviving in the Demon Realm with nothing but their bodies to rely on.

It wasn't easy to survive in this land teeming with evil creatures in all directions. They would most likely die or disappear after wandering these barren lands, and even if they did manage to adjust, they would have to lead the life of a primitive animal. Sungchul managed to eat and live freely because of his strength; ordinary people equated the Demon Realm with death.

"You traitors have forsaken your brothers in arms to save yourselves. You have added a heavy crime on top of the crimes you've already committed. I cannot forgive you, and thus I will kill you to appease the grievances of the spirits of warriors long gone."

Aaron flogged the three constrained deserters toward the brink of death. However, they did not die. An unexpected guest arrived as they were about to meet their end; the reinforcements from the south. There were about three hundred in all.

According to rumors, there was a mass desertion that occurred along the battlefront supervised by the Order of the Iron Blood Knights, and so a portion of them had been sent here.

Sungchul eyed one of them and tossed over a warm drink when the time was appropriate. "Why did the massive desertion happen?"

"Hesthnius Max. The Demon King came out personally on the battlefront."

The new recruit trembled with fear etched into his face. It all made sense if he was telling the truth. According to the man, Max led an elite army composed of the strongest devils and demons and attacked the forward base to the west operated by the Order of the Iron Blood Knights. They burned thirty percent of the fortification to the ground, and after a drawn-out battle, the Iron Blood Knights suffered a harsh defeat.

The Order of the Iron Blood Knights, who were one of the key players in holding the front line against the Demonkind, were losing control of the battle line they were in charge of.

They were in no immediate danger since the hibernation period had begun, but it would be difficult to hold the line in spring due to having already lost all of their strongholds.

"An unfortunate rumor is spreading around."

After roll call, Sungchul heard about the rumor spreading around the unit from Arkaard.

"Marquis Martin Breggas is preparing for an all-out attack to rescue the Order of the Iron Blood Knights."

This was nothing more than a death sentence for the Penal Unit if the rumors were true, due to the fact that the unit was meant to be sent to the bleakest and the most dangerous of missions. But this was good news for Sungchul since Deckard, his source of information, was safe in the rear and Sungchul had no one to worry about but himself. Sungchul was also planning on clearing the dungeon defended by the exploration team within a week, no matter who or what awaited within.

The main problem was that the entrance was guarded by the explorers from the Ancient Kingdom, but Sungchul even had a solution for this.

The next day, Sungchul left the rowdy unit behind him and headed into the Demon Realm. There, he challenged one of the Demon Lords and escaped after pretending to lose.

Excited at the idea that he had defeated the man responsible for reducing Hesthnius Max to spirit form and put him on the run, the Demon Lord gathered his army to give chase. Sungchul had thousands of demons at his tail as he fled toward the exploratory unit's camp. What happened next was obvious.

The demons that had hounded Sungchul discovered the Exploratory unit and attacked. Sungchul hid in a ravine out of view and watched the scene with a baked potato as a snack. Sungchul believed that the exploratory team would simply retreat, but they made an unexpected decision. Instead of abandoning the dungeon and escaping, they opted to enter the known danger that was the dungeon. The demons did not give chase. The high-ranking demons looked once at the entrance, shook their heads, then retreated their army. "These are the grounds of a race who were tributed to the gods as a sacrifice. We will only share their fate if we follow."

The demons fell back, and Sungchul felt great curiosity once again. He felt drawn to this dungeon that had caused even the demons to shake their heads and retreat. However, he chose to fall back again. He chose to head toward the south toward the field hospital that Deckard was committed to and snuck in.

"What is the identity of that dungeon?" asked Sungchul.

He even told Deckard that the entrance of the dungeon had already been discovered by the Ancient Kingdom's scouts and was being actively explored. When Deckard heard the story, he could hide the truth no longer.

"What did you say? The Ancient Kingdom's scouts already arrived? Shit…!"

He then spilled everything he knew.

"The dungeon is actually the land of a race eaten up by a Calamity."

"A race eaten up by a Calamity?"

"Races which succumb to the Calamities are enslaved by the Gods. In the case of the ancestors that constructed the Underground Kingdom, they became the slaves of the Ancient God."

"The slaves of the Ancient God…"

Deep wrinkles formed in Sungchul's brow.

There were five main gods within the Other World's Pantheon. The God of Order who ruled over goodness and justice. The God of Chaos that sought evil and entropy. The God of Mediation that maintained the world as it was. The Ancient God which was the manifestation of the eternal flow of time. Finally, the prearranged deity that was not yet born. It was known that the Ancient God was the most incomprehensible among all of these deities. Sungchul had once fought against the attendants of the Ancient God. They were revolting and twisted existences that he never wanted to see again.

***

One day passed. The Penal Unit was put on high alert in response to the reports of the overall movements of the Demon army. Aaron gathered the members of the unit to speak.

"All of you know this, that an unexpected army of demons has begun moving southward. According to the Gryphon scouts, the demons have retreated but the possibility of them preparing an ambush can't be ignored. We need scouts. I am looking for volunteers."

It wasn't easy to look for volunteers in a unit composed mostly of new recruits. Aaron naturally looked towards the veteran members. Sungchul raised his hand.

"Number 34? Aren't you a recruit as well?"

Sungchul shook his head. "I'm better than those guys. I have also been exploring the vicinity every day anyways. You can leave this to me."

"You sure?"

There was no reason to hold someone back from volunteering. Aaron assigned Sungchul as a scout then looked for soldiers to support him, but no one stepped up. It was because all the soldiers knew that demons never cleanly retreated in the Demon Realm battlefront. They might have left behind countless traps or ambushes in wait, or even some man-eating demonic beast might be lurking around. It was one thing if the whole army moved, but for a small patrolling party, they would easily become prey to some demonic beast or become a demon's plaything.

"If you successfully patrol the area once, I'll count it as a successful mission. Anyone willing to step up?" Genghis put out an offer that no one in the Penal Unit could scoff at, but even still, no one volunteered, showing the risk this mission carried.

In the silence, Sungchul spoke to Aaron once again. "It's enough with me alone. I'll be back in three days. If not, then consider me dead."

"Well, I don't plan on reducing your number of missions because you volunteered. Is that ok with you?" Aaron spoke with a dirty grin on his flat face. Sungchul nodded in return.

"If I fail at scouting, wouldn't we all die the same?"

"You know very well. Ok. Go on then, Number 34."

Sungchul was given a signalling scroll along with some rations and water before he headed out. It was nothing short of suicide in the eyes of other soldiers, but it was great news for Sungchul.

Looks like I won't need to join roll call for three days. I don't know what the scale of that dungeon is, but I should be able to determine its value within three days. Sungchul immediately left and headed toward the dungeon. There were a lot of traps and patrols around the dungeon as expected. Sungchul avoided detection and traps as he snuck his way toward his destination.

WHAM!

He bashed a mob of demons lying in ambush with a pebble, then looked below the rocky mountain. There were only barracks lying abandoned around the dungeon with no traces of human life. The barrier that had been cast everywhere was also shattered and had long since lost its effectiveness. Fortunately, the pulley system operating within the dungeon was still quite active. Unfortunately, there was no way the demons would simply pass it by. They had left behind a devious little trick on the machine. Anyone who operated the machine would be caught in an explosion.

"…"

Sungchul didn't lay a finger on the trap; he simply jumped down the bleak hole. Utter darkness swallowed him completely as the sensation of falling that numbed his feet pervaded throughout his body. During the seemingly endless fall, Sungchul noticed a faint ray of light and threw his fists toward the darkness.

BOOM!

The hard rock crumbled like tofu as half his arm was embedded into it causing his body to become fixed onto the rock wall. Sungchul pulled it out and leaped toward the bright light, which led him into a corridor with no end in sight.

The faded rock wall stained with dirt and green lichen combined together to create a dark atmosphere and a musky smell that could only be found in a charnel house pierced his nose.

"This place… I don't like it." Bertelgia trembled within his pocket, so Sungchul took her out and said, "From this point, you don't have to stay inside the pocket."

As soon as he finished speaking, Bertelgia popped out of his hand and flew around vigorously as she regained her normal size. "Ah. I wanted this feeling to be more refreshing than it is!"

"Do you know where this place is?" asked Sungchul.

Bertelgia shook her head at his question. "Nope. This is my first time here, but I do have information about the Nahak that you guys call the birdmen."

"Nahak? What's that?"

"They are a race that flourished in the Other World in the past but are all extinct now, so you can't find them anymore. Still, according to legend, they had massive wings which they used to soar the skies and used their beaks engraved with runic letters to control destructive magic at will."

"Are they a different race than the birdmen that can be found in the demonic army?"

"I think they might be a distant cousin? The Nahak aren't this shoddy."

As Bertelgia shared her story, Sungchul entered the dungeon one step at a time. There were traces of the exploratory squad all around. Sungchul carefully took each step as he looked at his surroundings. The Eye of Truth observed a magical existence far beyond in the darkness. It was a magic trap. One with a frost attribute. Anyone that accidently stepped on it would be overwhelmed by a chill that would freeze the entire body.

This was done by a human mage, thought Sungchul.

Footprints were scattered all around the trap. It appeared as though there was a huge commotion here. According to the number of footprints, there looked to have been about thirty humans within the dungeon. It was a combined number of both the exploratory squad and the troops prepared for defence. Sungchul continued on.

He soon found a trail of blood stains which led him to two corpses lying about on the floor. They were the corpses of soldiers. The group must have met a difficult enemy as they couldn't even observe the proper formality for their dead comrades. Sungchul left behind the corpse whose eyes were wide open and continued forward.

"An enemy." Bertelgia spoke briefly.

Sungchul sensed the lingering hostility lurking not too far away. With Fal Garaz gripped in his hand, he glared at the existence standing in the darkness and spoke curtly. "Crawl out."

Finally, something revealed itself in the darkness. It was a monster with a human body and the skull of a bird with an endless stream of green pus flowing down its skin. It had no eyes or nose, but it acted as though it was looking at Sungchul. As though it was a normal person. Sungchul knew exactly what it was.

It's a servant of the Ancient God.

It wasn't an opponent that he couldn't overcome, but it was one that he'd rather not fight. He swung his hammer and spoke briefly. "Get lost."

"..."

The creature dripping with slime stood blankly while looking at Sungchul before disappearing silently into the darkness.

Bertelgia who had been hiding behind Sungchul slowly popped out with a question, "Just what is that?"

"It's a Despair of the Abyss."

"A Despair of the Abyss?"

Sungchul nodded. "When it meets an existence weaker than itself, it tries to drag its victim into its pit regardless of whether the victim is a human or a demon."

And even the dead. A deathly stillness surrounded anywhere a Despair of the Abyss claimed as its own.

"Uuu... it's scarier because I think I know what you mean." Bertelgia trembled once again. "Do you think the soldiers before were this guy's doing?"

"Unlikely. Anyone that a Despair of the Abyss drags away is erased from existence. Not even a corpse would be left behind."

"Does that mean there are other monsters here too?"

Sungchul nodded as he began to think. *The power in my body must have lured this creature. It shouldn't have revealed itself to the exploratory squad.*

Sungchul remembered the report that they gave to Willie, if they had run into a Despair of the Abyss, none of them would have been left to tell the tale. Sungchul recalled what a nightmarish creatures the things called Despair of the Abyss truly were, even though they weren't a match for his current self.

Sungchul continued forth. He continued to discover more corpses of soldiers. One corpse. Two corpses. Then ten corpses. Sungchul could find traces of a fierce battle around each corpse: singe marks from magical flames, carved out walls where a Sword Master's sword aura would have sliced through, and splinters of shattered spear tips strewn about the floor. However, he couldn't find even a single trace of whatever the opposing monster might be. It was truly a strange occurrence. In cases of such large-scale battles, it would be normal to see at least a clue about the opposing side.

"..."

Sungchul stopped hiding his presence. He pulled out a torch from his Soul Storage, lit it, then began walking in loud footsteps. Surprisingly, he could hear some rustling noise in his surroundings soon after. He could see the teeming mass of monsters beyond the darkness. Two legs and both arms, also a pair of wings. Altogether, it was a disfigured corpse of an avian that walked on six legs.

"..."

The avian corpse crawled up silently like a centipede and leaped toward Sungchul. Its head with its lifeless eyes began to peck him fiercely. Fal Garaz split the air.

WHAM!

When the avian corpse was struck with the destructive blow from the divine hammer, it disintegrated into dust. Sungchul finally discovered why there were no corpses of the monsters.

The musky smell resembling a charnel house must be from the disintegrated corpses.

Dozens of Avian corpses began to crawl around like centipedes as they carefully eyed Sungchul.

"Uu! I wanna go back!" Bertelgia hid in Sungchul's pocket. Sungchul's hammer flew with even more vigor.

WHAM! WHAM! WHAM!

The grotesque spirits were no match for him. They turned to dust, and the remaining spirits fled into the darkness. Stillness returned to the dungeon.

When the battle ended, Bertelgia left the pocket once more and opened herself up to a page.

"What's that?" asked Sungchul.

A simple map that looked as though it was drawn hurriedly with a pen appeared on the page.

"I tried making a map," replied Bertelgia.

"A map?"

"Yep. This dungeon… it doesn't look small."

Sungchul agreed with her on this point, but there was a secret method that could allow him to easily break through this maze.

WHAM!

An opposing wall crumbled, and a large hole formed within it. Beyond the wall, there was another corridor. Sungchul walked across the corridor, then swung at another wall. BOOM! He continued this process until a dead end of the dungeon appeared.

"Mmm…" Bertelgia, who had spent some effort in drawing a map on one of her pages, let out a sigh. "It's quite handy if you're strong, isn't it?"

"…"

Sungchul fixed his grip on the hammer, then turned toward the north and began his excavation once again. When a total of four walls were smashed, he stood before a cliff. The pit surrounded in darkness was shrouded in an indeterminate green fog that obstructed his vision of the other side.

Sungchul tossed down a rock and listened for a sound. It was quite a deep pit. He thought as such and turned to a different direction.

Bertelgia spat out a question. "What's so great about making holes like this?"

"I'm making my own path. It's too easy to lose your way in a maze like this."

If there was no path, make one. It was Sungchul's method of clearing dungeons. Also, making this kind of a ruckus would draw out creatures hidden within the dungeon without forcing him to seek them out.

STEP STEP.

Before long, he could feel another presence. It was the presence of humans. Sungchul put away Fal Garaz into his Soul Storage and waited for the group of humans to arrive. Beyond the darkness, a female mage surrounded by a translucent fog appeared before him. There were five armor-clad homunculi around her feet. Sungchul was already aware of her presence, but he pretended not to have noticed and continued to stare ahead.

She took some time to observe him. His appearance, attire, equipment, and even his stats. She checked everything that could be secretly observed. After a complete inspection, the female mage removed her magical veil and revealed herself.

"Who are you?" asked Mimi Azrael, the leader of the exploratory squad.

Chapter 4 – Those who Swallowed the Nahak

Mimi had the outward appearance of a woman in her mid-20s. The gleam of her cold blue staring eyes was visible under the hood she wore over her head.

She raised her staff. "I'll ask again. Who are you?"

"Number 34." Sungchul pointed toward the cloth number that was attached to his coat. Mimi did not understand the meaning behind the number.

"I see, Mr. 34. Ok. How did you get here?" Mimi looked toward Bertelgia who was flying about behind Sungchul.

"Ms Mimi! The book flies! It's so wondrous-yeyo!!"

"That's called a familiar. Don't flap your lips if you're ignorant-yeyo!"

The homunculi that had been playing about beneath her skirt grew rowdy. When she lifted her staff, the homunculi lowered their head and immediately quieted down. Azrael looked at Sungchul again with an interrogating glare as silence returned to the dungeon.

"Now. Your answer is?"

Sungchul looked at her without any trace of hesitation as he answered her in a firm voice. "…I am currently investigating what is inside this dungeon."

When she heard his reply, she revealed a cold smile. "Big balls on this one. I don't know where you herald from, but I advise you to retreat from here within a week."

"For what reason?" asked Sungchul.

"The Seventh Champion of the Continent. Willie Gilford is on his way here."

"…"

Nothing would change whether he was here or not, but Sungchul remained silent.

Mimi looked over at the hole created by him. "What is this? Did you perhaps do that?"

Sungchul neither admitted it nor denied it.

"A living book type familiar… you appear to be a mage." She had already looked over his stats through the translucent fog. It wasn't anything impressive. It was why she chose to reveal herself without anyone to support her.

"What's it to you whether I'm a mage or not?" Sungchul finally spoke. Mimi looked at Sungchul with a chilling glare before turning around with a nod.

"Chief Investigator Ujira. Use the veil," she said to one of the homunculi.

Mimi and the five homunculi were then surrounded by an invisible fog which removed them from sight.

"I'll warn you again, but it's to your benefit to leave quickly. There are mighty Sword Masters here as well, then in a week's time…"

She let her words intermingled with hostile intent linger in the air as she disappeared into the darkness. However, Sungchul had the Eye of Truth within his Soul Contract. The figures of Mimi and her five homunculi veiled by the invisible fog reappeared into his sights.

"…"

Sungchul hid his presence and quietly tailed Mimi.

—

Mimi walked along silently like a cat before arriving at a specific area. It was an empty plot that was surrounded on all sides by hastily made fortifications. There were about fifteen soldiers and members of the exploratory squad catching their breath.

"Ugh…" There were quite a few wounded soldiers as well. One of the soldiers was muttering something to himself as he punched the air. Perhaps he had been critically wounded. He was gradually dying by himself in a dark corner as even the mage tending to him had given up. Mimi took off her invisible veil at this point.

"One human has died-yeyo!"

"He was a human who harassed us; it's good riddance-yeyo!"

The calmed homunculi began to grow rowdy once again.

"Ms Mimi said we should abandon the ruins and retreat-yeyo, why does this dumb human not listen to Ms Mimi?"

"That is because they are dumb-yeyo!"

"At least the day when we become real fairies is arriving sooner due to that-yeyo!"

Annoying voices poured out in all directions from the empty plot. It was at that moment one man suddenly shouted, "Can't they keep their mouths shut?!"

It was Willie Gilford's son, Mikhael Gilford. The confident youth with an elegant armor that was fitted to his form made his way toward Mimi with anger on his face. "How many times do I have to tell you to muzzle those fucking homunculi? Hm? What are you going to do if those monstrous creatures show up again, you damned witch?"

"… Your voice seems to be quite a bit louder?" Mimi didn't show any change in her expression even in the face of Mikhael engaging her so aggressively. Mikhael glared at her response as though he wanted to tear her apart with his bare teeth for a long while before chewing on his lips and taking practice swings with his sword.

"This was why we shouldn't have brought a fucking witch! Garbage that uses taboo magic should always be cut down with a blade!"

"If you cut me down, you might as well put an end to this scouting mission. I'm the only one that knows the way."

Mikhael's face twisted a degree further. It was then a man stepped up to hold him back. The man in his forties with a large scar across his face was in a servant's attire that didn't suit his solemn expression.

"Young master, there is no good that will come out of this anger."

"Mmm… Old man Ord."

Surprisingly, Mikhael looked as though his anger had washed away as the man stepped in. He had an unnaturally rapid change of heart as he looked back toward Mimi with a refreshing smile as he offered her an apology. "I was in the wrong, Scout Leader. It looks as though the tense situation made me lose control of my temper. It was immature of me."

Mimi heard his apology, yet made no reaction to it. "…I'll give you my scouting report." She instead made a report on her scouting mission with a frozen expression as though she was looking at an inanimate object.

Mikhael leaned onto a rock as he nodded.

"…When I arrived at the source of the noise, I ran across what appeared to be a male human mage."

"A human? His affiliations?" Mikhael looked surprised and quickly made his inquiry.

"I can't determine his affiliations. He called himself Number 34. However, he was dressed like a beggar in a pitiful attire of a Summoned. He also had a living book familiar," responded Mimi.

"A living book, eh? What a rare item. How is his strength? Is he up to a mid-grade mage?"

"I did peek at his stats, but it wasn't outstanding. However, I can't discount the possibility that he might be disguising his stats. It could also be some devil disguised as a human."

"Devils don't come to this place. They can't come here. It is a place crawling with their natural predators," said Mikhael with a smile.

"I tried to look around for his companions but found nothing." The report ended here. Mikhael made a gesture for Mimi to stand down before he gathered his subordinates and personal servant to discuss.

"Another explorer. Who do you think sent him?"

"There shouldn't be any new developments regarding the Underground Kingdom. We should consider all possibilities. It is most likely that he's from the Human Empire, but we can't discount the Kingdom of Etteria. No one is thirstier of magic than the elves."

"But, if they can find that, they should be able to produce a monster on the level of the Enemy of the World."

Sungchul, who was quietly hiding in the darkness, eavesdropped on their conversation. He could discern two facts: the exploratory unit within these ruins was seeking a particular item, and the information regarding the Underground Kingdom was publicly available.

It appears as though Deckard was not the only one to have discovered information relating to the existence of the Underground Kingdom.

Rather, Deckard's information was only baby steps at this point. He couldn't even find the entrance to the Underground Kingdom. It looked as though this exploratory unit knew much more. They knew what was hidden in this dungeon and the dangers lying within. Sungchul could now understand why Willie Gilford had hesitated in stepping in personally. He knew that a Despair of the Abyss had been sighted here. There was no other explanation other than this.

Sungchul left his hiding spot and returned to the darkness of the dungeon. He walked from the entrance back to the path he had created.

When Sungchul arrived at a point devoid of people, Bertelgia spoke again. "Those homunculi. It looked as though they were strengthened artificially."

"Is that so?"

Sungchul had perceived that those homunculi were different than the average ones, but he didn't pay much mind to it. At his level, homunculi would always be homunculi.

"But that woman is amazing. Seeing how loyal they are to her despite having done quite horrific things to their bodies," continued Bertelgia.

"Horrific things?" asked Sungchul.

"Those homunculi. Do you remember that their bodies were completely clad in armor? It isn't just to protect them. It was probably to prevent them from looking at their own appearances."

It was nearly nonexistent in Sungchul's time, but empowered homunculi must have been commonplace during the era Bertelgia was from. The population was decreasing, but they needed the power of magic. They had begun to modify the homunculi that had a human's intellect to make them proficient enough for combat and support. The biggest drawback was that the known techniques for strengthening would horrifically disfigure the homunculi's appearance.

"So that was a thing." Sungchul had confronted countless mages, but he had never seen any that had strengthened homunculi.

"It was probably banned. Such a horrific method was fated to be entered into the list of forbidden spells someday…" said Bertelgia.

"…"

Sungchul who had been listening to Bertelgia's story in silence finally discovered a red light beyond the darkness. There was a mound of human corpses. The red light emitted from a magic staff held by one of the corpses.

Sungchul carefully inspected the bodies. *A year? Maybe 2? These bodies are in a better condition than the avian corpses.*

These corpses mummified upon death and retained much of their former appearance. The cause of death appeared to be suicide. There were some with a bluish hue indicative of having taken poison, and others had died with a self-inflicted knife wound to the throat.

Sungchul discovered a worn-out diary on the body of the mage looking most noble among the corpses. Parts of the record were too damaged from the fluids leaked from the corpse to be read, but the final page had been preserved. Sungchul read through the last page with a nose full of revolting smells.

[Day 14]

Everything is proceeding smoothly. I already await the day that his imperial majesty sounds the news of his victory.

[Day 15]

Jara and Wesley, who had been getting along very well since long ago, requested that I act as their officiant. They requested to hold their ceremony in the Audience Chamber of the Nahak King. The audacious ideas of the Summoned often astound me.

[Day 16]

Jara had disappeared. Wesley left without notice in search for her. I only pray to the God of Order that everything is ok.

[Day 17]

[Day 18]

42325 54423 99832 31125 34238

88823 42321 11232 44235 19321

88768 11132 08323 13578 69180

The records ended at this point. Bertelgia who was reading beside him asked with a quizzical expression, "What is that last set of numbers?"

"It's an encrypted message."

"Encrypted message?"

Sungchul pulled out a faded book from his Soul Storage.

It was a book printed from a rotary press of the modern world. The old book contained a lot of numbers within, but there was also an explanation preceding them. It was a solution manual for sending secret messages via encrypted broadcast. Sungchul had received this book directly from the Emperor of the Human Empire, William Quinton Marlboro. Before their relationship deteriorated, anyways.

Sungchul opened the book and began to seek out the random numbers along with the explanation following them to decipher the message. The deciphered message was as follows:

[Third Floor Underground, Existence of Massive Cavern, Large Number of Eyeless Monsters, Attacked, Relay Farewell to Family, This is my final request.]

"What was it trying to say?" Bertelgia hurried him by poking on his shoulder. Sungchul closed the book and returned it to his Soul Storage before speaking.

"It looks as though there is definitely something underground. Monsters without eyes seem to be inhabiting the place."

The avian corpses were just the prelude to what was to come. There were creatures more bizarre and grotesque lurking beyond them. Sungchul put down the record to continue his exploration of the dungeon. When he finally discovered the stairs leading down to the floor below, Bertelgia diligently recorded Sungchul's path in her pages. "Map complete!"

Sungchul descended the dark spiral staircase which was littered with skeletons of the avian race. An obsidian door blocked his path at the end of the steps. The Eye of Truth reacted to the magic cast upon it.

This is dangerous.

It was a destructive magic that was powerful enough to cause the entire dungeon to collapse if he activated it carelessly. This was not something that a hammer could solve.

Sungchul approached the door and once he did, text soon appeared before him.

[This is a place that only the holy and majestic avian, Nahak, may enter.]

[Display the symbol of the Nahak.]

"What should we do? It doesn't look as though it'll just let us pass." Bertelgia circled Sungchul's vicinity while speaking with a concerned voice. Sungchul looked around the door's surroundings.

Before the door was a small altar with a hole and just below it was an obsidian shard. The obsidian, which still contained magic energy, looked like it might partially fit into the hole built into the altar. Sungchul placed the shard inside the altar as a test.

Immediately, magical energies of the altar enveloped the shard then dissipated once more.

[Display the proper symbol]

A statue in the shape of a bird man standing next to the door began to emit red lights from his two eyes.

"…"

Sungchul retreated up the stairs for now.

"What should we do now?" asked Bertelgia.

He ignored the endlessly talking Bertelgia who was following beside him and took a few steps forward once he reached back to the stair entrance.

This looks good.

It was an ordinary bedrock with no reaction to magic whatsoever. Sungchul pulled out Fal Garaz and swiped at the floor. When the hammer struck the ground, the large bedrock cracked and broke off.

As the entire dungeon shook, hundreds of avian corpses appeared before him. Sungchul resumed his work after the one-sided slaughter. A large hole appeared where he had been pounding away with his hammer, and he jumped into it.

BOOM!

A weighty landing. The back of the obsidian door that had refused to open stood behind Sungchul.

"Bertelgia. Draw out the map for the second floor starting from here."

***

BOOM! BOOM!

Sungchul continued the same way he did on the first floor. However, he noticed something different compared to the walls on the first floor as he worked his way through. There were bones of what appeared to be of animals, perhaps even human.

A pile of bones emerged from between the brick and mortar masonry wall. Considering more than a few bones were coming out, Sungchul couldn't help but be curious.

He stopped working for a moment to peer inside the area where he broke the wall. There were countless skeletons stacked within. Sungchul gripped the surface with his hand and easily pulled it apart, and, when he did, he discovered a skeleton that had managed to keep its original form intact.

"..."

Sungchul's pupils shrank. These were human skeletons trapped between the walls. They weren't from the avian race. Perhaps, they were buried alive as they were constructing this dungeon. It wasn't just one or two people, but it seemed that thousands or tens of thousands of individuals made up this graveyard.

Sungchul finally said, "It looks as though the Nahak were quite the cruel race."

"According to legend, the Nahak were known to be an arrogant and cruel race. More than anything, they didn't have a shred of mercy toward the other races. These corpses were probably once slaves." Bertelgia flew about the intact skeleton and explained what she knew. "Even if that was the case, they did something unimaginable: burying all these living people inside a wall. Those birdbrains."

"Why did they do this?" asked Sungchul. There was a gentle fury beneath his voice.

"Couldn't it be to gather their magical power? You know, using their pain and anguish as nourishment?"

"I would really like to see a living Nahak." Sungchul fixed his grip on his hammer as he muttered. His work began once again. The wall fell, and the skeletons within poured onto the floor. This was repeated several times until he reached the end of the second floor. Sungchul put his back to a bedrock and took a brief rest. It had been a while since he had used his strength like this, and he was feeling a bit peckish.

Should I make a meal?

However, this was not a good place to eat. Sungchul didn't eat just anywhere.

He turned back towards the path he had created but witnessed a strange occurrence along the way. Something was huddled over in the distant darkness, gluttonously eating the bones on the floor.

CRUNCH. CRUNCH.

Bertelgia tensed her body at the definite sound of chewing bone coming from the distance. "Uuu… What is it this time? I really want to leave now."

Sungchul walked over to the creature in question without another word. The creature lifted its head as Sungchul drew close, then let out an ear-piercing scream.

"Kiiiii—!!"

It was a sound that wasn't quite human nor beastly, but almost mechanical in nature. Sungchul acknowledged the intricacies of the sound but focused more on the creature's appearance. It looked quite human, but the skin was sickly pale, and the face was so grotesquely twisted that it was difficult to look at without grimacing.

The creature's most striking features were the empty spaces where eyes should have been and the rows of what should be called teeth. The teeth grew randomly and chaotically all over its mouth, and some even punctured through and stuck out of the face tissue.

"Hiii…" Bertelgia dropped out of the air as if she had fainted when she saw the hideous appearance of the monster.

Sungchul picked her up off the floor and placed her into his pocket before glaring at the creature. "Get lost."

But the creature did not move. It let out a monstrous cry instead and lunged at him.

WHAM!

His hammer destroyed the creature's skull and sent it flying off back into the darkness. The broken teeth scattered and made clinging noises as they fell onto the floor.

"…"

Sungchul glanced into the darkness. An incalculable number of those creatures was silently and stealthily approaching his location.

He briefly took a moment to think. The question was whether to kill all of the incoming monsters or to simply retreat from here. In the end, he chose to erase his presence and retreat from this place. He was feeling a bit hungry, and it might reduce his long-awaited appetite to deal with the grotesque monsters. He put the gathering creatures behind him and climbed back up through the hole he had created before. There were several members of the exploratory unit loitering outside the hole. When they saw Sungchul, they asked a question out of surprise, "W-who are you?"

Sungchul looked at every one of their faces. There were five in all. A party composed of two mages and three soldiers. He couldn't see Mikhael or Mimi. Sungchul pointed towards the piece of cloth attached to his person then spoke. "I am Number 34."

"Number… 34? Just what are you doing down here in a place like this?"

"I just came down because I saw a hole. Some fun things seem to be crawling around."

"Something… fun? Are you talking about the Nahak skeletons?"

Sungchul shook his head. "The monsters were blind and had a humanoid form, crawling around in droves."

The faces of the exploratory unit members who heard Sungchul's words became serious and twisted.

"It sounds like he's seen the Cave Elves."

"Cave Elves?" inquired Sungchul.

"Well, they were once creatures known as Cave Elves to be exact. Their race was enslaved and brutally exploited by the Nahaks, but after their extinction, it's the Cave Elves that control the dungeon now. They are strong, persistent, and still have some level of intelligence. They are extremely dangerous."

It was at this moment that a piercing shriek rang out. "Kiii—!"

It was the cry of the blind monsters. The members of the exploratory unit turned pale as sheets, then hurried to leave the place.

"L…let's return quickly. What scouting, schmouting? We're all about to die here!"

The members of the exploratory unit disappeared into the darkness as if their pants were on fire. Sungchul gave them a small service; He blocked the hole with a large boulder just in case the blind creatures emerge from it. After blocking his personal entrance, Sungchul continued to follow the path he created and left the dungeon.

—

The brunch for the day was fish. Sungchul jumped into the ice-cold water with a harpoon in hand. There were massive dark creatures swimming in the shadowy water. They were known as the Demon Fish, and they lived in the seas along the frontlines of the Demon Realm. They were about as large as an adult male. One of the fish discovered Sungchul, opened its maw, then leaped toward him.

STAB!

The harpoon pierced its forehead. The blood pouring out from its wound dissipated into the water like smoke. The large fish struggled once or twice, but as Sungchul's fist came down upon its head a few times, it gave up.

Sungchul grabbed the massive fish that was about his size with just his arms. A swarm of sharks that smelled the blood in the water began to gather. He grabbed the fish's gills to tear off its head, which he fed to the sharks, then headed leisurely toward the shore. The cooking utensils were already prepared on land.

"Goodness. At least you're diligent in preparing your meals," Bertelgia, who could not consume food, said while flapping in the air.

"…"

Sungchul pulled out a blade from his Soul Storage. By the bluish light emitting from it, it was obvious at a glance that it was a renowned sword of great repute. There was a beautifully engraved symbol of a lion representing the Human Empire on its grip. It was a gift from the Emperor that was coveted by every knight within the Human Empire, but to Sungchul it was just another tool for his cooking. The blue tinted blade plunged into the silvery scales of the Demon Fish, then was expertly wielded to rapidly remove the scales. Sungchul put the fish down and headed to the boiling pot once he was finished descaling the fish.

Within the pot were dried vegetables, fish, mushrooms, and various other things for a soup stock. Sungchul scooped a bit of soup with a bowl to test the flavor. "Mmm."

The flavouring was proper. He cut away a portion of fish and chopped it into paper thin slices before arranging it onto a plate. Chopsticks appeared from the Soul Storage.

Sungchul grabbed a slice of fish, dipped it briefly into the boiling soup, then put it in his mouth. The deep flavour of the soup along with the rich flavour of the fish melted together deliciously in his mouth.

[The score of this recipe is... 63!]

The score appeared before his eyes, but he didn't mind it. He solemnly gazed out taking in the scenery of the Demon Realm as he continued his meal alone. When Sungchul was starting to feel sated, he added dry noodles to the fish broth and let it boil.

Once the noodles softened up, Sungchul moved it to a bowl and poured the soup on top. Blowing on the steaming noodles, he gulped them down.

"Mmm." It had a great taste. He could feel his mind and body being reinvigorated.

When the meal ended, Bertelgia began to pout as though she had been waiting for him the entire time. "Quite the dedication to food. Really. Every meal."

"It is important to eat well," said Sungchul and he grabbed the half-eaten fish by the tail, then tossed it toward the ocean. It made a huge splash and made some waves. He then extinguished the fire beneath his pot and washed his dishes in the ocean. It was always wonderful to cook, but dishes were always annoying. Sungchul didn't particularly like to do it.

"I wish I had a familiar to do my dishes," Sungchul muttered to himself as he cleaned the pot and placed it into his Soul Storage.

"Hmph! In your dreams! I am a privileged lady who has never soiled her fingers with chores in her life!" retorted Bertelgia.

"That doesn't really sound like something to boast about."

"Keep a homunculus or two if you want someone around to do your dishes."

"I don't have a hobby of keeping those noisy things."

"How about a Cave Elf? I think they'll be quiet as long as they aren't shrieking."

"Well... Those monsters might be preferable to a homunculus when it comes to noise."

Sungchul suddenly recalled the woman who herded around the five homunculi. She held the title of "Captain of the Exploratory Unit," but she was simply a puppet. The actual authority seemed to be held by Willie's son, Mikhael.

That woman. Her eyes were fierce.

He had yet to see her capabilities, but to be placed as the Exploratory Unit's Captain by Willie personally meant that her abilities would be comparable to a court mage. Someone of that level quietly enduring insult from a greenhorn Sword Master was unheard of, and that is even after taking into consideration the characteristics of the Ancient Kingdom. That group was bound to have problems in the future. Not that he cared one way or the other.

Sungchul, who had satisfied his hunger, returned to the dungeon. However, the dungeon he returned to had changed in several aspects. The blind monsters were now present in every corner.

"..."

The monsters could not see Sungchul who stood in front of them. They had no eyes. Instead, the monsters differentiated objects through sound and smell.

"Sniff, sniff!" A monster's upturned nose began to sniff the air. Sungchul snuck through them like a ghost and headed toward the second-floor entrance. The stone was still in the place he had left it. This meant that nothing had left through this hole.

Sungchul changed his path to descend down the stairs. There were a large number of Cave Elves lingering around the vicinity of the stairs. He slipped by them soundlessly toward the second floor. When he reached the second floor, he found out how the cave elves were able to climb up to the first. It was because the immovable black door had been flung open. There was a spherical proof of the Nahak placed in the hole. The spherical mark of the Nahak gave off a brilliant light as it sat in the alcove of the altar.

When Sungchul pulled away the symbol of the Nahak from the altar, the obsidian door immediately shut again. He put away the symbol into his pocket and began to ponder on a question.

Who opened this door?

Nothing was confirmed. It was at that moment when a sharp shriek began to chorus on the floor above.

***

Sungchul ran directly to the first floor. Sensing a presence, the blind monsters waved their arms in search for him, but Sungchul had already moved past them. He passed by them like a gust of wind and the only thing that remained in Sungchul's eyes were the wide-eyed corpses of the Exploratory Unit. One of them was the man who had explained to Sungchul about the Cave Elves. The man had died with his eyes still open, and below his head were two

Cave Elves, busily drinking his blood and devouring his flesh. The corpse of the young man shook each time the hideous cave elf moved its jaw.

"..."

Sungchul pulled out a single whip from his Soul Storage. The whip was ten meters long with steel cleats embedded along its length that gave off a red light. The Demonic Whip Cassandra. It was an infamous demonic weapon once wielded by the leader of the Balroqs. It was capable of ripping apart the armor and flesh of holy knights with a single blow and was magically enchanted with the ability to sear the enemy with the fires of hell. The reason Sungchul put away Fal Garaz for Cassandra was simple.

SWISH!

The ten-meter long whip cracked in the air and struck dozens of Cave Elves with enough force to pound them into the ground. One swing was enough to scatter them all, and the magical enchantment on Cassandra caused the corpses of the Cave Elves to burn from the fires of hell. It was a suitable ending for their evil deeds.

What kind of a reaction would the rest of the Cave Elves have to the smell of their burning kin? Sungchul wondered as he kicked away two Cave Elves that were dumbly searching around his feet. The monsters had their skulls caved in and died a distance away before they could even scream.

"..."

Sungchul gazed into the darkness. Dozens of Cave Elves were drawn by the sounds and smells to his location. Sungchul sharply struck the ground with Cassandra for them to hear.

WHAP!

The sharp sound echoed in the dungeon, and the mass of Cave Elves began to reveal themselves. Cassandra split the air with one sharp motion. A single strike struck down dozens of Cave Elves like blades of grass. Not even five minutes had passed before corpses of the elves were burning all around Sungchul. It was at this moment the Cave Elves realized that the man with the whip was not someone they could mess with.

"Shiiik! Kahiiik!" A Cave Elf let out a sharp shriek from the rear. It caused the other Cave Elves to abandon the corpses of their kin and flee into the darkness. Sungchul who had just finished a round of massacre stood still to focus on the sounds in the cave. He could hear the faint sounds of a battle raging on nearby.

Sungchul immediately headed over there. The Swordsmen of the Ancient Kingdom were engaged in a fierce fight against the Cave Elves. The Cave Elves had oppressive numbers, but there was a Sword Master on the side of humans. Mikhael swung his blade which emitted its bluish sword aura as he drove into the center of the formation of the Cave Elves.

"3… 2… 1… Go! Shoot!"

He spun like a top and began to blindly slaughter the enemy leaving nothing but chunks of corpses in his wake. However, the Cave Elves didn't take the assault lying down. An elderly cave elf with bone piercings around its face waited until the moment Mikhael's spin grew weaker to fire a bone arrow toward him. It flew with a terrifying force toward his neck like lightning.

At that moment, a man appeared protectively and knocked away the arrow with a staff.

Quite a skilled fellow. Sungchul's eyes lit up with curiosity.

He had wondered who it was, and it turned out to be the man in his forties in the attire of a butler.

"Young master. The winner is he who captures the final five seconds. Please do not forget."

"I appreciate it, Odrias."

After expressing the proper formalities, Mikhael prepared for the final assault with his subordinate Sword Adepts. The battle ended the moment the old cave elf with the piercings died.

The elves ran away, never to attack again.

Mimi revealed herself once the battle was over by ripping off the veil covering her and her homunculi and walked over to where Mikhael stood.

SLAP!

Her hand struck Mikhael's cheek. The moment Mikhael's eyes were about to show hostility, Odrias kept him in check. He was already standing behind Mimi and shaking his head.

"Why did you open the door?" asked Mimi. "Just why did you open the door?" she aggressively pressed on.

"It was a door that had to be opened anyways." Mikhael answered as he rubbed the cheek that had been struck.

A bone chilling hostility rose from Mimi's eyes. "Can you even call that an excuse? Can you be so shameless after looking at the tragedy you've caused?"

"Tragedy? What tragedy? The real tragedy hasn't even occurred yet." Mikhael spat on the floor as he turned around. He peered at Mimi who was glaring at him through the corner of his eyes as he spoke in a frosty tone.

"It appears that you're not familiar with my father, Willie Gilford. You shouldn't interpret his words so literally."

"… what does that mean?" asked Mimi.

"My father said thus: 'Secure the area around the dungeon for a week.' But was that really all that he wanted? I don't think so."

"…"

"My father probably desired us to finish exploring the deeper areas of the dungeon, rather than wasting our time for a week doing nothing," continued Mikhael.

"I don't understand why we have to follow orders that weren't even given?"

"This is the proof that you don't truly understand the social conventions of the Ancient Kingdom." Mikhael treated her as though he was scolding a child. Mimi gazed at Odrias who now stood behind Mikhael. The man in a butler attire met eyes with Mimi, then spoke in a low voice with a nod.

"As young master has said, we must hurry. If Master Gilford discovers that we didn't manage to gain any results by the time he returns, he'll write us off. I hope you'll keep this in mind as we progress from this point on."

Mimi did not speak any further. Even as Mikhael and gang disappeared deeper into the dungeon, she stood blankly staring at the floor with an expression that showed that she didn't quite understand the situation around her. Sungchul didn't disagree with her sentiment, but the Other World was full of irrationalities such as this. There were bound to be one or two psychotic organizations.

"Miss Mimi, are you upset-yeyo?" a homunculus lingering around her feet carefully asked the question.

"…"

She didn't reply.

The other homunculi who had been keeping quiet began to speak. "You do not have to worry! Miss Mimi, as long as you have us, completing this dungeon is nothing too difficult-yeyo!"

"Since things have gone this way, let's complete this dungeon and take the prize for ourselves-yeyo!"

"And then you'll make us into real fairies-yeyo, not homunculi!"

At that moment, a man stepped out from the darkness in front of her. It was none other than Sungchul. Mimi was momentarily shocked, but she regained her calm expression and spoke in a soft voice. "You. You're still alive?"

"…"

Sungchul brushed past her and took in her face, expression, the emotions in her eyes, the magic hidden within her thick robe, and each of the homunculi huddled beneath her feet.

She definitely is not someone to be taken lightly.

She was ready. In many different ways. He couldn't see her stats, but regardless, he could clearly see that Mimi was an experienced mage even without having to see them. The sparkling eyes of the homunculi beneath their iron masks further reinforced the idea.

After finishing his cursory observations, Sungchul opened his mouth to speak. "I won't die to something like Cave Elves."

"I see. Also, it seems that you are quite capable in stealth seeing as even my little guys couldn't detect a thing."

Sungchul didn't respond to unnecessary inquiries. Instead, he moved on to the reason he'd revealed himself to her.

"What's that about? That thing your homunculi were speaking of."

A look of surprise appeared briefly on her face. "Did you come here not knowing about it? Or are you sizing me up?"

"..."

"Well, it's fine either way, considering that you and I have different circumstances. I'll tell you what they were talking about because allies can be found in all kinds of circumstances."

Mimi created a small sphere and sent it toward Sungchul. It was a marble of knowledge. Sungchul snatched the marble and accepted the information within. His eyes were soon filled with bright letters.

[Crown of the King of the Nahak]

The mighty avian race, who commanded the heavens and the earth, were buried underground and annihilated. The sole survivor, the king of the avian race, had sacrificed the entirety of his species in exchange for a magic power never before seen in history, but he too succumbed to ruin. Find his final resting place. And obtain his crown. The one who obtains the crown will experience a small fragment of reality only the Nahak knew.

Reward – Indeterminate

Sungchul, who read the long message, looked back at Mimi with a cold gaze and spoke bluntly. "Is this what you all are looking for? The crown of the Nahak race?"

Mimi nodded. "The crown commands an incredible amount of magic power. There is a legend that tells us that whoever obtains the crown will be granted that incredible strength."

"Why are you telling me this, I wonder."

"I don't know. Maybe it's because there is no way you'll get your hands on it even if I tell you." Mimi spoke as such and then lightly tapped her head with her finger. "If you don't have the knowledge I have, that is."

She made a meaningful smile, then spoke again. "You. You're hiding your strength, aren't you?"

It was a straightforward question. There was no reason to hide it now. Sungchul nodded. "A bit."

"I like your honesty. Why not be a bit more honest at this point?"

The atmosphere around her shifted slightly. The cold hostility in her voice warmed up, and the wariness in her eyes went away. Mimi spoke in an indifferent tone. "How strong are you?"

Sungchul didn't hesitate in answering her question. "I'm probably the strongest human in this dungeon."

Mimi looked a bit surprised, then asked with a bit of mischief in her tone. "Even more than Willie Gilford?"

Sungchul opted to remain silent on that question.

Mimi made a bitter smile. "That last question was a joke. Although I'm a bit surprised that you're stronger than those idiot Sword Masters." She held a soft smile as she led her homunculi forward.

"I don't think we were done speaking," said Sungchul as he glared at her back.

Mimi turned slightly and answered with a smile in her eyes. "If you're as strong as you say, we'll meet again at some point. We'll pick up the story where we left off then."

Mimi disappeared into the darkness with her homunculi while Sungchul gazed at her fading figure with indifference.

It looks as though this dungeon is definitely hiding something beyond my expectations.

Something within him began to ignite once again.

Chapter 5 – Tomb of the Avian King

After a bit of preparation, Sungchul proceeded to clear the second-floor basement. The large number of Cave Elves weren't a problem.

FWISH! FWISH!

After a couple of massacres, the Cave Elves fled in a panic at the mere sound of Cassandra flicking in the air. They seemed to possess a certain degree of intelligence as they launched a mass attack with hundreds of individuals hiding in ambush and a traditional upfront assault with a smaller group of elite soldiers. But no matter what tactic or strategy they employed, it was all for naught in the face of Sungchul and his demonic weapon Cassandra.

FWAP! FWICK!

The blind creatures began to tremble at the sound of death itself that this intruder wielded, and did not dare approach him.

"… You're quite experienced at this." Bertelgia who had been silent during all this spoke quietly.

"You shouldn't be careless while dealing with primitive races. They are cunning and savage to the point of fairness. You'll be fighting them forever if they think you're weak or if you give them an inch."

SLAP!

Sungchul spoke as he slapped the whip across the floor once again.

"I guess you've done this a lot," replied Bertelgia.

Sungchul nodded at her comment. "I've been around a few dungeons and mazes."

Memories of dungeons he could barely even remember flashed before his eyes. There were some that made him feel nostalgic at the mere sight of them, while others were just nightmarish.

"Anyways, this dungeon. There is a plentiful amount of mana flowing in here, unlike the outside. Do you feel it?" asked Bertelgia.

"A bit," responded Sungchul.

A much more dense concentration of mana existed here in the Underground Palace of the Nahak compared to the outside to be exact. Plentiful environmental mana meant that the same spells would be cast with more power and lost mana would be recovered much more quickly.

"While we're in this situation, why not use spells to break through instead of the whip? Wasn't your goal magic proficiency anyways?" suggested Bertelgia.

"That is something to consider."

It was definitely more convenient to proceed using the demonic equipment Cassandra, but it was more appealing to use magic for training as magic, like the body, improved with use.

"The environment is also good for Alchemy because high-level Alchemic Items require a lot of mana. You should be able to make up to level 5 Alchemic Items without chugging down Mana Essence like before," said Bertelgia.

"You make a good point."

Bertelgia flew up and down at Sungchul's rare compliment while pretending to clear her throat in pride. "Of course. Who do you think Bertelgia is? I am the embodiment of knowledge itself!"

Sungchul placed the whip into his Soul Storage as he continued the exploration. He saw a group of Cave Elves loitering about. Sungchul used Glare on the Cave Elves; the beam of light tore through their flesh, burning away their innards.

"Kiiiii!" The Cave Elf that was struck directly with Glare flailed about wildly before falling. The rest of the Cave Elves determined Sungchul's location and lunged to attack.

Sungchul leisurely dodged their attacks while piercing their vitals with Glare without error. Every time a beam of light sprouted from his fingertips, a Cave Elf fell.

"Kiii!" The only one who remained looked like the boss of the lot. Unlike others, it wore a metal armor over its chest and held a weapon and shield made to look like claws by using what appeared to be interwoven beaks.

He looks like an adequate opponent to test my current level of strength.

Sungchul slowly extended his finger to cast Glare. The Cave Elf was instinctively wary of Sungchul's finger movements and raised his shield.

CHIIIII.

Glare's beam of light struck directly at the surface of the shield, but that wasn't all.

"Kiiii?" It went on to pierce the shield and the breastplate, searing the Cave Elf's flesh. It didn't pierce him all the way through, but it was enough to leave the Cave Elf in poor spirits.

A faint smile rose on Sungchul's lips.

It looks like the offensive punch went up because of the environmental mana here.

The Cave Elf boss lunged forward with his claws made of beaks after taking the hit. Just as the claws reached him, Sungchul stepped to the side to evade then kicked at the elf's foot. The Cave Elf fell straight to the floor in a mess, and Sungchul aimed at the back of his neck where his helmet and breastplate met with Glare.

"Kiii…!!"

The Cave Elf shook a single time violently before falling limp. Sungchul repeated the feel of that recent bit of combat in his head as he walked forward. Two more bouts occurred following that. Sungchul brought down every mob of Cave Elves with only his Glare and finally arrived at a large room.

The room was grand enough to be the audience chamber. The decoration and ornaments that once adorned this room had long since rotted off or been stolen. However, the throne made of obsidian and the large avian sculptures around it still possessed the imposing aura of the mighty Nahak race that once dominated the Other World.

"It looks like this is the audience chamber of the Nahaks. Wow, it is quite different… to human sensibilities anyways." Bertelgia looked around her surroundings as she spoke with great interest.

Sungchul also checked his surroundings as he walked into the chamber. He didn't see any relic that stood out particularly.

Sungchul took a look at the throne. The fact that it had space made specifically to accommodate wings was particularly memorable. It was a shame that all of the gems and ornaments had been stolen from the throne. Sungchul discovered a dust covered sack left beneath the throne. When he opened the sack, the jewels and gold shone brilliantly beneath a layer of dust. It looked as though someone had ripped out everything valuable attached to the audience chamber and gathered it into the sack. But that someone didn't manage to escape to the outside...

"..."

Sungchul dusted off the sack before placing it into his Soul Storage.

"Uuu... this isn't right," Bertelgia protested, but Sungchul didn't bat an eye. After tucking away the jewels, he discovered two skeletons behind the throne. A single spear made of bone pierced through the corpses who lay embraced, like two lovers. Sungchul took the pendant from around one of the skeleton's necks. There was a picture of a man and a woman during their happiest moment within the cheap trinket made of brass and silver. Sungchul put down the pendant and pulled out the spear which had impaled the couple and threw it aside.

He then left the audience chamber to soon discover the stairs heading down to the third floor basement. On the third floor basement, there was an obsidian door similar to the one on the second floor. The sculpture attached to it lit up as he stood before the door and displayed a message.

[Display the symbol of the Nahak.]

Sungchul brought out the symbol of the Nahak that he had pocketed earlier. It was an object possessing magic made of obsidian. Sungchul placed it into the gap in the altar.

When he did, a gentle green light flowed out from the symbol and the obsidian door that had obstructed him began to open. The stale air that had been trapped behind the door blew toward Sungchul's face.

"Woah. The mana concentration is even thicker here."

Sungchul was thinking the same thing. The deeper one went into the Underground Kingdom of the avian race, the denser the concentration of mana was in the air. Sungchul tore down a wall to confirm his suspicions. Innumerable skeletons poured out of the third floor wall like the walls of the second floor.

"How many thousands of people were stuffed into this dungeon?" Bertelgia spoke with a slight shudder.

"It's not in the scale of thousands. It seems more accurate to count them in the tens of thousands," said Sungchul, but he even thought the figure might be in the hundreds of thousands.

The layout of the third floor was comparatively plain. There was a line-shaped corridor beyond the door, and several hundred doors alongside it. There didn't seem to be any need to break down the walls. Sungchul simply followed the corridor.

The atmosphere of the two floors differed as well. The concentration of mana was one thing, but not a single Cave Elf lingered here. He soon discovered the reason. There was something massive wandering the corridor. It was an obsidian golem with the skull of a bird.

When the golem discovered Sungchul, it fired off a long-range magic attack. Five balls of fire flew toward Sungchul in a spiral formation.

"Hiii!" Bertelgia immediately shrunk down and dug into Sungchul's pocket. After Bertelgia had been secured, Sungchul pulled out Fal Garaz as usual. However, he changed his mind slightly as he held the hammer.

This golem. How about I try to take care of it with only Glare?

Golems had strong resistance to magic. It wasn't something he would normally dare to do, but the situation wasn't a normal one. Wasn't this place overflowing with mana? Sungchul's Magic Power surpassed a beginner's and nearly reached into the realm of mid-grade mages', but he might be able to harness a greater power than normal while he was in this underground dungeon-

BOOOM!!

-Like the ferocious explosion from the fireball launched by the golem just now.

Sungchul hastily put away Fal Garaz, and ran toward the obsidian golem. It looked massive from a distance, but up close he could fully appreciate its height that reached at least eight meters. It was a size that mages would have categorized as a war golem.

"Enemy of Nahak. Exterminate."

The obsidian golem let out a metallic sound as he extended his hand made of stone. There was a magic crystal embedded in the center of his palm. A complex magical formation bloomed from the crystal. Sungchul's eyes reflexively read off the pattern of the magical formation.

Frost magic.

He immediately evaded to the side. A white frost enveloped the space where Sungchul had once stood and froze everything in place. He circled around toward the back of the golem. The arm that had fired off the frost tried to follow Sungchul's movements, but its speed was lacking.

Sungchul stopped at the edge of the frost's range and aimed the beams of light toward the weak points of the golem, such as the connection between the arm and the shoulder.

Glare fired off with greater brilliance and thickness than usual. Its power was several times higher than before. However, the beam of light only managed to heat up the golem's joint and failed to pierce it.

If only I had more power.

Meteor was not something he could repeatedly use, and the benefits of Glare were the short incantation and ability to fire in rapid succession. Sungchul continued to cast Glare at the joint in succession until the golem's right arm separated from its torso.

BOOM!

The golem, who lost its arm, began to swing its remaining arm in in a frenzy and tried to engage in close quarter combat while spewing blue flames of hellfire from its mouth.

Sungchul kept resisting with Glare, but he could feel his mana running out and so he retreated. This space, however, was filled to the brim with mana and he recovered what he had lost quickly. Sungchul readied himself to try against the golem once again after recovering his mana from behind a pillar; this process was repeated three times. After a long battle that lasted forty minutes, Sungchul managed to defeat the golem with solely his magic.

"Enemy of Nahak... Extermin..."

The core of the fallen golem, who had lost his limbs, lost its light. Sungchul opened his status window as he appreciated the rapid recovery of his mana in front of the shattered golem.

[Stats]			
Strength	999+	Dexterity	853
Vitality	801	Magic Power	191(+52)
Intuition	173	Magic Resist	621
Resilience	502	Charisma	18
	Luck	18	

His Magic Power had risen by more than 50 by simply being in this space. Not only that, his Magic Power had grown significantly. He was definitely within the mid-180s during the last time he had checked, but he was now at 191. At this rate, it wouldn't be an exaggeration to hope to surpass the hallmark of a mid-grade mage which was a Magic Power of 200.

This is better growth than I expected. I knew that the concentration of mana would help mana recovery and strengthen spells, but does it also supplement growth?

Sungchul suddenly felt an urge to use other spells. He felt that it might allow for greater growth by using up more mana with more powerful spells against even more formidable enemies, but the only other offensive spell he knew from Cosmomancy was Meteor, and that required an Intuition higher than 210.

Bertelgia who was watching him from the rear spoke up. "It might be good to start by taking a break at this point." She continued saying, "Your mana might recover quickly, but your body is still using it. Just because the tank fills up more quickly doesn't mean your body got stronger."

"I agree." Sungchul decided to stop the exploration here for today. He still had two days left. Since he had cleared down to the third floor in a day, he should be able to go much deeper and perhaps even discover the Nahak's crown. Sungchul left behind the remains of the golem without regrets and left the dungeon.

FWICK!

He slapped Cassandra the demonic weapon along the floor as a warning as he left. After leaving the dungeon post-haste, Sungchul found a rocky mountain upon which he could keep an eye on the dungeon and took a bit of rest. A good rest was a crucial part of any training regimen. However, it wasn't long before a deep ringing sound could be heard in the air. Sungchul looked up toward the sky. An airship was heading his direction from the south. It was Willie Gilford's airship.

What? He returned this quick? That doesn't make sense.

The airship descended at a location near the dungeon. A rope web flew down from the deck following which several dozen people disembarked from the ship and landed onto the surface. However, Sungchul's eyes grew wide when he saw who they were.

What? Aren't they... the Penal Unit?

It was unmistakable. The worn-out clothes with the prisoner number stitched on with ragged cloth. They were most definitely the Penal Unit.

How did those guys get on board that boat?

Sungchul soon discovered the reason. There was a familiar face next to Willie Gilford. It was the leader of the Penal Unit, the rock-headed Genghis Aaron. He was standing next to the Seventh Champion of the Continent with a modest posture.

Willie looked back toward Aaron with a smile. "If I had known you were here, I would have requested help a lot sooner."

"No! If I knew the Duke was near here, I would have come to meet you at all cost!"

When Sungchul saw this exchange, he was reminded of something he had briefly forgotten. *Ah, that guy used to be a Sword Master of the Ancient Kingdom too.*

Their goals weren't clear yet, but it was obvious that the two Sword Masters were conspiring something. A small explosion sounded from the entrance. A few members of the Penal Unit had activated the explosive trap that had been set by the devils as they descended using the pulley-operated lift.

"Uwaaaa!!" Five members of the Penal Unit fell in free fall with the lift toward the bottom.

"My my. We've already lost precious soldiers at the beginning." Willie clicked his tongue as he spoke, but Aaron looked magnanimous. His eyes sparkled as he spoke energetically. "There are still plenty left!"

***

The situation had quickly grown dire, but Sungchul did not hurry. In fact, he even went so far as to retrieve a seldom-used sleeping bag to have a more comfortable rest. Once a day passed, Sungchul headed not toward the dungeon but to the Penal Unit's encampment. He asked Prisoner Number 0, Arkaard, about the current situation, and to his surprise, Arkaard wasn't aware that a detachment of the Penal Unit had been redirected to the underground dungeon. All he knew was that the hard-headed Aaron had spun his rusted gears to concoct another foolhardy plan that was assuredly suicidal.

"He led a group of new recruits on a supposed assault on a demon fortress. What did he say? He'll cut down the required number of missions by three on success? He uttered some bullshit that convinced about eighty of those newbies to board the airship."

Firstly, the destination was wrong. Those that remained believed that Aaron had led the soldiers to the demon fortress, not the underground dungeon. Secondly, the number of soldiers was also different. Arkaard had said eighty men, but Sungchul had only seen about fifty in total. It was unclear what exactly happened to the thirty or so people, but Sungchul had a good idea what could have happened to them.

It seems that he compelled the members of the Penal Unit into the dungeon through violence and coaxing.

Sungchul headed toward the Underground Kingdom once again. There was a small number of soldiers and an airship defending the entrance. Willie and Aaron were nowhere to be seen, and there was no barrier in place as well. It was most likely because the mages that had been maintaining a barrier had met their end within the dungeon. Sungchul walked calmly over toward the entrance of the dungeon. The soldiers of the Ancient Kingdom raised their spears and shouted, "Who goes there?"

At their question, Sungchul pointed toward the ragged cloth number attached to his torso before he spoke. "I'm a member of the Penal Unit."

"Penal Unit? They all went in with the Duke. What kind of horseshit are you spouting?"

The two soldiers approached Sungchul and waved their spears threateningly. Sungchul replied without hesitation, "I was a scout sent out by Mr. Genghis. I have something to report to him personally, so I followed him here."

The soldiers became less wary when Aaron's name was mentioned. Their spears shifted toward the sky, but one of the soldiers remained dubious and asked, "Are you really a scout?"

Sungchul nodded. The soldiers huddled together for a brief moment before they decided to let him through. They assumed, by his desire to enter the monster-infested dungeon, that Sungchul had no idea what lay within, and, even if he was up to something sinister, Willie Gilford the Seventh Champion of the Continent whose name was recognized throughout the lands was inside the dungeon anyway. He was not someone any ordinary Penal Unit member could oppose. For all of these reasons, the soldiers simply opened the way for Sungchul.

"Thank you," said Sungchul. His voice was half laced with genuine gratitude.

If they had attempted communications with an empath or some other method, he would have had to kill them all.

Sungchul took the lift attached to the pulley to enter the dungeon. The scenery had vastly changed since the last time he went in. There were torches installed periodically along the path with a thick rope affixed to rocks to mark the way. There were also food and weapons strewn about the floor. Although it had been a small group, the area certainly looked like an army had passed by.

The rope led directly to the second floor. Once he reached the second floor, Sungchul witnessed familiar sights.

"Ugh... could I have some w-water..."

"Save me! Please!"

"Aaack! My leg! My leg!"

Injured soldiers who had been shoved to the side were screaming out in pain. Two priests were tending to them, but it looked woefully lacking. Sungchul moved past the second floor entrance that had been turned into an infirmary and continued following the rope. He observed traces of fierce battles and a mountain of Cave Elf corpses along the way. It seemed while Sungchul was sleeping without a worry in the world on the surface, the Penal Unit members and the Ancient Kingdom's Sword Masters had battled through the night against the forgotten race which dominated the dungeon and had emerged victorious.

The rope continued down toward the third floor where Willie and Genghis could be seen from the entrance. They didn't look very amicable.

"This is exactly why I can never trust you!" Willie's thunderous scorn echoed throughout the dungeon. Sungchul stopped his steps to observe the situation. Mikhael and Mimi stood before Willie with their heads down looking uncomfortable. Willie was reprimanding Mikhael.

"Just how much disappointment am I supposed to endure from an idiot like you?"

Mikhael stood silently with his head down.

"Due to your incompetence, I lost the majority of the Exploratory Unit in a single day. Those mages took significant investment to gather."

"I have nothing to say in my defense," replied Mikhael.

Sparks of Willie's anger soon spread over to Mimi as well.

"Mimi Azrael. I have been told that last year you were in charge of an important mission for a scouting unit of the Human Empire, so I invested a large sum of money to hire you. The mages you led were likewise hired for large sums of money to assist you, but what did I get for it? Is this the limit of what you can do?"

Mimi did not stay quiet like Mikhael. She immediately raised her head to defend herself. "I did not open the second-floor door. That man… no, your son was the cause. I do not understand why I must be blamed alongside him."

"Aren't you the squad leader? What is a leader? Isn't it a position of responsibility?"

When she heard those words, Mimi's face twisted as though it would swell up and explode. Willie must have known it. Mimi had no real authority in this team. Despite this obvious truth, he had chosen to reprimand her all the same. Mimi could not endure it much longer. She pulled out a symbol from her possession and placed it in front of Willie's feet. It was an extravagant symbol made of gold that represented her as an ally of the Ancient Kingdom.

"Ok. I'll bear the responsibility for this and remove myself."

However, Willie's expression remained frosty. "How will you take responsibility?"

"Isn't it enough for me to quit? I'll return all of the fees that were paid for the contract when I return."

Willie Gilford had somehow placed the sharp tip of the sword against her tongue in the short pause between her words despite the fact that she had been in the middle of speaking. Her face turned white from fear, but she didn't say anything more. If she had moved her tongue even slightly, the sword aura contained within the blade might have cut it to pieces.

"..."

Once Mimi was forced into silence, Willie looked down at the woman below him with a haughty expression. "In the Ancient Kingdom, taking responsibility means forfeiting your life, mage. Did you think that I would let someone like you to quit midway? Never."

Willie removed the sword from her mouth, then continued speaking. "I'll repeat this so you all can understand. Shut up and listen to it all the way to the end, and once I've finished speaking, remove those repulsive little homunculi from my vicinity and lead me to the tomb of the Avian King."

Mimi had no other option but to nod her head. The humiliation made her head swell, and her legs tremble, but she could do nothing against absolute strength. Willie placed her on display in the front while continuously scolding her with degrading speeches. His derision was never ending.

I suppose this is his hobby, thought Sungchul.

Unfortunately for Willie, his lectures didn't last much longer. A short shriek from the rear stopped him from scolding any further. At the same time, Sungchul felt a threatening presence on his back like a sticky substance.

"W-what is that?"

"It's a monster that we've never seen before!"

The monstrous creature in the form of an avian that was covered in a layer of mucus appeared from a distance. The Despair of the Abyss. The creature had revealed itself once again. However, the Despair of the Abyss didn't have its eyes set on Sungchul this time. It was headed toward Willie Gilford. The monster walked toward the man who had been blaming and chastising a child of another for the mistakes of his own. On seeing the approaching monster, Willie quickly pulled out his sword.

"Shit. These actually were here. I thought they were talking out of their asses."

He was deeply startled. He was peerlessly powerful in comparison to Mimi, but to the Despair of the Abyss, he was no different than any other soldier shitting themselves from fear. Despite this, he quickly regained his composure as expected of a man worthy of the title of a Champion of the Continent.

He backed up slowly with his sword emitting an aura as he pulled something out from his Soul Storage. He soon held a small lantern which contained a blue light. He pointed the lantern toward the Despair of the Abyss and spoke in a loud voice.

"Specter, lost and adrift with no knowledge of where you are, swept away by the flow of time and wandering through the ages, heed me. If you have eyes, lift up your face and gaze into this flame imbued with ancient moonlight!"

When the blue light drew closer toward it, the creature, who had been steadily moving forward, stopped. The creature looked mesmerized by the light and did not make any further movements. The others slowly began to regain their senses from the panic, and they could now clearly see the dark creature, which even omitted from the legends, known as the Despair of the Abyss.

When Sungchul saw this, he muttered something under his breath. *Ordinary people are not supposed to look at the Despair of the Abyss...*

The Despair of the Abyss was not only terrifying due to its hideous appearance and its ability to drag beings into oblivion, but also because weak minded creatures looking directly at it would lose their minds and go insane. It was difficult to express the levels of horrors that comprised this terrifying creature.

"Kyaaaaa!" One of the Sword Adepts who stood looking directly at the creature suddenly held his head and screamed. Willie Gilford who had been preoccupied in dealing with the creature realized his blunder too late and shouted a warning to all around him.

"Everyone, retreat! Do not put your eyes on this creature!"

However, the command was a moment too late. Many of his men had already looked at the creature and had their minds shattered.

"Uwaaaa!!" A dwarven Penal Unit member suddenly lifted his axe and decapitated his comrade whom he had just fought alongside. Fountains of blood spurted in every direction, and a bellowing battle cry roared simultaneously in the surroundings.

Wille did not lose his composure in the chaos and continued to face the Despair of the Abyss. "Begone from my sight, you who are buried by endless time!"

The Despair of the Abyss stood dumbly for a while before it turned and disappeared into the darkness. The monstrous existence that had caused the chaos had left, but the chaos had only just begun.

"Calm yourselves, everyone! All those who still hold their sanity hide behind me! Hurry!"

Willie shouted in a thunderous voice with the hope of reigning in the chaos, but it was already far too late. Mad men that had already lost themselves to the insanity were cutting down their comrades in full force, and the situation continued to deteriorate.

At that moment, Sungchul noticed a few people fleeing into different directions. One of them was Aaron Genghis. He was fleeing with the empath that always accompanied him along the rope toward the exit.

"I thought I had hit a jackpot, but it turned out to be a trap!" muttered Aaron.

The man had no qualms about abandoning his subordinates, but it looked as though he also didn't hesitate to abandon his superior.

The other fleeing the chaos was the one that had been wrongly disciplined by Willie Gilford, the female mage.

"...worthless human beings," said Mimi as she wrapped herself in the invisible veil and continued into the dungeon.

Sungchul had nothing more to see here. He evaded the blades flying in all directions with minimal movements in order to pass Willie. When he was passing by, Willie unintentionally looked toward Sungchul's direction.

That guy?

Looking at Sungchul's face and the cloth number attached to his coat, Willie turned his attention away. He shouted in a commanding voice instead, "All those who retain their sanity, listen well. Proceed to retreat to the second-floor entrance. All those who wish to live, follow at my rear!"

Sungchul ignored the command and stood before the stairs that lead to the third floor. There was nothing in his way. He re-entered the massive corridor inside which he had battled the golem.

"Krrrr..."

In the distance, another magic golem lifted its body from the ground. There was a feeling of *deja vu*, but the result was drastically different.

WHAM!

Sungchul's Fal Garaz struck against the golem's head, and it was smashed to pieces in a single blow.

"..."

Sungchul didn't intend to play with it leisurely this time.

Training is important, but I cannot afford to take my time.

There were too many guests to attend to. He didn't like having too many guests. Sungchul hurried across the corridor and smashed five more golems in a similar manner. It had taken forty minutes last time to deal with an obsidian golem with magic, but now it had taken only three minutes to smash all of them and reach the massive obsidian door.

"…"

Sungchul stopped before the door that obstructed his path. The door was rigged with explosives. It wasn't suitable to break through the ceiling like last time either. The booby trap was set not only on the door, but also on all sides of the ten-meter cube room. It looked as though it was meant to obstruct any path leading down the stairs.

Sungchul put away Fal Garaz and placed the symbol of the Nahak into the altar, but the door did not open.

[You cannot enter with the symbol of the lowly.]

[Return with the symbol of the noble.]

Sungchul felt lost, but at that moment he could feel a faint presence behind him. Sungchul simply waited for them to approach. Finally, the hooded woman underneath the invisible fog revealed herself.

"I guess you might actually be strong?"

Mimi appeared with her homunculi.

"Can we become fairies if we cross beyond this door-yeyo?"

"We can take off these heavy and stinky helmets once we become fairies! I want to quickly become a lord that rules over humans-yeyo!"

"Miss Mimi! Let's ignore that human and continue down this path-yeyo!"

The homunculi began to shout excitedly. Mimi struck the floor with her staff and spoke angrily. "Everyone quiet down."

At her scolding, the five homunculi became terrified and shut their mouths.

"I apologize. My familiars were excessively loud." Mimi put on a pretentious smile as she gave a small nod toward Sungchul. Sungchul pointed toward the obsidian door. "Can you open this door?"

"Yes. I can open the door. Not only that door, but I can also open the doors of antiquity that lie beyond this door."

Mimi handed Sungchul a platinum-plated stick about the size of a finger.

"This is the symbol of Nahak nobility. This is my gift in return for you having taken care of those pesky golems."

Sungchul extended his hand to receive the symbol which he inserted into the slot on the altar.

[One of noble blood, you may enter]

[His Majesty awaits impatiently]

[For the restoration of the Nahak]

The eyes of the avian statue lit up and the door opened with a small tremor.

"It is quite dangerous starting from the fourth floor. I wish you luck. Even if we meet in the Tomb of the King, let us refrain from fighting. We are seeking different things."

Sound of military boots was then heard from a distance. Sungchul and Mimi both looked back. The Sword Masters of the Ancient Kingdom and the surviving members of the Penal Unit had entered the third floor.

"Find Mimi Azrael! She must be somewhere around here!" The one leading the group was not Willie Gilford, but his son, Mikhael. He was gritting his teeth.

I have to get results this time; otherwise, my brother will take my place and I will be cast into the cold.

Willie Gilford had three sons. They had all grown into brilliant Sword Masters, but their relationship couldn't be considered friendly. It was well known that Mikhael, the second son, was far lacking in terms of talent among the three. He was inferior in every way to his brothers; in character, in intellect, and even in skill with the sword. Mikhael wasn't one to listen to this gossip, but he could also feel that his father's paternal devotion and expectations were dwindling as of late. He had thrown himself into this dungeon in order to regain his value. To the dungeon where almost the entire expedition of mighty veteran warriors and mages of the Ancient Kingdom had nearly been wiped out.

"Young master, do not feel rushed. As long as Master Willie has plugged the exit, Miss Azrael is but a rat in a corner. Don't rush; instead, track her carefully, and you'll eventually be able to find that female mage," advised Odrias.

Butler Odrias was Mikhael's sole ally. Mikhael, who was arrogant and self-righteous, just like his father, listened to the old butler's word without hesitation.

"We've got an unwelcome guest. It might be best to split up," said Mimi before she made a gesture after which one of her homunculi muttered an incantation which veiled them in an invisible fog. She used a teleportation magic within the fog and disappeared to another place. Her destination could not be determined.

Sungchul also hid his presence and melted into the darkness. A spiralling staircase extending down to the fourth floor was waiting for him. Sungchul quickly descended to the fourth floor.

When he reached the bottom of the stairs, glints of emerald light brilliantly shined from all directions.

"Wow…" Bertelgia couldn't help but whisper in admiration. There were clusters of green gems lining every wall along the fourth floor basement, including the ceiling.

"These are Green Luminous Ores. They are all entirely made from Alchemy!" Bertelgia spoke as she carefully examined the green gems exuding light before her. Sungchul slowly walked down the corridor filled with emerald lights until he noticed something lying ahead. Whatever it was, it was waiting for him. Sungchul stopped his steps and projected his voice further down the corridor.

"Who is it? Reveal yourself."

Upon hearing his voice, a shadowy figure appeared beyond the bright lights. A hint of curiosity flickered in his eyes. What appeared within the emerald brilliance was something unexpected. A blind creature; a Cave Elf had appeared before him. It had an appearance different than the Cave Elves Sungchul had seen before, wearing a circlet made of beaks and a dress decorated with feathers. Sungchul's Eye of Truth, his Soul Contract, activated itself.

Is it an illusion?

What appeared before him was an illusion of the Cave Elf, but it wasn't just a simple illusion; it breathed and gave off a foul stench. It was a spell that he hadn't come across yet.

Sungchul finished his conclusions of the situation as he spoke while looking directly at the Cave Elf. "I said to reveal your identity."

When Sungchul asserted himself, the Cave Elf swung his staff and opened his mouth. "Kii... I-I have not c-come... to f-fight..."

Surprisingly, the Cave Elf spoke in the language of the Other World. His vocalization was airy, and the timbre of his voice sounded metallic, so it was difficult to understand, but the crowned Cave Elf undoubtedly spoke the common language of this world.

Sungchul glared at the Cave Elf and spoke in a low voice. "What is your purpose then?"

"I-I have... thoroughly witnessed... your strength. You are one... that we could never oppose... despite this... you cannot go further..."

"State the reason, blind man."

The Cave Elf shook as though struck with fear then spoke with great difficulty in a trembling metallic voice.

"Beyond here... lies... the King of Feathers and Beaks..."

"King? The King of the Avians?"

"T-That... is correct... The accursed king... who not only buried alive... millions of my kind... but also swallowed up his own kind..."

"Are you saying that the King of Avians still lives?"

The unfamiliar cave elf muttered something unintelligible in response to this question from Sungchul. Not even Sungchul was able discern a meaning. When this undecipherable mumble came to an end, the Cave Elf slowly continued his speech.

"The King... of Feathers and Beaks... Not even you... can oppose him... He has already far surpassed... the mortal limits... and has stepped into... the realm of lesser gods... If... that thing is awakened... great disaster... will befall us..."

Those were the final words of the crowned Cave Elf. After speaking, the Cave Elf collapsed, and his entire body went up in black smoke. Another Cave Elf with a different appearance was lying in its place when the smoke had cleared.

He must have cast an illusory magic on a living body of his kin.

It was magic that he had never heard of. It could possibly be the secret magic passed down among Cave Elves from the forgotten ancient era of the past. The Cave Elves must be feeling desperate to use such a magic to warn Sungchul.

Quite an unusual thing. The King of the Avians might still be alive according to what that Cave Elf had said, but Mimi hadn't mentioned a word about it.

He couldn't determine which side was lying, but things like this did not bother Sungchul. As long as there was a way to gain more power, he had no choice but to push forward. Sungchul erased all suspicion from his mind and walked forth. New enemies soon blocked his path. They were the mummified avian corpses. They had a sinister aura about them which was incomparable to the one emitted by the skeletal swarm roaming on the first floor. Sungchul could feel the chill of an insidious black magic from these corpses.

Cassandra, the demonic weapon, made another appearance from the Soul Storage.

FWICK!

The heavy blow from the whip left the corpses in pieces.

At that same moment, another battle was going on somewhere nearby. Sungchul could hear an explosion rather close by along with the scream of homunculi. He headed toward the noise.

Mimi looked at the limp corpses of the avians with a cold stare. There was not a scratch on her person, but she wasn't without losses. One of the homunculi had lost its leg and was crawling along the floor.

"Miss Mimi... Miss Mimi... leave behind this Head of Investigations Ujira! I can't go on-yeyo."

The homunculus had dragged himself toward Mimi as it bled from its severed limb and whispered in a quiet voice as it grabbed her skirt. Mimi looked hesitant for a while, but soon arrived at a decision.

"I'm sorry," she said as she looked toward the other homunculi.

"New Head of Investigations Ujicha! You'll be casting the veil this time."

She disappeared into the darkness with the other four homunculi.

When their presence faded away, Sungchul approached the homunculus that had lost its leg. The iron mask that had covered the homunculus's face had been crushed revealing a portion of its hideously twisted face. On seeing this, Sungchul began to wonder if these homunculi had been formed by some other method than the one he was familiar with.

"Enhanced homunculus... poor thing." Bertelgia spoke in a sad voice. The homunculus who had heard her voice looked toward Sungchul's direction.

"Why are you looking at me? Are you perhaps pitying me even though you're just some human-yeyo?" The Homunculus revealed a completely different attitude from when it was talking to Mimi, filled with hostility and aggression.

"..."

Sungchul didn't rebuke it and tossed the creature a bandage. It was some cheap styptic.

"I don't need such things-yeyo! I don't need cheap pity!"

The bone-chilling eyes of the homunculus revealed through the crumpled iron mask began to spasm, but the homunculus applied the medicine to the critical injury. It must have felt unbearable pain as it let out a peculiar cry in agony.

"Te-e-e-e-e!!!"

After applying the styptic, the homunculus began to hurriedly crawl into the darkness with its two arms.

"I must... I must repay Miss Mimi for giving us life... I must..."

More grumbling could be heard from the restless homunculus that faded into the darkness. Sungchul left the scene.

In front of the dungeon, there were countless avian corpses lying in wait. These hollowed creatures from an ancient time had no thoughts and no fear as they had their souls plundered through some sinister dark magic. They only knew to exterminate anyone that dared to intrude upon the tomb of their king.

There is no end to them.

He could fight them all day, but a lot of time was wasting away. He decided to change his method. Sungchul pulled out Fal Garaz from the Soul Storage. He held Cassandra, the demonic weapon, on the right and Fal Garaz on the left.

WHAM!

The hammer didn't strike the avians, but the stone wall. The wall crumbled to open a path which allowed countless more avians to lunge towards him.

FWICK!

Cassandra, the demonic weapon, split the air with an earsplitting noise. Dozens of corpses were torn apart in the air as they were struck by the whip's oppressive strength.

WHAM!

When one mob fell, he broke down another wall. Another mob of avians appeared, and Cassandra shrieked to disassemble his enemies once again. Sungchul repeated this process ad nauseam. Finally, he came across what appeared to be the end to this seemingly never-ending process. A square room rigged with a destructive magic appeared before him. He made quick work of all the avian corpses rushing toward him and stood before this room. A message of bright letters appeared before him.

[The Tomb of the Immortal King.]

[Spill the hot blood of the Nahak]

[Do so and the King shall respond to your call]

Sungchul's pupils shook. It was because the tomb of the king was asking for the impossible. The Nahak were already extinct. There were no living Nahak left.

Chapter 6– The Last King

"…"

It was utterly hopeless. Sungchul looked around his surroundings to see countless bodies of Nahak strewn about on the floor, but none of them had hot blood flowing through their veins. However, it would be a waste of too much time and effort to give up now.

Sungchul circled around the area of the burial chamber looking for even the smallest of gaps in the construction, but it couldn't be found. Forcing it open with his strength would cause an explosion that might cause the entire dungeon to collapse.

Is there any other way…

He knew of only one person that might know something: Mimi Azrael. He needed her. Sungchul immediately took action. He turned back toward the path of rubble that he had created and sought out the young woman with five… no, now four homunculi. He soon found a clue. It was the charred remains of a homunculus. There were similarly charred corpses of a pair of Sword Adepts beside it.

"This woman. They managed to get on her trail," Bertelgia said as she saw the remains. Sungchul observed the scattered footprints on the ground. Mimi had fled north, and at least ten people were following behind her. Sungchul followed them quickly toward the dungeon filled with emerald light.

It didn't take long before he discovered another two soldiers resting on the floor. They were part of the Penal Unit. They didn't even have enough energy left to speak and simply nodded toward Sungchul when they saw him passing by.

Soon, he discovered another homunculus corpse. It had been torn apart and scattered beyond recognition. Sungchul discovered another homunculus in a similar state before he found their owner.

"Ughhh…"

What he discovered was a woman in such a pitiful state that her continued survival was a form of punishment itself. Both her hands were nailed to the wall with swords instead of stakes and blood dripped from her body that gathered in a pool beneath her like water from a well. Three Sword Adepts were gathered around her snickering as they swapped stories.

"..."

Sungchul walked up to her.

"Who goes there?!" The three Sword Adepts discovered his presence and pulled out their swords.

Sungchul's response to their question was Fal Garaz.

WHAM! BLAM! BAM!

He ignored the three corpses with their skulls bashed in and approached Mimi.

"My God... how could anyone do such a thing," said Bertelgia who hid behind Sungchul's back as though she couldn't bear to watch.

Sungchul pulled out a healing potion and fed it to Mimi.

"Uu... Uh..." It would not have been surprising for anyone else to have died already, but Mimi's resilience was incredible.

"O-one more...!" She bit down on the bottle's opening like a hungry baby onto a nipple and struggled to get every last drop. Sungchul gave her another potion as she asked, "T-thank you... but who are you?"

Sungchul then realized. Eyes that should have been sparkling from between her disheveled hair had been stabbed and had already lost their light.

Darkness leads to fear. Truly a despicable method. I don't know who's done it, but it isn't their first time.

Sungchul contemplated this as he revealed his identity. "I'm Number 34."

"Ah... it's you... I thought as much. Hold on a moment."

She had attempted to stand up and walk, but she collapsed before she could fully extend her knees. There was an injury behind her ankle where a knife was used to gouge out a portion of her leg.

"It looks as though your Achilles tendon was removed. That can't be healed with potions. You'll have to get it healed by a high priest personally."

"Shit… shit… those bastards…"

Mimi was collapsed onto the floor while muttering profanities under her breath. Sungchul waited for her to calm down before speaking.

"Who did this? Willie Gilford? Or Mikhael?"

"It was neither. Mikhael does not know more than how to slap someone in the face. It was the butler that he carries around. Who knew that such a quiet old man would know such diabolical torture methods."

The nightmarish moments flashed by her eyes once again causing her to shudder in fear. "…we have to hurry. They know everything!"

"About what?" asked Sungchul.

"About how to find the tomb of the Nahak King. Everything happened in a flash."

"To open the tomb of the Nahak King, you need the blood of a living Nahak. Can that problem be solved?"

"I gave them the location of a living Nahak. They are most likely headed that direction," Mimi replied.

Sungchul eyes lit up and he further inquired, "Just where is that exactly?"

Mimi wiped the blood dripping off of her forehead with her sleeve as she spoke. "Take me with you. I'll lead the way."

Sungchul slung her across his back. "Can you hang on?"

"I am strong enough for that at the very least."

Soon, Mimi revealed everything she knew to Sungchul. The location of the last remaining Nahaks. Sungchul's eyes shook when he heard it.

"They are at the dwelling of the Cave Elves?"

It was difficult to swallow, but even if it was hard to believe, he had no choice but to listen to Mimi. Sungchul stood before the small opening on the entrance to the fourth floor. It looked as though a typhoon had passed through it. There were frightening amounts of Cave Elf corpses strewn about the floor.

Sungchul followed a trail of blood in the direction the human expedition had traveled which led to a massive cavern beyond a dark cave. In this space of utter darkness where not even a single strand of light broke through, there were an uncountable number of huts made of feathers, bones, and the hides of insects and reptiles. It was the city of the Cave Elves.

Mimi spoke as they entered the city. "There is a breeding farm over to the Southeast."

"A breeding farm?"

It sounded jarring.

"An enemy!" Bertelgia shouted. As expected, a mass of Cave Elf warriors stood before Sungchul. Sungchul struck the ground with the demonic weapon Cassandra. Its unique cry resonated in the air causing the Cave Elves to lose their will to fight and flee. They had already acknowledged that this human was not an opponent on their level.

After passing through countless waves of Cave Elf warriors in a similar manner, they ran over to the breeding farm in question. The rancid smell of feces filled their noses, and they could hear something similar to the cry of a bird. They headed over to the massive tent made of bones and feathers where they finally spotted them.

"Buckaw!" The beings that inhabited this massive bone cage had the beak and wings of a bird and the body of a human. They were the Nahak.

However, the beings of legend were trapped in a small cramped chicken cage, making bestial noises.

"Bawk... Bawk..."

It wasn't just the one. The Nahak trapped in the hundreds of cages within this tent were no longer the Nahak of legends that ruled the skies and land; they were lowly livestock. Sungchul could see decapitated Nahak corpses dangling from a corner of the tent designated as the butchery.

Mimi who was being piggy-backed smelled a sharp stench of bird droppings and said, "After the Nahak kingdom collapsed... the Cave Elves grabbed the children of the Nahaks and raised them as cattle. Here, the Nahaks are immediately thrown into these coops at birth, treated like animals for their eggs, then butchered when they come of age."

"In some ways, this might have been the ultimate revenge," Sungchul spoke as he recalled countless corpses of Cave Elves that had been buried alive within the walls he had broken through.

"Where did you find the clues that lead here?" Sungchul asked as he looked around his surroundings.

"I focused on the weapons that a few of the Cave Elves were using. They seemed to have been adorned with feathers and beaks."

"That does seem to be the case."

The Cave Elf that had appeared before to warn Sungchul was similarly decorated.

"But where would there be a bird in a dungeon this deep? Even if the Cave Elves wandered outside, they would never be able to catch any flying birds with their blindness. This line of questioning led to the correct hypothesis."

"Impressive." Suddenly, a thought entered Sungchul's mind. "You've been here before, haven't you?"

"Yes."

"Why did you fail then?"

"It took far too long until we learned of this truth."

"I see."

Sungchul grabbed one of the Nahak within the coop.

"Bawk, Bawk!" It was still a young beast, and like the other Nahaks, it showed no signs of intelligence.

Bertelgia looked around the area surrounding that Nahak with curiosity and spoke. "Hmmm. These are the Nahak of legends? Looking like this, they aren't any different from chicken in a poultry farm."

"Bawk Bawk!"

Suddenly, the young Nahak made a fuss and began to peck at Bertelgia.

"Hey, hey! It hurts, you birdbrain!"

Sungchul looked at the scene and spoke in a firm voice. "Bertelgia. Get inside my pocket."

"Why?"

"Because we're going to move at full speed."

Bertelgia didn't say anything more and stuffed herself into his pocket. Sungchul took a deep breath and propelled himself forward with the godlike strength in his body. The caves elves could sense, even though they could not see, that a being they could not hope to win against was crossing their lands at an unbelievable speed.

Sungchul who had returned to the dungeon through the opening stopped his steps and reassessed his directions.

Mimi, who had been on his back, opened her mouth to speak. "Excuse me."

Sungchul didn't bother looking before replying. "What is it?"

"You. You're really strong. I can feel it. Even though I can't see it."

Sungchul could feel a sigh spilling out of her onto his back.

"If it's small talk you're after, I'll have to refuse."

"What's the color of the feather of the Nahak you just caught?" she then asked in a different tone.

"White," replied Sungchul.

"Ah, I see."

"Why do you ask?"

"I was suddenly curious. Last time, we grabbed some blue ones and some white ones."

" … "

Sungchul didn't feel a need to respond. Mimi already had another question. "Could I ask a favor?"

"This is the last one. We don't have time for small talk."

"Did you perhaps see my homunculus? Not the dead ones, but ones that are still alive."

"I only saw three dead corpses."

"I see. That means there's still one living. No, is it two?"

Mimi suddenly let go of Sungchul's neck.

THUD.

Her body fell beside his feet.

"What are you doing?" asked Sungchul as he looked down at her fallen form.

"I'll remain here. I don't want to meet the people that did this to me."

"They are not on my level."

"Even if you say that, the fear that has been carved into my body is difficult to erase."

The blind and lame Mimi looked around as she screamed with a pitiful voice. "Ujicha! Ujicha! Where are you! Ujicha!"

"…"

Sungchul left her behind and moved toward the tomb of the Nahak. As he followed the path that he had created, a square-shaped burial chamber revealed itself. However, there were some unwelcome guests in front of the chamber. They were the soldiers of the Ancient Kingdom. Mikhael Gilford and the man named Odrias stood in the center of them.

"Now, spread the blood of this chick on the altar."

There was a baby avian fluttering in Odrias's bloodied hands. It was also white like the one Sungchul had brought.

Odrias slit its throat without hesitation.

"Bawk BAWK-!!"

Crimson blood spilled from the avian. Odrias held the avian's bleeding corpse on top of the altar. The concave space on top became filled with blood.

Was I a step too late? Sungchul observed the situation from a short distance. A geometric pattern formed on the surface of the obsidian burial chamber. It was a magical formation… no, something similar to one.

It's a magical formation I'm not familiar with. Is it some magic technique of the Nahaks?

The surface began to tremble. Something was about to happen. It was the burial chamber. The blackened square burial chamber split perfectly in half and revealed what lay within. Mikhael clenched both his fists as he looked at the black burial chamber with a face swelling with pride.

"Finally. I did it! I finally did it!" He approached Odrias while still holding the avian corpse and shouted, his voice filled with happiness, "Old man Odrias! We did it! We really did it!"

"Not quite. It's not yet the time to lower your guard. Didn't I say so before? You can only climb up if you do everything right to the very end."

"Yes. You did say that." Mikhael laughed awkwardly before returning to his tense expression. The rumbling finally stopped. The burial chamber opened. Everyone held their breath as they approached the newly opened chamber. Sungchul quietly moved closer to them.

There were two sarcophagi within the burial chamber.

"Two sarcophagi? Are there two Kings of the Avians?" Mikhael scratched his head as he spoke. It was unexpected, but he continued optimistically, "It's better with two sarcophagi. More for us to take."

As his words left his mouth, the two sarcophagi began to open. The swordsmen of the Ancient Kingdom held their breath as they watched the sarcophagi open before them. Uncertainty rose in the hearts of all present. The corpses within the two sarcophagi wore extravagant garments with equipment adorned with gems indicating their prestigious heritage, but everyone could see a single critical error. The ones within the sarcophagi were not avians. They were without beaks or wings. They were Cave Elves.

***

The Cave Elves were almost identical in appearance, but the weapons that they were wielding were different. One held a sword, while the other held a staff. They also had one critical difference from the other Cave Elves: their eyes. They possessed artificially inserted eyes that shined like brilliant rubies.

"Who was it?" The Cave Elf wielding a sword spoke as his eyes flashed a deep crimson. The voice was both dreary and authoritative. The humans surrounding him felt pressured from just hearing his voice.

"Young Master." Odrias leaned in toward Mikhael's ears. "I have a bad feeling about this."

Mikhael had recognized that there was something strange about the way things were going, but he hadn't thought of retreating. "No. I don't think so."

Mikhael didn't want to err by throwing away this opportunity that had taken great efforts to achieve. His only thoughts were on how he could return the spoils of victory to his father as quickly as possible.

Victory is within my grasp! Did you think I would back off when I am this close to my goal?

The shameful days in which he was criticized and scorned for being average passed through his eyes like a film.

"Are you both the Kings of the Avians?" Mikhael broadened his shoulders as he shouted with foolhardy confidence, and the two Cave Elves with shining eyes stopped their movements and turned to look at Mikhael.

"I have revived you two, so I demand a suitable reward. A being with the title of 'King' must keep its word, no?"

125

He stared them down without flinching. The Cave Elves returned his gaze and made no further actions. Meanwhile, Mikhael felt as though his heart would explode in this moment of silence. *Hurry up. Bring me my reward quickly. The Crown of the Nahak which will prove my worth to all!*

The sword-wielding Cave Elf pointed his finger toward Mikhael. Delight and heightened expectation brightened up Mikhael's eyes, but only for a moment as the Elf spoke.

"We are not the king. We are but his most faithful servants."

The Cave Elf wielding the staff finished their introduction. "We are the guardians protecting the tomb of the great king. We seek out the false ones and strike them down."

Mikhael's mouth twisted into a weird shape. His expectations had been shattered. Odrias hurriedly tugged on his sleeve from the side. "Young Master."

The situation had turned sour. Mikhael understood this mentally, but his heart could not accept this truth. He continued to waddle in shock when both of the Cave Elves pointed towards Mikhael and his group.

"How dare you sacrifice the blood of some lowly commoner to the monarch of the skies and earth!" The Cave Elves let out a thunderous roar as even the air around them seemed to chill. A silence full of hostility filled the air. The Ancient Kingdom's swordsmen, who had been looking in on the situation from a distance, finally began to realize that the situation was worsening and exchanged glances while the Elves continued.

"There is only death for those who disturb our king's resting place with foul blood."

"We shall wash away the unclean blood you have brought with your own."

The two Cave Elves raised their weapons.

"Young Master!" Odrias pulled out his sword and stood protectively in front of Mikhael.

"Now! You must es-…!!"

He didn't even manage to finish his warning when an unseen magical shackle constricted his body and a sword adorned with gems pierced his throat.

"O-old man!!" A sharp screech echoed throughout the tomb of the Avian King. Odrias, who had been a powerful Swordmaster, had been killed by a single strike of a blade, causing the swordsmen of the Ancient Kingdom in the vicinity to lose their will to fight. Mikhael was no exception.

"I am no match for them! I-I have to get Father!'

He immediately turned around to escape, but the Servants of the Nahak weren't sitting idly by. The magical chains bound his torso, and the sharp blade severed his leg.

"Aaaaah!"

Mikhael Gilford cried out like a wild beast when both of his heel tendons were cut and rolled about before the burial chamber of the king. The two Cave Elves that had suppressed Mikhael began to attack the remaining swordsmen of the Ancient Kingdom. It didn't take much longer to clean up the riffraff. The other five, excluding Odrias, were dragged into the burial chamber with their legs severed.

"A peaceful death is a pipe dream for the likes of you."

"You will listen to the sound of your own breathing as you suffocate to death in utter darkness."

The Cave Elf wielding the staff chanted a spell that caused one of the walls to crumble and the skulls within to pour out. The other wielding the sword threw them into the wall one by one.

"N-no!"

"Stop this!"

"F-Forgive me! Mercy!"

Their cries of mercy were swallowed up by the wall that magically sealed itself. The bleak desolation and shrieks of pain rang out beyond the wall like an echo.

" … "

Sungchul had been watching everything. *Mimi must have seen a similar spectacle. She must have escaped by herself somehow.*

The Cave Elf wielding a sword turned its head towards where Sungchul was hiding. "Who is hiding there? Identify yourself."

Sungchul did not reveal himself from the darkness. The Cave Elves looked over in his direction for quite a while before they walked towards their tombs. The Royal Servants could not find Sungchul.

So they're only around this level. Sungchul let out a shallow sigh before quietly revealing himself.

"Bawk! Bawk!"

The young Nahak in his grasp cried out as it flailed. The Cave Elves heard this and turned their heads. The red rubies embedded into their eye sockets let out an eerie light.

"Who are you?" The two Cave Elves spoke simultaneously.

Sungchul revealed the young Nahak in his hand as he spoke. "As you can see, I am here to make a sacrifice."

The Cave Elves looked toward the Nahak held in his hands. It was a beast that possessed white feathers.

The eyes of the Cave Elves flared angrily once again.

"You dare bring another pathetic white-feathered one? Did you not witness what happened after the mistake of your kind?"

"It just shows that this is the level of these inferior humans."

Sungchul silently listened to their rumblings as he contemplated their words. *So it was the color of the feathers that was the issue.*

Sungchul tried to recall the scene back at the poultry farm. It was difficult to parse due to the poor lighting, but he could recall that there were only white-feathered Nahaks there. It meant that Nahaks with feathers that were not white in color were rare.

As expected, the woman must have known everything.

Regardless, there was a problem at hand to attend to: the servants of the Royal King that were fuming with hostility towards him. Sungchul released the Nahak in his hands.

The young Nahak began to look at the foreign surroundings with wonder and curiosity until he discovered Odrias's corpse and pecked out his eyeball with its beak. In the time it took for the bird to swallow the eye loudly, Sungchul extended his right hand. Fal Garaz suddenly appeared within it. The divine tool which was crafted from the shards of the sky itself.

"...!!"

The two Cave Elves that witnessed its majesty began to hesitate. Its might was something that didn't require explanation to be felt. They could feel that there was power and history behind that weapon.

Bertelgia, who had now grown accustomed to this pattern of events, began to shout from Sungchul's back. "Both of you! You're done for!"

Sungchul hefted the hammer to his shoulder as he walked toward the Cave Elves.

The Cave Elf with the staff began to utter an indecipherable incantation. A mysterious magical formation began to ripple out from his lips. Sungchul hadn't known what it was when he first arrived here, but he figured it out now. *Is it some kind of restraint?*

Suddenly, invisible shackles bound his arms and legs firmly. Sungchul's Soul Contract, The Eye of Truth, revealed to him that the shackles were made of vengeful souls of the deceased.

Such vile magic.

The sword-wielding elf began to rush towards him. It was the same tactic that had caught Odrias off guard, but that method wouldn't work on Sungchul. God-like power coursed through his veins. He could feel that wave of power and began to lightly move his body.

"Kwaaaaa!"

"Gyaaaaak!"

Hellish screeches and cries of agony could be heard as the restraints formed of souls that bound his four limbs began to tear.

"...?!"

The staff-wielding Cave Elf suddenly froze. Something impossible had occurred. The sword-wielding Cave Elf had been completely focused on the task of piercing Sungchul's heart and waited for the sensation of the sword digging into his chest and piercing his heart. However, his expectations didn't come to pass. A blunt force lightly shook his body.

GRIP.

The powerful hands of a human wrapped around his neck. Shock and terror appeared in the Cave Elf's ruby red eyes. When strength passed through the hand that gripped his neck, the Cave Elf dropped his blade and used both his arms in an effort to free himself from the human's grasp. He tried to scratch the man with his sharp nails, but it wasn't enough to even leave a mark on the firmly gripped hand.

Krrrt!

The Cave Elf lost consciousness along with the sound of something snapping echoing in the halls. And after a loud impact, its body was forever destroyed.

"…"

Sungchul tossed away the Cave Elf corpse with a crushed skull and moved to face his next enemy. The remaining Cave Elf began to wave his arms while quickly rushing to speak.

"Wait, human! I'll tell you a method. A blue-feathered…"

WHAM!

The number of crushed heads grew to two.

"So it's the blue feathers?"

The pieces of the puzzle fell into place. All that was left was for Sungchul to return to the poultry farm to seek out a blue-feathered Nahak.

"Hey, what are you going to do about that guy?" Bertelgia looked toward the young Nahak that was chewing on Odrias' corpse as she continued, "You're not going to use him in one of your recipes, are you?"

"I don't eat intelligent creatures."

"Really…?"

"…except dragons."

Sungchul put away Fal Garaz into his Soul Storage and headed toward the poultry farm, but as he was about to step out of the room with the still burial chamber, he could hear someone's voice from another entrance.

"Miss Mimi! It's over here! The black square is here-yeyo!"

It was a homunculus's voice. Sungchul stopped in his tracks and looked over in the direction of the voice. From the corner of a hidden entrance, an armored homunculus was leading a bloodied woman. It was the blinded Mimi Azrael.

The woman who could no longer see in front of her moved her head as if trying to look around her surroundings and spoke. "Ujicha. Are you sure that the Swordmaster is dead?" She asked with her voice thick with genuine fear.

"Yes! This Ujicha saw it himself! Miss Mimi! The Swordmaster died to the Cave Elves with the shinies-yeyo! There is that bad guy's corpse over there-yeyo!"

"What about the Tomb Guardians?"

"Ara? I thought I saw them enter the tomb, but now they're all dead-yeyo."

"Dead? The Guardians?"

"Yes. All of their heads were caved in-yeyo."

"How did that happen? For the Guardians to die… could it be Willie Gilford himself…?!" Mimi sucked in her breath and focused on her hearing. There was only a deathly silence with no sounds of the living. "Let's move quickly, Ujicha."

"I understand-yeyo!"

The homunculus led Mimi towards the altar. Mimi reached out to feel for the altar, then when she managed to find it, she pulled out two magic staves from her Soul Storage to use as crutches to stand with all of her strength.

"Urrrk…"

Mimi, who now stood in front of the altar, looked down towards the homunculus who should be standing beside her feet and spoke in a soft voice. "Ujicha. Can you give me a big hug?"

"What? Miss Mimi is going to hug me-yeyo?!" The homunculus spoke with a tearful voice.

"I just have one last request," said Mimi.

Sungchul and Bertelgia were watching the scene quietly from a distance.

"What could they be doing?" Bertelgia asked Sungchul who was beside her.

Sungchul also had the same question. *What could this woman be trying to do?*

He continued to watch Mimi's actions. The homunculus went into her embrace.

"Take off your helmet." Mimi spoke softly.

"Can I really do that-yeyo?"

When the homunculus asked carefully, she put on a magnanimous expression and nodded her head. Soon, the homunculus removed his iron mask. The grotesque appearance that lied within was completely exposed without any filter. Rather than a face, it looked more like several grotesque pieces of meat had been sewn together to form the face tissue.

"Urk…"

Bertelgia couldn't bear looking at the appearance any longer and hid behind Sungchul, but Sungchul didn't miss a single moment of that enhanced homunculus' bare face. One thing stood out as odd. It looked fundamentally different than a normal homunculus. Sungchul's eyes were drawn to something hidden behind the hideous scars and the countless boils, something beyond the severely burnt skin.

It wasn't a normal homunculus as expected. More than that… that mouth… did she rip a beak out of its face?

At that moment, the homunculus' body suddenly stiffened. A sharp dagger had been stabbed into its neck.

"Miss… Miss Mimi…?"

The homunculus stuttered like a clockwork doll as it turned its head with red blood pouring out of its neck. Mimi pushed the homunculus down onto the altar and shoved the dagger deeper as she spoke softly. "I'm really sorry, but there's no other way."

"This life was given by Miss Mimi anyways. It's only right that Miss Mimi takes back what she gave-yeyo, but everything is growing so dark. It hurts so much-yeyo…"

"…when I get stronger, I'll revive you guys," said Mimi as she twisted the dagger embedded into its neck. Something seemed to snap as the homunculus instantly died, and its blood began to fill the altar.

Surprise overtook Sungchul's eyes. *Could that homunculus have been created with the blood of a blue-feathered Nahak?*

The ground began to tremble, and a deep rumbling that pierced the dungeon in its entirety could be heard by everyone within. The black gravestone began to rise into the air. Within the burial chamber, the real burial chamber of the Avian King finally revealed itself.

[All those living and dead, kneel]

[make way for the Final King, Marakia]

At the same time, there was a relic upon the Tower of Recluse, an ancient tower revered as the most mystical and holy structure of the Other World, known as the Scripture of Calamity. There was an all-important change occurring to this relic which can only be altered by the divine will.

"What the…! Are you saying that a new clause is being added to the Scripture of Calamity?!"

The tower's owner, Saint Porpyrius, began to head towards the sacred citadel in which the Scripture of Calamity was held in such a hurry that he paid no heed to his clothes becoming disarrayed. He witnessed it. Along with the alteration of the previous five calamities, a new calamity was being recorded on the first line simultaneously.

[The King of Feathers and Beak that devoured his own kin will spread his wings of sin once again to swallow the world in darkness.]

***

The fog lifted and the being within the burial chamber slowly revealed itself. The face and wings of a hawk and the torso of a human. It was an avian. Most noble of all avians, it was the King of the Nahaks. He had pitch black feathers and a shining golden beak, and purple eyes so deep, they looked as if they would suck everything in.

As he stepped down from his burial chamber, he looked toward Mimi who was holding herself up precariously with two staves.

"I am Marakia. Who are you, foreigner?"

If one ignored the dignified and dominating aura which wrapped his entire body, his voice seemed rather young, perhaps even childish. Mimi could not see what was in front of her, but she knew that a great and destructive being of legends was standing before her.

"My absolute monarch of the earth and skies." Mimi put both her hands together in a grovelling gesture as she continued, "This pathetic and insignificant Mimi Azrael of the humankind greets you."

Marakia tilted his head slightly to look at her. "You are blind in both eyes."

He extended his hand filled with rings adorned with gems and brushed across her face as though stroking it. Then a miracle occurred: Mimi's two eyes returned to their formal state.

"Ah...! Your highness!" She suddenly realized that she could see once more and threw herself at Marakia's feet out of gratitude.

"However, where are my servants and my people?" asked Marakia.

"Your Highness' servants and people... have long since disappeared."

"What did you say?"

A small creature began to linger in the corner of his eyes. It was the white-feathered baby Nahak that was feeding upon Odrias' corpse.

"Isn't that one of my people? He might be of low blood with his white feathers, but he is still one of my subjects nonetheless. Where are my blue-feathered nobles and advisers?" asked Marakia.

"They... have already... become extinct for the sake of raising your highness to your god-like status."

"Ah!" Marakia let out a short exclamation. He thought back to the days before his long slumber, to the time when his race had flourished. In the bleak moment before the Calamity came down upon them, the King and the Council had decided to bet everything they had on Marakia who was born with the black wings of legends said to be the mark of the one destined to bring salvation to their race and committed to performing a ritual as their last act of desperation.

And that was where his memories ended.

"I see. I had fallen into an eternal slumber after that moment."

"That's correct, your majesty." Mimi adjusted her mangled legs to grovel before Marakia. She looked up towards him carefully and spoke again. "And I have woken you from that eternal slumber despite countless dangers and obstructions."

"Is that so? Then I suppose it is only correct to bestow upon you something appropriate."

Marakia raised his hand, and overwhelming power gathered into it. At that moment, slow but firm footsteps could be heard from the darkness on the opposite side of the room.

"..."

It was Sungchul. Curiosity rose within Marakia's eyes. "Who is that?"

Mimi desperately evaded Sungchul's gaze as she answered his question. "That man is one of those that did not want your majesty's rebirth. It might be good to rid yourself of him."

Bertelgia scoffed as though it was the most ridiculous thing she had ever heard. "What?! Listen, lady! How can you be so ungrateful to say that we are the enemy after we saved you? Are you even human?"

Sungchul calmed Bertelgia who was buzzing about in anger with a wave of his hand, then looked alternatingly toward Marakia and Mimi and spoke calmly. "Mimi Azrael. I have come to receive the crown as promised."

Mimi did not give Sungchul a single glance. She continued to kneel before the Avian King and pleaded to him. "Just look your highness. They aim for your majesty's crown. You mustn't show mercy to the irreverent ones without beak or wing who covet the crown of the Nahak."

Marakia was barely listening to Mimi's words. His violet eyes were focused intently on this foreigner with a strange attire composed of a dusty coat and a pair of worn-out jeans. *This human. He is definitely not normal.*

It was at that moment when another figure leapt into the burial chamber.

"What is going on? Mikhael Gilford! Odrias!"

It was the Seventh Continental Champion, Willie Gilford. He had been outside the dungeon when he heard the strange rumblings that shook the entire dungeon leading him to follow his suspicions to this place with a small group accompanying him. However, the son he was looking for was nowhere to be found in this tomb. Instead, in the main chamber of the tomb, there was a strange young man that appeared to be from the Penal Unit, the Exploratory Unit leader Mimi Azrael, and an avian with black-feathered wings.

His eyes were locked onto Marakia. With the grand outfit and decorations that surrounded the avian's entire body, the overwhelming oppressive feeling that pushed against his entire body, and the avian's appearance, there was only one guess that he could make.

Could it be? Mimi Azrael... did she awaken the Avian King? And just where is that idiot Mikhael?

His son was nowhere to be found.

"And who is that?" Marakia directed his question towards Mimi.

She hesitated slightly but made her resolve before answering. "That man is our enemy."

"Lies! That person is my employee." Willie raised his voice as he spoke. Mimi trembled as she felt fearful of the overwhelming strength in his voice. This was what it meant to have the strength to hold the title of the Seventh Champion of the Continent.

Willie glared at Mimi as he questioned her. "Mimi Azrael! Where is my son?"

As he spoke, a weak voice rang out from the wall.

"Kuu... S-save me..."

It was the voice of his subordinates trapped by the servants of the king. Willie immediately went towards the voice and split the wall with his sword. The wall split cleanly allowing the people trapped within to spill out. Mikhael was among them.

"Mikhael!" Willie quickly embraced his son's body and shook him. Mikhael was already dead. His mind broke much earlier within the darkness to despair, causing his body to follow soon after.

"This damned…"

Willie's eyes lit up with intense flames, but he was also a person of great caution. He didn't have any desire to fight with the King of the Nahaks whose strength couldn't be determined. He quickly calculated in his mind to coordinate with the Avian King for a benefit or to cut his losses and leave with his son's body. However, he couldn't locate his most useful pawn.

In any case, where did Odrias go? I stuck him with my son to watch over him. Where is he now?

He looked around his surroundings and soon a single corpse abandoned in a distant corner came into his view.

That attire…?

Willie, whose eyes were drawn to the corpse's face due to the familiar outfit it wore, was beyond shocked with what he saw. "Odrias Sikoro!"

His former comrade and most trusted subordinate was in the middle of being pecked to pieces by a white-feathered avian chick.

"This bastard!" Willie flipped out. Who was Odrias to him? He was the most loyal of followers who had been with him from the start and had fought with his back against his in many battles, even though Willie was a summoned that everyone looked down upon. They were so close that Willie hired Odrias as Mikhael's mentor after Odrias's retirement. It might have been odder for him to retain his calm after seeing such a man being pitifully pecked apart by some chicken.

Willie grew furious and booted the young chick that was pecking at the corpse.

"Bawk bawk!!" The avian bounced away like a ball until it hit the floor, then thrashed about a bit and died.

"How dare a fucking chicken try to eat my comrade's corpse." It was an immediate reflex that occurred before his head had time to think. He was known to be a selfish man, but he deeply valued those close to him and treated them with great care.

But due to his actions, the previously calm burial chamber began to stir. The mood of Marakia, the King of the Nahaks, had shifted. A dark and chilly air flowed from Marakia who had been quiet and agreeable despite his title as the Last King.

"You dare kill my subject in front of me?" Marakia grew enraged. Mimi who had been hunched over in front of him was wearing a meaningful smile beneath him.

Shit!

Willie realized that he had made a critical error, and to make matters worse, a being appeared from the shadows that he wished to never meet again. The Despair of the Abyss revealed himself as though he had been here from the beginning.

"T-that thing!"

His followers who had already had their share of troubles due to the creature immediately turned their gaze away from it.

"…"

Sungchul silently looked at his surroundings. Marakia was in the center of the room, Mimi was hunched over beneath him, Willie and his followers were at the entrance, the Despair of the Abyss sat in a shaded corner, while he stood in the middle of them all. All of the key figures within the Underground Kingdom had gathered in one spot. When it rains it pours, and this powder keg was ready to explode.

Marakia moved first.

"Which race rules the world now?' he coldly asked Mimi who lay at his feet.

Mimi answered while still in her grovelling pose, "Several races share dominion, but the most dominating among them… are humans."

"Is that so?" Marakia let out a cold laughter. His starry eyes were looking directly at Willie.

"Those that crawled the ground when we flew the skies have now become arrogant because they managed to gather some strength. To dare treat a subject of the King of Nahaks in such a manner."

"…"

Willie began to retreat slowly but looked ready to pull out his sword anytime. Marakia who had seen this mocked him. "Do you truly believe that you could harm a feather on my body with a cheap toy like that?"

"…It is true that I have harmed one of your subjects, but it is also true that your young subject had desecrated the corpse of my subordinate." Willie did not back down an inch, and the Avian King broke out into laughter.

"The creatures that once crawled on the ground as prey are now barking so indignantly. Human, I will let you experience again the fear that had since been forgotten."

Marakia's wings burst open. The massive magic power instilled within his black wings flooded the room, creating an uneasy atmosphere so tense that it felt ready to burst at any moment.

"I shall leave this place and lay waste to each and every human nation and drive them towards extinction. I shall burn the unworthy to death with the flames of purification, and the human kings will be forced to watch as I devour their own livers in front of them. If I repeat this enough times, the human race may remember once more what these black wings symbolize."

Things escalated quickly, thought Mimi as she continued to lie bowed with her head to the ground at the king's feet.

Meanwhile, Willie Gilford, who was receiving the full force of the Avian King's rage with his body, felt extreme terror. *This is not an enemy I can defeat.*

What stood in front of him exuded so much oppressive strength that it relegated the Despair of the Abyss to the status of bystander.

Maybe if I gathered all 13 Champions of the Continent… but I can't do this by myself.

He had wiped clean all notions of taking the bodies of his son or his comrade with him. Survival was the first priority.

These thoughts were running through his mind as he clenched his sword tighter, but Marakia's wings suddenly moved. Marakia flew up to the ceiling with a single flap, and Willie, who could see the black wings of the Nahak King, couldn't fathom what he should do next. Soon, the air above burst into feathers and beams of black light.

Sungchul silently watched the two battle. *It is similar to Glare, but not quite the same. It's a more powerful version of Magic Arrow.*

Willie swung his sword to parry the projectiles or evaded them completely, but the deadly magical arrows continued to pour like rain, causing small and large cuts all over his body. His followers were long since dead within the confusion of the battle.

"Gasp… Gasp…"

There was no way to retaliate for Willie. He would simply be whittled to death at his rate, and it was too much of a risk to leap toward the Avian King.

A way… is there no way at all? Something most likely to succeed?

In a fight without the possibility of victory, everything had to be put on the line. Willie had only involved himself when the odds were with him. This was his first fight where the odds were against him from the start. He attempted a counterattack within the baptism of countless arrows, but it was already far too late as his body was exhausted and riddled with injuries. He was struck in the abdomen with a black magic arrow, and he fell. It was a mortal wound.

Willie wiped his lips and tried to catch his breath. The shadow of death was looming over him.

"You insect." The Avian King gradually descended to end the life of the Seventh Champion of the Continent personally. A short staff that looked more like a pitchfork rather than a blade appeared in his hand. It was the Sceptre of the Avian King.

Marakia approached Willie who was desperately gasping for breath on the floor and raised the sceptre above him. "Die."

It was at that moment when a man appeared before them. A man who had such a small presence that everyone had forgotten him and in his hands was a hammer. It was Sungchul.

The man who had naturally stepped in to block the Avian King's path approached Willie and spoke in a calm voice. "Willie Gilford. Do you remember me?"

Chapter 7 – Echoes

"Who are you?"

It was an unfamiliar face, but when Willie noticed the hammer in this strange man's hands, he recalled where he had seen the man. It was in front of the Demon King's Palace. It was the man who was losing his mind before the heroes of Other World such as Girasung, spouting curses towards them.

Sungchul, the Enemy of the World? No… How could it be? His face is different. He looks younger than before, and his physique is different as well.

The most important aspect wasn't his face, but rather the Divine Weapon, Fal Garaz, that he held in his hands. Sungchul looked down on Willie with a chilly gaze and opened his mouth again.

"You haven't changed at all in eight years. Or rather, you might have regressed."

At that moment, Marakia shot down dozens of magical arrows from the sky like rain. Sungchul struck the earth with his hammer. The surface cracked, and an entire sheet of bedrock popped out. He held it in place with just one hand. The bedrock was as large as a house, but the hand which held it up was unwavering.

PEWT! PEWT! PEWT PEWT PEWT!

Multiple Magic arrows landed on the bedrock, but none managed to penetrate it all the way through. After he had managed to block the first round of attacks, Sungchul threw the bedrock and mightily swung his hammer. It caused a sound reminiscent of an explosion along with a tremendous rush of wind. The Avian King was temporarily disoriented due to taking the resulting wind head on, and the bedrock Sungchul launched into the air came crashing down to the ground.

BOOM!

The ground shook wildly, but what shook even more was the Seventh Champion of the Continent's eyes.

What is that strength? I knew that he forsook everything for the sake of physical stats, but that strength... what is this?

For a moment, a goal that he once chased but had long since come to accept as infeasible popped into his mind.

Could it be... did that man exceed Superhuman levels and step into the realm of Transcendence?

Transcendent One. It is the highest attainable state for a mortal. There were only three known Transcendents among the Thirteen Champions of the Continent: the First Champion of the Continent, Emperor William Quinton Marlboro, the Second Champion of the Continent, Mediator Aquiroa, and the Fifth Champion of the Continent, leader of the Assassin's Guild Shamal Rajput.

Sungchul who had been the 10th Champion of the Continent was known as a powerful warrior, but he was too simple. People believed his upper limits were all too clear. He had no particular skills or techniques and chose to throw himself into battle with just his own body. This method was crude and predictable. But the martial prowess Sungchul just demonstrated in that short period of time was on a completely different level from his past self.

Could it be that he overcame his limits?

Suddenly, Willie spat out a glob of blood from his throat and curled up like a shrimp. It was because the shadow of death was looming over him.

THUD.

Sungchul's military boots passed by him.

"Selfishness has clouded your judgement and made you fall into the pitfall called complacence."

KONK.

Fal Garaz's head fell lightly onto the ground's surface.

"Look well, Willie Gilford. This is how the Enemy of the World fights."

Sungchul ran out with his hammer in hand. Willie, who didn't even have the strength to move a finger, couldn't do much else than to watch Sungchul fight while his head still lay on the ground, forcing him to breathe in the loose dirt.

When the battle began, Willie fell into a huge shock. Sungchul and Marakia fought on equal footing. No... Sungchul had an air of leisure about him. It was unbelievable. A summoned, a mortal, was fighting evenly with a figure of legends.

Sungchul. He was definitely weaker than me. Just how did he manage to get his hands on such massive power? And... and for what reason?

Sungchul's words were correct. While Willie had become complacent after obtaining the title of "Regent of the Ancient Kingdom" and the Seventh Champion of the Continent, Sungchul had become unfathomably stronger. He was forced to fight and struggle to survive every day for eight years, to the point where death would have been a much kinder fate.

"Receive the fury of the skies!"

Marakia formed several magic formations all across the ceiling and summoned a part of a storm cloud to cause lightning to strike down with abandon. It was a terrifying magical attack that hadn't been seen before, but Sungchul's response was quite simple. He rapidly smashed Fal Garaz into the bedrock, shattering the ground around him causing the debris to float up into the air. He then struck the floating chunks of the bedrock faster than the eyes could see, launching them towards and destroying every magic formation Marakia had created, even scattering the thunderclouds that had formed.

Marakia was impressive, but Sungchul's response was simply breathtaking.

Just how did that man... for what reason did he reach that level...

In that moment, Willie's sight began to fade. Death was quickly approaching him. All he could hear was the sound of battle, and even that was starting to grow distant. Within the tranquil darkness, Willie lay dying in humiliation and regret. The last thing he heard was Marakia's outburst.

"You lowly pest of a human!"

It was an all-out attack. Marakia brought forth all sorts of damnable forbidden spells from within his feathers by muttering their incantation in his beaks before he thrust his wings forward. His entire body began to emit a black magical aura that swept through the entire Underground Kingdom like a torrent, causing all the corpses caught within to reawaken.

CLACK. CLACK. CLACK.

The countless Cave Elves buried within the wall broke through and began to stumble forth. It was an undead army of thousands… no, tens of thousands.

"My slaves. Exterminate that vulgar insect!"

The skeletal army began to rush towards Sungchul like a river.

"…"

Sungchul stood his ground and watched the tidal wave of skeletons overwhelm him while Marakia looked over the scene from the ceiling with his arms crossed.

The river of white skeletons quickly began to surround Sungchul and eventually enveloped him entirely. These dead beings had the magical ability to drain the life force of the living simply by being near them. Although each of them was weak, but what would happen if few dozens or few hundreds of them suddenly came rushing all at once to drain away life energy? No human warrior, no matter how powerful, would be able to withstand the onslaught. Marakia's skeleton army also numbered in the tens of thousands. It might have helped to have wings to fly, but those without the ability to fly would be simply doomed to die without a struggle.

However, tremors began to rumble within the mass of skeletons. Marakia's eyes caught something moving.

SWECK~

Within the river of white below his feet, something small and white began to fly over in his direction. Marakia immediately began to move his wings to back away.

FWIK! FWIK!

Something sharp flew past where he flew and became embedded into the wall. Marakia turned his head to take a look at what it was. They were fragments of bone.

BOOM!

Another muffled tremor exploded below him followed by the sound of the air splitting that shocked him to his core.

Did that bastard actually…?!

Marakia could not hold back his surprise and quickly descended. Skeletal fragments shot out like a shotgun and embedded themselves everywhere.

BOOM! BOOM! BOOM!

The swarm of skeletons moved in unison. More fragments flew toward Marakia than he had expected.

"Urk!"

One of the fragments caused an injury. The wound wasn't deep, but it bled and caused ripples of pain. Marakia began to tremble. He was a Nahak; a race believed to be chosen by God. He was also the most revered and powerful among the Nahaks, but he was injured by a mere human.

However, that attack was only the beginning.

BOOM! BOOM! BOOM! BOOM! BOOM!

Consecutive muffled explosions resonated from the mass of skeletons.

What is he? Why is he fine while being surrounded by the Army of Death?

He had been the one showering black arrows like rain, but now he was on the receiving end, being exposed to the flying fragments of bone. Marakia now stood at a crossroad.

Do I release the Army of Death and put up a defensive barrier? If I do that, I'll lose one of my methods of attack. The might of the Army of Death isn't explosive, but it is unending. No matter how strong that human is, he will not be able to resist the Army of Death indefinitely.

Marakia was not only a powerful mage, but he was also a powerful warrior. He also had more confidence than anyone in his ability to fly. He looked down to the ground as he sustained the Army of Death.

BOOM!

Another explosion. A shotgun of bone fragments began to fly out. Marakia tracked every fragment and began to maneuver in the air. With a single flap, he majestically and agilely tore through the air to evade every fragment.

BOOM! BOOM!

Sungchul, who was buried within the skeletons, continued to shoot out fragments.

He is struggling, but his attacks will not work on me!

Marakia had faith in his wings and the precision of his eyes; he continued to evade the attacks easily.

BOOM! BOOM! BOOM!

Bones continued to fly towards him. Marakia put on a beautiful display of flight as he continued to evade the fragments, but as he dodged the fragments for the third time, another attack flew his way with a slight delay. Marakia scoffed at him and descended quickly.

Do you think these kinds of attacks will work?

The fragment flew by harmlessly over his head, and with that, Marakia was confident in his victory. But the moment he lowered his altitude to dodge the projectiles, something shot out of the pile of skeletons like a bullet. It happened so suddenly that Marakia could not respond in time.

Could it be?

He had a good guess of what had happened to him. The attack which he thought he had easily evaded was actually meant to drive him into a checkmate.

GRIP!

A human hand gripped onto the avian king's wing. Marakia quickly tried to shake the human off, but the human hand was faster.

RIP!

The rough grip proceeded to separate his wing from his body. Following the traumatic pain shooting through his body, a fountain of blood shot out from the wound. Marakia's vision grew dim as he fell towards the ground. What appeared next in his sights was the Army of Death that he had raised himself. Corpses of Cave Elves, ones on whom he wouldn't even waste the words "lowly" on, began to envelop him as he lost consciousness.

BOOM!

The Avian King crashed in the middle of the mass of skeletons. The skeletons that had been animated due to the king's power began to collapse as they lost their source of power. Sungchul lightly landed onto the surface made of bones. His usual appearance remained intact without a single injury nor any clothing out of place.

"…"

He turned his head and looked back towards a specific spot. Willie, who had been lying in that place, could no longer be seen under a mound of skeletons of nameless Cave Elves. It was a pitiful end to someone praised as the Seventh Champion of the Continent as well as the only one in over 500 years to have achieved the rank of Grand Swordmaster.

Sungchul walked over slowly toward Marakia, who was lying on top of the skeletal mound.

"Uuu… Kuuu…"

Marakia, who had one of his wings torn off, was trembling and groaning from pain. The sound of Sungchul's military boots grew closer and closer. And for the first time in his life, Marakia felt fear blossom in his heart. He pushed aside the pain and immediately flipped himself over to look at the man who was silently approaching him with his violet eyes.

How could this be? This doesn't make sense. This strength that I acquired at the cost of my entire race and era couldn't overcome this lowly human?

Sungchul continued to walk towards him. The avian king had to swallow the insult of having to use his two arms and legs to crawl on his back to postpone the destined moment. He suddenly had a thought.

That's right. This guy can only resort to physical attacks.

Within his body was near infinite amounts of magic power. The problem was that the vessel of this immense magical power had sustained a critical injury. It would be difficult to heal himself in the current circumstance. He needed something he could immediately use. A potion or another living creature.

Marakia who was now crawling on his back caught something in his sights. It was a human. The female mage who had claimed to have revived him. He may have been reawakened by that woman, but humans were nothing more than a snack to Marakia.

That looks good. The mage would also work great as nourishment.

Marakia was capable of sacrificing his own subjects; it would be impossible to expect mercy from him toward another race entirely. His eyes were those of a predator looking at his prey.

"W-What...?!" Mimi quickly figured out the intent behind Marakia's gaze toward her, but by then, it was all too late. The sharp beak tore through her flesh and became lodged into her heart. Marakia's throat gulped down the warm blood of a freshly killed human.

"..."

Sungchul only watched the scene with an indifferent expression.

***

Sungchul stood in front of Marakia, then raised Fal Garaz onto his shoulders as he spoke.

"I heard that you were in the class of lesser gods, but I guess you haven't quite gotten there yet."

"...What do you want?"

Marakia wiped off the blood off his beaks as he asked, looking exasperated. Sungchul looked down at the Avian King apathetically as he held his hand out.

"Crown."

The Crown of the Nahak King was believed to possess an unimaginable amount of magic power. The crown was the sole reason that Sungchul hadn't already torn Marakia to shreds. However, Marakia appeared as though it was the first time he heard of a Nahak crown.

"The Kings of Nahaks don't wear crowns. The color of their feathers symbolize their royalty, and also…"

Once enough vitality returned, Marakia quickly chanted an aria under his breath that caused a mysterious square barrier to form around him. He then laughed loudly within his barrier.

"Kuhahaha! I've already caught on the fact that physical attacks are all that you're good at. You will not be able to break through this barrier as long as my unlimited mana endures!"

Sungchul picked up his hammer and took a swing at the barrier as a test. He felt no vibration nor impact, but the hammer did not budge any further than the boundary of the magic wall. Sungchul's Soul Contract, the Eye of Truth, activated which let him peek into the nature of the barrier.

A barrier technique that nullifies all physical attacks. It can be sustained for as long as the caster desires.

In other words, it was the perfect defense. However, it is impossible for mortals to make something perfect. Marakia had to place a critical weakness in exchange for a perfectly sustainable defense against physical damage. Sungchul used the Eye of Truth to look into the constraints.

The barrier can nullify all physical attacks, but he had to include a form of weakness, so he increased his vulnerability to magic by several times.

In other words, even the weakest of spells would become quite powerful once passing through that barrier. That was the vulnerability placed within his own technique. It was because the power of the spell increased proportionally to how crippling the weakness was and so Marakia took advantage of this method.

This would have been effective a year ago, but Sungchul had gone through a similar ordeal and had been looking far and wide for a method to break through this obstacle. Now was the moment of truth, to find out if his efforts were not in vain.

Sungchul put down his hammer and extended his finger.

"Glare."

A magic formation flashed for an instant at the tip of his finger. Marakia's violet eyes grew wide as he saw this. *That bastard. He can use magic too?*

In the next moment, a beam of light extended from the tip of Sungchul's finger directly onto Marakia.

"Keuk!"

He used his last remaining wing to shield his body from the piercing light from Glare. Bone-numbing pain scraped through his entire body. In addition to the plentiful mana in the surrounding area, the barrier further amplified the enemy's magic attack. One factor weakens him and the other strengthens the enemy. It was the worst possible situation. But Marakia was not just anybody. He who was called the Last King calmly calculated and assessed the situation despite it being seemingly hopeless.

This guy's magic power is insignificant. It's a low-grade magic that doesn't even reach the third circle. It might hurt like I'm dying, but this isn't lethal.

As he expected, Sungchul's magic attack stung, but it didn't leave a mortal wound due to Marakia's exceptionally high magic resistance. Generally, mages with extraordinarily high magic power would have equally remarkable levels of magic resistance. Marakia was no exception. His magic resistance reached the levels only a Transcendent could, around 600. Most half-assed magic wouldn't even be enough to put a scratch on him. If it had been anywhere other than inside the barrier, or if he had been hit by Sungchul's magic outside of the dungeon on the surface, the Magic Resistance that covered his entire body might have nullified the spell entirely. He sustained this much of an injury because he was within the barrier and because he was in the underground labyrinth overflowing with mana. But Marakia would not die from this level of damage.

He thanked the corpse of Mimi Azrael that was sprawled out in the corner and refocused on the battle. A shadow wrapped around the burnt flesh that Sungchul's Glare had seared, and it quickly healed.

If I hadn't resorted to emergency measures by eating that human, it might have been really dangerous.

Sungchul was pouring in Glare from beyond the barrier. Marakia felt intense pain on every strike, but the shadow continued to heal him every time.

"…"

Sungchul felt annoyed.

This guy. He recovered his Magic Fingerprint.

When Sungchul tore away Marakia's wing, he felt that he had torn away one of the pillars that supported Marakia's magic system. However, it had recovered after Marakia devoured Mimi Azrael.

"Why did you just watch him eat that rotten woman?" Bertelgia who was somehow already out of the pocket asked bluntly.

Sungchul sighed lightly. "I wanted to see the potential."

"The potential?"

"…"

Sungchul didn't reply. Instead, he circled around Marakia who was still behind the barrier and tried Glare several more times. Marakia spat out cries of pain, but as time passed, he regained his confidence and began mocking Sungchul.

"Your flesh might be fearsome, but your magic is pathetic. This place might be overflowing with mana, but how long can you continue to fire off blindly with your pathetic amount of magical talent?"

He had a point. Sungchul had also been thinking on that point, and he knew the answer. He pulled out a sleeping bag from his Soul Storage and laid it out on top of the skeletons. Marakia, who did not know what a sleeping bag was, watched puzzled as to what Sungchul was up to until Sungchul lay down on it.

Wait, is this human planning to…

His speculation soon became a reality when Sungchul turned his back and spoke in a composed voice. "It's ok. I've got a lot of time. I'll just take a snooze and knock on you some more afterwards."

It wasn't just empty words. Marakia could feel the truth in his voice. That stupid oaf with more brawn than brain would never give up before he got what he wanted. And thus, Marakia asked the question, "I do not have a crown. But if there is anything other than the crown that I can give, I wish to make a deal with you. What is it that you desire, human?"

Sungchul, who was facing away from Marakia, turned his head over his shoulder. He looked at Marakia indifferently and put forward his demand. "Magic Power."

"Magic Power?"

"That's right. There is a conniving one who's exactly like you, and I think both of you have similar levels of strength. I want to get rid of him with magic."

"Are you perhaps telling me to give you my Magic Power?"

"Anything is fine. Magic Power or relic. As long as it's acceptable to me, I'll take it," Sungchul said as he lay back down.

Marakia closed his beak and began to contemplate. Something acceptable. The weight of those words fell heavy on Marakia's shoulders. The human in front of his eyes was a being that even he could not contend with. How much would such a person require before he could be satisfied? Marakia, who was thinking carefully, came to such a very shocking conclusion that he couldn't breathe.

Could it be… does this human want my entire Magic Power?

In other words, stat transference. Dreadful suspicion rose in Marakia's eyes as he continued to contemplate what this human could possibly want.

There were largely two ways through which a being transferred stats to another being. One was through quests, but the creation of a quest required a long time and effort as it required the permission of a god and the stats that could be given were limited. Creating an Objective, which was a superior form of quests, or using quest as a way to set up a gamble with stat points as wager were some of the few ways to raise some stat points, but it would not satisfy someone like Sungchul. In order to hand over the acceptable amount of plentiful stats, it required another method: Soul Inheritance.

But this method had a dreadful unavoidable prerequisite: It resulted in the death of the one giving his stats.

The Soul Inheritance required strong will, desire, and the death of the giver. This was considered as the greatest form of inheritance a denizen of the Other World could leave for their posterity.

Even if the amount of stat that could be transferred via Soul Inheritance was roughly a tenth of the sacrifice's original stats, being able to raise stats by even one for those who are close to becoming Transcendent was an immense boon. But as already stated, this method requires the death of the one transferring the stat; a prerequisite Marakia could never come to accept.

Do you really think I would hand over my Soul Inheritance to some lesser species like you, who isn't even my child?

No, it would not matter even if he were his child. Marakia made up his mind inside of the barrier and resolved himself.

First, I have to heal my wounds in here till my wings recover. Once my wings recover, I'll find a way, human. I'll show you that time is not only on your side.

At that moment, something at the edge of his sight began to stir. It was the green monster with the avian skull that was covered in mucous. It was the Despair of the Abyss.

Why is that accursed monster in my kingdom? And it's even in the form of a Nahak. How strange. Our kingdom has nothing to do with the Ancient God.

The Despair of the Abyss dug through the skeletons that blanketed the ground to seek out a single corpse. It was Willie Gilford's corpse. The creature lifted the corpse, opened its maw, then swallowed his body whole. It was an unrealistic scene that couldn't be believed, and it sent shivers down Marakia's body.

Sungchul rose from his knapsack a bit later. Feeling a bit rested, he began shooting out Glare without warning. Marakia continued to endure Sungchul's attack and ultimately managed to protect himself. This continued for a while longer until Sungchul realized that he was making no progress.

Do I have to bring Deckard? No, he's too weak. He might crumble to some mental attack before he can use any magic.

Sungchul rethought his plans as he turned to his rectangular friend. "Bertelgia."

"Hm? Why do you seek me, Bertelgia, Oh Mr. Scary, Scary Man?"

"Do you know any way to resolve this situation?"

Marakia who was hunched over within the barrier lifted his head to see Bertelgia flapping behind Sungchul.

Is that a living book? Wait, now that I look at it, it's not just a normal living book. I can feel a faint trace of life force and a soul within.

Curiosity rose within Marakia's eyes as he could hear Berltegia's voice from afar.

"Mmmm… how about you keep bashing at it with your hammer? That bird brain's mana can't be infinite, so just keep bashing away at it until it breaks."

"Wait!"

Marakia's voice interrupted her.

"Do you think that method will work? My mana is infinite."

To this Bertelgia flew listlessly around Sungchul and replied as if she was disappointed with Marakia's answer.

"Well, this mister's strength is also infinite."

"Ah, that's a good idea."

Sungchul picked up Fal Garaz once again, and fear rose within Marakia's eyes.

Shit.

Bertelgia's words were correct. He may call his mana infinite, but it was something earned through the death of tens of thousands of Cave Elves and the lives of his own kind. There was an end.

However, what about the man that stood in front of him? It wasn't clear how he obtained his strength, but each and every strike of his hammer seemed to possess the might of a god. What would happen if he were to engage in a battle between infinities against someone like him? Marakia already knew the answer.

STOMP.

Sungchul stood before the barrier with his hammer in hand. Marakia's eyes grew wide, but Sungchul stopped and placed the hammer before the barrier.

"On second thought, I want to use a different method."

It was an unexpected opportunity. Sungchul wanted to dominate the Avian King through a method other than his own strength.

Marakia fought with all his strength to maintain his expression, but the danger had not yet passed for him. When Sungchul put down the hammer, he asked Bertelgia another question.

"Bertelgia, do you know of any way to enhance magic in your alchemic library?"

"Why wouldn't there be?"

Bertelgia spun up into the air with vigor as she answered. Marakia felt intense desire to tear apart that chattering book in the air, but despite his wishes, Bertelgia's mouth did not rest.

"There is a drink and a powder. Which do you prefer?"

"Doping, eh? I personally don't like strengthening up temporarily by drinking. I'm not weak," responded Sungchul.

"How about the powder?"

"It is a type of item that lowers enemy magic resistance?"

"No, it is a powder that enhances the might of the magic."

"The description itself does not seem all that promising."

"What a rude thing to say! It's one of the popular items that the Seven Heroes that you like so much came to Dad's shop for!"

"Hoh?" Sungchul's eyes lit up. The method didn't sound all that promising, but if the Seven Heroes used it, it was another story. Sungchul felt like things were going his way as he asked in a slightly different tone. "And the ingredients?"

It was the critical problem with alchemy. No matter how good of an Alchemist you are, your hands are tied without the ingredients. Thankfully, there wasn't an issue this time.

Bertelgia flew above Sungchul's head as she flapped her pages with one swoop. "Not all the ingredients are here, but the critical pieces are lying around. Yep, it's those things sparkling above your head."

Sungchul looked up. Above his head were as many gems embedded in the ceiling emitting a green light as there were stars in the night sky.

***

Marakia watched Sungchul and his living book craft something from his self-made prison. Sungchul pulled out Eckheart's Portable Alchemic Cauldron first. It was usually in a miniature form that would fit into a pocket, but once a hidden feature was activated, it grew to a massive size that even three adults might struggle to move. It was one of Eckhart's genius inventions that he had created based on his theory of how Soul Storages worked.

Sungchul crushed the rock with a green glow from the ceiling into the Alchemic cauldron. An ordinary Alchemist might require tools such as a mortar or a mill, but it was unnecessary for Sungchul.

"Now, keep crushing those luminous ores into powder-yeyo!" Bertelgia continued chattering away beside him.

159

"Why are you mimicking a Homunculus?" Sungchul, who didn't particularly like the homunculi, glared at Bertelgia as he asked curtly. However, Bertelgia must have not sensed the danger.

"It is not a homunculus-yeyo! I am mimicking a fairy-yeyo!"

She continued to imitate a homunculus.

Sungchul crushed another luminous ore with his grip as he spoke again. "If you keep at it, I will stuff you back into the storage." It was a calm voice, but he was a man of his words.

Bertelgia immediately stopped. "O…ok-yeyo!"

Some time had passed, and a considerable amount of glowing green powder was amassed inside the cauldron.

"What now?"

"Ahem. The luminous ores possess powerful mana of their own. In other words, it is emitting light on its own due to its abundant mana! We can learn two things from this! Can you guess what they are?"

"…"

Sungchul was about to tell her to cut to the chase, but he internally fixed his attitude and began to contemplate on the answer to her question. "The luminous ores must be capable of storing mana."

"And the other?"

"Mmm…"

"Why does it emit light on its own?"

"Not only can it store mana, but it can also emit the stored mana in some form?"

"Exactly!" Bertelgia let out a whistle as she flew around Sungchul once. "Well, I did give you a hint in the end."

Sungchul grabbed a handful of the luminous ore powder and took a whiff. It was to activate the Observation ability of the Alchemists. However, the powder was already an Alchemic item created through some ingredients and not an ingredient on its own, so it was not something he could initiate inspection or analysis via smelling it. Sungchul grabbed one of the intact luminous ores and stared at it piercingly. An information screen regarding the green glowing ore appeared before him.

```
                    [Luminous Ore (Green)]
    Level: 4
    Grade: B
    Attribute: Earth
    Type: Valuable
    Effect: A gem capable of emitting a green light on its own
```

"It is a level 4 Alchemic Item."

It was a rather high-level item when considering the fact that being able to create a level 5 item was enough to be called a professor.

"Yep, correct. It's a level 4 Alchemic item. The ingredients are fairly rare, and the method of creating them is quite intricate. Looking at how they were able to fill the ceiling with them like stars in the sky, I suppose the legends about the Nahak race wasn't for nothing."

When she finished speaking, a sharp laughter could be heard from the other side of the cauldron. It was Marakia within the barrier.

"We, the Nahaks, are one of the most noble of the mortal races. This Underground Kingdom is but one of countless wonders we've created. To be surprised by mere glowing stones that serve only as decorations within this palace. How pathetic."

He was like a bird trapped in a cage, but his pride had yet to fall. He had lost, but the belief that the Nahak race didn't share in this loss remained iron-clad in his heart.

Bertelgia looked over at his mocking figure and retorted bluntly, "So what? They've fallen now."

"Fallen? The Nahak race? Hahaha! Don't make me laugh, you pitiful book-shaped human," retorted Marakia.

"Who are you calling pitiful? You birdbrain!"

"My eyes see all. Even that pitiable and pathetic form hidden under the guise of what is visible."

"Oh, yeah? What do you see?" Bertelgia snorted, and when she did, Marakia made an undecipherable smile as he stared at Bertelgia as if to look through her. His purple irises contained several complex and exotic magic formations which were shuffling among themselves until one of them rose to the surface and remained fixed in place. It was the All-Seeing Eye that saw through all things.

Now let's see.

He first looked at Bertelgia. A faint figure was lingering behind her appearance as a large book. It was a human girl with a slim stature. The girl had both her eyes closed and was hunched over like a fetus.

So that is the true form of the book. She must be hiding her true form in the space between reality and the netherworld and interacting with the world by projecting a false appearance. Truly a complex and creative magic technique for a mere human. I praise thee.

Marakia's gaze turned toward Sungchul next, but the moment his All-Seeing Eye locked onto Sungchul, his beak went slack.

W…what is that…?!

All strength in his body left him, and he felt enough trauma to give him a heart attack briefly. Marakia immediately turned away. It was because he saw within the man's body something that mortals were forbidden to see. His heart still showed no sign of settling down.

After quite a bit of time had passed, Marakia spoke with a trembling voice. "Hey, human."

Sungchul, who was stirring the cauldron with a large spoon, turned his gaze toward Marakia. Marakia tensed up when their gaze met, and spoke in a sonorous voice.

"Just what are you planning?"

"What are you talking about?" asked Sungchul.

"Just what are you planning to do that you carry such a horrible baggage inside your body?"

"…"

Sungchul was silent, but Marakia's eyes flashed as he asked accusingly, "You. You've stood before a god, haven't you?"

Sungchul finally replied in a calm voice, "What are you trying to say?"

Marakia laughed weakly and lightly moved his remaining wing. When a single black feather fell slowly onto the floor, he spoke again. "Me? I don't have much to say. I have been nicknamed the Final King, but I still was unworthy to stand before a god. Though I do know one thing."

Marakia let out a low-pitched laughter before he continued to speak. "That all who stand before a god meet a tragic end."

"..."

"The sin of seeing what mortals must never see. The sin of hearing what must not be heard. Finally, the sin of trying to speak of what must not be spoken. It is an age-old teaching that those who commit these sins will face divine punishment far worse than death and the punishment will extend to all eternity."

Marakia began to laugh like a madman when he finished. Sungchul continued to stir the cauldron silently as he laughed, and a bright light began to pour out of the cauldron soon after.

[Synthesis Success!]

Sungchul took the final product out of the cauldron. It was a pitch-black crystal that seemed to be made of darkness itself. The crystal without lustre felt cold as ice and heavy as a lump of iron. Bertelgia approached the final product and began to observe it. Soon her judgement was made.

"Ahem. Quite good. I only taught you the basic methods, and you managed to make a level 4 item."

Sungchul immediately began to inspect the black crystal in his hand.

[Black Crystal]
Level: 4
Grade: C
Attribute: Fire
Type: Magic Tool
Note: If dispersed as a powder, spells passing through it will be amplified.

"So it was like that." He looked at the Black Crystal as he continued, "That is how it is. Alchemy isn't just for making something new, but also turning something into something else."

Sungchul stared at the Black Crystal in his hand once again. Unlike the luminous ore which shined brightly, it absorbed light from the surroundings, with a dark unreflective surface. It had only taken a simple alchemic process to bring about the polar opposite characteristic of this object. Sungchul had felt that the alchemic process had consumed significant amounts of mana, but he took it as a test of his newfound magical prowess.

"Now. Marakia. I'll be starting up again. It'll be different this time."

"Give me your best shot, one who stood before a god." taunted Marakia from within the barrier.

CRUNCH.

The Black Crystal became crushed in his hand and turned into fragments. Sungchul waved his hand with the fragments toward Marakia. The fragments in his hand turned to powder and were dispersed around Marakia's surroundings.

"It's not even funny. Do you think anything will change with but a simple powder?" Marakia continued to taunt him, but Bertelgia lightly shook her body and whispered like a prim lady.

"It might sting a wee bit more this time!"

Sungchul's finger was extended toward Marakia within the black dust of the crystal.

Glare.

He recited the incantation of the spell in his head. A beam of light containing the power of the skies shot out from his fingertip towards Marakia. It wasn't much different than before up to this point, but everything changed once the beam of light began to interact with the black powder floating about in the air.

As the thin strand of light passed through the gap between the particles of the black powder, it grew thicker and brighter as it transformed mightily. The transformation that occurred in a blink of an eye was observed clearly by Marakia.

What's this? The magic is being amplified again?!

The beam of light pierced through his barrier and directly struck him.

"Kuuek!"

Marakia tried to protect himself with his last remaining wing, but the beam penetrated the wing and struck his body. He immediately felt immense trauma and pain coursing through his body, but Marakia continued to callously calculate the damage and the rate of his recovery even through the pain.

I can hold on from this much. I can hold on!

Sungchul was also thinking the same thing. His magic power had been amplified through the black crystal, but it wasn't enough to bring Marakia to his knees. Even if the difference was as thin as a sheet of paper, the difference between having overcome that wall and not was as great as the heavens and the earth. He needed something different. Something more to supplement his power, but something to amplify his magic power in this moment didn't exist.

The beam of light gradually became thinner. It meant that the effect of Glare was running out. The dark presence that was held within Marakia's body continued to heal him rapidly. Sungchul would not be able to make Marakia surrender even if he were to fire another round of Glare.

Deep disappointment could be seen on Sungchul's face.

Is this my limit?

It was at that moment Sungchul's magic became drastically drained, and a bright message appeared before his eyes.

[The first Echo]

When the message appeared, another beam of light replaced the fading beam with even more strength and ferocity than before. It wasn't caused by another Aria. The magic had manifested itself as though it was sentient. When Sungchul saw this, he instantly recalled a class that he had relegated to the back of his mind. The Echo Mage class.

One of the Seven Heroes of legend, Vestiare's echo overcame the immense gap of time and had manifested itself into the world through Sungchul.

Is this the echo…?!

This new beam of light that had swallowed up the fading beam critically struck Marakia's recovering wing consecutively.

"What's this?!"

Marakia's eyes grew wide as plates. It might have been different if there had been a pause between attacks, but it was another attack even before the first one could end. This was beyond any of his expectations. To make things worse, Sungchul recited another spell in his mind.

Glare.

The finger that was already shooting out a beam of light shot out another beam. He felt his mana hit rock bottom, but Sungchul did not relent. The fading beam of light, the second beam born from within the first, and a third new beam of light all struck Marakia's body at the same time. When all three instances of Glare attacked the Avian King's body simultaneously, even the being called the Final King could not bear it much longer.

"S-stop! Stop!!! I concede! Stop!!!"

The urgent shouts of defeat rang out in the tomb, and the barrier collapsed. Sungchul stood before the king of Nahaks who was kneeling, defenseless.

"Now, I will have what I came for."

Chapter 8 – The King's Request

"What do you want? I will not give you the Soul Inheritance. I'd rather choose death."

Marakia was feeling hopeless.

In a crumpled posture and with voice lacking energy, his appearance revealed the despair which had settled in his heart.

Sungchul gazed upon Marakia in such a state and spoke in a calm voice. "I never asked for the Soul Inheritance. I would happily receive it if it was offered, but what I want is an adequate increase in Magic Power and Intuition. Just those two things."

"Am I not in this state because I can't give you those things? Someone of your calibre should be aware how difficult and inefficient it is to transfer status points to someone else," responded Marakia.

"Is there truly no crown? Something that would grant power by wielding it?"

Sungchul had already suspected that Mimi had made up the story about the crown of the Nahak King, but he asked once again with a fleeting hope. Unrealistic expectations were always meant to be broken. Marakia shook his head.

"I told you there is no such thing. This is the truth."

"I see."

It was all futile. He had spent a great deal of effort in subjugating Marakia to his will, but he had gained nothing from it. However, nothing could be done if the other was not willing to give. It is easy to kill someone, but it was impossible to steal their inherent power and accomplishments.

"I have nothing to give you, but if you desire, I can perform a ritual that might supplement your power," Marakia said as he saw Sungchul's stiff profile.

Sungchul turned his head slightly. "What kind of ritual?"

At this, Marakia made a sinister expression as he answered. "Haven't you already seen it? What happened to the Underground Kingdom?"

"Are you asking me to offer a sacrifice?"

Marakia nodded.

"I see that there are countless Cave Elves still lingering in the Underground Kingdom. If you offer their lives to a god as sacrifice, wouldn't it be enough to get what you desire?"

"…"

Sungchul shook his head.

"Why? Why refuse this?" Marakia couldn't understand at all. He had given Sungchul the greatest offer that he could muster, and Sungchul had denied it without a second thought.

Sungchul immediately gave his reply. "Unlike you, I do not wish to sacrifice the lives of others for the sake of power."

"I thought you were wise, but you also have a foolish side to you. Why concern yourself with the lives of a lesser race that is not even your own?"

Sungchul didn't respond to that question. No, he didn't feel that the question needed an answer. It was because he was feeling that there was an unbridgeable gap between Marakia and himself. Instead, Bertelgia answered during Sungchul's silence. "You speak as if you're so great, and yet because of you your species is no more."

"What? They are no more? How can you utter such nonsense while I still stand?"

"It looks like you still aren't aware of what had happened to your people."

As Bertelgia and Marakia continued their meaningless debate, Sungchul took a step back and began to contemplate on his next steps.

Is training the only method? If I use him, I should be able to gain at least some… no wait.

A thought crossed Sungchul's mind. His eyes turned toward Marakia. The black-feathered king of the Nahaks could not overcome Sungchul, but he was still a powerful and fearsome existence. Especially in magic power where he was even superior to the Demon King.

If I use this guy, I might be able to take care of Hesthnius Max, the Demon King, without having to go through all that trouble of learning magic.

Sungchul, who had let Max slip from his grasp, had been contemplating on many different ways to resolve his situation. A method was to bring a capable mage to deal the critical blow, but it hadn't been possible due to two reasons. Firstly, there wasn't a mage that would help him. Next, he wasn't confident in being able to escort the mage safely to the Palace of the Demon King even if he did manage to recruit someone.

There are thousands, tens of thousands of demons swarming about in the Demon world. As long as the demons weren't completely brain dead, if Sungchul were to bring a Mage such as Altugius Xero along, the demons would focus all of their attacks on the Mage. Mental attacks, ambush, sensory alteration, large scale magic area bombardment, and mass attack with a great army. They would utilize each and every tactic and method available under the heavens.

Marakia was different. If it was someone as skilled as Marakia, then he will be able to withstand the threat of the demonic forces and be able to protect himself as well as annihilate the ghost form of Hesthnius Max.

As Sungchul reached this conclusion, he heart grew light.

This is the most assured method.

Sungchul immediately stood before Marakia. "Let's bargain."

Marakia, who had been tongue wrestling with Bertelgia, shut his beak and looked up towards Sungchul. "A bargain?"

"Come with me to the Demon Realm to kill the Demon King."

"The Demon King? Are you talking about Fuhrst, the Fire Eater?"

"That demon has been gone since ages ago. The demon I speak of is Hesthnius Max."

"Hesthnius Max? I've never heard of this demon. Ok. Is this demon strong?"

"He's weaker than you."

"Then why do you need to take me?"

Sungchul concisely described the circumstances between Max and himself. Marakia laughed out loud after hearing the story.

When the laughter finally died, Marakia's violet eyes grew bright as he spoke. "Ok. You want to use my magic to take care of that vile demon. What do I gain from this?"

"If you cooperate with me to kill Max, I'll grant you your life and freedom."

"Life and freedom you say?" Marakia asked in a ridiculing tone, and Sungchul's eyes grew a degree colder.

"Or I could just kill you right here."

It was a quiet and calm voice, but it bore an unbearable weight to it. Marakia, who had been mocking the offer, suddenly felt the threat of death press down upon him. The man named Sungchul possessed enough power to kill him with ease. However, a question filled Marakia's mind.

"Just why do you wish to kill this demon king? Is it out of vengeance? Or maybe you wish to secure peace within the kingdom you rule over?"

At Marakia's question, Sungchul unhesitatingly made a short reply. "It's to end the Calamity."

Curiosity filled Marakia's eyes. "I did not realize that the one who defeated me is a being who wishes to call himself the Savior of the World."

"Your answer?" Sungchul's voice rang out once again, and Marakia nodded.

"I accept. I swear upon the name 'King of Nahaks' that I will help you, human." Marakia pulled out a single black feather on his body and held it toward Sungchul. "It's a symbol of my promise. It is a royal gift from the great king of the Nahaks, so receive it well."

"I don't need it." Sungchul raised Fal Garaz. When Marakia saw the hammer once again, he was reaffirmed in his need to keep his promise.

"Let's take care of it right away." Sungchul left the tomb with a few dexterous movements. Bertelgia flapped her pages to follow after as Marakia wrapped his one remaining wing around his body and followed them with his two feet.

The Despair of the Abyss, who was now left alone within the tomb, looked toward the departing party and disappeared into the darkness.

The second underground floor was filled with countless Cave Elves. He didn't know the objective, but it couldn't possibly be good. Sungchul pulled out Cassandra, the demonic weapon, from his Soul Storage. Marakia who saw this scene, stepped forward, and opened his beak letting out a clear and loud sound. The long and crystal-clear call that sounded like the cry of a Black Kite rang out throughout the dungeon, causing all the Cave Elves residing within to respond simultaneously. It was out of pure terror.

"Ki….Kiiiiiii!"

The Cave Elves that simply ran away at the sound of the demonic whip Cassandra began to shriek as they scattered in all direction in utter panic and chaos. It was not a rational fear. It was an instinctual terror that was residing deep in their blood. They were responding to the fear sealed within their bloodline.

It was the genuine and inhumane cry of their masters and predators.

"How's that?" Marakia who was watching the Cave Elves scatter like rats in panic asked in a relatively cheerful voice.

"Not bad." Sungchul moved forward as he put away Cassandra which had been made redundant. The party eventually made it through the dark and long corridors of the Underground Kingdom and reached the entrance. The shuttle connected to the pulley was waiting for them. However, an unwelcome guest awaited them. It was the Despair of the Abyss.

"…"

The strange being stood in the center of the passageway as though it had something to say to Sungchul's party.

"Why does that thing exist within my kingdom?" Marakia spoke in annoyance.

Sungchul held Fal Garaz and walked toward the Despair of the Abyss. "Begone, creature of oblivion."

It was a troublesome enemy, but if it stood in his way, Sungchul wouldn't hesitate to fight. However, the Despair of the Abyss began to move past Sungchul unsteadily in a grotesque manner. It looked like it was going to back off like last time, but the Despair of the Abyss stopped before someone; it was before Marakia

"Hey, can't you do something about this monster?" Marakia took a step back as he asked Sungchul. As Sungchul walked toward him with Fal Garaz in hand, Marakia saw it. He saw the beak of the oozing Despair of the Abyss slowly open.

"D…n't lea…"

It was speech. The Despair of the Abyss was speaking. Both Marakia and Sungchul immediately froze at this unexpected situation.

While everyone was stunned, the Despair of the Abyss with an avian head continued to speak, this time more coherently, "D…Don't…L…leave…"

In the next moment, Fal Garaz struck the creature's head. The Despair of the Abyss was knocked far away following a rather weak sound of impact. But it deformed for a moment before it regained its original appearance again.

"What is that thing?" Marakia asked in anger, but Sungchul didn't respond. It was also the first time he had witnessed this situation.

A Despair of the Abyss spoke. I can't believe it. It should have had its body, mind, and soul taken away as it became the Ancient God's servant. This one managed to hold onto its consciousness?

It was not something that could be figured out. It was not something that should be figured out. Sungchul thought as he got onto the lift. Marakia followed after.

"How long has it been since I came up to the surface?"

Marakia spoke in a relatively cheerful voice as though he had forgotten about the incident just moments ago. The mechanism of the lift activated, and the lift rose. When they went up the hole shaped like a well, the blinding sun greeted them. A sharp scream rang out the moment they arrived at the entrance.

"Kyaaa!"

It was Marakia's scream. He fell to his knees and let out a wretched cry of agony like that of a bull's.

Sungchul immediately stopped the pulley and inspected Marakia's state.

"What's wrong?"

Sungchul's eyes were filled with shock as he became covered in spots. Black spots blossomed all across Marakia's body like a flower of death as Sungchul watched.

Isn't... isn't this the Curse of Extinction?

The scene that he had never wished to see again reappeared before him in a flash.

"Kyaaaaaak!!"

Marakia continued to scream and thrash about in agony. Rotting discharge poured out like a fountain from the stump of his severed wing, and a disgusting stench began to spread.

Sungchul immediately lowered the lift. Once they reached the Underground Kingdom, Marakia's condition stabilized. The spots that had spread on his body receded and the discharge from his wound no longer flowed. However, Marakia did not speak as he remained hunched over with his arms and wing wrapped around himself as though the memory of the pain still haunted him.

Sungchul spoke to him after a considerable time had passed. "Were you afflicted with the Curse of Extinction?"

He nodded at Sungchul's question as his body lightly trembled. "That's right. The curse cast down by the god afflicted my people without warning. It was the reason that the Nahaks that once roamed the skies were forced into the ground like moles."

"You must be younger than you appear?" Bertelgia offered a question toward Marakia in a soft voice. Marakia didn't deny it.

"One year. I was cursed by a matter of a single year. My older brothers were fine, but my younger brothers and I were at the risk of death. However, my father, the king, wished to hand the crown to me, who had the black feathers. That is why the ritual was performed, and I continued to live, but…"

Deep concern filled Marakia's violet eyes. "Why does the curse still remain?"

"…Because god is cruel," Sungchul responded.

Marakia snorted in amusement, but the fact that his body was cursed remained.

"It appears as though I am fated to die anyways."

The spots that covered his body had faded, but it didn't disappear. Marakia smiled helplessly as he looked up at the sky. "Tens of thousands of years had passed, but my fate remains unchanged."

Soon, fearsome anger began to burn in his eyes.

"Since this is the way things are, it wouldn't be bad to go out with a bang and just do whatever I want until I die."

"…"

"Burning the humans and crumbling their kingdoms. Who knows? Maybe, after I'm done, they'll remember me… and remember the Nahaks?"

Had Sungchul not been there next to him, Marakia might have done exactly as he had said. But Sungchul was, indeed, there.

"I won't leave you to do this." He glared at Marakia and spoke clearly.

Marakia laughed out loud. "I am to die anyways. What does it matter to me if I die in one way or another?"

"I will stop the Calamity. Help me. If so, it will also free you from the curse on your body."

"That's nonsense. Mortals cannot overcome the Trial of God. Also, Calamities are not to be overcome. They are meant to be endured like the passing seasons."

"There are those that have managed to overcome it."

"What?"

Marakia didn't look convinced. Sungchul recalled Vestiare's laughter as he replied, "They are the humans that you have looked down on."

Sungchul expounded on his reply a bit more. "Specifically, by beings called the Seven Heroes."

"What? Mere humans managed to overcome the Trial of God? I cannot believe such a thing."

"You're free to believe as you will, but let me just say one thing. I am stronger than all of the Seven Heroes combined, and haven't you peered into me already? You should be more than aware of what kind of commitment I have made to this."

"..."

Marakia didn't admit nor deny anything. Instead, he simply waited for the aimless rage boiling inside of him to dissipate.

Time, as it had always done, calmed down the anger.

When the flames of rage inside of him pacified, Marakia spoke once again in a tired voice. "How do you plan on overcoming the Calamity? You will not be enough to stop it on your own."

"There are five Calamities in total. I should be able to overcome three of them on my own at the very least."

Sungchul spoke in a calm voice as he described the Calamities looming over the world currently. The First will arrive from the Demon World. According to the Scripture of Calamity, it is prophesied that the Demon King will lead a massive army of devils never before seen in history, burning everything as they make their way south.

The Second Calamity will come from the past. The return of the Seven Heroes that overcame a Calamity of the past. The Scripture of Calamity prophesied that they will return as enemies of mortals and spread anguish, distrust, and death across the world.

The Third Calamity will come from suspicion. The survivors of the two Calamities that have swept through the continent and turned it into a wasteland will be filled with suspicion for one another and start a war which will only conclude at everyone's demise.

The Fourth Calamity and beyond are not known. Some have spoken of the advent of the lesser gods or the stirring of the Dragonfolk as the Calamities to follow, but nothing had been confirmed as of yet. It was because everything after the third Calamity was blank when he saw the Scripture of Calamity last. It was likely that the details in the Scripture of Calamity will only be filled in after the Calamities progress along to a certain extent.

"Half of the Calamities on your own? What great confidence," Marakia responded coldly.

Sungchul continued to try to persuade him. "It isn't all that difficult for me. As long as the Demon King is taken care of, the rest of the Calamities will be resolved soon as well."

However, Sungchul's words were woefully lacking in trying to turn Marakia's mind. Marakia snorted in laughter as he threw out a series of questions to shoot down Sungchul's request.

"But what about the Fourth Calamity? And what if the Fifth Calamity turns out to be something that fundamentally cannot be resolved by your strength?"

"…"

Sungchul didn't respond further. He knew that anything he would say will come off as being desperate.

Marakia simply smirked and rose from his place. "If you have nothing more to say, then I'm going to go rest. After my rest, I shall head out and bring ruin to the human kingdoms. I feel that if I do not, then the wrath of the insulted Nahak can never be sated."

Marakia spoke in a clear and bright voice as he leisurely walked deep into the dungeon. He would most likely keep his promise. He had already given up on his own life and had nothing more to lose.

Sungchul's eyes were filled with concern. *Things that can't be dealt with by strength are such a hassle.*

In his eyes, there was only one option. He had to eliminate the enraged Marakia with his own hands before Marakia left the dungeon. It was the worst possible outcome which nullified all the effort he had put in.

It was just when Sungchul believed firmly in his failure that someone unexpectedly stepped up.

"Hey, you birdbrain! I have something to say!"

It was Bertelgia.

This kid? Sungchul considered restraining Bertelgia, but vague hopes kept him taking a step back from the situation.

"Can't you hear me? Birdbrain! I said I have something to say!" Bertelgia continued to scream, and soon Marakia stopped his steps and turned his head slightly.

"Book. Your words are too crude. Even if you have that human guarding you by your side, it might be better to know your own place."

The instant he was done speaking, a magic arrow accompanied by a black feather came flying towards Bertelgia. Bertelgia froze in this immediate change in circumstance, and could only watch as the magic arrow flew at her. As the arrow was about to be embedded into her body, a rough hand appeared to protect her.

Sungchul's steely arm had protected her. The Magic Arrow managed to pierce his clothing, but when faced with his oppressive battle aura and his magic resistance, it dissipated without a trace.

"Keep talking." Sungchul whispered to her in a low voice.

Bertelgia shook her body once toward Sungchul and continued in a clear voice without a trace of fear. "You say that you were insulted as a Nahak?"

"So?" Marakia turned around and nodded with his arms crossed.

"How can someone who places such importance on the pride of the species not look after his own kin?"

"What? My kin?"

"That's right. Do you even know what kind of situation that the Nahaks like you are in right now?"

"What? What nonsense are you saying now?"

When Marakia let out a hollow laughter, Bertelgia broke free from Sungchul's protective arm and spoke boldly. "Then follow me, O Great King of Nahaks!"

She moved away from Sungchul and led the way down the dungeon.

This kid… she's quite something. Sungchul was looking at Bertelgia's back in a new light. He quickly followed after and escorted her down the path. Marakia didn't look convinced, but he trotted behind as though Bertelgia's words bothered him.

Bertelgia led Marakia to none other than the city of the Cave Elves. Looking at the dirty and damp city, Marakia frowned.

"Truly a lowly dwelling for a lowly race. I shall burn down all of these insects before I part from the Underground Kingdom."

He said as such before letting loose a high-pitched bird cry. The clear and high-pitched cry of the Nahak rang out within the entire area causing all of the Cave Elves to tremble in terror. Some of the Cave Elves began to collapse foaming at the mouth while others started to shit themselves where they stood.

While passing through the city, Marakia entertained himself by using telekinesis to lift passerby Cave Elves into the air and making them explode on the spot. Bertelgia didn't say anything as she led him to their destination.

They stood before the poultry farm. The area reeked with some unknown foul stench intermingling with the smell of rotten flesh, and Marakia tilted his head in confusion as he stood before this massive tent.

"So what's supposed to be here?"

That was when something caught his eye. It was the white feathers decorating the tent. They were smaller and much duller than his, but they were similar to the feathers he knew very well. Marakia extended his hand and examined one of the feathers.

"This… a Nahak's feather…?!"

An ominous feeling arose as Marakia suddenly had a terrible thought. Feeling shock and goosebumps form all over his body, he turned his eyes towards the interior of the tent. Sounds of low-pitched bird cries, sounds of beaks repeatedly striking metal, and sounds of feathers ruffling could be heard. Marakia entered the tent as Sungchul and Bertelgia watched, and he finally saw it with his own eyes.

He witnessed the fallen state of the "proud and noble" people of Nahak who were now being raised as livestock by what he considered as an insignificant and enslaved race.

Something holding him together inside had crumbled. A horrible shriek filled with a mixture of shock and anger reverberated within the tent followed by the sound of an object being shattered. Soon, a different Marakia came out of the tent.

Bertelgia let out a groan. "The spots… grew darker."

Was it due to the shock? Marakia's spots grew much darker. Sungchul could smell the stench of death from his body.

"How did this happen?" asked Marakia with a shaky voice.

"Your race fell after performing the ritual held for you, and those that remained were captured by the Cave Elves and raised as livestock," responded Bertelgia.

"Livestock… I can't believe it."

At that moment, a single young Nahak crawled out of the tent. He was one of the rare blue Nahaks among the countless white feathered ones. Marakia believed it to be a sort of divine revelation.

He spoke as he held the young Nahak. "As long as I live, the Nahak will rise again and reclaim the skies."

Marakia created an Orb of Knowledge. It was the physical manifestation of the language and the secret of the Nahaks. The orb was soon absorbed into the blue-feathered chick.

The blue Nahak that had been making cries of an unintelligent animal shivered once and then looked at his surroundings with a different set of eyes. Different than before as though he had regained a bit of his intellect, but when the chick recovered its intelligence, black spots like those of poisonous mushrooms quickly spread across its body.

Sungchul muttered in a low voice. "The moment he was freed from being livestock and regained his intellect, the Calamity of Extinction returned."

The young Nahak whose entire body was covered in spots let out a shrill scream before it became limp in its king's grasp. Marakia stood dumbly as he looked at the young Nahak's corpse with eyes filled with disbelief.

"This is too cruel. Simply too…" He couldn't manage to finish his words. He fell to his knees with the young Nahak's corpse in his grip.

In this moment of silence, Bertelgia spoke in a soft voice. "They can only preserve their race as cattle…"

"…"

Sungchul moved toward the kneeling Marakia. Marakia who felt his presence looked up. His violet eyes held a single tear.

"Is this what a Calamity is?" Marakia asked.

"This is also a Calamity," said Sungchul.

"Also?"

"That's right. It is in the Calamity's nature to destroy all manner of hope and leave behind only a cruel reality," Sungchul responded. "This is why I wish to destroy the Calamity."

Fal Garaz appeared in Sungchul's hand. When he swung Fal Garaz, the cloth covering the poultry farm blew away and tens of thousands of Nahaks within were revealed. When the cloth that was obstructing their vision disappeared, the young and curious beasts began to flee from the poultry farm and spread out everywhere. The white-feathered Nahaks looked towards Marakia with curiosity. These Nahaks flapped their underdeveloped wings and drew closer towards him.

Marakia did not reject their touch. Instead, he rose from where he sat and extended his hand towards Sungchul. "I will put my faith in you, human."

"..."

Sungchul wordlessly extended his own hand and met Marakia's. There was warmth no different than one between two humans in this grip.

"What is your name?" Marakia finally asked.

"Sungchul Kim."

"Sungchul Kim, eh? What a strange name. However, I don't think I'll be able to forget it."

Marakia looked back toward the Nahak chicks once again before looking at Sungchul. "I leave my people to you."

Sungchul nodded.

Marakia closed his eyes. His one remaining wing covered his upper body, and soon he began to glow in a bright light. He was burning the last bit of life energy that remained in him to transform the vast power contained in his body into a single object. Marakia, who was covered in blinding light, disappeared and all that remained in his place was a large egg and a fist-sized sphere emitting a mix of black and white energies.

"..."

Sungchul first lifted the large egg. It was a black egg. When he held it, a faint smile formed on his lips.

[Marakia's Egg]

"I have heard a legend that some Nahaks can return to the form of an egg at the time of their death... like a phoenix."

Bertelgia spoke beside him. Sungchul carefully placed the egg inside his Soul Storage, and lifted the orb that had been beside it.

[Soul Inheritance]

It was an object that held Marakia's will. Sungchul showed his respects towards Marakia by lowering his head then gripped the hand that held the Soul Inheritance tighter. When he did, the marble shattered and the power within it was absorbed into Sungchul. Messages flooded his sight in a bright light.

[Your strength is higher than the inheritance, therefore your strength did not increase.]

[Your dexterity is higher than the inheritance, therefore your dexterity did not increase.]

[Your vitality is higher than the inheritance, therefore your vitality did not increase.]

…

After all the messages that he had expected had flowed past, the words Sungchul was waiting for appeared.

[You will inherit the magic power within the inheritance.]

[You will inherit the intuition within the inheritance.]

…

When the inheritance ceremony was complete, Sungchul opened his status window. It was a status window which excluded bonus stats originating from external sources; a status screen showing only his base stats.

[Stats]			
Strength	999+	Dexterity	853
Vitality	801	Magic Power	323
Intuition	334	Magic Resist	621
Resilience	502	Charisma	18
		Luck	18

Magic Power and Intuition now exceeded 300. He had broken through what was commonly called the threshold of Superhuman in a single blow. Immediately, a long list of things that had suddenly become possible came to mind, but Sungchul had something he had to do first.

—

"Look after these Nahaks. If I can't hear the cry of Nahaks when I return, it will be the day that your entire race will meet extinction."

Sungchul made his ultimatum in front of the Cave Elf elders. The Cave Elves had already experienced his godlike strength and were simply bowing their heads in agreement. Sungchul visited the poultry farm once again before he left the Underground Kingdom. In front of the poultry farm lay the remains of Marakia left behind after his death. An unwelcome guest waited for him there.

It was the Despair of the Abyss, but its actions were strange. The oozy creature stood before Marakia's remains and simply stared at it. Sungchul observed it for a while and saw no change. The creature simply stared at the ground where Marakia had disappeared like a statue. Sungchul and Bertelgia left the scene.

"What was that?"

Bertelgia popped her head out and spoke while they were in the shuttle on the way to the surface.

The salty winds of the surface were blowing with force. Hair and clothes were fluttering wildly, and Bertelgia let out a short scream before hiding her body behind Sungchul.

A ray of light pierced through the darkness and fell across Sungchul's eyes.

"Well."

Sungchul brushed aside his fallen hair and spoke in a calm voice. "It might be someone like me." He could hear the familiar cries of demons off in the distance.

Chapter 9 – Crusaders of Salvation

The serene area around the Tower of Recluse was teeming with an unprecedented amount of people. In the sky above the tower were many airships with flags of many countries, all tied and anchored down to alters, and on the ground were rows of lumbering mobile fortresses. There was only one possible reason for all of these representatives of prominent nations to have been gathered at the Tower of Recluse. It was due to a single piece of news.

[The contents of the Scripture of Calamity have been altered]

The Kings and the feudal lords of the many nations were gathered because of the letter sent out in the name of Porpyrius, the master of the Tower of Recluse. The visitors gathered at the holy site of the Scripture of Calamity, filled with concern and fear. They had witnessed it with their own eyes; the new contents detailing a brand new Calamity.

But soon, the tower became filled with murmurs.

"Hm?"

One man tilted his head from confusion. It was because the contents were no different than before. The contents were listed in order as they were in the past: the Calamity of the Demon King, the Calamity of the Seven Heroes, and the Calamity of the War. There was nothing new.

Porpyrius' face froze. He immediately called over one of his servants that kept the grounds of the holy site and spoke in a low voice.

"What happened?"

"I…it… disappeared."

"What?"

"The Calamity of the Avian King suddenly disappeared."

"What kind of nonsense are you uttering? How could that be possible?"

Despite his disbelief, the Scripture of Calamity was, without a doubt, showing that his subordinate was speaking the truth. The atmosphere within the holy site was growing restless. No one spoke as such, but the gathered sovereigns looked towards Porpyrius with eyes of reproach.

Within these piercing gazes that were sharp and painful as arrows, Porpyrius swallowed deeply and attempted at an explanation.

"T-that is to say… The Calamity ended up disappearing due to an… unexplained circumstance."

Porpyrius the Reclusive became the boy who cried wolf. The reputation that he had built for half of a century crumbled overnight. That day, he had to swallow more insults than he ever had in his life, so he decided to use the strongest card in his hand.

"The Scripture of Calamity does not lie. Therefore, what we saw was not false which means that an unknown power has interfered with the Scripture of Calamity. Your task will be to find out exactly what it was."

The one who was prostrated before Porpyrius lifted her head. Her red draconic eyes glowed underneath her deep hood.

"…Understood, incapable old man."

The half-man, half-dragon Kha'nes. Her name wasn't widely known, but all those who were well-informed knew it. This woman whose blood was mixed with that of the dragons, the most powerful race, was a being who existed outside the boundaries of the ordinary. This exceptional figure had just received a special command and now set forth from the tower for the first time in several centuries.

However, Kha'nes's personality was anything but diligent.

"Wouldn't it be human of me to graciously accept all the delicious food out there since this is my first outing in a long time?"

This is how the most powerful Recluse, Kha'nes, began her hunt for famous restaurants in search of the most delectable food.

—

Frontlines of the Demon Realm

The Penal Unit was caught up in an ominous silence. The reason was simple. The vice commander, Aaron Genghis, was in a foul mood. He had taken a hundred members of the unit on an airship, and he only managed to return with the single mage who followed him. There were no other survivors.

Although it was a common occurrence, Aaron seemed to have been greatly shocked this time; he had withdrawn to his tent and did not emerge for an entire month. The veterans of the Penal Unit who had seen this assumed that Aaron had realized his own shortcomings, but only a single man, number 34, knew the inside story.

He is right to be scared now that he abandoned Willie Gilford. He's not a man known for his forgiving nature.

This man, Sungchul, had returned to the Penal Unit. There was no special reason behind it. The unit didn't particularly restrict his activities and allowed him easier access to information, but these weren't decisive enough reason for him to return. In truth, he returned without much thought and spent his days following a stable routine.

Recently, he had become acknowledged for his Alchemy and had begun to make Alchemic items for his fellow soldiers. He left the unit early in the morning to gather materials and returned to synthesize the items in his cauldron later in the day.

He had made everything from antipyretics to decorative lightings and all sorts of miscellaneous sundries in between. And no one rebuked him for spending his time this way because he did everything on his own. He was sometimes commanded by the higher-ups to create healing potions or other medicines, and this was met with favorable reception as they were known to be highly effective.

Sungchul who made the transformation from a bold patrolman to a talented Alchemist in one month's time had a secret nobody knew about. He snuck out once a week to test his magical prowess on the Deep Sea Demon known as the gatekeeper of the entrance to the Demon World.

He had mastered a new spell since the time he absorbed Marakia's power. Meteor: a powerful offensive spell that symbolized the might of Cosmomancy. He ruthlessly struck the back of the demon's head with this fearsome spell whose power had few equals.

"Guuuuh!!!"

Glare could only singe the creature's skin before, but the situation had changed now. The meteorite that fell from the sky possessed enough force to cause the Deep Sea Demon's body to go weak. He also gained another boon through his empowered magic power.

[Echo – 1]

He was now able to activate the Echo Mage's skill. Although he was limited to a single Echo, the might of consecutive descent of the meteors was destructive.

One month ago, it was a target he could not deal any kind of damage to, but he was now able to deal a considerable damage to it with nothing but the power of magic.

Even the basic magic, Glare, had become intensified by the multiplicative effects of the echo and grew powerful enough to pierce through the thick skin and burn the soft tissue underneath, spreading the sweet scent of freshly cooked meat through the air. Sungchul pounded the Deep Sea Demon to within an inch of death before leaving.

"Hm. Not bad." Bertelgia who had been floating in the air observing the fight gave her thoughts.

However, Sungchul shook his head and downed a magic essence. "It's still not enough. I am only at about the level of a court mage."

It was clear that he was far superior to someone like Dolorence Winterer whom he had met in the Summoning Palace, but if he were to compare himself to a mage of the calibre of the Dean of Airfruit, then there was still a long way to go. Sungchul could guess that Altugius' magic power was 450 at minimum. He wanted to exceed that number and reach at least 500 before he headed to the Demon King. The reason was simple. Sungchul wanted to finish this in one go. If he made a half-assed attempt and failed, he might not get another chance. The Demon King was extremely crafty. Sungchul wanted to ambush the Demon King at a time he wouldn't expect with an attack he didn't think was possible. This was Sungchul's overall strategy.

Primordial Light. That is my only answer.

This is why Sungchul chose the demon of the deep sea to mark his progress. If he could kill the Deep Sea Demon in one blow, then he would also be able to kill the Demon King in one blow. Especially since Sungchul assessed that the Deep Sea Demon had similar or superior magic resistance to the Demon King's.

The Intuition required to learn Primordial Light was 500. Sungchul was currently over half way through at 340. He still needed 160 more points in Intuition, but Sungchul did not rush. He switched between combat and Alchemy to slowly train his own capabilities and would calmly gather information within his reach in the meantime.

And then one day, he heard a strange rumor within the barracks. It was a rumor that had been circulating for a while, but the information had gained fresh momentum as of late. It said that there was about to be an expedition sent to attack the Demon Realm.

"I've heard they've organized the Crusaders of Salvation." Prisoner 0, Arkaard the Dwarf, spoke in a sigh.

"Crusaders of Salvation you say?" Sungchul's expressions darkened. The origins of the Crusaders of Salvation went back to the days of the Seven Heroes. Various countries had ceased their wars and hostilities at the time and had joined forces in an effort to face the upcoming Calamity with their most elite of elite warriors. This was the birth of the Seven Heroes. They met and overcame the Calamity of their era.

The Crusaders of Salvation was a facsimile of the Seven Heroes. The countries would gather the elite and create punitive forces to oppose the Calamity as was done thousands of years ago in the past.

The problem was the quality of these elites. The great powers of the Other World did not send their best anymore. They sent subpar or completely untested rookies and claimed that they had done due diligence. This is what was told to the residents of the Other World that were trembling in fear.

Sungchul, who had been listening quietly, suddenly asked Arkaard a question, "Which attempt is this one?"

Arkaard thought for a moment before relaying that this was the 13th Crusaders of Salvation.

"Number 13..."

This meant that the previous twelve returned as failures. This begged the great question: How many people were killed or sacrificed in the name of salvation.

So they're still doing things like this.

They were likely to continue this practice into perpetuity since the ones in power were all fine as long as the world was in status quo for the duration of their lives. They only thought of the Crusaders of Salvation as a cheap sacrifice to this end.

Sungchul thought all these thoughts but ultimately kept them to himself before leaving the area.

But the next day, Aaron called up every member of the Penal Unit. He looked emaciated as he had shut himself away for the past month, but those that had been with him for a while realized that he hadn't changed much from the rockhead that he was before. Especially that overly confident smile on his face before he revealed a suicidal mission.

As expected, Aaron began his announcement in front of 300 soldiers.

"Lord Marquis Martin Breggas has permitted the 13th Crusaders of Salvation to pass the Frontlines into the demon world. Countless units competed for the honor of providing support to their cause, and rejoice! We, the 8th Penal Unit, were chosen to become their support unit."

The announcement was like a bolt out of the blue, but no one brought up any objections.

—

The Crusaders of Salvation entered the Penal Unit's encampment in the late afternoon. Sungchul who had been synthesizing in front of an Alchemic cauldron saw their large flag with a greatsword in the shape of a cross fluttering in the air and knew that what had to come had finally arrived.

They came quickly. It must mean that this matter was already agreed upon beforehand.

Sungchul scanned the Crusaders to estimate their numbers. They were approximately three hundred members, similar to the Penal Unit, but the number of combat-capable soldiers was barely over a hundred. Experienced men were far and few between, and they were mostly comprised of untested youth. They looked to be mostly sons and daughters of prestigious families.

Complicated emotions ran through Sungchul's mind as he watched Aaron head over to greet their leader.

"Oh, my. You've arrived? It must have been rough travelling for so long."

Aaron was full of smiles as he continued bobbing his head up and down in an attempt to suck up to the leader of the Crusaders. But the apparent leader of the Crusaders of Salvation was a youth who just barely looked like he reached the cusp of adulthood.

"You're Aaron Genghis? I've heard that you begged to escort us along our journey."

The youth, who was riding on top of a pure completely unmarred white stallion, had a graceful and suitably haughty expression on his face. He spoke his mind and didn't care about the opinions of those around him.

"Truthfully, I wanted to enter the Demon Realm through the battlefront kept by the Elves rather than the Storm Battlefront managed by the Dwarves. I personally dislike dwarves."

Aaron's face became visibly distorted at the youth's words, but he could say nothing in response. The boy looked over the bleak encampment of the Penal Unit and spoke as if he was spitting. "Goodness, what an inelegant unit in an inelegant place. Does such a unit really deserve the honor of escorting the Crusaders of Salvation?"

This was the moment that signified the end of the peace and the coming of the storm for the Penal Unit.

***

The Crusaders of Salvation set up their camp in the dead centre of the Penal Unit's encampment. The retinue was responsible for their manual labor.

Here and there, the sound of posts being driven into the ground and the sound of workers shouting could be heard. The Crusaders of Salvation, who had little else to do, gathered in small groups for idle chat or wandered around their surroundings. Some of the Crusaders visited the tent where Sungchul performed his Alchemy. Three men and two women, all so young it looked as though they had narrowly avoided the Curse of Extinction. One of them discovered the Alchemic cauldron and called the others into the tent in excitement.

"Hey, look over here! There's an Alchemist here!"

"What? There's an Alchemist in a place like this? Weird."

"Should we go check out what he's making?"

Sungchul was standing right before them, but they continued without according him any respect. It was because of the prisoner number attached to his ragged coat. Sungchul peeked over at the unwelcome guests and continued what he was doing. He was making a Level 4 alchemic item called the Jug of Purification. It was a jar created from the clay found in the Demon Realm mixed with the Kaolin clay found further south.

The Jar was able to purify water into drinkable water, no matter how dirty or impure it was. It was an invaluable item within the Demon Realm where fresh water was difficult to find. Not only that, its Alchemic level was four. In the Other World where Alchemy was looked down upon, it was a significant level of difficulty.

WHOOSH. WHOOSH. WHOOSH.

Sungchul continued to grow the flames beneath the Alchemic cauldron by stepping on the bellows with no particular expression on his face. The jar inside the lidded cauldron was beginning to take a solid form as it was baked. When the jar was properly baked, Sungchul opened the lid. The steam that had been circulating within flew out with fearsome vigor. Sungchul placed a spoon inside the cauldron with the jar and began to stir.

The act of stirring was more for the purpose of allowing the mana to flow into the Alchemic item, which granted the item a life of its own, rather than actually mixing the ingredients. He wasn't aware of it at first, but it was knowledge he acquired through continued practice. The spoon appeared to touch the jar, but it didn't. The spoon simply passed through the jar and stirred the bottom of the cauldron as though the spoon and the jar were on separate planes of existence. It was quite literally a miracle that was taking place inside of the small cauldron, but it must have appeared unremarkable to the onlookers.

"Boring."

"I thought it might be interesting, but it's some useless jar?"

"I thought he was making a bomb or something."

"It looks cheap."

Each onlooker made their complaints before leaving the tent.

"…"

The pride of Sungchul, for whom everything had been going well recently, crumbled. It affected the results poorly.

[Synthesis Failed!]

With a poof, the jar inside the cauldron shattered into countless pieces before turning into black dust.

"Those fucking bitches…!!" Sungchul's face became twisted as he headed towards the members of the Crusaders of Salvation.

"Woah, calm down." Bertelgia shook her body within his pocket and spoke to him softly as she continued, "Failure is the mother of success! A true Alchemist can create the Philosopher's Stone even in the midst of a busy market place."

"…"

Sungchul clenched his teeth as he left the tent. Non-commissioned soldiers nearby saw Sungchul and threw out their greetings.

"Hey! Alchemist! Is it going well?"

"So-so."

Sungchul went towards the back of the tent. There was a separate brazier and preparatory table installed here. It was a private kitchen which Sungchul sometimes used to cook. He glimpsed around his surroundings before he pulled out the ingredients from his Soul Storage. It was the Mandragora kimchi he had made in a small pot with blood pudding made of the blood of the Man-faced Beast he had beaten in the Demon Realm.

The meat of the Man-faced Beast was tough like leather, and when one bit down on it, the abscess within it exploded with unpleasant flavor which made it impossible to eat. However, blood pudding made of cooled and hardened fresh blood of a recently killed Man-faced Beast was an excellent cooking ingredient.

He pulled out the ingredients onto a simple counter to the side, then headed over to the food storage with three low-grade healing potions.

"What? Another trade?" The storage manager, prisoner number 132, peeked over at Sungchul's healing potions then handed over a portion of the rations. Dried sausages, ham, and an unknown bird's carcass were traded for three healing potions. Sungchul took the exchanged materials to his own barracks to begin cooking.

Even though it was called cooking, there wasn't much to it.

The mountain bird's bones were boiled to make meat stock and left to simmer as the alchemic cauldron's lid was set upside down and used as a pan to fry the blood pudding of the Man-faced Beast.

Once the blood pudding was cooked to a certain extent, succulent juices burst out from within. Sungchul put the Mandragora kimchi and the sausages and ham he had obtained earlier on top of the juice, and over everything he poured in the broth he had made by cooking the bones of the mountain bird and brought the mix to a boil. After it had boiled enough, he added in the spices and adjusted the flavor. This was the Demon Frontline version of sausage stew.

Unfortunately, Sungchul's cooking wasn't popular within the barracks. It was because the food was seasoned heavily with spices that the Other Worlders weren't familiar with. Their opinions might have changed if they had given it a chance, but the soldiers of the Penal Unit weren't feeling very adventurous when it came to their meals.

Sungchul gave no heed to such criticisms. His food was made for his sake anyways. However, unfamiliar onlookers arrived as he was putting the finishing touches. He briefly wondered who they were, but quickly realized it was the same five members that watched him do Alchemy.

A freckled girl with blonde hair looked over at the bubbling sausage stew and popped her question. "Huh? What's this, Alchemy?"

To call it Alchemy... thought Sungchul.

The fact that the girl called his dignified cooking Alchemy meant that she didn't see Sungchul's food as food.

"Whatever it is, it reeks. Is he making something dangerous?" A blond youth oozing with pomp clenched his nose and made a disgusted expression. The fellows next to him had things to say as well.

"It looks like some kind of food? Look. There's some sausage and ham floating on the red liquid."

"Uwek."

The conversation between the five fell right into Sungchul's ears. Sungchul felt humiliation on a level he had never experienced before.

Making such judgement of a High-Class Chef's dish. What arrogance, when the most they amount to are mere nobles.

Judging strictly by ability, Sungchul was a level above the average royal chef. Chef itself was a rare class, and not just anybody could become a high-class chef which was a rarity among the chefs. Sungchul had actually spent considerable effort to become a high-class chef, and he had great pride in his own recipes, and those five had dared to mock his food.

Bertelgia could feel something big rumbling from Sungchul's psyche and began to shake strongly as she whispered softly, "Hold it. Woaaah… Relax."

However, Bertelgia's words didn't reach Sungchul's ears. Sungchul turned to face the group of five. An incredibly heavy aura exuded from his person, and the five leaped up from the sudden change in atmosphere. Sungchul slowly opened his mouth. "Why not give it a try?"

He held a ladle with the Man-faced Beast stew with pieces of ham and sausage within towards the group.

"Go ahead and eat some."

The faces of the five froze at Sungchul's sudden suggestion.

Sungchul continued to insist. "Hey. Why don't you have a bite before you make a judgement? See if it tastes good or not."

Despite Sungchul's repeated insistence, the group of five remained distant.

"Let's go." The blond youth spoke coldly before turning to leave. The other four followed suit without question. Callous voices could be heard from their backs.

"How could anyone eat something like that?"

"Not even dogs would eat that slop."

Sungchul was unperturbed. He only smirked to himself. "Rejecting a meal prepared by a High-Class Chef; they're throwing away a once-in-a-lifetime opportunity."

Sungchul returned to his place and swallowed the stew in his ladle in a single gulp. The clotted blood exploded with savory flavors and melted on his tongue like soft tofu as the sausage and ham that had a chewy texture filled his stomach. The Mandragora kimchi complemented the soup nicely with a deep vinegar flavor. It was truly a feast of flavors in his mouth. Sungchul wore a satisfied expression on his face.

I give it an 87.

However, his class didn't rate it so highly.

[This recipe is… 34 points.]

I don't know who is managing this class, but I really want to see his face just once, Sungchul thought to himself as he pulled out a bottle of hard liquor from his supplies and downed it. The bursting flavor in his mouth mixed with the strong drink as it moved into his stomach. It was heavenly. It felt like all the fatigue he had built up had evaporated all at once.

They rejected something this good. They're truly pitiful.

Sungchul was still dining in this way when he felt someone's gaze. He turned around to see if the five from before had returned, but it was someone unexpected.

This guy is…

Curiosity rose in his eyes. His visitors were the blond male who was the head of the Crusaders of Salvation and a blonde woman who looked just like him.

"I thought I smelled something funky. It looks like it was the cooking of a Summoned," said the youth as he approached

Sungchul then looked over at the boiling sausage stew in the cauldron lid with a sharp gaze. Sungchul didn't reply and continued to look up at him.

The youth looked young and delicate, but his eyes were bold and prudent.

He looks like he's got some spunk. I don't know how it'll be in reality though. Sungchul shifted his gaze toward the girl who was standing behind the youth protectively. She had similarly pale blonde hair and piercing blue eyes, and she was already looking at Sungchul. The moment their eyes met, Sungchul was reminded of a freshly honed blade of a knife.

The siblings are quite something despite their age. Sungchul finished judging the unwelcome guests as the youth who was observing his food began to speak.

"Hmm. This red soup, and this provocative smell. It feels similar to the food they serve at the Order of the Iron Blood Knights."

"…"

"The food didn't taste good, and I forced myself to eat it, but it was quite spicy and striking. It felt like I was looking at the Order of the Iron Blood Knights itself; elegant facade with no substance behind it."

"What do you want to say?" Sungchul downed another shot of alcohol as he retorted. Even dogs should be left alone during their meals. He wasn't feeling hospitable as these unwelcome guests were buzzing around him during his meal.

The corner of the youth's lip rose as the hand of the girl behind him reached for the hilt of her blade. A thick aura of hostility flew out from her. The youth waved his hand towards her.

"Sophia. Stop. I am the one in the wrong here." He slightly bent his neck towards Sungchul to express his apology for his disrespectful behavior.

"I apologize, unknown soldier. I smelled the scent of such foreign food, and I unknowingly overstepped my bounds."

The fact that the same man who treated even Aaron like a bug was now apologizing to a no-name low-rank soldier was a very unusual occurrence. He seemed to be a better man than he looked. Sungchul took a ladle and offered a portion of the soup towards the youth. "Don't just apologize with words, try some."

At Sungchul's sudden action, the youth briefly froze.

"Brother." The woman behind him had a worried expression and approached him. She glared towards Sungchul with a frosty gaze and shouted, "You. Summoned! Who do you think he is that you can shove your slop of garbage towards him?"

Her blade was already pulled halfway. Sungchul made a bitter smile as he saw the shining blade and put the ladle back into the pot. "Don't eat it, if you don't want to."

His words brought forth a great rage upon the lady's face.

"This bastard…"

The youth restrained the girl once again. "Sophia. Restrain yourself. How long do you intend to remain hysterical?"

Unlike the fuming girl, the youth sat next to Sungchul with a relaxed expression on his face and said, "Could I give it a taste?"

Sungchul made a faint smile and handed over a small bowl filled with the stew. The youth made an indecipherable expression as he stared at the contents of the bowl for a long while.

"It won't taste as good if it goes cold," said Sungchul.

"Brother. You can't eat this." The girl objected, but the youth smirked and swallowed Sungchul's dish in a single gulp. However, his attitude was like that of someone forcing himself to try and eat something that wasn't food. It was like the characteristic recklessness of youth.

The youth who had the stew in his mouth began to chew a few times before his face turned to stone. The girl who was watching the scene became pale. "Brother!"

At that moment, the youth let out a soft exclamation, "Huh…?!"

Sungchul crossed his arms and made a smug expression on his face as he observed the change. *I made it. There is no way it'll taste bad.*

The youth who had a mysterious expression on his face looked behind him with a happy expression and spoke in a cheerful voice. "It's good!"

The mood changed completely.

***

"Delicious! Sophia, you must give it a try! The way this black clump melts in your mouth... this is a delicacy!"

"I don't believe you."

"It's the truth. It's really good."

Sungchul silently listened to the bickering of the siblings while taking in his drinks. He could feel the injured pride of a high-class chef slowly being healed. After the brief intermission, the youth formally introduced himself.

"This has been thoroughly enjoyable, Mr. Number 34. It wasn't my original purpose in coming here, but I was treated to a gourmet meal. I am Elijah Breggas."

Curiosity filled Sungchul's eyes. *Breggas?*

A particular man's face appeared in his mind. The Sixth Champion of the Continent, Lord Marquis Breggas. It was because the youth had the same family name as the man who supervised the frontline of the Demon Realm, but the chances of him being the man's son were low. There was just no way that Martin Breggas, who knew the survival rates of the frontline of the Demon Realm better than anyone else, would send his direct family into the Crusaders of Salvation which had less than 10% chance of survival.

Elijah and Sophia Breggas took their leave during Sungchul's silence. After finishing up his meal, Sungchul headed toward the medical tent where the veteran soldiers were gathered.

It wasn't hard to distinguish the medical tent. All of the tents looked similar to each other, but the medical tent was adorned with the numbers of the fallen soldiers. Sungchul noticed the number 700 among the countless numbers attached to the large tent as he entered and figured that the Penal Unit had been much larger in scale before.

Once he entered the tent, he could see that the veteran soldiers were having fun gambling. Playing dice was one of the favorite pastimes of bored soldiers.

"Haha! Sorry, but my senses are off the charts today!"

Sungchul stood behind an enthusiastic Dwarf who was deeply immersed in the dice game and watched him toss his die. It was a losing throw.

"Shit!"

The most veteran among the Penal Unit, Number 0 Arkaard, laughed heartily as he pushed his share of the rations towards his opponent, then looked up towards Sungchul.

"Is something wrong, Alchemist?"

"I have a couple of questions."

Arkaard was not only the most senior within the unit, but was also quite friendly, which earned him a lot of friends with the logistics team, his superiors, and especially the Dwarven engineering corp. Thanks to him, it was possible to hear fresh news about the outside world. However, nothing in this world was free. Sungchul handed Arkaard a freshly brewed hangover cure.

"Exactly what I wanted," said Arkaard looking extremely happy as he passed the baton over to Sungchul.

"Now, what are you curious about?"

Sungchul avoided asking anything too sensitive or secretive. It didn't look all that important on the surface, but being able to earn the trust of an informant and build and maintain a relationship with him was an important conversational skill.

Sungchul asked about any updates or development on the frontlines of the Demon world as well as a brief summary on the new arrivals: the Crusaders of Salvation. Arkaard gulped down the hangover cure in a single breath and spoke.

"Mm. There haven't been many changes overall regarding the frontline. The winter has come, but the demon army is still stationed within the territory of the Iron Blood Knights, and the Order of the Iron Blood Knights are moving in full force to repel them. It looks like hard battles are ahead. Well, none of that matters to us anyways."

Arkaard followed up with information regarding the Crusaders of Salvation.

"I don't know what Aaron Genghis is planning, but don't worry too hard about it. Do you know who the leader of the Crusaders is this time? It's Elijah freaking Breggas. They tell me that he's the eldest son of Lord Marquis Martin Breggas who could be considered as the head commander of the entire Demon Realm Battlefront!"

Sungchul immediately doubted his own hearing. It would have been shocking enough for the man to have sent his close relative, but his own eldest son?

Martin Breggas isn't known to have such a strong sense of duty...

Sungchul had fought several battles with Martin Breggas. The farthest back he could remember was fifteen years ago struggling together during the earth-shattering awakening of the black dragon Groteus, to about eight years ago when they fought shoulder to shoulder sharing their life and death on the battlefield in an expedition against the demon king. Sungchul recalled that the man was rather selfish and self-centered during those hard-fought battles. The only reason that he had taken over as Lord Marquis of the Demon Realm Battlefront was to be able to brag loudly with minimal interference from others. Would this kind of man send his eldest son and daughter to the Crusaders of Salvation, an act which was nothing more than a glorified execution? That would be irrational. There had to be another side to this story.

"What are you thinking so hard about?" Arkaard prodded for conversation as he was in a great mood. The dwarf usually had a friendly demeanor, but he was on another level today.

"Did something good happen?"

When Sungchul asked, Arkaard lifted his drink up and let out a lively chuckle.

"Indeed indeed! I might be able to leave this damned Penal Unit thanks to Martin Breggas' son!"

A faint smile rose on Sungchul's lips at the news. "Ho. This is the last one?"

Arkaard nodded vigorously. "I've been through hell and back nine times already. I've even been all the way into the central regions of the demon world as well. Time has come for me to return to the home of my heart, the Storm Battlefront, and defend that black rocky mountain."

It was easy to enter the Penal Unit, but it wasn't so easy to graduate from it. The chances of survival might increase with a brilliant commander of good character, but with someone rash and incompetent like Aaron Genghis, it was next to impossible. To be able to survive 9 missions through those unfavorable conditions meant that Arkaard was no ordinary fighter.

"Even if he's a rockhead, he shouldn't be able to pull any of his stunts now that the Marquis' son is here."

"His usual stunts, eh…" When Sungchul's trailed off his words, Arkaard made a mischievous smile as he checked his surroundings before leaning in to whisper.

"What do you think I mean? Leading his subordinates to their deaths is what I mean. That guy might be nicknamed rockhead, but he's more like a fox."

Sungchul knew that Aaron was a cunning and underhanded fellow. He purposely set forth on impossible missions to sacrifice his men to not only make the battles seem more difficult than they truly were to artificially boost his military merits, but also monopolize all the credit. He might appear like an incompetent rockhead of a commander to his subordinates, but to his superiors, he was a sly dog they can't get rid of.

"…I might be the first to graduate from the Penal Unit under that rockhead. Truthfully, this place wouldn't be so bad if it weren't so dangerous." Arkaard spoke for quite a while about the beauty of his homeland and the strength of the Dwarven people. After the lengthy story came to an end, his eyes lit up as though he finally recalled something and handed something over to Sungchul.

"Look at me. I completely forgot that Deckard asked me to deliver a letter to you. Read it carefully. The letter has not been inspected."

Sungchul acknowledged him with a nod before reading the letter. The contents of the letter weren't anything new. It was mostly a letter about how he was still in the infirmary and was thinking of his family, but he also packed the end of the letter with a full list of all quests he discovered within the Demon Realm Battlefront that were Magic Power related. It might be Deckard's style of being considerate. Unfortunately, Sungchul no longer had any use for these quests.

[Your Magic Power is too high.]

The quest that he tried as an experiment told the full story. Sungchul was no longer considered an average mage, and could no longer raise his stats through normal quests. Only those made by the likes of the Seven Heroes or Altugius, at the very least, would supplement his growth.

"…"

Sungchul gave up on Deckard's list of quests without hesitation.

I should work more on the collection journal before the winter passes.

He had already completed all the quests that were worth doing. All that was left were the quests related to the Creationist that he had been putting off. According to Bertelgia, what Sungchul needed now as a Creationist was experience. The difference between "being able to do" and "having tried it" for an alchemist was like the difference between heaven and earth. So, to improve as an alchemist, he had no choice but to make anything and everything, and a lot of it.

"I've recorded all of the Alchemic items you've created so far. You've only completed 40% of the illustrated works recorded within me, and although you've surpassed the average Alchemist of this world by leaps and bounds, you're still lacking in my eyes. Only those who have filled out at least half of the list can call themselves a real Alchemist!"

Sungchul let Bertelgia's words pass through one ear and out the other, but he did keep one thing in mind. Completing certain milestones towards the completion of the alchemy collection journal caused a rise in status points. It was an important opportunity for Sungchul, who could no longer benefit from ordinary quests.

Sungchul started by reattempting the Jug of Essence that he failed before and succeeded. He placed the Jug of Essence in the corner of the tent and tested it with some seawater he got from nearby. The bright gray color of the jug grew a bit dull, and the seawater within became purified.

Sungchul tasted a cup of the water within the jug.

"It's not very tasty, but it really is drinkable."

When he said so, Bertelgia immediately retorted angrily, "How naive! If you can make an S-grade Jug of Essence, you wouldn't be able to find a better tasting water anywhere in the world!"

"I noticed that an S grade item is extremely difficult to make," said Sungchul.

"To begin with, the ingredients have to be good. The quality of the ingredients is directly linked to the grade of the Alchemic Item, but it's hard to get good quality ingredients," responded Bertelgia.

"I always feel this way, but Cooking and Alchemy seems to be very similar," said Sungchul.

Cooking was the same. It was possible to make something tasty with poor ingredients, but there was a limit. Top-grade recipes were only possible with top-grade ingredients. High-grade chef and

Alchemist. They looked like two unrelated classes, but Sungchul began to realize that the two classes were two sides of the same coin.

After a bit of rest, Sungchul rose from his seat and headed toward the Alchemic cauldron.

"Bertelgia. Next recipe."

"My, you're planning on making two things today? Aren't you overworking yourself?"

"Why not just get it over with while I'm still at it. I have enough Magic Power."

Thanks to the Magic Power he had obtained from the Underground Kingdom, Sungchul could now hold much more mana within his body than before, which in turn allowed him to synthesize more Alchemic items. Not only that, but he could also see higher grade Alchemic item recipes thanks to the Intuition he earned at the same time. The increase in Magic Power and Intuition supplemented Alchemy and the rise in Alchemy was, in turn, supplementing Magic Power and Intuition. Sungchul didn't rush himself, but he also did not relax.

Although Sungchul had hit something of a plateau in his growth, he was with the mindset that he was going to do whatever he could every single day.

"Well, I won't stop you if you insist. Bertelgia's Illustrated Alchemic Collection Journal! The next item is…"

It was when Bertelgia was about to open the page feeling smug that a sharp sound of a trumpet rang from the outside. It was the call for the Penal Unit to sortie.

"It looks like we'll have to put off the next synthesis for another time."

Sungchul stuffed Bertelgia into his coat pocket and left the tent.

"Attention."

The one to sortie the members of the Penal Unit was none other than Aaron Genghis. Sungchul discovered a familiar face next to him. It was the leader of the 13th Crusaders of Salvation and the eldest son of the Sixth Champion of the Continent, Elijah Breggas, standing behind Aaron with no particular expression on his face while his younger sister, Sophia Breggas, stood beside him protectively. Aaron Genghis spoke as the Penal Unit watched on.

"We the members of the Penal Unit have been given the duty and honor to escort the Crusaders of Salvation, heroes hailing from every corner of the continent, to the dangerous gateway to the Demon Realm in three days' time. This mission has been ordered by the Lord Marquis Martin Breggas himself, and thus it will count as three successful missions for those members who wish to participate…"

Arkaard, who had been listening so far, spat on the ground and began to complain. "What? What the hell is this about? It's one mission, so it should count as one mission!"

On the other hand, his closest companion, the Elven archer Faagan, had a delighted expression. "It looks as though we'll be leaving this place hand in hand, Mr. Dwarf."

"This is bullshit!" Arkaard was full of complaints, but his expression betrayed his true thoughts. Faagan played along as well.

"Anyway, that kid Deckard. He'll miss this golden opportunity."

A trip to the Demon Realm's entrance was treacherous, but it wasn't too difficult. Not only that, the winter season meant reduced activity from the demons. The veterans of the Penal Unit treated this mission as a rare gift bestowed by the gods.

"…"

Elijah Breggas looked upon the celebrating soldiers with an indifferent gaze. Aaron stood at the front shouting something with veins in his neck popping out, but all of his words went ignored.

"Brother. Is this really ok?" In the middle of all the excitement, Sophia leaned in to whisper to her brother. "If we arrive at the Demon Realm and fail, he will just get what he wants."

Deep concern drew over her face. A sigh escaped from Elijah's mouth. "It can't be helped, Sophia."

His eyes were looking beyond the razor-sharp mountain ridge, toward the northern skies in the distance that was just beginning to take on a red tint. The Demon Realm. The land of the Devils. It was the forbidden land that was synonymous with death to humans, but it represented a unique opportunity in Elijah's eyes. His delicate hands caressed an ominous book dyed in the color of blood beneath his cloak.

"There should be another way. A way that doesn't involve this method."

Sophia still seemed skeptical, but Elijah's resolution was unshakable.

"Our opponent is one called the Sixth Champion of the Continent. We have no other choice in the matter, Sophia." He spoke in a quiet, but firm voice. "Only the devil's quest can bring us salvation."

Chapter 10 – Invasion of the Demon Realm

On the day of the expedition, the weather was fair and clear like no other. Three hundred members of the Penal Unit and three hundred members of the Crusaders of Salvation. Under the bright morning sun, the army of six hundred men began their march towards the demon world along a previously planned route. It would take three days by foot to arrive at the entrance of the Demon Realm.

The first terrain they encountered was the rugged mountain region under the jurisdiction of the Storm Battlefront. The region was littered with ideal ambush locations, so Aaron took extra precaution with scouting. Even Sungchul was sent to scout several times, but no ambush lay in wait as Aaron had feared. Even if it did, the ambushers were crushed by Sungchul's hands and were left unreported.

By the end of the cautious march when they reached the tip of the mountainous region, the sun was already resting atop the eastern mountains. It wasn't wise to move within the darkness that the Devils favored, so Aaron ordered the group to make camp.

"…"

Sungchul who finished making his tent before anyone else left camp to roam the areas close to mountain regions. The snowfields dyed red by the setting sun looked to be empty, but Sungchul's sharp gaze landed on a small leaf poking out from the crimson snow. He brushed off the snow to grasp the grass hidden within. An information screen appeared before him as he took a whiff.

[Blind Man's Grass]

Level: 1

Grade: A

Attribute: Wood

Effect: None

Note: It is commonly seen along the roadside, but due to its stabilizing nature, it acts as a neutralizing agent to otherwise reactive ingredients.

Blind Man's Grass was plentiful around the Other World. It was a common ingredient that Sungchul had collected endlessly, but if there was one thing that made the Blind Man's grass in this region unique, it was its grade. It had reached A grade.

"Hoh."

"How is it? It's as I said, right? Blind Man's grass can grow anywhere, but its potency rises proportionately to the harshness of the environment it is found in!" exclaimed Bertelgia.

Sungchul tossed the Blind Man's Grass into the gunny sack on his back and continued to seek out more. He discovered another clump of Blind Man's Grass buried in the snow. Sungchul pulled it out forcefully.

"This…" Sungchul's eyes lit up in curiosity. The clump in his hand had the top grade of S. Bertelgia flapped her pages as she spoke.

"We should be able to make the most powerful buffers! The highest grade of neutralizer not only suppresses two ingredients that have high reactivity with each other, but it also affects the item's grade!"

"Not bad."

He had been making more than one type of item per day, but none of them could be considered higher than B grade. It might have been from his pride as a High-class Chef, but he felt determined to make an A grade item, and the expedition into the Demon Realm provided the perfect opportunity to collect high-quality alchemic materials. He had left to hunt for ingredients every day, but he was always short on time, and it wasn't possible to leisurely seek out the top-grade ingredients.

While he was stuffing his sack full of top-grade Blind Man's Grass, he noticed something moving quickly on the far side of the snow pile. It was a deer of a heavy built with massive horns. It appeared to be a normal deer, but because it lived near the Demon Realm, its strength could be compared to mystical creatures with resilient life force. Its meat was on another level.

Sungchul felt some drool pooling in his mouth at the sight of the deer, but he noticed something else. There was an arrow stuck onto the deer. Blood dripped from the wound, dying the fluffy white snow red.

Is he being hunted by someone?

A hunter appeared from beyond the snow-covered mountain. The hunter turned out to be a slim woman wearing fancy equipment. Sungchul recognized her face.

"That kid. Isn't she the sister of Elijah Breggas? What was her name?"

Sungchul turned to ask Bertelgia. She had a much better memory than him, and she spoke in a cheerful voice as she loved to boast about it. "Sophia!"

"Ah, yes. It was Sophia."

Sungchul had trouble with the names of women. He just didn't care about them. Sophia wielded a bow carved from Faerie wood used by the Elves and was chasing her prey at high speed. She pulled the string of her bow. The arrow fired from the taut bow, flew out in a line, and pierced the deer's neck. It was a flawless and honed performance.

"Hoo…" Sophia saw the deer fall, put her bow on her back, and approached it.

I should be able to serve a decent meal to Brother with this.

A faint expression of joy appeared on her usually indifferent face, but there was another guest standing near the deer already. It was none other than Sungchul. Sophia's indifference face filled with animosity. "Hey, you. What are you doing here?"

Sungchul revealed his gunny sack filled with Blind Man's Grass and spoke in a neutral voice. "Gathering ingredients."

"Ah." She opened her lips a bit before heading over to the deer and throwing it over her back in one motion. The beefy deer, easily weighing more than one ton, was balanced on top of Sophia's rather slim physique. It was an admirable amount of strength, but she would not be able to ignore the uneven distribution of weight due to its size. Not long after she hefted the creature onto her shoulder, Sophia lost her balance and was forced to put the deer back down.

Should I use the Soul Storage? No, something this big won't fit. And most likely it will completely dry out, thought Sophia. Breathing heavily she looked down on the carcass, then decided to cut off a portion of the beast. Suddenly, she heard a clear voice beside her.

"Excuse me, but may I have a share of the beast?"

It was Sungchul. Sophia peered over at the member of the Penal Unit and his ragged clothing out of the corner of her eyes and scoffed at him. "No need to be so roundabout in saying that you want to die."

She didn't like him from the beginning. Even Aaron Genghis, the leader of the Penal Unit, wagged his tail like a dumb puppy in front of the siblings; it was pure disrespect for a mere criminal to stand with a straight neck before her.

There were only two types of people who would act this way before members of the Breggas family, the most powerful family in the front lines of the Demon World: those who did not have common sense and those who did not know fear. It didn't matter which it was to her. Neither was acceptable in her eyes.

"If you want, I'm willing to give you a hand in butchering the beast," Sungchul suggested.

Although she disliked him, his request was reasonable enough to let him to soften her up. Sophia was skilled in hunting, but she was clueless on the work afterwards. She usually left her servants to handle the meat, but because of where she was headed, she didn't bring any with her. Considering all this, Sungchul's request seemed reasonable.

"I won't hand over any of the good portions. What I can allow you to take is the head, feet, and maybe the hindquarters." She spoke with her frosty gaze trained on Sungchul. All the regions she mentioned were of poor taste or too sinewy and unpopular. Sungchul didn't mind at all.

"I don't need all that. Just his internal organs are fine."

Sophia scoffed again. *Figures.*

Unless it was the liver of geese, intestines and organs were food only commoners ate. She couldn't help but laugh when he asked for parts that she was thinking of throwing to the dogs.

"Fine. If that's what you want, then do as you wish, but in turn, butcher the meat ahead of time. I'll send someone for it."

"I'll just take it to you personally. Not like it's heavy," said Sungchul.

"Oh really? I won't stop you if you want to bring it over. If you can, that is. However, if I find that any more than the portions discussed are missing, then there will be harsh punishment," warned Sophia.

After she relayed her threat, Sophia left the snowy mountain quickly.

"What a rude woman," said Bertelgia who emerged from the pocket as soon as she was gone.

"…"

Sungchul didn't care about the attitudes of common people as always. All of his attention was focused on the carcass that was rapidly cooling in the snow. "This guy's quite rare around these parts. I got lucky."

As the region was infertile, vegetation was rare which meant game animals were also rare. It would be hard to find a deer of this size after a week of hunting. Sungchul took out a treasured sword of the Human Empire from his Soul Storage and sliced through the deer's belly. Blood and viscera contained within poured out. He pulled out a bright red-colored organ to examine the texture in the light.

"Truly an impressive liver. Top quality."

Bertelgia observed the innards from right next to Sungchul and commented, "Uuu…. you eat liver? I can't eat that stuff. Maybe if it was the lean meat."

"You have the preferences of a child," responded Sungchul.

"I don't risk my life for food, unlike you!"

"Only people who have tasted it know how delicious it is. It's also quite the impressive specimen."

"Hm. Is that right? I don't know anything about it. How would it be as an Alchemic ingredient?"

"S grade," Sungchul answered briefly as he buried the fresh liver in the snow. He lifted the limp deer with a single hand and tossed it over to an evergreen tree nearby. The massive deer that easily weighed over a ton flew in the air like a light game ball and landed on a beautiful conifer tree. He then threw sharp branches that pierced the deer and embedded it to the pine tree, firmly securing the deer corpse in place.

"Hiii..!" Bertelgia recoiled in fear. It was a common sight at this point, but today's preparation method was more vigorous than average. Sungchul decapitated the beast's head with its magnificent horns, then threw it to the side. He began to strip off the hide with experienced handiwork.

RIIIP! RIP!

Powerful strength combined with skillful handwork allowed the leather to be stripped away like the peel of a banana. Sungchul tossed the hide over toward the severed head as he began to open up the arteries to drain the blood. As the blood was draining, Sungchul used the time to gather more Blind Man's Grass.

Bertelgia, who was watching from the side, commented, "I don't know about anything else, but I can't deny that you're diligent."

Sungchul tossed the leather onto the gunny sack which he stored in the Soul Storage before speaking. "Of course."

When enough of the blood was drained, Sungchul hefted the deer carcass onto his shoulder and returned to camp.

It wasn't difficult to recognize the tent of the Leader of the Crusaders from a distance. Sungchul carried the deer toward the camp before a sword-wielding youngster of the Crusaders of Salvation obstructed his path. "Who are you?"

"I'm just here to deliver the meat," replied Sungchul.

Suddenly, he could hear the voice of Sophia Breggas from one of the tents. "Wait a minute, I'm coming out."

Sophia came out of the tent while brushing her flowing blonde hair. Sungchul dropped the deer down before the tent when he saw her.

THUD.

The carcass hit the ground with a blunt sound.

"You've got some muscle on you," said Sophia.

"…"

Sophia carefully scanned over the deer that he brought to see if any of the portions were missing. Other than the innards removed from the belly, there was no problem. The most important portion, the tail meat, was safe and there was no sign of any other cuts being removed. Sophia nodded after a long inspection. "You've done well. You can leave now."

At that moment, the voice of a young man could be heard. "Hey, Sophia. The guest went out of his way to visit us; it is not proper to send him away like that, right?"

It was the voice of Elijah Breggas. Sophia quickly turned away and muttered to herself, "Shit. Did he overhear?"

"…"

Sungchul didn't refuse the invitation and made his way to the tent. By the time Sophia hastily tried to stop him, he was already half way inside.

The tent was roomy and looked comfortable. At the center burned a tribal style campfire with stylish furniture, and carpet decorated the interior. It was an opulent scene befitting the name Breggas.

"We meet again, Mr. Number 34." Elijah was showing Sungchul favor for one reason or another. Sungchul nodded to greet him and asked a question.

"What do you want from me?"

Elijah smiled brightly at this question. "Nothing much. The memory of the delicious dish you served last time lingered with me. Especially the black mass that softly melted in my mouth still lingers on my tongue."

Sungchul wordlessly silently listened to his words as he thought, *Is he talking about the Man-faced Beast stew? This kid knows how to appreciate good food.*

Elijah continued to speak, "I've lost my appetite of late, and I haven't enjoyed any tasty food. It's not something to boast about, but we had a rather hard-to-find chef class cook at our Trowyn mansion."

"A Chef class?" asked Sungchul.

"Yes. You might have never heard of it. They are people blessed by the God of Taste. Regardless of everything else, they are at the peak in cooking. Anyways, I just can't seem to regain my appetite regardless of food or scenery. But, I seem to have regained some of it after having tasted your food."

"I see."

It wasn't wrong to say the sour taste of kimchi helps with appetite.

"Seeing as I have been treated by you before, I want to treat you this time. My sister says that she wants to show off some of her skills. How would you like to try it with me?"

It was a sudden proposition. Sungchul immediately began to suspect whether Elijah was plotting something sinister. *I didn't detect any malintent nor suspicious activity. Did they discover my identity?*

Sungchul held his breath and began to sense his surroundings. He didn't feel any noticeable aura that might be able to harm him.

"Brother, why are you saying such nonsense? This man is just one of the prisoners."

As Sungchul was carefully scanning his surroundings, he could hear the annoyed voice of Sophia who had been standing to the side. Elijah laughed without restraint while calming his sister. "Didn't Mother say that what goes around comes around regardless of their status? I was treated to a meal, and didn't that bring back my appetite?"

Sophia didn't look satisfied, but she couldn't win against her brother's stubbornness.

"Consider yourself lucky, criminal!" After throwing her harsh words toward Sungchul, she left the tent.

"My sister has her flaws, but she is truly a kind child." Elijah smiled with his eyes as he spoke softly. Sungchul still couldn't determine his motives.

Why is this kid trying to hold me here?

Elijah didn't seem to have anything waiting in ambush nor did the boy have much personal strength. Sungchul couldn't understand with what audacity Elijah was trying to tie him down here. It was a rare moment when Sungchul felt deeply puzzled by his circumstance. A plot so completely concealed by fog to the extent that its intent could not even be guessed was a feat only someone like the Emperor of the Human Kingdom could match, but he decided to handle this calmly. He had faith in his strength to break through any deception or plot.

He shut his mouth and waited for time to pass. Sophia entered the tent again after some time. There were servants carrying dishes with food behind her. Sungchul's eyes grew wide in terror the moment he saw the dish.

T-this is…?!

Rather than food, it was something closer to a pile of charcoal. Sungchul held the fork with trembling hands as he put whatever this mass was to his lips. A surprise even larger than the previous passed his eyes. The basic ability of Chef, Taste Appraisal, did not activate.

... This isn't food!

***

Elijah Breggas had a magnanimous expression on his face as he struggled to chew on whatever inedible thing it was with a smile in his eyes. Sophia was watching him like a hawk. Sungchul discovered that Elijah's eyebrows trembled each time he put that black charcoal into his mouth. It was patience on a superhuman level. Or at least that's what Sungchul believed.

After eating about half of this thing that couldn't even be called food, Elijah turned to Sungchul and said in a soft voice, "This is truly delicious, but I feel like I want to try something different. I am truly sorry for asking this of a guest, but could I try another one of your dishes?"

It was only now that Sungchul fully realized the circumstances surrounding him.

This guy... he called me over so he could eat some human cooking.

Fine. Sungchul pushed aside the food he only took a single bite of and rose from his seat.

"You're not trying to make that rank smelling red dish, are you? I'll say this once. I hate food like those of the Order of the Iron Blood Knights."

Sophia's cold words struck him in the back as he prepared to leave the tent. Sungchul looked over his shoulder to gaze at her cooking. The charcoal on her plate hadn't shrunk at all from the time it had been first served.

217

This woman… He had a lot to say, but he suppressed it all. True chefs speak with their food, not with their mouth. Sungchul pulled out the fresh liver from the gunny sack placed outside the tent.

This should do just fine.

The kitchen was a bit off from the back of the tent. Despite being a mobile kitchen, it was still fully stocked with various kinds of spices, vegetables, and wines as expected of upper nobility. Sungchul grabbed one of the bottles and called over to the servant manning the fire. "Can I use this?"

The servant nodded. Sungchul popped the cork and took a whiff. It wasn't a high-class wine, but it wasn't cheap either. It was adequate for cooking.

He smeared the pan with butter, and then he began to stir fry some onions and tomatoes. When the onions and tomatoes were ready, Sungchul pulled some Worcester sauce that was prepared before from his Soul Storage and added it to the pan. He waited for the sauce to reduce before he began adding the wine without restraint.

The eye of the servant who was tending to the flames with an equivocal expression automatically focused onto Sungchul's pan. There was an indescribable smell emitting from it. As the red wine was being simmered, Sungchul sought out the rest of the ingredients. He found potatoes and rice. He diced the potatoes and powderized the rice.

WHAM! WHAM!

His hands alone were enough to crush the rice grain. The servant's eyes grew wide.

"Wow, you must be quite strong."

"…"

Sungchul prepared another pan with plenty of oil and began to fry the freshly cut potatoes coated in rice powder. While the potatoes were cooking, the red wine sauce had reduced somewhat and was giving off an appetizing scent.

Sungchul placed the saucepan over the center of the flame and began to prepare the long-awaited liver. The main point was searing the surface with strong heat and then simmering the liver in the previously prepared red wine sauce.

"Do you have sugar?" Sungchul suddenly asked the servant.

"Yes. Right over here," replied the servant.

"Thanks. By the way, I was wondering something. What's your lady's favorite dish?"

"That is... what did she call it? I heard it was a dish from the other world. She enjoys eating fried cod battered in flour with a side of fried potatoes."

"An English palate," Sungchul retorted coldly before focusing on cooking once again.

It would take a while until the fresh deer liver would properly and fully marinate with the sweet red wine sauce. In the meantime, Sungchul prepared a simple salad that was to be served along with the breaded fries as the sides to the soon-to-be prepared marinated deer liver and then began plating.

The whole world seemed like it had plunged into a serene silence while he simmered the sauce on a weak flame.

The servant suddenly asked a question, "Your cooking ability must be quite impressive?"

"Of course. I'm actually..." Sungchul smiled faintly as he pulled out a brooch from his Soul Storage. It displayed a cute dragon holding a knife and a fork while radiating a golden light and a mysterious aura.

The servant asked, "What is this?"

He must not know about the Chef's symbol.

What Sungchul had pulled out was the Chef's symbol that could only be possessed by those of the Chef class. It couldn't be passed on to anyone else and provided no inherent benefits, but to chefs, this item was as precious as one's own face. This symbol was the proof of one's culinary abilities. Average chefs would have one with a cast iron tint, but as one's skills improved the brooch's color

219

became more brilliant. In the case of Sungchul, it was the golden light of a High-Class Chef. It was a level that one could not help but be proud of.

"...it's nothing." Sungchul spoke as such before pinning the brooch onto his front pocket.

"Ouch!"

While he pinned the brooch onto his pocket, it must have poked Bertelgia.

"W-what was that sound?" The servant who heard the scream jumped up and began to look around frantically.

"Could it be a rat?" The servant grabbed a broom and quickly left the kitchen.

"That hurt!" As soon as the servant left, Bertelgia complained furiously.

"..."

Sungchul didn't apologize. Instead, he quietly stirred the pan and focused his attention on cooking.

"Arr... Really! Have some decency!"

The sauce on the pan was slowly but surely simmering down. Sungchul didn't rush and continued to watch over his cooking as he waited for the right moment.

It was in this quiet moment when he heard sounds of whispers from the tent.

"I heard that the battle line held by the Order of the Iron Blood Knights had completely crumbled when I was preparing the meal. Two of the Mobile Fortresses that they boasted about were destroyed, and the villages were being raided."

It was the voice of Sophia Breggas.

Sungchul began to contemplate the news as he lightly stirred the pan. *I also heard that the state of the Order of the Iron Blood Knights wasn't so good, but for it to have reached the point of the villages that maintained their supplies to have been raided... There's no better way to describe them than a candle before the storm.*

The strangest part about the ordeal was Martin Breggas' reaction. Rationally, one must pull together the excess forces from the other frontlines towards any breakages, but he had leisurely sent away the Crusaders of Salvation. It might be less odd if the Crusaders had been sent to the Order of the Iron Blood Knights.

"Couldn't we just go back? I'll be honest. I don't trust that mage." Sophia continued to speak, and a mumbling voice followed. It was a voice that was too quiet to be heard clearly, but Sungchul focused on his hearing to listen in. It was Elijah's voice.

"… We don't have many chances left. Just think of this as our last resort. If we go back now, it'll only go the way that man wanted."

"But…"

"That mage… even I don't have much faith in him, but remember this, the only method to our salvation lies in the Demon Realm."

That was all Sungchul was able to hear from their conversation.

The sauce was done simmering. The faint smell of burning food brought Sungchul's attention back to pan.

Those siblings definitely aren't going to the Demon Realm on a whim.

He couldn't determine what they were seeking yet, but even the discovery of their motive of entering the Demonic Realm was a great boon. At the very least, this trip into the Demonic Realm wouldn't simply be to collect some Alchemic ingredients.

Sungchul placed the deer liver soaked in steaming wine sauce last.

"H-how could this… this flavor…! I'm touched." The effect of the dish was great. Different than the practiced smile Elijah held during his sister's cooking, his face exploded with life as he devoured his meal.

"How dare you serve liver as food for nobles!" Sophia didn't look pleased. Sungchul quietly revealed the golden brooch hidden under his coat as he spoke.

"Why not just give it a try?"

Sungchul let his brooch peek out as he crossed his arms and looked toward the sibling with an expression full of leisure.

"Sophia, what's wrong? Just try it. It's truly delicious. This might even be better than what we ate at our home." Elijah spoke after he had already finished half his meal as he took another sip of his wine. Sophia didn't look pleased, but she finally sliced off a piece of the dark liver and took it to her lips.

"...?!"

It was only for a brief instant, but the pale skin of her cheeks became rosy pink. *D-delicious...?*

The moment it entered her mouth, the deer liver melted on her tongue and all of the meaty juices hidden within performed a symphony of flavors with the wine. The ill-willed sister who had been intending on taking a bite before tossing the rest away found herself addicted to this strange man's dish.

It wasn't only the deer liver that was delicious. The fried potatoes battered in rice powder that adorned the outside of the dish was crispy and synergized well with the softness of the deer liver, and even the salad offered a refreshing sensation that didn't fall behind.

The Breggas siblings emptied their dishes not long after. Elijah wore a satisfied expression on his face as he wiped his lips and turned to ask his sister, "How was it? Wasn't it amazing?"

Sophia let out a haughty snort in reply as she answered, "It's not inedible."

She gave a twisted reply but the fact that her plate was completely cleaned did not give her much credibility. When the meal had ended, Elijah praised Sungchul's skills as he handed him a gold coin as payment.

"It's not much, but it is the least I can do." As he said so, he continued to request another meal despite Sophia's glare in protest. Sungchul readily accepted. He found an interest in the offspring of Martin Breggas. He figured that, although he did not know why the children of a celebrity decided to head into the Demon Realm despite the dangers, following them could potentially lead to great rewards.

"Call me any time. I'll be happy to put my skills to use," Sungchul said as such before he let the golden brooch under his coat peek out a little more. However, the siblings never noticed it.

—

A day passed and the Crusaders of Salvation and the Penal Unit continued on their path towards the Demon Realm. They passed through the rugged mountains after an hour and found themselves in front of a desert surrounded by a crimson light that extended toward the horizon. This land, known as The Land that Swallowed the Sun, had little sunlight and high precipitation with frosty winds which was starkly different than a normal desert, but it was still quite a vast desert. The secret of the heat was buried in the sand.

The red-colored sand which covered the whole landscape was warm all year round. It was because the sands were being cooked from below by geothermal activity which is why the demons remained active in this region despite being winter. Furthermore, the infamous "Sand Hell of Death" spawned here as well. The terrifying monster Sajators had seen several thousand years ago still infested these parts. Anyone with half a wit would know to never step foot in this land that swallowed the sun, but instead, would choose to walk the waterfront with solid earth and lower temperatures. However, this expedition ignored such sound logic.

"Time is money. We shall take the shortcut through the desert to save time!"

A guide in name only, Aaron Genghis had chosen the worst possible marching route. One through the crimson desert. The veterans caused a small ruckus, but they were a minority. Also, Aaron led the charge in order to assert his decision.

"As long as I am in front, we shall overcome any obstacle!"

A dark shadow loomed over the veteran soldiers as Aaron shouted his words of inspiration.

"Can someone talk to the young leader? It is looking like that rockhead is going to throw everyone including the Crusaders of Salvation into the maws of the Sand Hell!"

Arkaard looked around and cried out words of protest, but he was just a criminal. It was impossible for him to gain an audience with the leader of the Crusaders, the heir of the Breggas family. There was just one exception: Sungchul Kim.

He snuck in to seek Elijah and reported the situation.

"Hmmm. Is that the truth?"

Elijah looked indifferent on the outside, but the effect of Sungchul's words was clear. Sungchul watched the Breggas boy scolding Aaron where all the soldiers could see.

"Do you think of me as an idiot, Aaron?"

Aaron could only keep his head down as Elijah continued to scold him. A new marching path through the waterfront was decided.

***

Broken chariots and military equipment under canvas had a thick layer of dust on them as they lay littered all over the field. These were debris left behind by previous incursions into the Demon Realm. The seaside was known to be safer when compared to the crimson desert, but that didn't remove its inherent dangers.

There were monsters with bodies that of half-man and half-fish along these shores of the Demon Realm that were lying in ambush by the command of the devils. They were the Merfolk with the body of a fish and the limbs of man. Whenever they prepared to spring their ambush, the shores would be covered in a sickening stench.

Just like now.

The terrible fishy smell came from all sides. Aaron felt the ambush was imminent and ordered the forces to take defensive positions. Sungchul and the veterans stood at the center of the formation as they watched the shores. Between the black waves, the ominous sight of writhing scales was visible. The Merfolk must be looking for an opportunity to strike as they prepared their battle formations.

As this uneventful confrontation was unfolding itself, Arkaard held a picture before Sungchul. It was the illustration of a female dwarf that resembled him.

"How is she?" Arkaard asked all of a sudden. "It's my little girl. Isn't she beautiful?"

The aesthetic sense of dwarves differed greatly from the other races.

"..."

Sungchul didn't say anything. Arkaard simply muttered to himself as though he had never expected a reply to begin with and gazed sentimentally over to the endlessly stretching red desert. "I suppose this'll be the last time I get to see this blasted desert."

"..."

"The way I see it. You're a good man, Number 34."

Arkaard had suddenly begun to act like someone staring death in the face. Even Bertelgia, who had been listening to the conversation from her pocket, began to shake lightly and whispered to Sungchul, "Why is that dwarf acting like that? He's raising a death flag all by himself."

"...leave him." Sungchul seemed to not mind either way.

It finally happened. Piercing shouts rang out from all directions.

"Merfolk! The Merfolk are here!"

Large fish heads began to fill the shore. The Merfolk trod onto the sandy beach on flimsy human legs, each wielding primitive weapons such as metal hooks, clubs, or rusted spears. Their individual combat strength wasn't anything impressive, but their sheer number made up for that. The shoreline was soon filled with thousands of Merfolk.

"There is nothing to fear." Aaron stood at the front as always. He held his hand over his scabbard waiting for the Merfolk to attack. It was to take advantage of the fact that the further they left the water the weaker they became.

On the other side, the Crusaders of Salvation were positioned in the rear of the Penal Unit. Elijah had expressed his wish to join the fray, but Aaron reassured him that the Penal Unit would be enough for such pathetic enemies and positioned him in the rear.

"Will it be ok? To leave them to that person?" Sophia who stood protectively at Elijah's side quietly questioned the decision.

"Aaron is a petty man, but his skills are dependable. There was a time when it was expected that he would someday take an important position within the Ancient Kingdom, if he had only exercised more restraint in accepting bribes that is. But…" A thread of suspicion lingered in Elijah's eyes.

The one to nominate that Aaron Genghis as the escort was my father, Martin Breggas. I don't know what kind of under-the-table dealings went on, but I will not lower my guard until the very end.

Elijah relegated himself to the safety of the rear, but he still commanded his unit to be prepared to enter combat at any moment.

Even during this brief exchange, the Merfolk were continuously being reinforced. The scouts that had been counting the number of Merfolk gave up and announced a rough estimate in a booming voice.

"Merfolk have exceeded five thousand! I repeat, over five thousand!"

The rookies of the Penal Unit who heard the figures began to tremble. They were more than a bit outnumbered. The estimated number of the Merfolk kept climbing, nearing eight thousand.

The wide-open shore became filled with Merfolk and the atrocious stench that followed them. Arkaard, who did not eat fish, began to gag.

"Shit! Those fish heads! They gotta learn to wash themselves!"

The number of Merfolk eventually stopped at eight thousand. The new recruits trembled at the mere number, but Aaron began to laugh in a loud voice. "Just enough to get warmed up!"

He positioned his unit behind the dunes protruding from the sand and protected them by building a barricade from the flotsam scattered on the shore. The unit formed a rectangular formation with the most veteran soldiers and him in the front where the attack was expected to be most concentrated, while the remaining three sides would be defended by the rookies. It was a decent strategy, or so Sungchul believed.

The Merfolk soon began their attack with a strange battle cry. Thousands of Merfolk crawled along the hot sand. The recruits were filled with terror, but the veterans like Aaron looked unfazed. The Merfolk were not only weak and wielded primitive weapons, but they were also quite dumb.

"Byurururu!"

They only had a single strategy in their arsenal. Continuously pummel the enemy with sheer numbers. The Merfolk were making their monstrous cries as they assaulted every side, but they didn't even manage to make the slightest dent in the defensive formation as they fell before the shield wall.

STAB! SLASH!

The shield wall took the initial charge of the Merfolk after which the axes and spears tore through their flesh. The Merfolk bled out as they rolled back down the hill, falling on top of their comrades that were making their way up. Another group of Merfolk were making an attack toward the defenses, but the results were the same.

"All those who can use magic! The time is now! Hit them with all you've got!" Aaron saw a crack in the enemy's battle formation and ordered all of his forces to concentrate their attack. They bombarded the Merfolk with fireballs causing them to fly off with force. The faltering assault of the Merfolk was obliterated in a single magical barrage. Everything was exemplary… up to this point. But soon problems began to arise.

"Good! Very good! Let's make use of this momentum and drive these bastards back to the sea!" Aaron pulled out his sword without hesitation and shouted a foolhardy command.

"All forces! Follow me! Charge!"

He ordered all his men to leave the sturdy defenses behind and charge directly into the Merfolk's ranks as he leaped and led the charge himself.

"Die!"

Aaron's sword, steeped in Sword Aura, mowed down dozens of Merfolk with a single swing. The Merfolk were not a threat to a powerful Sword Master like Aaron. There were fountains of blood everywhere he went as corpses of Merfolk began to pile.

"Go! Let's sweep them up in a single blow! I'll immediately graduate anyone from the Penal Unit that is able to stand out!"

The recruits grew excited after hearing those words and broke the defensive formation to follow behind him toward the center of the Merfolk army. The Penal Unit with Aaron at the helm split the Merfolk army down the middle. It was a heroic charge in every sense of the word, but it was also extremely premature. The Merfolk's overall forces were still intact, and had only barely lost their vanguard.

"Why's he acting like this again?"

Only the veterans were left guarding the dune. They felt the ominous feeling that came chronically with being under Aaron Genghis' command.

"…"

Sungchul looked objectively at the situation, and it cemented his previous suspicions. *Is he doing this purposely?*

Because Aaron had always stood at the vanguard fighting bravely, it wasn't evident before, but this time Sungchul clearly saw it: the insidious malintent hidden behind his courage and valor. Sungchul wasn't sure what his motives were, but he was sure that Aaron was leading his own troops to their demise. He had done so before, and he was doing it again. And soon the consequence followed.

"Byururururu!!!"

"Byururu!!"

The Merfolk that had been split in half regained their composure and surrounded the Penal Unit that had charged deep into their forces. And at the same time, Aaron's lion-like ferocious confidence evaporated as if it was a lie.

"Everyone organize! Organize! Maintain the ring formation and face the enemy!"

The Aaron in Sungchul's eyes had more than enough strength to meet the enemy. If he desired, he could force his way through the enemy forces to save his own troops and break open a path. But this did not come to pass.

"Kwaaak!"

"Uwaaak!"

One by one, the members of the Penal Unit succumbed to the unending tide of the Merfolk army. Even the veterans that had not followed the charge were met by the resumed assault of the Merfolk.

"That damned rockhead bastard!" Arkaard swung his axe mightily lopping off three Merfolk heads as he spat out curses. Another Merfolk leaped at him in this brief interim. Arkaard, whose eyes had been half closed, suddenly glared. Right at the moment he was about to die, an arrow flew like lightning and struck the Merfolk in the skull. He turned toward the direction from which the arrow came. A woman wearing a white coat with an elegant motif over her breastplate was nocking another arrow. It was Sophia Breggas, the sister of the leader of the Crusaders of Salvation.

"Keep fighting, Dwarf."

The Crusaders of Salvation that had been observing from the rear had decided to join the battle. They might be younger than the average soldier, but each one of them was a fighter trained from their childhood as they were all from respectable families. Once they entered the fray, the situation improved, but the combat did not end right away.

When the Merfolk finally retreated back to the sea, leaving behind countless piles of corpses on the sandy beach, the three hundred-member Penal Unit was reduced to less than half of their original number. Aaron returned once again without a single injury on him. He approached Elijah with a defeated expression on his face after a brief mourning of his troops that were sent tragically to their graves early. "I have no excuses."

At this point, Elijah made a cold decision. "I don't need your help anymore. We will go our own way from this point on, so I would appreciate it if you could disappear from my sight immediately."

Aaron had already lost more than half of his forces, and his incompetence was openly revealed. There was not a single reason for the two units to remain together. Aaron retreated without raising his head. His cheeks were burning at this public humiliation, but he didn't immediately order his men back to base. The sun was setting, and they had to make camp for the night.

He set up camp apart from the Crusaders of Salvation, and once darkness arrived, Aaron covertly ordered all his men to gather into one place. It was a pitiful number that barely broke one hundred thirty, so it didn't take very long. When all of the men were gathered, Aaron finally revealed his face. It was a face filled with confidence which was in contrast to his expression during his humiliation.

"Shameless bastard."

Several soldiers mocked him under their breath, but Aaron didn't mind it at all. Instead, he smirked. He smirked widely enough to show his pearly white teeth. It was then that a question arose in the soldiers' minds.

Did he finally snap?

On the contrary to the popular opinion, Aaron did not go crazy.

"You all have survived the last battle and thusly have proven yourselves as worthy warriors."

It was an unexpected sermon. Aaron noticed several soldiers looking at him quizzically, and so he continued his speech, "Today, I sifted out the main forces. As a result, the incompetent and stupid were filtered out. Thankfully, our shares of the rewards have also increased."

The soldiers couldn't grasp at what Aaron was alluding to, but as they kept listening, Aaron's announcement made their blood freeze.

"Tonight. We shall strike the Crusaders of Salvation."

Everyone's mouth became shut as they stared blankly at Aaron's face, but Aaron remained indifferent. One of the men raised a hand. It was the stocky Dwarf, Arkaard.

"You're going to strike at the son of Martin Breggas? Are you preparing to turn us all into traitors?"

All anyone could think was that Aaron was trying to exact revenge for the humiliation he endured, but the truth was far from their expectation. Aaron pulled out a single document from his possession.

"The one that made this order was Martin Breggas. The Lord Marquis himself."

Aaron left it at that and opened the document for his subordinates to see.

[I command Aaron Genghis thusly.]

[Kill all of the Crusaders of Salvation. Leave none alive.]

[Especially, Elijah Breggas, the Follower of Calamity, must die.]

[Lord Marquis of Trowyn, Martin Breggas]

It was a formal document adorned magnificently with specks of gold that was not something that could be forged overnight on a whim. Sungchul could also see with his Eye of Truth that the magical signature on the document was authentic.

"The purpose of sacrificing half of the unit was as I stated before. It was to cull the weak and make the enemy lower their guard."

Aaron's tone drastically changed. In stark contrast to his nickname, he smoothly continued on like a cunning snake

"Tonight, those brats in the Crusaders of Salvation shall meet us completely unprepared."

Aaron looked toward the camp of the Crusaders situated not so far away. There were delicious aromas and sensuous music flowing from that direction. There were a few sentries standing guard, but overall, their vigilance was more than lacking.

Aaron glared toward the camp of the Crusaders as he continued speaking. "Kill those brats in their beds. Rape the girls if you want. All the valuables on their persons will be up for grabs. Finally, every one of you will be granted freedom upon success of this mission. By the name of the Lord Marquis."

Chapter 11 – Tome of the High Devils

When a situation progressed independently of his will, Sungchul always had the same answer: nip the problem at its source. As the Penal Unit was preparing for their midnight raid, Sungchul approached Aaron.

Aaron was sitting in his chair while wiping his sword with a solemn expression on his face. As was befitting of his title as a Swordmaster, he glared in Sungchul's direction the moment he sensed his presence. He then spoke in a commanding voice. "Who is it?"

"..."

Sungchul simply slipped out to reveal himself. Aaron finally remembered who Sungchul was as he entered the tent.

"You… you're that patrolman, right?"

He had completely forgotten about Sungchul. As the incident within the Underground Kingdom had been so traumatic, Aaron didn't have the peace of mind to care for each and every scouting report. "Yes. What is it, Number 34?"

Sungchul kept his points brief. "I came by the order of Willie Gilford."

CLANG.

The sword clattered to the floor. Not a single drop of blood remained in Aaron's pale face.

"W-what did you just say?" He spoke in a trembling voice.

"Willie Gilford has sent me." Sungchul's expression remained unchanged, and Aaron's spine broke out in cold sweat.

Did… Willie Gilford survive?! He had abandoned the powerhouse of the Ancient Kingdom, Willie Gilford, to die in the Underground Kingdom. Willie was not known for mercy; he was famous for seeking revenge for even the pettiest of grudges. It was because Aaron knew Willie best that he had been suffering from anxiety for a whole month in his room after returning from the Underground Kingdom.

Thankfully, there was no news from the Ancient Kingdom's side and he struggled desperately to form any kind of relationship to ensure his survival and eventually successfully managed to do a favor for Martin Breggas. He believed that after this mission he would be under the protection of a powerful ally who could shelter him from Willie Gilford, but the name he did not want to hear ever again was mentioned in the middle of carrying out the mission.

"W-w-why did Willie Gilford s-send you here?" Aaron asked as he reached for his fallen sword with a trembling hand.

Sungchul replied with an apathetic voice, "He has already arrived nearby."

"Waaak!" Aaron let out a scream.

Sungchul laughed to himself upon seeing Aaron squirm. As expected. He's deathly afraid of Willie.

Sungchul spoke again in a softer voice towards the terrified Aaron. "Sir Willie Gilford said to convey this to you. He has no intention to bring you harm and simply has a request to make of you, so be at ease and come. Immediately."

"A r-request?" Aaron's eyes which were drowning in despair came back alive. Relying on him for a task was equivalent to saying that he was forgiven.

"Yes. Immediately." Sungchul emphasized that last word. Aaron quickly sheathed his blade and rose from his seat.

"Where is he now? Willie Gilford that is…"

"He and Mikhael Gilford are currently at the seaside," replied Sungchul.

"Is that right? I got it. I'll head toward there now."

Suddenly, Aaron felt a twinge of suspicion rise in his mind. Why and how had this soldier become a messenger of Willie Gilford? The only person that was aware of his brief service under Willie Gilford was the Empath that he kept beside him. The rest were killed within the cold corridors of the Underground Kingdom. However, this was not the time to mess about with these minor details. Regardless of whether this was the truth or not, he had to investigate the matter. If not, he would forever live in agony worrying about Willie Gilford behind his back for the rest of his life.

"So, where is he?" Aaron rushed Number 34. Number 34 walked quite briskly, but to Aaron, he might as well have been walking at the pace of a tortoise. "Run, Number 34! I'm in quite the hurry!"

"I understand." Number 34 began to run. It was a fast pace, but it couldn't possibly compare to Aaron's. No, it is more correct to say that it shouldn't have been possible for him to outpace Aaron. But when Aaron tried to close the distance by speeding up, Number 34 quickened even further and kept the distance the same. It was good that Number 34 was moving quickly, but something was not right.

Why the fuck is this kid so fast? Did he eat the wrong medicine?

The two of them finally arrived at the seaside filled with rotting Merfolk flesh.

"It's here," said Sungchul.

A scarlet moon hung in the sky as the blood-stained tide washed upon the sandy beach. Aaron looked around his surroundings. The only two people standing were Number 34 and himself. As the clouds slowly covered the moon, Aaron spoke again. "Where is Willie Gilford?"

Number 34 turned around in reply. Something popped out of his pocket and began to flutter about, flying up into the air. On a closer inspection, it was a book.

What is this?

As things were growing odder, Number 34 pulled something from the air. It was a hammer with a long handle.

A Soul Storage?!

As the clouds retreated, the moonlight fell upon the sand for the second time. The light shone upon the hammer revealing its full form in all its glory. All the alarms went off in Aaron's mind as he saw the hammer.

I have to run.

Someone like Willie Gilford was long since gone from his mind. The person standing before him was the Enemy of the World who made the world tremble with his name. Someone that little Willie couldn't compare to.

Aaron, who always fought on the frontlines against mob creatures but retreated at the first sight of a powerful foe, found no way out this time. His escape ended not even three steps later when he was caught from the back and thrown upside down into the sand.

Aaron who was embedded with his entire upper body into the soft sand desperately pulled himself out from the ground.

SSSSSK

His face which was messy from the sand blushed bright red.

"S-spare me!" Aaron prostrated himself onto the beach and begged for his life.

"..."

Sungchul looked at him apathetically for a while before opening his mouth to speak. "Explain everything that's happening right now."

Aaron followed the command to the letter. He revealed everything that he knew was occurring and will occur with no details spared. From his report, Sungchul learned two things: the internal struggles within the Breggas household and the situation regarding Elijah Breggas. It appeared that Martin wanted to make his bastard son his heir, and when he pressured Elijah, it was said that Elijah turned to the Followers of Calamity. The personal accounts of each side weren't known, but the rumor is that Elijah met with the head of the Followers of Calamity.

"The leader of the Followers of Calamity?" This was the first time Sungchul had heard of this. The Followers of Calamity was cult-like in its creation and would arise spontaneously; their organizational structure didn't allow for a leader. Grand Mage Balzark, the man who Sungchul killed a while back, might have held enough importance to be called the center of the movement, but other than him, there wasn't anyone worthy of being called the leader.

I will have to talk to Elijah directly about this one. A cold light appeared in Sungchul's eyes. Aaron who was still prostrated before him continued to pour out his heart in a pathetic voice.

"Yes. This expedition into the Demon Realm was requested by Elijah Breggas, who had come in contact with the Followers of Calamity, of Martin Breggas. There definitely is some kind of scheme in play here. It was why Lord Martin left the disposal of this problem to me."

"I see." Sungchul began to fidget with the handle of the hammer as he lorded over Aaron. Aaron's heart trembled at even the slightest movement of the shadow drawn by Fal Garaz. He tactfully gauged the mood as he carefully spoke once again.

"T-that is all I know, Destroyer."

Sungchul gave Aaron a frosty glare. The man was cunning and selfish, but he could be used exactly for that reason.

Sungchul chose to keep him alive for now.

"Cease the attack on the Crusaders of Salvation."

"What…? That's…" Aaron showed some resistance, and so Sungchul pulled out a box filled with various gems, gold, and silver treasures before him.

"T-This is?!" Treasures worth more than what he could possibly obtain in his entire life were laid out before him. Aaron's eyes grew wide.

"I heard that you were chased out of the Ancient Kingdom on bad terms. Is that true?" Sungchul asked in a low voice.

Aaron lowered his head and replied, "That's correct, sir."

"Can you return to the Ancient Kingdom with this?"

"Of course!"

Anything was possible with this amount of wealth. It was enough to restore his place within the Ancient Kingdom as he truly wanted. The wealth that lay before him was enough to make even the worst of enemies into the best of friends.

Sungchul stared at Aaron's constantly changing expression and said coldly, "Also, Willie Gilford, who you were so deathly afraid of, died in the Underground Kingdom."

"W-Was it done by the hands of Sir Destroyer?"

"I didn't lay a finger on him, but he did die."

A brief expression of relief passed over Aaron's face. The greatest obstacle in his path had disappeared. Aaron finally had to weigh his options. The answer was clear.

"This Genghis Aaron shall follow the will of the Destroyer."

The situation drew to a close with this. Aaron ceased the attack on the Crusaders of Salvation and withdrew his troops. The men who were excited at the prospects of plunder began to complain, but Aaron paid them no mind.

"That person. Is it ok like this? Shouldn't we get a covenant out of him or something? He might blab to someone that you're here." Bertelgia made her concerns known, but Sungchul looked indifferent.

"We don't have to worry. He won't say anything, even at the cost of his life."

If the truth that he had had dealings with the Enemy of the World was revealed, then Aaron would be finished anyways. It was unlikely that this truth would ever be leaked except as a very last resort.

Sungchul watched the Penal Unit's retreat apathetically. *I no longer have a reason to stay in there.*

He had stayed as long as he had wanted and accomplished a fair bit. A part of him wanted to say farewell to his squadmates with whom he had spent time, but it was too much of a luxury for someone who had turned away from the world like Sungchul. Sending the Penal Unit back was the most he could do for them. Sungchul's eyes were now set on the other side where the Crusaders of Salvation were camped.

—

When the sun rose, the Crusaders of Salvation planned to resume their journey toward the Demon Realm. Sungchul and Bertelgia followed their tracks from a distance. Half a day later, the Crusaders of Salvation left the crimson desert and entered into tundra filled with glaciers and canyons.

The entrance to the Demon Realm: It was the invasion path of the Devils. Tension rose within the Crusaders of Salvation since they didn't know when they might come into contact with a large host of demonic forces. However, there was a well-known gatekeeper to the entrance of the Demon Realm; the Deep Sea Demon.

The monster that Sungchul had been beating up once a week with spells heard the footsteps of the Crusaders of Salvation and emerged from the ground to overwhelm them with intimidation. This creature was nothing more than a training dummy for Sungchul, but it was a formidable enemy to the Crusaders.

Should I see how they handle this?

Sungchul watched the confrontation between the Deep Sea Demon and the Crusaders of Salvation from afar, but it turned out to be a disappointment. The Crusaders couldn't even properly fight the creature before their morale broke and they routed. It was an indescribably pitiful defeat.

The Crusaders of Salvation had, as a result, lost a considerable number of servants and supplies, but their tribulations were yet to end. An army of demons appeared before them after having barely managed to escape from the Deep Sea Demon. They were cavalry units riding on Helldogs. The Crusaders might have been able to defeat this foe effortlessly, but that would have been before they met the Deep Sea Demon.

Countless members of the Crusaders were torn apart by the Helldogs and lost their lives to the serrated blades of the demon soldiers.

"Everyone! To positions! Maintain your formation!"

Elijah flailed about trying to maintain order as the demon cavalry weaved through their formation with ease, but it was to no avail. He would have long since become a cold body had it not been for Sophia who vigilantly protected his side.

It looks like they're having a hard time avoiding complete destruction. Sungchul couldn't stand it much longer and stepped in himself. He suddenly appeared behind the leader of the demons, who was directing the troops, and snapped his neck with his powerful grip. When the devils saw their leader had been instantly killed by a monstrous stranger who appeared out of nowhere, only one name popped into their head as they fled in panic.

"It's the Destroyer! The Destroyer is here!"

The demon cavalry ceased their attacks and scattered as they ran. Sungchul leisurely approached where the Crusaders of Salvation had been earlier. There were bodies of Helldogs, demons, and Crusaders strewn about the battlefield. He couldn't find any of the surviving Crusaders, but there were scattered prints stretched out towards the south.

It looks like they used the moment when I killed the demon to retreat.

Regardless of how chaotic the battle had seemed, it was the eldest son of the Sixth Champion of the Continent Martin Breggas. There was no way the boy would die here. As he began to contemplate such thoughts, something caught his attention.

"Hm? What's that?" As Sungchul continued his path between the corpses, Bertelgia popped out of her pocket to speak. Sungchul turned his head to notice that Bertelgia was hovering over a specific point on the ground. A single book lay under her. It was bound in dark red leather colored like blood and had an ominous presence.

"This thing here. This thing. It smells really evil?"

Sungchul nodded as he noticed the book. "It definitely isn't a normal book."

Sungchul bent his knee to take a second look at it. When his fingers touched the book, its texture felt familiar.

It was bound with human leather.

The book looked appropriate for demons to use. Sungchul held it and activated Inspection. Information on the book appeared before him.

[Tome of the High Devils: Volume 7]

Grade   : Epic
Type   : Equipment – Book
Effect   : On Equip – Increases Magic Power 20, Vitality 20
Note   : Those who wish to obtain the power of the High Devil must open the tome before The Altar of Ten Thousand Demons.
Restriction : Mage-related Class

It had low stats considering its grade as an Epic item, and it didn't even have any additional effects. However, something within the information screen couldn't be overlooked.

Power of the High Devil?

As he reflected on this new information, he sensed the desperate steps of people approaching. Before long their voices could be heard.

"Brother. This place is dangerous! Let's go back, please?"

It was Sophia's voice. Sungchul hid within the fog hanging over the battlefield and quietly observed them. He soon heard another voice.

"We have to find that book! All of our efforts will be for nothing without the book!"

It was Elijah's voice. He was crawling along the ground with bloodshot eyes searching the battlefield.

Sungchul looked at the book bound with human skin in his hand.

***

THWOP.

Sungchul dropped the book where it could easily be seen.

Bertelgia saw the book left on the ground and asked in surprise, "Huh? What are you planning?"

"I think it'll be good to see how this plays out." Sungchul left the book on the ground and hid once again in the fog hanging over the battlefield. Elijah soon arrived.

Elijah had been stumbling around the ground of the battlefield like a blind man when he suddenly broke out into a cheer. "It's here! It's here!"

Only after he had hidden the Tome of High the Devil beneath his cloak and fastened it to a clasp on his belt did Elijah sigh in relief.

"I had thought that it was all over. Really. It would all have been for nothing without this."

Sophia just silently guarded her brother as she followed. The siblings immediately headed back after recovering the book. The Crusaders of Salvation were situated on a hill not too far from the battle site; their lifeless eyes looked towards the Breggas siblings. Lacking the strength to even raise their arms, they simply stared at the siblings without saying a word. It was fine as long as the intruders were human; this was the thought shared between every member.

Sungchul roughly counted the remaining members of the Crusaders of Salvation as he gazed at them. None of the non-combatants remained and not even half of the original hundred members had survived. Most importantly, they had abandoned all of their supplies when they had faced the Deep Sea Demon. Their current state was dire and anyone could easily see that further progress was impossible. Despite all of this, Elijah ordered them to continue once again.

When people began to complain, Elijah yelled for those wanting to leave to leave. This led to deserters and the Crusaders of Salvation were degraded to a pitiful party that didn't even have ten members. However, Elijah's will wasn't broken. He stroked the Tome of the High Devil hidden beneath his cloak and walked deeper into the Demon Realm with the few that still followed him.

And, of course, there were many difficult-to-overcome obstacles scattered before them. To begin with, they needed to first pass through the Deep Sea Demon that guarded the entrance to the Demon Realm.

The small group gathered their heads and formulated a plan to sneak past the gatekeeper before he woke. It was a plan that had not even a semblance of a chance of success. The area surrounding the Deep Sea Demon was teeming with imps. The imps themselves were no stronger than a rabid dog, but they would charge towards anything that wasn't a Demon and die with an earsplitting scream. In other words, they were like literal living alarms. And trying to stealthily pass through terrain that was overflowing with those things was close to impossible for the Crusaders of Salvation.

Sungchul went ahead of the Crusaders to where the Deep Sea Demon could be found. In order to call out the Sea Demon, he killed several of the imps that charged towards him.

"Gwuuuuuh!!!" With a loud bellow, the Deep Sea Demon shot up towards the surface and found itself recoiling in fear at the sight of his guest. It was the bastard that had savagely pummeled it every week. However, Sungchul didn't use magic this time. He pulled out Fal Garaz and struck the creature with just enough force to keep it alive. A one-sided and terrifying beating began. Only after its skull was cracked and both of its arms were broken, did the Sea Demon fall back below the surface.

Bertelgia carefully asked after witnessing Sungchul's intense beating, "You sure it's not dead?"

"Deep Sea Demons are dim-witted, but they have extremely strong vitality. Their regeneration is second to none." Sungchul turned to look towards the south. He could see the Crusaders of Salvation bumbling about in the distance trying to walk silently like assassins. Sungchul left the area.

"Kiiiii!!"

One of the imps discovered the Crusaders and rushed towards them.

"Shit!" Elijah quickly drew his blade and cut off the creature's head. His swordplay was precise and accurate, as expected of Martin Breggas's son, but it wasn't quick enough to stop the imp's death throes.

"Kii…? Techaaaaaaaaa!"

Surprise filled Elijah's eyes. "I cut through his neck directly. Where is this cry coming from?!"

The stealth mission was thwarted before it even began.

"Brother. Let's retreat," Sophia said with a low tone of voice, but a small miracle appeared before them. Despite the imp's terrible scream, the Deep Sea Demon did not reveal himself. Elijah was skeptical, but he pushed forward cautiously once again. Another group of imps discovered them, attacked, and got annihilated. This time not just one, but several of them released their death throes as they fell to the ground and died. However, no Deep Sea Demon appeared. In the face of such unexpected good luck, Elijah decided to act boldly.

"Let's break through quickly."

His decision was ultimately the correct one. They were able to safely pass through the territory guarded by the Deep Sea Demon. The land of fire and ice where lava flowed beyond frozen glaciers entered their sights.

"It's the Demon Realm. We finally made it into the Demon Realm."

Elijah was overcome with emotions as he took in the view of the land of the Demon Realm. The roars of demons could be heard from all directions, but he wasn't discouraged. He stroked the book hidden beneath his cloak and pressed forward once again.

An army of Devils could be seen approaching in the distance; their marching emitted a cloud of dust behind them. Elijah and his unit hid themselves behind rocks which were as sharp as knife blades. Thankfully, the Devils did not discover them.

They continued their march in this fashion. Their progress was slow, and the sun that shone in the hazy skies of the Demon Realm had begun to set. Night was approaching. Once the night fell, all sorts of demons that were hiding underground or in clouds came out and roamed above the surface of the Demon Realm. They sniffed in search of prey or weaker demons.

The time for the Devils of the Demon Realm, governed only by the rule "survival of the fittest," had begun in earnest. The weak only existed to feed the strong or die to amuse them. Elijah and his group were quite strong among the humans, but they were nothing compared to the swarms of Devils. Human flesh and souls were popular among the Devils. There would be nothing left of them; their body and soul would be plundered by the Devils upon discovery. However, fortune smiled upon them that day.

"…"

The divine armament forged from a fragment of the sky, Fal Garaz. A man watched over them with such a fearsome weapon. A gigantic demon wearing a vicious smile emerged from the clouds as it discovered the Crusaders of Salvation below and was diving down when it noticed Sungchul. The Devil didn't recognize Sungchul's face, but it recognized the weapon in his hand. It immediately turned its gaze elsewhere and flew toward the sky once again.

Similar scenes continued to occur within the pitch-black darkness of the night, and the Crusaders of Salvation were able to survive through their first night in the Demon Realm. But the problem occurred after the sun had risen.

It was when Sungchul had chased away the last devil with his stare before taking a sigh of relief when he heard a short cry of pain ring out from the direction of the camp of the Crusaders.

"Uwaaak!"

It was Elijah.

Was there a hidden Devil? It can't be. No Devil should have been able to sneak past by me. Sungchul immediately headed toward the camp. The guilty party wasn't a Devil, but a fellow human. Seven of the Crusaders were fleeing toward the south. Sungchul looked and confirmed that one of them was holding the Tome of the High Devils.

"Kuuh…"

Elijah's laborious breathing could be heard coming from the back, as if he was on the brink of death. Sungchul immediately headed toward the noise. Elijah had a large sword wound to his abdomen and was lying on the floor.

"Brother! Stay awake! Brother!"

Sophia performed emergency aid beside him, but she herself wasn't faring that well. There were several cuts of various sizes along her body, and her white outfit was damp with blood.

Sungchul checked his surroundings. There was no one left but the siblings. They were thoroughly betrayed and abandoned. Sungchul revealed himself and Elijah's eyes turned towards him.

"You are…?"

When Sophia heard her brother's words, she turned her head and harshly glared at Sungchul. Sungchul took a look at Elijah's injuries. The affected area was starting to turn black. The poison in his body was weakening him faster than the cut of his wound.

"Move."

Sungchul commanded. His voice contained an irrefutable authoritative quality to it, and Sophia moved out of the way as if she was possessed.

Sungchul grabbed a sharp dagger from his Soul Storage and cut open the affected area.

"Krrrk!"

Blood as black as ink poured out of the wound. It was blood tainted by the poison. When Sungchul drained enough of the blood, he applied the antidote to the injury before applying some healing salve on the affected area. It was a very beneficial medicine for the body but was extremely bitter, making Elijah scream out in horrible pain. But proving his worth as the heir of an important family, he was able to endure it all. Elijah was soon able to overcome the critical juncture.

When the situation had resolved itself to a degree, Sophia opened her mouth first. "Why are you here?"

"..."

Sungchul didn't answer her. His gaze was fixed on Elijah as he asked, "What do you seek in the Demon Realm?"

"How did you...?" Elijah asked, but Sungchul spoke again with a bit more force.

"I ask again, what are you looking for here?"

His question contained that undefiable authority once again. It was at this moment that a sharp blade was held at Sungchul's neck. It was Sophia's blade.

"Put it away."

Sungchul simply spoke, and Sophia found her body freezing in fear. However, she was also the offspring of the Sixth Champion. Despite the overwhelming fear, she held on. In the midst of this tension, an earsplitting cry of a monster rang out from the sky.

"KREWAAAAAAA!!"

A gigantic bird roaming the skies had discovered a prey on the ground. Sophia saw the massive wingspan that covered the sky in darkness and was frozen in shock.

Could that be an Omen of Calamity?

An Omen of Calamity was one of the most infamous creatures residing in the Demon Realm. They were known to be the most terrifying life-form and didn't quite belong to the realm of humanity or the Devils, and they followed above the army of Devils so that they could devour the human and Devil corpses alike at the end of every battle. They were a scavenger of sorts, but they were carved into the minds of every human as a terrifying symbol of the Calamity due to their incredible size and strength. That Omen of

Calamity was flapping its wings as it rapidly dove toward Sungchul's group. Sophia's face paled in fear.

I can't stop it! She had already lost a majority of her strength fending off the deserters. Her injuries of varying sizes were a drain on her recovery. She might be able to move out of the way to save her own neck, but she wouldn't be able to save Elijah.

The mysterious man known as Number 34 pulled out a whip that seemed as black and red as a burning coal from his Soul Storage. It was a long whip that seemed to extend ten meters from a quick glance. He swung it toward the rapidly descending Omen without a moment of hesitation.

Idiot. How can you stop that thing with just a whip? All of her rationality argued that his actions were meaningless, but Sungchul's strength defied all logic. Cassandra, the Demonic Weapon, accurately wrapped around the Omen's neck whose talons were bared toward the ground.

"Kweh?"

The moment when the Omen tilted its head, the whip pulled it with overwhelming force, slamming it into the ground.

WHAM!

The Omen's head struck the solid piece of bedrock and shattered the ground while its wings were crippled to the point where pieces of broken bone were piercing through its flesh.

Sungchul's hand that was gripping the whip moved again. The Omen was flung towards the opposite side and it struck the ground once again.

BOOM!

"Krweh…" The Omen convulsed in pain, but Sungchul was a man that knew no mercy.

BOOM! BOOM! BOOM!

With each of Sungchul's movements, the Omen was continuously smashed onto the ground like a dog, killing it by causing its entire body to be broken.

"Hiiii…" Sophia's face grew paler. She had lost all ability to form words in the face of this unbelievable sight.

This human… who is he? Countless ideas ran through her mind, but there was only one name that felt possible. Horror filled Sophia's eyes. *Could this man be…?*

The blade held in her delicate hand clattered to the floor. Finally, she managed to speak with a trembling voice. "You… are the Enemy of the World?"

Sungchul looked directly into her eyes as he nodded. "Yes, I am."

***

The Demons were the first race that awakened their magical potential. The Demons had an affinity towards magic that allowed them to understand it better, and they possessed greater talent toward it. Obsession over magic had eventually led to their fall, but magical knowledge and powerful spells had been the target of admiration and worship among the Demons. They had all but disappeared now, but there was a time when there were many Devil worshippers. The goal of the Devil worshippers was to escape the lowly and servile destiny as a human and turn into a Devil themselves. The Tome of the High Devils recorded the secrets of such Devil worshippers.

"…It contains a Devil's quest."

They could hide it no longer, and there was no point in doing so. Elijah revealed everything he knew to the Enemy of the World.

"The book acts as a guide to the city of the Devil worshippers hidden within the entrance of the Demon Realm, and if the book is opened on the Altar of Ten Thousand Demons that is said to exist in the city, then he who was once human could receive the quest of the High Devil."

"It is not a wholesome quest. Must you really do such a thing?" Sungchul asked in a calm voice.

"I want my revenge even if I have to use the power of the Devils. That man drove Mother to her death and tried to have us killed as well." A cold fire of vengeance burned in Elijah's eyes. Sungchul could feel truth within it.

"...Follow me." Sungchul led the way. He followed the footsteps of those that fled towards the south. The siblings, who were confused by the unexpected actions of the Enemy of the World, simply followed suit. They soon found a single human corpse torn to shreds. It was one of the Crusaders of Salvation. Those who had left Sungchul's protection were immediately subjected to the ambush of Devils and had met pitiful ends as prey.

"Lucas..." Sophia recognized the corpse and trembled lightly.

Sungchul looked at the mass of bloody hair and flesh on the ground and asked, "Do you know him?"

"...He was a childhood friend. Even though he did betray us in the end," answered Sophia.

Sungchul continued forward. They soon found another corpse. Not just one, but two of them. The corpses had been caught by an insidious-looking devil with a hundred teeth, and had become its plaything. Sungchul looked callously toward the demon who had cut up the corpses and was now trying to piece them together in different combinations.

The siblings grimaced at the sight.

"Gil, Jinte..."

These members were also long-time friends of theirs. They had also betrayed the siblings, but their pitiful deaths still left a great shock in the hearts of the Breggas siblings. When the hundred-toothed devil saw new humans, it tossed aside the corpses it was playing with and revealed its hideous teeth. "Kiii! Kiii! Kiii!"

However, things did not go as the devil had planned.

WHAM!

Sungchul's fist met the devil's face and all one hundred of its teeth shattered as they poured out of its mouth, carried out by a stream of blood. Sungchul grabbed a fist full of razor sharp teeth that littered the ground and rubbed them into the devil's eyes.

"Kiiiiii!"

He then pulled out the devil's arms in its entirety and threw the crying devil off into a random direction. The Omens of Calamity began to circle around the devil that was squirming while stuck in the ground.

"…"

Sungchul, who had taken care of the devil, began to walk forward once again without any words. The Breggas siblings could only watch the back of this man with god-like strength with wide eyes and follow along. As they walked, a sudden thought crossed by Elijah's mind.

Could it be that we only managed to get this far… because this man was nearby?

His guess was right on point. This was why Sungchul didn't chase after the deserters right away. Leaving the veil of protection Sungchul provided in the Demon Realm, which equated to hell in this world, meant that these deserters would simply return to the bottom rung of the food pyramid becoming just food.

Sungchul and the Breggas siblings continued to discover more corpses. They had all met pitiful and gruesome deaths. They had found a single survivor, but he was in a state worse than death

"K-kill me…" The man begged for death as he had been injected with the eggs of a giant insect, and the larvae of the insect were now eating him from inside out.

WHAM!

Sungchul's hammer immediately shattered the man's skull. A parasite about as large as a finger bared its fangs as it wriggled about within the skull.

"Uwek…" Bertelgia who was within Sungchul's pocket began to wriggle.

"…"

Sungchul left behind the corpse and pressed on. *There are two left.*

It didn't take long to find the final two: one male and one female. They were alive, but barely. A pale-skinned devil wearing a necklace made of limbs hovered near them as if he were a cloud. The devil laughed mechanically as he descended, creating thunder and lightning around him. A terrifying electric shock struck them. Sungchul immediately smashed the devil's skull with his hammer, but it was only after the pair had already been critically wounded.

"Uuugggh."

One of them immediately died. The other, a man with long sideburns, let out a pained cry as he looked out toward nothing in particular with his rapidly fading vision. Elijah and Sophia hurriedly ran to his side.

"Kruut!" Elijah propped him up and hugged him. The man's eyes had already lost their sight at this point.

"Elijah. Is that you?" asked Kruut.

"Yes. It's me."

"I'm sorry. I'm… really sorry."

The man died after leaving behind those words. A heavy silence soon followed. Sungchul recovered the Tome of the High Devils from the dead woman's corpse within this silence. When he held the tome in his hand, a faint line appeared in his vision. It was a faint beam of light that would be easily missed without focus. The light extended towards the south.

Sungchul handed the tome to Elijah. "Take it."

"…"

Elijah had a befuddled look as he accepted the Tome of the High Devils. *This guy… what are his intentions?*

It was impossible for him to even guess what Sungchul's heart deeply desired. The man's motives and goals were all veiled in mystery.

Sungchul read the confusion that was raging behind Elijah's eyes and said with a low tone of voice, "Lead on. Towards the Devil's quest."

Elijah finally understood a bit of what Sungchul wanted. He nodded and led the man to the location where the Devil's quest awaited them. After crossing several glacial mountains and rivers of lava, they arrived before a foggy sea. Curiosity rose in Sungchul's eyes. *Are you saying there is something in this foggy region?*

The Sea of Fog was one of the places that Sungchul recalled from his days when he wandered the Demon Realm. The area had nothing special. There were pits of mud scattered about the ground, with monsters resembling drowned corpses waiting to drag victims into the pits. However, Sungchul had the Tome of the High Devils now. The beam of light extending from the Tome of the High Devils acted as a guide that led them through the Sea of Fog where vision was completely obstructed.

CRUNCH!

Around the time Sungchul crushed the tenth monster with the sole of his military boots, the annoying fog began to dissipate. Sungchul and the Breggas siblings could see towers that seemed to pierce the sky as they left the fog.

There were eight towers in total. The precarious walkways strung like spider webs between the eight towers were dizzying to the eye. Sungchul took another step forward as he looked at the towers. *So there are places like this in the Demon Realm.*

Sungchul discovered a figure lingering at the bottom of a tower. Surprisingly, it was a human. Its body had become twisted and disfigured from horrendous torture and body modifications, but Sungchul could easily recognize that the creature carrying a gunny sack was a human. He looked back toward Elijah as he asked, "Where is this?"

Sungchul thought that Elijah, who held the Tome of the High Devils, would know something. He was bound to have additional information from the person who had given him the book. Some information regarding this city in the Demon Realm that even Sungchul had never seen before, and he had guessed correctly.

"This place… is a city of humans," Elijah responded honestly, and curiosity rose in Sungchul's eyes once again.

"There is a human city in the middle of the Demon Realm?"

"That's right. It is a city of those that wished to escape their mortal destiny. A gathering place of those that desired to become Devils," answered Elijah.

"You're saying that this place is a so-called hideout of the Devil worshippers?"

Elijah's eyes grew dark before he nodded to Sungchul's question.

So a place like this exists.

There weren't many people among the humans who knew more than Sungchul regarding the Demon Realm. At the very least among the people of the same era as he. However, Elijah Breggas… no, the person that handed him the book knew of this city's existence. This was no ordinary person.

Sungchul turned towards Elijah. "Who gave you that book?"

It was a question that had to be asked at one point. Sungchul felt that that moment had been drawing close, and it had finally arrived.

Elijah also knew that Sungchul would ask that question at some point. After organizing his thoughts in his head, he made a complete and calm reply. "I would like to first begin with an apology. There is very little I know about her. It is because she appeared before us without warning. We also don't know whether the identity this person revealed to us is true or not."

It was not a satisfactory answer. Sungchul's arm twitched slightly, but to Elijah, that movement felt unreasonably large. He gulped and continued to speak again. "She gave the name of one of the Seven Heroes."

"Seven Heroes?" Sungchul's lips that had been tightly shut came loose. Elijah immediately followed up the question.

"Yes. The woman called herself Vestiare."

Vestiare. One of the Seven Heroes, and the one who had handed Sungchul his Echo Mage class. Elijah continued to explain what he had seen when Sungchul's hand shot up. It was a signal for silence. He then turned to look at Sophia. Sophia's figure trembled slightly, but her dignified eyes met Sungchul's.

"Have you also seen this woman?"

Sophia was about to shake her head when she realized it was a pointless attempt and nodded instead.

"What did that woman look like?" asked Sungchul.

Sophia combed through her memories at his question. "It was a blonde High Elf."

Sungchul's eyes lit up.

"She had pale skin like a ghost. Enough to be able to see her veins. She also had a serene voice as though she was from a dream." Sophia's recollection of Vestiare roughly matched up with his. It didn't seem like a lie. Sungchul immediately fell into thought.

The Calamity of the Demon King hasn't ended, but the Seven Heroes are already active?

The words of the Breggas siblings couldn't be trusted completely, but most of what they said seemed to be truthful. Sungchul glared at the high rising tower of the Devil worshippers with suspicion. *It has become clear that something is happening here.*

But it was more important right now for him to resolve the problem at hand. He quickly concluded his thoughts.

A firmly shut doorway stood before Sungchul and the Breggas siblings. It was a massive steel door that didn't look like it could be forced open by human strength. But it opened with a thunderous noise once Sungchul's hand, instilled with godly strength, took action.

"Follow me."

Sungchul walked towards the interior of the tower, which shone with an ominous light.

Chapter 12 – Lords of the Tower

Within the tower, a short path appeared with opaque windows on either side. It was an empty walkway, but the busy murmurs of conversations could be heard without pause from every direction. There stood another door on the opposite end of the path. Sungchul flung that door open.

As soon as the door opened, an overwhelming stench of perfume that could paralyze the senses flooded his nose. Sungchul held his breath and looked around at the surroundings. He had arrived at a crossroads this time. Ahead were several pathways which were surrounded by glass walls. The sound of murmur which hung in the air of the walkway like a fog was now clear enough to be discerned.

"Hey, Good-lookin' Oppa. Come and play."

"Ten gold coins. Anything below ten gold coins could be worked out too!"

"It's the same, regardless of where you go, so just come into our shop!"

It was a commotion that was commonly heard in any marketplace. There was no change to Elijah's expression, but Sophia looked deeply disturbed. Sungchul's indifferent face looked toward the wall where the noises came from. Behind the cloudy window, there was a shadowy figure in the shape of a human whose eyes lit up in a reddish hue.

"Where's the Altar of Ten Thousand Demons?" Sungchul asked Elijah.

Elijah opened the book and nodded as he arrived at the answer. "At the top of the tower."

"Typical," responded Sungchul as he pressed forward.

After walking a few steps, a masked woman whose clothing barely covered the most important parts appeared. "Oh, my. How cute. It looks like we have a couple of new faces here."

Sophia, who noticed the woman's vulgar appearance, paled. "Orabuni! you can't look!"

She hurriedly rushed towards Elijah and covered his eyes. Sungchul, on the other hand, was glaring at the unfamiliar woman with the most unconcerned of expression. *Something that is neither a devil nor a human.*

The feet of the masked woman didn't touch the floor. She appeared to float like a balloon through some magical force.

"State your purpose," Sungchul demanded plainly.

The woman's rosy lips formed a curious smile beneath her mask. "Oh, my. A young man that doesn't even bat an eye at the sight of me? Maybe I'm not your type?"

"I said state your purpose." A hint of annoyance mixed in Sungchul's voice.

The woman licked her lips in disappointment at Sungchul's cold response and straightened her body once again. "I don't have any particular purpose. I just wanted to be the first to greet the new faces."

Then her eyes settled on Elijah. Elijah, whose eyes were still covered by Sophia's hands, had the Tome of the High Devils in his embrace. The woman's eyes revealed a strange light when she saw the book. "My, my. You've got the book."

The voice of the masked woman changed. "Hey, good-looking Oppa. That book... could I have a look?"

She drifted towards Elijah's direction and pushed her body towards him.

"Be gone! Perverse harlot!" Sophia drew her blade in revulsion. When she did so, the woman retreated with a mischievous smile on her face.

"My, my. A baby just weaned off of milk is trying to interfere? Do you want to die?" She flew back but quickly raised both of her manicured hands. As she did so, Walls of flame formed around Sungchul. The woman's coy voice could be heard beyond the flames.

"Hand over the book if you wish to preserve your life. Otherwise, you can burn with the book."

At that very moment, Sungchul jumped into the flames. He burst through the flames in an instant and stormed toward the masked woman standing behind them. The masked woman tried to recite another spell in the face of such unexpected behavior, but Sungchul's hand was faster. His hand gripped her neck.

"Kk-kuuu…" Her arms and legs, supple with beautiful youth, began to flail. When Sungchul began to assert a bit more strength, the woman's appearance started to change.

Sungchul firmly asked his question without releasing his grip, "Who are you?"

"I-I am…! Cough! Cough! A resident… of this tower!"

"Why do you covet the book?"

"I-I can become… a real De… Devil with it…!!"

"I see. This is the final question. Where is this place?"

The masked woman answered Sungchul through great pain, "This is… the Tower of Euphoria… It is the territory of the High Devil Miriadora…!"

Sungchul's interrogation ended here. He threw the masked woman towards a wall. Her body broke through one of the opaque windows and dispersed the shadowy figure behind it before she turned into smoke herself. A massive maggot with the head of a human wriggled in her place when the smoke dissipated. It was a disgusting life-form that conjured revulsion at the mere sight of it.

"It looks like this was the true form of that harlot." Sophia held her blade as she headed towards the direction of the wall. Fearsome hostility poured out of her eyes. Sungchul held her back.

"Leave it. Life itself is a punishment for their kind."

There were many different forms of immortality. The ideal form of immortality was to live eternally while retaining your original appearance, but that kind of lifespan was the privilege of those who have surpassed mortality. An inferior being, therefore, had no choice but to resort to repulsive and wretched dark magic which often resulted in a grotesque and freakish appearance. Sungchul immediately understood that this maggot-like creature was one such pitiful result of their experiments with immortality.

When he gained some more distance from the paths filled with opaque windows, he was able to see more residents of this tower. They each had overwhelmingly charismatic appearances. They were either handsome youths or voluptuous women, and they all attempted to entice Sungchul's party.

"Hey, miss. Do you want to play with me? We can just swap stories for a bit?"

"Little boy with the red book. You're totally my type! Do you want to have a meal together? Or maybe something else…?"

When Sungchul's group ignored them completely and pushed on, the crowd of beautiful women and handsome men continued their vulgar jokes and suggestive tirade. A set of stairs heading upwards could be seen as the group moved forward.

A space filled with the sensuous aroma of food appeared as the group entered the next floor. Sounds of wine glasses clinking, food being chewed, and meat being grilled could be heard behind each opaque window. There were chefs holding ladles and wearing comically tall chef hats.

"Now now! You'll be missing out if you don't have a taste! These are the greatest delicacies, and they can't be found anywhere in the human world!"

"Hey, there is a single empty table just waiting for you! It'll be perfect if you guys come over here!"

All the people here were fighting to attract Sungchul's group towards their shop. Sophia, who had had a completely hostile attitude towards the masked pervert, now appeared to have lowered her guard. More than anything, the Breggas siblings hadn't had a decent meal since they entered the Demon Realm. Their tension began to wear down as the tempting aroma of food enticed them in their already hungry state.

"Let's go and have a little taste." Sungchul pointed towards the barbecue of an entire baby pig on a spinning rotisserie.

"Sounds great!" the siblings exclaimed.

The chef, with a comically tall hat of about two meters, laughed as he held out a leg of the baby pig. Sungchul inserted the food into his mouth with a serious expression.

Gulp. The Breggas siblings could only swallow their drool, but Sungchul's face was not pleasant.

[The Score of this dish is…. 0 points.]

[It might not be a good idea to put another dish of this caliber before me unless you intend to insult me.]

The abysmal score and the threatening message that appeared before him weren't the only problems. As expected, there was a serious conundrum behind this dish.

This is human meat. They also flavored it with sorcery and narcotics, Sungchul thought and immediately spat out the meat from his mouth.

"Hey! You dare spit out my top dish made with my heart and soul?! You lowly peasant with no discerning taste!" The chef roared in anger and pulled out something from his possession. It was a large kitchen knife caked with blood and dried maggots. "I'll cook you up!"

"…"

Sungchul easily evaded the knife of the rushing chef and held his collar before shoving his face onto the spinning grill.

"Chiiiiiii-"

The chef began to struggle along with the sound of burning flesh and his tortured scream, but Sungchul's powerful grip did not allow for the chef to escape.

"Kwaaaaa!!"

The Breggas siblings watched on as the chef let out a howling scream and turned into a grotesque maggot. The mouth-watering baby pig on the rotisserie also transformed into a human thigh before their eyes.

"Claiming to be a chef after declaring such garbage as a 'dish'… Your arrogance knows no bounds." Sungchul threw the maggot chef onto a wall and let something peek out from beneath his coat. And once that happened the golden broach that was hidden underneath gave off a brilliant golden glow. That light was blinding to all the other chefs who were watching Sungchul and company.

"Oh…!!"

"Is that the symbol of a High-Grade Chef?!"

"It's real…! A real one has appeared!!"

The other chefs on the floor immediately recognized the broach with a single glance, unlike the Breggas siblings. They looked at Sungchul surprised as if they saw a monster and let out words of praises.

"You must be feeling good. Real good." Bertelgia bluntly spoke her feelings which Sungchul completely ignored as he said in a firm voice, "Let's go."

Following this floor, several different areas appeared. There were some floors filled with comfortable beds, and Sungchul's group could see people lying on the beds with a happy expression on their faces. It was a place that was filled with boredom and languor that made anyone have the desire to head to bed and close their eyes subconsciously.

Another floor was filled with people on racks being whipped and tortured through various instruments. It was a crazed region filled with the tortured and the torturers who were all enjoying themselves.

The final floor was one giant gambling hall. The ones gathered at the gambling hall were like residents of any other regions and both the men and women boasted absolute beauty, but all of them were missing one or more of their facial features like eyes, nose, or lips. Sungchul could see the reason why as he crossed through the floor. It was because they would gamble their body parts to win the coveted parts of others. There was no other form of currency that would instill these immortal maggots with a similar thrill of gambling.

261

Is this the world sought so dearly by these Devil Worshippers? At the very least, the faces of those reflected in Sungchul's eyes looked happy. It wasn't discernible whether all of this was a facade, but it was not something Sungchul concerned himself with.

"It looks like the Altar is beyond this door." The final set of stairs awaited Sungchul, and when he climbed it, a massive space opened up before him. There was something similar to a gigantic blob of flesh occupying the space.

"Hm? That is…?!" Bertelgia shook her body lightly. Sungchul looked at the massive piece of meat with disinterest. There was a faint trace of what appeared to be a face on this grotesquely swinging piece of meat.

"Welcome, guests. I don't think I've met any of you before?" The slab of meat spoke in a soft voice. It was a low voice, but it held enough weight to fill the surroundings.

"I am the owner of this tower. I am Miriadora."

The eyes embedded into the flesh of this meat discovered the red book in Elijah's grasp and continued, "So you've brought the book. If you understood the hidden meaning buried within the book and still wish to undertake it, open the book before me."

The Altar of Ten Thousand Demons that the book was referring to was this massive slab of meat that looked to weigh dozens of tons.

"I will warn you before you open the book before me. My quests are different from others where there are only rewards. This means there are consequences for failure as well," said the massive blob. It shook as its arms moved to raise its stomach folds. A single maggot with a human head was revealed to be pressed within the folds of its stomach. The maggot worked hard to crawl out of the folds of the stomach after which he smiled toward Sungchul's party.

"The Tome of the High Devils that you've brought is the entrance ticket to receive this quest! You all will have a single attempt at this opportunity, and for additional attempts, you'll have to bring another Tome of the High Devils here again."

262

The maggot blabbed on excitedly. Sungchul silently focused on the maggot's explanation.

"Lord Miriadora has a total of ten quests, and one of them is an objective. Upon completion of the objective, you all will receive the privilege to become a High Devil like Lord Miriadora. This does not mean that the other quests can be overlooked! The authority within the tower will vary depending on how many of the ten quests you are able to complete!"

The maggot then began to laugh hysterically while rolling on the floor for some mysterious reason. Sungchul brought up a question. "What happens if none of the quests are completed?"

The maggot formed an eerie smile as he answered. "You'll be turned into livestock without even achieving immortality."

"…"

"However, do not fret! You'll earn the privilege to become a resident of the Tower of Euphoria upon the completion of even a single quest!"

Sungchul had another question. "Will we receive the quests together?"

"Yes." The maggot nodded his head and continued saying, "It is also fine if you take it alone. That is if you want to turn the others into livestock."

As he heard this, he couldn't help but think, *It has been a while since I did a quest as a group.*

They weren't really reliable companions, but he turned toward Elijah and spoke in a composed voice. "Open the book."

***

When the book was opened, glittering letters appeared before Sungchul's party.

> [Path to Euphoria #1]
> Requirement – Exterminate the residents of the Tower of Idiocy.
> Reward – Strength 5, Magic Power 5, Citizenship (Tower of Euphoria), Additional Reward can be chosen.

As the group read through the message, the maggot beside Miriadora began to squirm as he shouted, "The Tower of Idiocy is the blue tower standing directly next to the Tower of Euphoria. There is a path directly from the Floor of Sloth, but I recommend you enter from the first floor! There are a lot of powerful Guardians overlooking the entrance on the fourth floor, you know?"

Sungchul's group started by retracing their path back down. The group passed through the floors filled with avarice and corruption before the desolation of the Demon Realm greeted them as they exited the tower. They had simply crossed through a single steel door, but it felt like a whole different world.

"…Are you perhaps trying to become a High Devil as well?" Elijah mustered up the courage to finally ask the question that was burning in his mind as he gazed at Sungchul's back.

Sungchul immediately shot back his reply, "I refuse to become such utter garbage."

"But then why…?" asked Elijah.

"I only need Magic Power."

"Magic?!"

Curiosity rose in Elijah and Sophia's eyes. *Why would such a powerful man require magic?*

Sungchul lifted his head to scan the blue tower standing next to the Tower of Euphoria. *I better finish this quickly.*

Sungchul turned his head slightly before asking a question. "I remember something about an additional reward. Do you know of its requirements?"

Elijah shuffled through the Tome of the High Devils and calmly replied to Sungchul's question, "Murder 10 or more residents, or kill the Supervisor. These appear to be the conditions for receiving the selectable rewards."

"A Supervisor…" Sungchul walked towards the tower. The bluish door of the tower was closed as tight as the Tower of Euphoria, but there was a faint cold light shining through the gap.

Sungchul stood before the doors and flung them open. A neatly decorated white and faint blue interior greeted him. The tower had a completely different atmosphere to that of the Tower of Euphoria.

Sungchul opened another door that stood in his path and a wide hallway filled with countless pillars appeared. The place was as still as death. Despite the sheer size of the open hall, not a single shadow of a person nor their movements could be seen. It felt like a space frozen in time.

Sungchul slowly looked around the hall and searched for where the residents of the tower might be. It didn't take long for something to capture his attention. A single motionless man sat on a square stone chair next to a pillar.

Sungchul and his group drew closer. Their footsteps were loud enough to echo throughout the entire hall, and soon Sungchul could see the resident of this tower up close. It was a man that had a beautiful appearance and an imposing presence similar to the residents of the previous tower. The only difference between the inhabitants of the two towers was that the man of this tower was lost in deep contemplation.

Sungchul stood before him and addressed him, "Hey."

The man's eyes narrowed as he lifted his head at Sungchul's calling. "You all look to be new here, but it is against the rules to speak within the Pallid Hall."

He appeared disgusted as though he had witnessed something that he would have rather avoided before rising from his seat to leave. Sungchul did not lay a hand on the man.

Something is off. Sungchul lifted his head to survey his surroundings. He could see that there were people spread sporadically throughout the hall. They were dressed in the same blue and white colors of the hall and sat motionlessly, like inanimate objects. They were all sitting on a chair deep in contemplation without any indication of what they were thinking so deeply about.

Sungchul prodded another for conversation, but was given the same response as the first. He was told multiple times that speaking was forbidden or that it was against the rules.

"What should we do now?" Elijah asked in a quiet voice.

At this point, Sungchul began to pull out the Demonic Weapon Cassandra from his Soul Storage. He abruptly pulled out the whip and began to strike the marble floor of the hall fiercely.

SHRRACK!

The sharp noises reverberated through the entire hall. The residents who were contemplating in their chairs began to turn towards Sungchul. All of them looked at him with scorn and repulsion, but not a single one of them moved to restrict him. Sungchul continued to strike the floor.

Several marble tiles became shattered, sending fragments into the air, with each strike that Sungchul's whip made across the floor. The continuous chain of bone-chilling sounds of impact filled the Hall.

Why is he doing this? Elijah and Sophia simply stared at each other with dumbstruck faces, but it didn't take long before Sophia caught something in the corner of her eyes. Three large, dark beings approached the opposite end of the hall.

What are those? Sophia's eyes grew wide. The huge dark figures turned out to be humans. The mere size of these figures reached three meters, and they had an impressive physique to match. They were wearing the mask of an executioner over their heads while holding a hangman's noose and a metallic rake of unknown purpose. Their breathing was heavy enough to be heard across the other side of the hall.

"Who is it? Who dares to breach the rules?" Bloodshot eyes flared intensely through the holes on the black masks. "It must be YOU!"

Sungchul finally stopped whipping once they appeared and glared at them.

"…"

The giant holding the steel rake pointed the rake towards Sungchul and began to shout, "I announce a summary trial for the grave crime of violating the holy and preeminent laws of the Tower of Order!"

As the Giant shouted, the other two Giants began to surround Sungchul's group. The Breggas siblings pulled out their weapons as the situation began to deteriorate, but Sungchul continued to simply glare at the Giants without any other particular movements.

Soon, the Giant in the center pointed toward Sungchul and shouted his sentence. "The sentence is… Death!"

The three Giants each threw out their hangman's noose at the same time. Each of them was aimed accurately at the necks of Sungchul and his company, but before the nooses managed to catch their necks, Cassandra tangled all three of the nooses with one sharp movement.

"You bastard!"

The Giants roared in anger as they pulled at their hangman's nooses. They each pulled on their rope with strength befitting their massive stature, but the whip and the man holding the whip didn't budge. When terror filled the bloodshot eyes hidden behind the masks, Sungchul lightly moved his arm. The Giants were flying in the air within the next moment. Sungchul's god-like strength had lifted them into the air, but it didn't end there. After lifting the Giants, he pulled his whip taut to cause them to slam onto the ground with full force.

BOOM!

The ground was struck with a tremendous force that caused the entire tower to tremble. It goes without saying that the fallen Giants did not move any further.

But what was most unusual was the reaction of the residents. They had witnessed an incredible scene unfolding before them, but the residents of the tower didn't show any sign of moving from their seats and simply looked onwards.

As expected. This is a strange place. Sungchul looked at the message that appeared before him with disinterest.

[Exemplary. You have gone beyond simply killing the dumb residents of the Blue Tower, and managed to take out their guard dogs.]

[Accordingly, you have been deemed worthy of S-grade rewards.]

Basic Rewards:
Strength: 5
Magic Power: 5
Citizenship (Tower of Euphoria)

Selective Rewards:
Certificate for Doctor Madd's Plastic Surgery
Certificate for Doctor Psykko's Gender Change
Meal Voucher for Chef Minamoto's restaurant

"..."

The optional rewards were all complete garbage, and he couldn't even receive one of the basic rewards.

[Your strength is exceedingly high, and thus a portion of the basic rewards cannot be received.]

All he managed to receive was 5 Magic Power and a citizenship with unknown purpose. Sungchul opted to choose none of the rewards, but Doctor Madd's certificate for plastic surgery was automatically given to him. On the other hand, the Breggas siblings seemed to have chosen the meal Voucher for Chef Minamoto's restaurant.

THUD.

A red identity tag dropped by Sungchul's feet. It appeared to be the citizenship in question. Sungchul held the tag and carefully studied it.

[Citizenship (Tower of Euphoria)]
Grade: Common – Mid grade
Type: Held Item
Effects: None
Note: It is possible to receive an eternal body when holding the citizenship before the Altar of Ten Thousand Demons. However, it must be noted that the current body is offered as a sacrifice and cannot be recovered.

It looks like a ticket to turn into those maggots, thought Sungchul and didn't hesitate to throw the citizenship to the ground and crush it with his military boots.

Elijah carefully opened his mouth to speak. "Excuse me. I have something to tell you."

Sungchul turned slightly to respond. "Speak."

"The second quest has been revealed in the book." Elijah opened the Tome of the High Devils in front of Sungchul. Another message appeared before Sungchul's eyes.

[The Path to Euphoria #2]
Proof – Break one of the scales that can be found anywhere on the second floor.
Reward – Magic Resistance 10, Intuition 10, Standard Body, Additional Reward can be chosen.

Sungchul who had watched until here realized that his expectation was proving to be correct. *This quest. There is something more to this.*

It wasn't explicitly written anywhere, but Sungchul believed that the Tower of Euphoria, the tower he first stepped into, had a hostile relationship to the blue tower where he currently stood. More than anything, it was strongly implied within the contents of the quest itself.

Let's just go along with it for now, Sungchul thought, as he continued toward the second floor.

The second floor of the blue tower was a space filled entirely of pure white. The walls, the floors, the ceilings, and even the decorations attached to each surface were entirely white. Sungchul who felt his eyes beginning to strain pulled something from his Soul Storage. An item brought over from the Modern World. It was an old and faded pair of sunglasses.

Bertelgia saw the item and shook her body to ask a question. "What's with the colored glasses?"

"It's an item called sunglasses," answered Sungchul.

It was an item given by an old friend that had become a Returnee. He had said that he was a bus driver with 20 years of experience without a single accident on his record before he was brought over to the Other World. He had a problem with his temper, but more importantly, he had been rather kind-hearted and dependable. Sungchul continued to walk forward while reminiscing about his old friend.

A door appeared not before long.

When he went through the door, a large space similar to a courtroom appeared. In this courtroom, there were Giants lined up along the judge's stand whose end could only be seen through straining your neck, and there was a haggard human sitting on a plain chair beneath them. The judges looked down at the accused with magnanimous expressions and spoke. "According to article number 284 of Sharique Law… the accused is sentenced to be executed."

The moment the words were spoken, the gigantic executioners put a noose around the haggard human and began to spin it around. The accused that was being spun around like a tied balloon lost consciousness before reverting to his maggot form. The executioners pierced the maggot through with their metal rakes and disappeared somewhere.

Soon, another accused was sitting on the plain chair. The judges spoke again in their magnanimous voice. "According to article 53 of Sharique Law… the accused is sentenced to be executed."

The same scene began to replay itself. The executioners put nooses around the neck of the accused and stuck the now-maggot corpse with the rakes before disappearing from sight.

There were a lot of insane things gathered at the Tower of Euphoria, but this place also seems to be on a similar level, thought Sungchul as he observed the court session. He discovered an object shining in a golden light on top of the judge's stand. It was a pair of scales. Sungchul suddenly held a hammer in his grip. He addressed the judge's stand that was high up in the air.

"According to Article 1 of Sungchul's Law… I'm going to break everything here."

***

Sungchul's hammer swung towards the Judges' stand.
BOOM!
The stand was smashed to pieces following a powerful sound of impact. The judges sitting on the stand fell onto the floor along with a shower of splinters.

"Get that bastard!"

The executioners swung their noose as they rushed towards Sungchul, but they just weren't able to keep up with him.

BAM! BAM! BAM!

With every refreshing sound of impact, an executioner slumped to the ground like a frog struck by lightning as their heads were smashed to pieces. The slaughter didn't take long, and the entire courtroom was completely overtaken after a single minute.

A dense Book of Laws that had fallen beside Sungchul's feet was opened up to the middle. The pages were filled to the brim with articles of law written in tiny letters, and Sungchul chose a few of them to read.

[Section 234: Those that aren't sincere in their contemplation will be put to death.]

[Section 235: Those who do not diligently fulfill the assigned roles in the tower will be executed.]

[Section 236: Those that graffiti the walls will be put to death.]

There were countless references to questionable crimes listed within the Book of Laws, and every punishment was death without exception. There was no classification, standard, or fundamental basis.

Sungchul gazed towards a judge that was groaning on the floor.

"Krrrrr…"

There was no longer any trace of the magnanimous of expression he had been wearing, leaving behind only a hideous face filled with nothing but stubbornness and sadism. The scale was lying on the floor before the judge. Sungchul stood in front of the scale before turning around for a question. "What was the requirement for the optional reward?"

Elijah frantically scoured through the book upon Sungchul's question and made his reply. "It's to kill a judge."

"I see."

Sungchul's hammer rose towards the sky. It was then when the judge began to shout with a pitiful voice, "Mercy!"

"…"

Sungchul granted as much mercy as they did towards their accused. Spurts of blood spilled on his military boots, and Sungchul checked the messages that appeared before him.

[Amazing! You have taken care of the repulsive pigs while smashing the idiots' annoying symbol of justice.]

[You have been deemed worthy of S-grade rewards.]

Basic Reward:
Magic Resistance 10
Intuition 10
Basic Flesh Ticket x1

Selective Reward:
Ticket for Heaven Service from the Peerless Beauty, Su
Ticket for Fantastic Service from Peerless Host, Pu
Coin for Crimson Dragon Gambling Den x100 Gil

"…"

The optional rewards for this quest were garbage as well. Sungchul wondered whether or not he should seek any more optional rewards. But he chose to pick one this time instead of letting it default. He picked the third reward, the coins for the gambling den; it seemed more useful than the worthless service tickets.

The Basic Flesh Ticket appeared to be redeemable certificates which allowed the residents to hide their original maggot forms behind a beautiful facade. As he wasn't a human maggot that lived within these towers, Sungchul had no use for it.

"What's the next quest?" Sungchul asked as he grabbed the bluish coins that had fallen to the floor.

Elijah appeared to have gotten used to the pace of things and had an answer prepared before Sungchul asked his question. He revealed a new page to Sungchul.

> [Path to Euphoria #3]
> Proof – Tear or burn down the collection of 20 books located on the third floor of the tower of idiots.
> Reward – Intuition 10, Magic Power – 10, Ideal Citizenship (Tower of Euphoria), Additional Reward can be chosen.

Sungchul nodded his head in acknowledgement. *As expected. This quest as well. It's a struggle between factions.*

If Sungchul was accurate in his guess, this blue tower would also have another High Devil at the top floor similar to the tower with the High Devil Miriadora as a fight could only happen when both parties were on equal footing. Sungchul's group continued on to the third floor.

Like the Tower of Euphoria which was filled with different sorts of mental patients on each floor, this tower of idiots, or rather the Tower of Order, had different humanoid monsters partaking in all sorts of eccentricities. The only difference was that unlike the Tower of Euphoria where the residents sought to satisfy basic urges, the Tower of Order advocated strange beliefs like "knowledge is absolute," or discipline.

Sungchul took a different approach and began to complete the quest in quick succession. He burned away the books with Glare as soon as he saw the library where they were kept and even killed the librarian with a single blow from Fal Garaz for the optional rewards. When he finished the sixth quest, only the final mission was left for Sungchul's party.

> [Path to Euphoria #Final]
> Kill Karak Sharique, the King of Idiots.
> Rewards – Strength 30, Vitality 30, Dexterity 30, Skull of Modification (Epic)

Sungchul looked at the tome that Elijah held for him with indifference.

"..."

The rewards weren't all that enticing, especially the stat gains that were completely useless. Sungchul wasn't sure what the Skull of Modification was, but it didn't look like something he should care about.

"What do you plan on doing now?" Elijah carefully asked Sungchul.

Sungchul began to climb the stairs to the final floor in response. "We go to meet the owner of this tower."

The final floor was a massive parliament. There were countless judges and executioners sitting in their designated seats, and there was a gigantic devil with the face of a fly in a similarly large seat of power in the center.

"I welcome you to this place, intruder." The High Devil opened both his arms in greeting as he spoke. There were countless maggots squirming below his throne, and they were squirming to eat the skin flakes that fell off his body.

Sungchul took off his sunglasses, slung Fal Garaz onto his shoulder, and moved forward. Elijah felt his heart beating with excitement.

My God... so something like this could also happen. I thought we'd just die without resistance when we met the Enemy of the World... Instead, I managed to get amazing boosts to my stats and an opportunity to become a High Devil, thanks to him...

The martial prowess of the one called the Enemy of the World was absolute. His own father, Martin Breggas, could not compare. The Enemy of the World was more powerful and oppressive than the rumors suggested, and he was truly a man that couldn't be opposed. It now made sense to Elijah why every nation feared him so, and now that very person was standing before the leader of the Tower of Order. Elijah expected for Sungchul to fight the High Devil with the legendary Fal Garaz. It wasn't clear to him who would win, but Elijah would jump in and help Sungchul for the sake of victory.

However, Sungchul stood before the massive fly king and didn't show any further movement; instead, he looked up and spoke to the High Devil. "Do you know who I am?"

The master of the Tower of Order, Karak Sharique, shook his head as he answered, "I do not know of you, intruder."

Sungchul held up his hammer. But this object of fear of all demons within the Demon Realm did not seem to interest this High Devil at all. Instead, the devil clucked with laughter and simply spoke his mind. "Though if you managed to get this far in spite of being just an insignificant human, then you must be someone with skill. Are you a Warchief of a country? Or perhaps the holder of the Hero title?"

It looked as though this devil had no clue who Sungchul was. Sungchul then asked another question, "You are not very close to the other Devils, are you?"

"Of course, I couldn't get close. I might have become a High Devil, but I was formerly a human. Devils are quite the bigoted race despite their appearance."

"I see."

This explained why this High Devil did not fear Sungchul. The Devil Worshippers that lived beyond the Fog Sea had formed their own area, secluded from the rest of the world.

Why are they talking so much? Can't he just kill him already? As Sungchul and the High Devil's conversation prattled on, Elijah began to feel restless. He wanted Sungchul to immediately exterminate the High Devil and complete the mission, but not everything always went as planned. Sungchul put the hammer into his Soul Storage. It meant that he had no intention to fight.

A shallow sigh leaked out from Elijah's lips. Sophia simply continued to protect this restless boy's rear.

"Do you perhaps know why I've come here?" Sungchul asked the High Devil.

Karak haughtily nodded his head. "Were you sent by the owner of that animal pen? It appears that the book held by that human behind you is his."

Sungchul's eyes lit up as he asked, "Then do you have a book as well?"

"A book?"

"That's right. I'm asking if there is a Tome of High Devils that you've created."

The tome held by Elijah had the designation of being the seventh volume. Sungchul hadn't been able to figure out what that meant when he first noticed it, but he pieced together the obvious conclusion about the significance of this number as he continued the petty quests and met the people working for the High Devils. He speculated that it meant that there were several volumes of the Tome of High Devils, with each written by the High Devils that lived at the top of the eight towers.

The devil with a fly's head began to cluck with laughter and pointed his razor-sharp fingernail towards Sungchul. A magic formation formed at the tip of this fingernail which caused a book wrapped with blue leather to appear. It then floated towards Sungchul and landed in his hands. Sungchul stared piercingly at this new book.

[Tome of the High Devils: Volume 3]

Grade: Epic

Type: Equipment – Book

Effect: Dexterity 20, Intuition 20 upon equip

Note: Those who wish to obtain the power of the High Devil must open the tome before The Altar of Ten Thousand Demons.

Restriction: Mage Related Class

His suspicions were confirmed. The stats raised were different, but the capabilities matched with the red book held by Elijah Breggas.

"What an unpredictable one. To offer to complete my quests while in the midst of performing the quests of another High Devil."

It wasn't clear what was so funny, but the High Devil could not stop laughing. As he laughed, the countless executioners and judges mechanically laughed along. The chilling sounds of their laughter swept through the entire room.

Elijah felt extreme fear seeping in his mind. The realization that the goal he desired had been lost had left him in a desperate state already, but this unnerving laughter had driven him past his limits. He was now on the floor clutching the sides of his head. Sophia whose will was comparatively intact approached Elijah with concern on her face. "Brother."

It was then that a blue book flew towards her. Sungchul had thrown it at her. She managed to catch the book out of reflex and then glared at Sungchul with a hint of resentment.

Sungchul simply looked at her with his usual disinterest and commanded her with a single sentence. "Open the book."

"..."

It didn't sit well with her, but she couldn't refuse him. She let out a sigh before opening the book in front of the Altar of Ten Thousand Demons. A faint smile rose on Sungchul's face as another quest message appeared before his eyes. *This coven of devil worshippers might be another gold mine like the Summoning Palace.*

Sungchul had come to this place with low expectations. But despite the slim chance for gains, the result was better than he could have ever imagined. The key to rapid growth that he had been searching for was hidden here all along.

I'm not sure how many High Devils reside in this region, but I hope that all of them hate each other. Sungchul smiled to himself as the group descended the stairs of the blue tower. He decided to drain this place of every opportunity before leaving.

An emboldened Sungchul acted without restraint. He performed each quest Sophia revealed to him faithfully as he entered the Tower of Euphoria once again. He killed the pimp of the first floor, massacred the chefs of the second floor, and smashed every bed on the third floor. Similar scenes of destruction unfolded on every other floor, and Sungchul's party collected as many stats as the Tome of the High Devils gave. Sungchul finally checked his stats as he approached the final set of stairs for the top floor of the Tower of Euphoria.

[Stats]			
Strength	999+	Dexterity	853
Vitality	801	Magic Power	388
Intuition	375	Magic Resist	622

His eyes lit up. *Looks like I managed to raise Magic Power by a bit more than 30 here.*

However, Sungchul was still very thirsty for more.

Chapter 13 – The Abandoned

The eight towers within the land of the devil worshippers.

At the top of each tower, a human that had managed to evolve into a High Devil reigned. Every tower contained a small world in itself with different colors and personalities decided by the characteristics of the High Devil that ruled over the tower.

Decadence, order, vanity, flamboyance, etc. Their personalities and their conduct were vastly different, and it was difficult to place them into a single category. Each High Devil had its own nemesis, and they had created the Tomes of the High Devils in order to inconvenience their enemies or eliminate them outright (although the chances of the latter were quite slim).

Sungchul planned to get his hands on all eight volumes of the Tome of the High Devils. He had managed to get his hands on four of them in a single day, and he cleared all of the quests except the final mission at the end. Ordinary people easily lost track of time in the Demon Realm where the sun couldn't be seen, but Sungchul had an incredibly meticulous alarm: his stomach.

It was his principle to eat at every appetite. Sungchul who considered everyday diligence to be the highest of virtues, placed importance on rest as highly as progress. He set up camp on top of the hill overlooking the eight towers once he had completed his rounds of the four towers. Of course, the Breggas siblings acted along with him.

CRACKLE CRACKLE.

The campfire set up by Sungchul spit red ashes as it burned while the siblings sat in silence. Sungchul had disappeared off to somewhere and was yet to return. Sophia was the first to speak in this heavy silence.

"Brother. Are you ok?"

Her eyes were filled with deep concern. They were able to obtain an unbelievable amount of status points while traveling with the being called the Enemy of the World, but it was no different from being with a beast; no one could predict when the beast might suddenly get loose. He could suddenly feel dissatisfied and harm them, or demand something horrible of them. And, above all else, wasn't Sungchul a healthy male?

It must have been a while since that man interacted with a female.

She didn't want to imagine it, but fear was growing in her mind like a poisonous mushroom.

What if that man demands my body... what do I do then? In front of my brother... If I were to suffer such actions... I couldn't bear to live with such a body!

The mind is prone to distractions when the body is relaxed.

"It's ok, Sophia."

On the other hand, Elijah was struggling with a different issue.

The Enemy of the World... what is he thinking? Why is he forfeiting the opportunity to become a High Devil right at the cusp and only doing these lowly quests?

The increase in stats was worth celebrating. Elijah was often told that he was a late bloomer among the youth, but in a single day he achieved a great deal of progress. However, he had his sights on a much higher goal.

High Devil.

Elijah idolized the strength of Devils that transcended humans, but Sungchul didn't seem to have any intentions of joining him. He would have to see how things progressed for a bit longer, but it seemed like the man was more interested in the tomes than the High Devils.

CRACKLE CRACKLE.

The withered firewood gradually burned through and settled at the bottom. Elijah grabbed a dry branch from the pile beside him and used it to stir the stack of firewood before unintentionally swallowing loudly.

If that man doesn't take care of the High Devils, what should I do then? Do I have to face the High Devils on my own?

However, he didn't have the confidence to do so. The High Devils that he had seen personally were overwhelmingly oppressive, and he saw no path to victory. His struggle grew deeper within the silence. Soon, footsteps could be heard from nearby.

CRUNCH

The sound of military boots that was now so familiar. Sungchul was approaching. He was carrying something large on his back.

THUD.

He placed the object on the ground. It was some form of cow with long fur. The creature looked young, but its size was quite impressive. Sungchul pulled out a blade and began to butcher the cow without a word.

"Excuse me, but... are you preparing to cook?" Sophia carefully asked a question.

"..."

Sungchul looked back at her with sharp eyes as he nodded.

"If it's food, how about we consider eating over at the Tower of Euphoria? I have a meal ticket from a quest," said Sophia as she held out the meal ticket to Chef Minamoto's that she had received as an additional reward.

"Do you see a farm anywhere?" asked Sungchul.

This simple question caused Sophia to look around her surroundings carefully. Forget a farm, she couldn't see any sign of a single field anywhere. She shook her head.

"Where do you think the ingredients to feed that huge number of people comes from? If you still want to eat over there despite this knowledge, I won't stop you," said Sungchul and continued to prepare the meal.

The Breggas siblings looked over at Sungchul with complicated emotions. Sophia's eyes were filled with admiration.

Even his swordsmanship isn't average.

She practiced both sword and magic, but as her knowledge of the sword was greater than her actual skill, she could clearly see how proficient Sungchul was with his blade. There were no excess movements in his handling of the blade. A significant portion of the cow's carcass was removed with each movement of his sword, and it was disassembled in an instant and prepared.

Sungchul grabbed a portion of the cut meat as the blood dripped off and began to sniff it. "Mmm... the meat isn't very good."

It was quite savory, but there was a slight smell and was also a bit tough to chew. Sungchul grabbed a flat rock from his surroundings and started to mince the meat on top of it with a knife. As he began to chop at a rapid pace, Bertelgia, who was inside his pocket, became a hindrance to his movement.

"Come out," said Sungchul and pulled her out.

"No! I hate being seen by some strange kids!" Bertelgia struggled to stay in his pocket, but she couldn't overcome Sungchul's strength. She was eventually pulled out, and she began to flap herself into the air. Elijah and Sophia looked towards Bertelgia with surprise.

"A living book?" Sophia asked as she watched with curiosity.

"Is this your first time seeing a living book?" Bertelgia, whose mood was soured, shot back sharply.

On the other hand, Sungchul pulled out a secret ingredient from his Soul Storage. The cooking container with dried mushrooms, vegetables, pepper, and various herbs appeared before him. Sungchul mixed the ingredients from the container with the minced meat and continued chopping with his knife.

Elijah turned his gaze towards Sungchul's direction. Elijah, who had been sighing relentlessly, grew visibly brighter as he noticed Sungchul cooking. He hadn't had a proper meal in a while and recalled his previous experience with Sungchul's food; involuntarily, he began to look forward to the result.

Che...! Sophia who was watching this scene rose from her seat and approached Sungchul from behind.

"Um..."

"What is it?" asked Sungchul.

"Could I... help you?"

Sophia had made a once-in-a-lifetime decision before making her request, but Sungchul's response was callous.

"I'll decline."

He refused it point-blank. *I might as well starve before I leave any of the cooking to you.*

However, Sophia was not one to give up easily. She feared Sungchul, but she stood her ground and asked once more, "I'll help just a little bit, since we are eating as well."

At this point, Sungchul tore off a portion of the meat he had been mincing and handed it to Sophia. "Prepare your portion yourself then."

It was not her ideal resolution, but Sophia received the meat politely with both hands and celebrated in her mind.

Great. The time has come to show Brother my cooking skills!

Unfortunately, she didn't notice it. She didn't notice Elijah's eyes twitch in fear.

Sophia discerned that the dish Sungchul was preparing was a form of a Hamburg steak. The preparation of the ingredients and most of the cooking had already passed through Sungchul's hands, and she only had to mince the meat a bit further and grill it.

The mincing wasn't difficult, but the problem was in the grilling. It was difficult to find appropriate cooking tools out here. It took Sophia considerable amount of creativity to prepare an adequate cooking utensil. She noticed a branch rolling on the ground.

It'll be fine if I just stick this stick through the meat like a bone and grill the surface, right?

She looked over her shoulders at Sungchul who she considered her rival. He was still mincing the meat. It was almost a stupid level of persistence. Sophia reminded herself that the greatest spice was hunger and began to put her idea into action.

She washed a branch with an appropriate thickness and stuck the minced meat into its center, but the meat didn't stick properly. Perhaps it had lost viscosity as a result of being minced, but even when it was rolled into a ball it would fall apart constantly. She had to borrow the power of magic in the end.

Sophia, who had studied the art of Cryomancy, conjured an air of frost from her hand and succeeded in freezing the meat solid onto the stick.

"…That woman. What is she doing?" Bertelgia who had been kicked out of Sungchul's pocket was wandering the area, and she began to mutter to herself when she noticed Sophia's antics. Sophia was grilling the frozen meat, as it was, by placing it onto the cooking station attached to the campfire, but it was doubtful if the frozen meat could cook properly.

For a moment, the completely frozen meat seemed to withstand the heat pretty well until it suddenly and rapidly burnt up, transforming into a black piece of coal that gave off a black smoke. A plume of black smoke rose from the fire.

Sophia vaguely recognized that there was something wrong, but didn't take it seriously. She pulled out the black mass that was the source of the smoke from the fire, but the branch that had held the meat also suddenly caught fire. She quickly froze the meat, put out the fire, and served the frozen black mass to Elijah.

"Brother, you must have been starving? Eat up. It's been a while since I've last showed off my skills."

"…"

Elijah's face looked relaxed, but his mind wasn't. *Please… help me. I really don't want to eat… that thing!*

His personality did not allow him to say words that might upset his sister and was in turn bringing him unspeakable suffering. His gaze passed over Sophia and landed on Sungchul. Sungchul was throwing a fist-sized rock with a flat surface into the fire, but as he was doing so, he took a peek over at Elijah and Sophia.

"What's that? Is that edible?" Sungchul asked bluntly.

"Of course… it's edible." Sophia showed a bit of dissatisfaction, but Sungchul noticed that Elijah was backed into a corner, so he walked over towards them with a small sigh.

"Why don't you try eating it? That thing that you've made."

"What did you… say?"

"Just try it. That food you made yourself."

She would have normally ignored it, but her current opponent was the legendary villain that held the ultimate authority over life and death known as the Enemy of the World.

Sophia turned her eyes towards the food that she had made. The burnt lump that could not be called food was in her hands.

"It'll… be delicious?"

Sophia already realized her mistake. She already knew that the food she prepared herself was something that shouldn't be eaten.

Sungchul quickly lifted the flat stone with the minced meat and carried it closer to the fire. The meat was stacked up like a mountain peak. Sungchul split that meat into three parts and split it equally between himself and the Breggas sibling. Sophia who watched him do so spoke coldly. "You surely don't expect us to eat raw meat?"

Sophia may have thrown aside the dish she had prepared, but she still had an excuse left. *I burned it because I lacked the proper cooking tools. Could you really do any better?*

At her question, Sungchul's sword made swift movements. On his blade was placed the small and flat rock that had been previously thrown into the fire. He placed the steaming rock in front of them, and using the dagger, he placed the minced meat lightly on the rock as if it were butter.

SIZZLE

The minced meat miraculously began to cook with a savory sound. The rock that had soaked the campfire's heat acted like a frying pan. They had no sauce, and only minimal ingredients were used, but the moment that the grilled meat entered their mouths, an extraordinary flavor danced around their tongues.

"Mmm." Sungchul, who was the first to enjoy the meat, closed his eyes and savored the flavor.

[The score of the dish is… 68 points!]

He would have been able to receive a much higher score if he had additional materials like sauces or spices, but even this was not a score that an ordinary cook could obtain.

"…!!" A quiet exclamation escaped from Elijah's lips. The dish had tremendous flavor.

"!!" Sophia also felt shocked. *It was the same meat, but the flavor is this different?!*

She felt frustrated, but she couldn't stop eating.

Sungchul watched the Breggas siblings voraciously devour their meal. He felt his dignity as a chef slowly being recharged. Even if it was a momentary solace.

A familiar scene entered in his mind. It was that of a girl dressed like a vagrant. This child had abruptly approached him and had brought up the name of the woman that he had long since forgotten. Sungchul was caught up in conflicting emotions as he watched the girl hungrily eat up the food that a servant brought up. This was in Sungchul's glory days.

It was a time when Sungchul was spreading his name throughout the land as the Tenth Champion of the Continent and the newly appointed Commander-in-Chief of the newly formed Human Empire, bringing order on the continent that was becoming weakened by depravity.

But on the other hand, it was also the depressing period of time when he was feeling the insidious effects of internal power struggle that spread like an infection from within the empire. He had been quietly preparing to return to the original world along with his comrades, but the appearance of this child completely turned his life around.

"…"

Sungchul's reverie was interrupted by rustling noises in the background.

"Come out." A low, but heavy sound left his lips. The Breggas siblings that were completely occupied with eating looked surprised and began to search their surroundings. A dark figure revealed himself to Sungchul's party through the fog within this heavy silence. They had seen this figure before. It was the human that was lingering around the tower of the devil worshippers doing heavy labor.

The man was wearing black clothes like an undertaker and had his pitiful face covered with a bandana as he carefully walked over to Sungchul and spoke with a hideous voice. "Kekeke... Don't misunderstand. I am no enemy. I simply came over with a proposition."

"A proposition?" When Sungchul responded with disinterest, a grotesque smile formed around the man's twisted lips underneath his bandana.

"Do you wish to kill the High Devils? If so, I might have some information to share."

***

"Get lost," Sungchul retorted coldly.

The humanoid creature was suppressed by Sungchul's oppressive aura and backed off without another word. It seemed like the brief meeting with the creature might come to a close without any further development, but this was not the end of it.

"..."

Elijah had stopped eating his meal as he couldn't take his eyes off the creature. Sungchul had noticed this, but he didn't mention it.

—

The next day, Sungchul prepared to attack the final four towers. However, just as they were about to depart, Elijah appeared to be in intense pain. Sungchul had expected something like this, but he didn't quite expect Elijah Breggas, the son of a famous figure, to go as far as forsaking his own dignity. Unfortunately, he made the wrong choice. Sungchul already knew what becoming a Devil truly meant and had seen the end result of such a transformation with his own two eyes, but he also knew that nothing would change even if he said something.

"…"

He could physically restrain him, but he wasn't obligated to go that far for the boy. Sungchul chose to take the most indirect method for those reasons.

"I need an attendant to hold the book. I don't want to flip through the pages tediously. If you need medication to numb the pain, I can give you some."

When Sungchul said as such, Elijah turned towards Sophia without hesitation. "Sophia. I'm sorry, but you'll have to go in my stead."

"Brother!" Sophia was shaken, but she also understood the resolve in Elijah's eyes and nodded weakly.

"Hand over all of the Tomes of the High Devils to the girl." Sungchul silently moved forward.

Elijah obediently handed over every tome that he held to Sophia.

"Don't be concerned for me," Elijah reassured her as he handed the books over.

He said as such, but there was no way that she wouldn't be worried about him. This may be the territory of the devil worshippers, but it was still within the Demon Realm where demons roamed freely. Sophia looked towards Elijah with eyes full of concern as she thought about what to say, but she didn't know what she should be saying in this situation. Soon, Sungchul's stern voice could be heard from the front. "What's taking so long?"

In the end, Sophia simply lowered her head and moved to follow Sungchul. She turned back as she walked behind Sungchul. However, Elijah was not looking at her. The place he was looking at was the tower where the humanoid creature worked as a laborer. Sophia continued to look towards Elijah until his figure disappeared from her sight, but Elijah did not look in her direction even once.

"…"

Her heart quivered, but she didn't show weakness. Instead, she bit down on her lower lip and turned to look towards Sungchul's back who had flung open the doors of a new tower as she thought, *You knew that it was going to be like this.*

It was only recently that Sophia was able to use the Breggas family name. Elijah and Sophia were from different mothers. In contrast to Elijah's mother who was the esteemed daughter of an influential family, Sophia's mother was a country bumpkin that lived on a farm scooping cow manure. To Sophia, who had lived with the scar of illegitimacy since birth, her childhood was pitiful. It was none other than Elijah who had brought the light of salvation to this little girl. To Sophia, Elijah was far more than simply her brother. She was prepared to give up anything for her brother, even her meager life.

"…Becoming a Devil…"

The man who was leading her down an unfamiliar hallway finally opened his mouth. Sophia, who had been temporarily preoccupied with her thoughts, snapped to attention and gazed towards the back of the man with the fluttering ragged coat.

"It's essentially the same as throwing oneself away."

"…?!" Sophia's eyes grew wide. *Why is this person saying such things?*

Sungchul continued to speak, "The physique of a Devil is different than the physique of a man. If the human body is like the surface of a lake lightly stirring with the wind, then the body of a Devil is like a sea forever burning in the endless flames of compulsion."

"I'm sorry, but I don't understand what you're talking about." Sophia politely tried to push back, but Sungchul did not stop talking.

"Inside the body of a Devil, the mind of a human won't last even a year before turning to ash."

"…"

She already knew that the man was never one to speak empty words, and she knew what it was he was trying to tell her. She quickly regained her cool before turning to Sungchul with frosty words. "If we don't get stronger, we'll die. Martin Breggas. You have no idea how cruel and twisted the man really is."

"You probably won't die. If you give up everything, that is." Sungchul abruptly stopped walking and turned around. He pointed a finger towards himself.

"At least I'm still alive."

"But you're strong." Sophia spoke in protest, but Sungchul only let out a bitter laugh.

"I wasn't strong from the start. When I first became the Enemy of the World, there were ten people on the continent who were more powerful than me... no, over thirty including those that are not so well known."

"..."

Sophia shut her mouth and didn't speak any further. She knew the kind of manpower that was deployed to deal with Sungchul.

Fighting him required at minimum an Armada. Or perhaps the highest class of Assassins from the Assassin's guild. It was completely on a different scale from the Breggas siblings, who could be taken care of by a few second-rate Assassins.

"If you throw away the Breggas name and live in seclusion, Martin Breggas will not pursue you any further."

Sungchul said it. His words were all true. The reason why Martin was seeking to murder his own son and daughter was to allow for the child of the woman he loved to inherit everything.

"...It's better to die than to live without a name like savages." Sophia finally changed her words. Elijah likely felt the same as well.

"..."

Sungchul closed his mouth once again and proceeded to follow the tower's stairs to the top. He did not utter another word while they climbed the stairs, but when he arrived before the High Devil on the top floor, he spoke.

"Here is a demon who was originally a human. You must have seen it several times already, but this should serve as a suitable example."

What awaited Sungchul's party at the top floor of the green tower was the figure of a giant devil with iron nails embedded all over his body causing blood and pus to pour from the innumerous wounds. Sophia almost fainted because of the devil's ghoulish appearance and its even more disgusting stench, while Sungchul stood before it confidently and attempted another bargain. He appeared to be unfazed by anything.

As they descended the tower, Sophia recalled the words Sungchul had spoken to her over and over again in her mind. *Brother is going to become a monster like that? That can't happen. It can't.*

However, when she saw another High Devil residing in another tower, her mind lost the balance which had already begun to shake, and it began to develop more and more doubt. She searched for Elijah as soon as they exited the sixth tower after finishing all of its quests, but she could no longer see him hunched over beneath the blue tower. The creature that had been working below the tower was also nowhere to be found.

Could it be? Did brother already begin to act?

Sophia felt her mind growing restless and looked visibly anxious. Sungchul continued to press forward through the unnerving silence. "We're moving to the next tower."

"Excuse me…" Sophia mustered up some courage.

Sungchul turned toward her.

"I cannot see Elijah anymore."

Sungchul pointed to a location veiled by thick fog upon her words. Surprisingly, there was a shape of a human at the spot Sungchul had pointed to. It was Elijah. Sophia felt a single tear welling in her eye as she attempted to run toward that location.

"Where are you going?" Sungchul callously stopped her.

"I'm sorry, but I just want to check up on him," said Sophia and immediately ran towards Elijah while Sungchul continued to look indifferently toward that place.

Bertelgia crawled out of his pocket and spoke some rather cold words. "Hm. Do I smell the familiar scent of tragedy? Is it perhaps your hobby to enjoy these kinds of situations?"

"Why do you think that?" asked Sungchul.

"If it was me, I might have stopped them physically or something. But, you always seem to just leave people to make their bad choices."

"Choices have to be made on their own. The consequences of those choices are also on them as well. I do not have a reason, the right, or the obligation to convince them otherwise."

Sophia ran over to Elijah in a sprint. Elijah was digging the ground, and she could see several piles of dirt all around.

"Brother," Sophia called out to him.

"Oh, Sophia. You've come." Elijah put down the shovel to warmly greet his sister. There were tiny beads of sweat on his brow, but he looked quite elated.

"Listen, Sophia. That monster from before made quite a suggestion." He revealed a dark marble that he had dug from the ground to her.

"What is this?" asked Sophia.

It looked like a plain marble.

"It is a sealing orb capable of binding the power of a High Devil. This one is black since it's already been used, but I was told that an unused one would be colorless. If I find that, then getting rid of a High Devil would be as easy as twisting the arms of a child."

Elijah peeked over at Sungchul who stood tall on a plateau beyond the fog and spoke in a low voice. "What do you think about the Enemy of the World?"

"Well, he's no different than before." She tried to speak normally to the best of her abilities, but her eyes were trembling. Sungchul's words and the image of the hideous High Devils were swirling in her mind. Fortunately, Elijah didn't seem to notice in all of his excitement. He continued to speak to her in a hushed voice.

"Do you have any of the tomes?"

"Tomes?"

"I'm talking about the Tomes of the High Devils."

"Yes. We managed to gather about six volumes. That man is probably looking to gather the final two."

"That's good. Can you lend me just one? That... red one. The red one looks good."

"But if the Enemy of the World notices..." Sophia let her words trail as she lowered her head, but there was not a single hint of fear on Elijah's face. He was making a once-in-a-lifetime gamble. Although he was filled with flaws, the blood of Martin Breggas who could calmly face death flowed in his veins.

"It's fine. Aren't you going to leave it all in the Soul Storage anyways? It's enough with just one volume, so don't worry about it. It won't take long. I'll finish it before that guy notices."

"..."

Sophia felt conflicted, but she eventually relented. She covertly handed him the red Tome of the High Devils, but the moment she handed the book over, Sungchul's words and the image of the hideous High Devils reappeared in her mind.

"Um, Brother."

Before Elijah managed to take the book from her, Sophia's hand gripped the tome tightly.

"What is it suddenly, Sophia?" Elijah asked in confusion.

"Do we really need to become a High Devil?"

"What are you talking about? Isn't that the whole reason why we came here? Even at the cost of our friends' lives?"

"But... becoming a High Devil. It doesn't seem like a good idea."

"I think so too... But, Sophia, we have no other options."

It was the expected response. Sophia's breathing grew tight as she finally managed to convey the words that had been buried deep in her heart.

"Let's just run away. To where no one knows us. To where no one can find us."

It was something that she had wanted to say many times but didn't have the courage to. Unfortunately, her precious words were met with ridicule.

"What are you saying, Sophia?" Elijah wore a mocking smile on his lips as though she was speaking nonsense.

Sophia's eyes shook, but she managed to respond with a similar smile in kind. "It was a joke. I must have lost my mind or something."

She finally released the grip on the tome. The Tome of the High Devils fell into Elijah's hands.

"I'll meet you later." Elijah who managed to get his hands on the tome placed it into his Soul Storage and began to dig the ground once again. "Hurry back. That guy might notice."

"O…ok." Sophia weakly nodded her head and returned to Sungchul.

"…"

Sungchul asked her nothing as she returned. Instead, he moved to the next tower. He managed to conquer the last two towers before even half of the day had passed. Forty-eight quests from the High Devils were resolved within two days in his hands.

Sungchul opened his status window as he finished all of the ordinary quests.

[Stats]			
Strength	999+	Dexterity	853
Vitality	801	Magic Power	429
Intuition	422	Magic Resist	622
Resilience	502	Charisma	18
	Luck	18	

Magic Power and Intuition had both broken through 400. All that was left were the objectives. There were eight objectives that requested the extermination of each High Devil. Sungchul felt that it was possible to complete four of them at most at this point. It was because there was a high chance for the mission to disappear due to the death of the High Devil that created it.

Each of the rewards for the missions were different. Sungchul decided to prioritize the missions that gave Magic Power and Intuition.

I didn't check the fine details of the missions, but I might be able to break through the 500s for both Magic Power and Intuition if I'm lucky.

If he were to surpass his initial goal and reach a level where he could learn Primordial Light, Sungchul would immediately head over to the Deep Sea Demon to test its power, and then seek the Demon King.

Finally, the resolution to the First Calamity is in sight.

It wasn't that long ago when he had known no magic at all. But it did not even take a year to obtain enough Magic Power for him to have the right to call himself a Grand Mage. Sungchul could feel an excitement in his heart that hadn't been felt for a long time as he turned to Sophia with an order.

"Bring out all eight Tomes of the High Devils."

When she heard his command, her eyes shook like an earthquake.

***

Sophia laid down seven Tomes of the High Devils in order. However, the red tome couldn't be found.

"We're missing one?" Sungchul asked her bluntly.

"T-That is…"

"Tell me truthfully. Where is the book?"

"…"

Sophia did not answer. Bertelgia dug herself deeper into Sungchul's pocket. It was because she guessed what was going to happen next. *Corpses of pretty girls are more unpleasant for some reason… I don't wanna see it.*

However, Sungchul did nothing to Sophia. He moved past her trembling form towards the tomes on the floor and looked over them one by one.

I think the red Tome of the High Devils rewarded with Strength and Dexterity which I don't require.

He remembered the contents well as it was the first tome he had received. He turned toward the pale-faced Sophia and said, "Open the tomes and show the objectives to me."

Sophia uncharacteristically jumped up and scrambled to do as he ordered.

Sungchul arranged the books so that he could see them all lined up and compared their rewards. Intuition was the priority. He could make do with less Magic Power, but without sufficient Intuition, it wasn't possible to learn the final spell of Cosmomancy. So, he gave Intuition first priority followed by Magic Power. Then he made sure the target of the tomes and the benefactors did not conflict with each other. Through this method, he narrowed it down to the three missions that he had to complete first.

Tome of the High Devils: Volume 1 – Intuition 30, Magic Power 15, Charisma 15

Tome of the High Devils: Volume 5 – Intuition 20, Magic Power 10, Charisma 20

Tome of the High Devils: Volume 8 – Intuition 10, Magic Power 10, Luck 30

There were various items offered besides the stats, but Sungchul wasn't concerned with that part. He remained fixated on the stats.

That's 60 points for just Intuition. If I can complete all of them, I'll be able to get close to my goal of 500 for Intuition.

Sungchul's pace quickened as he ordered, "Grab the books and follow me."

Fal Garaz appeared in his hand, and he first entered the green tower. Sungchul gave Sophia an order before the entrance to the High Devil's room.

"Hand over the book and wait here."

Sophia handed over the book. It was then given to Bertelgia who carried the opened tome on top of her opened pages. "Hup!"

Sungchul entered the room of the High Devil with Bertelgia while Sophia stayed behind praying for his demise. *Please. Dear God, please kill that man. Only with his death can my brother and I survive.*

It was her first time praying. She did not know how to draw the cross or know any prayers, but her sincerity alone was enough to reach the heavens.

Meanwhile, there was a High Devil who had disassembled himself into a troupe of forty-two wooden marionettes; one was forty-two, and all forty-two were one. The devil then spoke through the mouths of the dolls in chorus.

"I plainly ordered you to exterminate the scum, so why are you defying my command?"

"We should make the defiant child into a puppet!"

"Puppets listen to orders very well!"

"Are you stupid? Aren't puppets created to follow commands?"

"Those are wise words!"

While the forty-two dolls clapped together and made a ruckus, Sungchul picked up Fal Garaz and leaped up to the ceiling where the strings connected to the dolls came from. There he could see a massive squirming brain. Sungchul rose up into the air with the hammer.

"Is it a fight?"

"If it's a fight, we gotta get in on it!"

The marionettes chased after Sungchul and impeded his path. But from the beginning, the High Devil had not been a match for him.

WHAM! BLAM! SMASH!

With a single blow, the marionettes, each holding a piece of the High Devil's flesh, were smashed to pieces. The marionettes continued to charge in fearlessly as if to prove that they were existences that followed commands, but all of it was meaningless. Every marionette of the High Devil's troupe was destroyed. The High Devil finally realized that his meager existence could not compare to the human before him when only his brain remained.

"Y-you are? Just what are you?"

"I've always liked rag-dolls more than wooden puppets."

Fal Garaz dealt the final blow. Sungchul read the shining message that appeared before him in the midst of a shower of brain viscera.

[You have dealt an execution befitting the objective.]

[Very Impressive! You have carried out the punishment of the serial killer obsessed with puppets, Herik Mas, in place of god.]

[High Devil Kadenburr is overjoyed.]

```
Basic Reward:
Intuition      30
Magic Power  10
Charisma      15
Worn-out Bone
```

The Tome of the High Devils that Bertelgia was clutching onto desperately began to leak an ominous light as the mysterious energies within were let loose, giving Sungchul the powers contained inside it and an item. Unfortunately, he was unable to receive everything.

[Due to an unknown curse, one of your stats, Charisma, is blocked from increasing.]

However, this was not important. Sungchul confirmed that the two stats he was concerned about had increased and then appraised the item he had received as a reward.

[Worn-out Bone]

Grade: Legendary

Type: Inheritance of Power

Effect: Upon usage, one's soul and flesh are used as a sacrifice to receive the power of the High Devil.

Note: Even the corpse of a great Devil contains great power.

Restriction: None

It was as expected. It was an item that granted the power of a High Devil simply upon its use. For now, Sungchul put away the Worn-out Bone into his Soul Storage before leaving the room of the High Devil. Outside, Sophia was kneeling in prayer.

"What are you praying so hard for?" Sungchul asked as he gazed at her with indifference.

Sophia looked at him with frantic eyes.

He came out so quickly without a single injury? No way. Even if the man is the Enemy of the World, his opponent was a High Devil...

She knew that Sungchul was powerful, but she didn't know how powerful. This was because the man named Sungchul was not someone she was capable of gauging the strength of.

He spoke bluntly to the blankly staring Sophia. "What are you spacing out for?"

Sungchul began to descend the stairs first.

As he was walking down, Bertelgia fluttered behind him and asked a question, "Why don't you kill that woman? You would have normally killed her several times over by now."

"..."

"Could it be... she's your type?"

"Don't joke around. I only let her live because I don't have any reason to kill her."

Fate shall take her life. Sungchul did not have the ability to look into the future, but he had a strong premonition with regards to Sophia. Those that treasured another's life before their own never lived for long.

When they left the green tower, a different scene appeared before them. The bases of the towers that had been completely desolate were filled with devil worshippers looking towards the green tower.

"The High Devil Troupe was killed. Who do you think is the new High Devil?"

"I hope a REALLY insane High Devil appears this time."

"The Troupe's hobby was childish. He was needlessly cruel too."

When Sungchul exited the tower, the devil worshippers gathered like flies.

"Could that human be the one who took care of the High Devil?"

"Couldn't be. If he had killed the High Devil, then he would have become one by now."

Sungchul lightly swung his hammer to scatter the devil worshippers.

"Get lost."

Most of them retreated, but one of them was filled with bravado and continued to approach Sungchul. He appeared to be daring Sungchul to strike him. When their eyes met, the devil worshipper allowed himself a smirk.

Sungchul pulled out a rope he liked from his Soul Storage. He grabbed the smirking devil worshipper's neck and quickly wrapped the rope around it, then hung him on a dried-out tree nearby. The foolhardy devil worshipper reverted to a maggot and struggled violently, but he soon fell limp.

" … "

The crowd of devil worshippers now parted to form a path wherever Sungchul walked.

Sungchul looked toward the gray tower which was his next target. The gray tower was quite different from the green. Half-human and half-demon monsters who looked like guards blocked his path on the first floor.

"Reveal your identity, Human!"

They hadn't been there on Sungchul's previous visit and looked to be numbered in the hundreds. It looked as though all the High Devils were raising their defenses in response to the death of their kin.

Sophia's face grew stiff as she drew her blade. She had come to the conclusion that the number of enemies would prove difficult, even for Sungchul. However, Fal Garaz moved quickly and...

WHAM! BAM! WHAM!

The monsters standing before them became blood stains. There was no forgiveness or mercy in Sungchul's blows. Only the fact that the hammer left behind a result each time it moved remained. The monsters tried to escape in a panic as they lost half their numbers. Sungchul gave chase, and Sophia stood awkwardly with her sword half-drawn before sheathing it once again.

Crazy. This is complete madness! She had felt that she had grown since she had arrived in this place, but Sophia realized now that she was less than a speck of dirt in relation to the man standing before her.

Sungchul continued to move forward again. He destroyed everything blocking his path until he found himself on the top floor of the gray tower where he took care of the High Devil.

In contrast to the last battle, Sungchul did not even give him a chance to speak this time. He entered the High Devil's room as though it was his own living room, beat the devil down with a single blow, then took the rewards before heading to the next tower.

The same process was utilized again except this High Devil seemed to be rather wiser than the previous two because it assumed a timid form and begged for its life. "Shall we make a bargain?"

Sungchul's response was a single blow of the hammer.

WHAM!

Bertelgia who looked at the High Devil's corpse that had been crushed with a single blow spoke as though she had been waiting for it all along. "Beep! You aren't good enough to trade!"

"..."

Sungchul again felt the ominous light spilling out of the Tome of the High Devils seeping into him, but an unexpected obstacle appeared.

[Warning! Your intuition is too high, only a portion of the Intuition will be transferred.]

He immediately checked his status screen.

[Stats]			
Strength	999+	Dexterity	853
Vitality	801	Magic Power	474
Intuition	477	Magic Resist	622
Resilience	502	Charisma	18
	Luck	18	

Sungchul who noticed the number confirmed something to himself. *It looks like the High Devil that gave this quest had 477 intuition.*

The High Devil that had given him the quest was the giant whose body was filled with large nails carrying a disgusting stench. The devil's appearance did not give off the impression that he was particularly clever, and it seemed that Sungchul was right. Not to mention that having over 500 points for any stat was also known as the realm of Transcendence.

As Sungchul saw it, the High Devils were merely at the cusp of Transcendence. The ones who specialized in magic probably had Magic Power beyond the threshold of Transcendence, but the ones who didn't, probably had Magic Power and Intuition below those levels.

In any case, Sungchul had completed all three missions that he had set as his goal.

I managed to do everything I wanted.

The other missions were unnecessary to him. He had never considered becoming one of these pathetic High Devils from the beginning. Sungchul left the tower without regret.

Outside the tower, there were more devil worshippers than before. Sungchul saw a man kneeling before him. The man had an emaciated appearance akin to that of a skeleton and looked similar to the people that would commonly be seen in the tower known as the Tower of Enlightenment.

"I-I have something to say to you. Hero of the Restoration Age!"

Sungchul quietly pulled out his favorite rope from his Soul Storage as he asked, "What is it?"

The man bowed his head low before speaking in a courteous tone. "I promise you that we are not your enemy. We may be called devil worshippers, but this was a choice that was forced upon us. We had abandoned our humanity and chosen servitude under the devils to escape the Curse of Extinction as there were no other options."

"Why are you telling me this? I don't recall asking about your situation."

"Please do not harm the High Devils, Hero of the Living!"

The emaciated man smashed his head onto the ground as he shouted with sincerity.

"They might be evil creatures deserving extermination in your eyes, but they are necessary evils in our lives who protect us from the other devils. Without them, we will become enslaved or eaten by the other devils."

"That isn't my concern." Sungchul callously spoke as he turned around. However, the man didn't relent. Even after having the rope tied around his neck his response remained the same. He was different from the others. That was what Sungchul thought as he released the man.

"I didn't have any intention of killing the other High Devils anyways."

A familiar form appeared before Sungchul's eyes. The black mask and clothes of an undertaker. A humanoid man with a twisted body was mixed in with the crowd.

That man?

It was the one who had whispered that he could teach them now to defeat the High Devils. Sungchul turned his feet towards the humanoid creature.

"You."

Sungchul stood before him. The man tried to retreat, but Sungchul's hammer blocked his path.

"Where is Elijah Breggas?" Sungchul asked.

The man already knew of Sungchul's strength and so he spoke quickly while trembling. "Te-eh-eh-eh... blue tower... He's challenging the master of the blue tower!"

Sophia was the first to act upon hearing the news. "Brother!"

Sungchul's arm stopped her as she tried to hurry forward.

"Follow behind me."

Chapter 14 – Order of the Iron Blood Knights

Sungchul headed towards the top of the blue tower, and no one dared to cross his path. The battle of Elijah and the High Devil of the blue tower awaited him on the top floor. By the time he arrived, the conclusion had already been drawn. The High Devil with the head of a fly seemed to be unscathed, while Elijah Breggas was tired and on the defensive. There was a black-colored marble rolling by his feet.

"Regardless of your schemes, you cannot win at your level of strength."

The High Devil who had been flying in the air landed in front of Elijah. He was close enough that Elijah could reach out and touch him, but Elijah could not respond. There wasn't even enough strength left in his body to lift a finger.

Shit. Is it because I only managed to find a single marble? I should have listened to the bastard and gathered at least three.

The information regarding the marbles sealing the strength of the High Devils turned out to be true. It acted as a sponge for the oppressive amounts of Magic Power that sustained their bodies, but it wasn't nearly enough with a single marble.

The twisted humanoid monster had recommended Elijah to wait until he had gathered at least three marbles, but the news of the death of the High Devil Troupe had spread panic among the residents of the towers. Elijah felt like he was running out of time, and so he challenged the High Devil before he was ready. And the result was the defeat now. Elijah who was out of mana and stamina couldn't do anything but watch the devil approach him.

It was at this moment that the massive doorway to the High Devil's room burst open, and the atmosphere of the room changed instantly. The one who entered the room was none other than the Enemy of the World.

"…"

Sungchul looked around the surroundings with disinterest and walked over to their direction while Sophia and Bertelgia followed behind him.

Sophia recognized Elijah and shouted, "Brother!"

The High Devil who had been preparing to deliver the final blow unconsciously stepped back. He could feel a fearsome hostility and fighting spirit radiating from Sungchul's body that he hadn't felt before. *Could it be... Was he the one who killed the High Devil Troupe along with the other High Devils?*

If that was the case, then the pathetic human before him did not matter. The High Devil looked towards Sungchul and said, "Why have you returned to this place?"

Sungchul did not answer. He took a step back and simply crossed his arms as he observed Elijah and the High Devil. It was an unspoken sign that he had no intention to interfere.

The cunning High Devil understood Sungchul's intent and turned his hideous fly head towards Elijah once again. It wasn't possible to actually know whether the High Devil was smiling or not, but he was definitely laughing.

"Kekeke... Have you been abandoned?"

"..."

Elijah's face grew twisted. He had nothing to say. Strictly speaking, it wasn't he who was abandoned, but rather he who abandoned them.

The High Devil took another step closer. In between the fancy robes reminiscent of a judge's gown, the mutilated hand of a corpse shot out. It held a large spoon in its hand.

"I'll suck your brain while you're alive!"

Elijah pulled out his blade and faced off against the High Devil, but the conclusion was quite obvious. He wouldn't last much longer. Seeing Elijah in peril, Sophia let out a short scream before quickly heading to Sungchul.

"I beg you, please save my brother."

It was the first time she had lowered her head to him.

"…"

However, Sungchul did not respond verbally or physically. Sophia was panicking and began to meaninglessly fidget with her arms. She managed to quickly take a deep breath and pleaded to Sungchul once again.

"I'll do anything, if it will save my brother. Please. Please save him! You have the power to do so."

"…It was his personal decision. I have no obligation to intervene." Sungchul spoke bluntly wasting no words.

A dark shadow passed by Sophia's eyes. She could see with a glance that he wasn't to be persuaded, and so she bit down on her lower lip and bowed her head once again. Her slim form was trembling slightly. She turned to face the High Devil as she drew her blade.

"… I have no excuse. I have shown you something shameful."

"…"

"I am grateful for your help this far."

Sophia turned again towards Sungchul and gave a polite nod before rushing towards the High Devil. Sungchul's eye lit up with interest. *She was unexpectedly a good kid.*

If it had been anyone else, they might have shouted profanities towards him before leaving. It was human nature to hold grudges for just one wrong even if they were treated well a hundred times before. However, Sophia Breggas was better than most regarding this. Her behavior was what ought to have been considered normal, but there weren't many good people in Other World.

"Hmm."

Bertelgia began to circle around Sungchul's back as though she had something to say.

"What is it?" Sungchul asked without taking his eyes off of Sophia who was wielding Cryomancy against the High Devil.

"That woman. She doesn't look so bad. She looks a lot more decent than that Elijah or whoever."

"So what are you trying to say?"

"Can't you save her? You went out of your way to save that Sarasa or Sarada girl from before."

"…"

"Is it because she's not your type?"

"Stop blabbering nonsense before I tear you apart."

"Hiii…"

When Sungchul let out a coarse language, Bertelgia shrank back and flew away. Sungchul turned back towards the battle when the annoying kid left his sight. Sophia was putting up a struggle, but she would not last long.

"Kekeke! Human trash! You're skittering about without knowing your place!"

Terrifying swarms of giant flies flew out from his robe and enveloped Sophia.

"Ice Storm!"

She used a spell in an attempt to freeze the fly swarm, but there was no end to them as they kept on flying out of the High Devil's robe. The flies managed to break through the spell and overwhelmed the siblings. Sophia's dancing swords dropped the giant flies, but Elijah was currently unarmed. She noticed Elijah's crisis and ran towards his side, but unfortunately, the giant flies aiming towards her back managed to tackle her with their bodies.

"Ugh!"

Sophia let out a shout, but she soon regained her posture and managed to reach her brother's side while repelling the swarm with magic. Fortunately, Elijah was still alive.

"Are you ok, Brother?"

"…"

Elijah nodded weakly. The swarm of flies surrounded both of the siblings. Sophia looked at the countless flies circling them and instinctively knew that they had no chance of survival. Now that she was facing imminent death, she broke into a grin. She began to recall an unforgettable scene from her past.

"Do you remember when we first met?"

She was a girl who lived with the pigs in the pigpen. A miracle came to visit this girl who had been looking after the livestock day after day without the possibility of a better future. Sophia could still remember the well-groomed boy standing in front of the pig pen with a shocked expression on his face.

"…"

Elijah didn't respond. It was because the situation didn't call for such leisurely conversation, but Sophia strangely felt the desire to say many things. She knew better than anyone that they would not have many more opportunities to have a conversation like this.

"There were swarms of flies around us then too, though none of them were this big!"

She began to laugh openly as though something was funny to her.

A few swarms of flies let loose a fierce attack. Sophia's sword cut through the flies and caused them to fall head first to the ground, but there were still hundreds more flying around her.

"I'll break through the front." Sophia spoke resolutely. "When I do, run to the Enemy of the World, Brother. Get on your knees before his feet and beg for your life."

"Sophia…"

"That is the only way to survive."

As soon as the words left her lips, Sophia poured the last ounce of her magic into a fierce magical assault to attack the swarm. The fearsome storm of frost roared as though it would freeze the entire room of the gigantic High Devil. Elijah ran out as the swarm of flies began to falter.

Sophia looked towards his retreating figure and allowed herself a quiet smile, but the swarm of flies quickly swallowed her up. Elijah clenched his eyes as he ran over to Sungchul with all of his strength.

"…"

Sungchul looked at Elijah groveling before his feet with indifference. "I beg you. Please… please help."

"Who are you asking for me to save?" retorted Sungchul callously.

Elijah looked at him as though he didn't understand, so Sungchul pointed his finger towards Sophia where the battle was still fiercely raging on. "There? Or here?"

"T-that is…" Elijah had nowhere to look. His eyes shook as he continued to stare at the ground.

Sungchul walked past him with disappointment hanging densely in his eyes.

Bertelgia flew past him as well, but allowed herself a single cold word: "Garbage."

Sungchul walked toward the High Devil who retreated in surprise when it sensed his approach.

"W-what is it? Are you trying to challenge me as well?!"

The High Devil's emaciated hand moved, and the countless flies swarming around Sophia began to attack Sungchul. But, their enemy this time was not on the same level.

Fal Garaz struck the air.

BOOM!

The hammer, when swung with his godlike strength, resulted in a concussion of air that destroyed everything within its vicinity. The thousands of windows in the room shattered simultaneously and the eardrums of the human maggots spectating the battle ruptured while the swarm of flies in the air popped into a bloody mass.

"…"

Sungchul continued to approach the High Devil, who had nothing left in his arsenal.

"N-negotiation! Let's negotiate!" The High Devil spoke in a panic, but it was already too late. Fal Garaz rose again in the air and then it fell. Sungchul put the smashed body of the High Devil behind him as he turned around. Sophia was lying on the floor; her body was riddled with injuries large and small. He approached her to gauge her condition. She was still breathing, but not for much longer.

Sungchul looked over at Elijah hurrying over to the High Devil's corpse to loot the item on the floor with disinterest.

"Look! Sophia! High Devil! I got the item that can make me into a High Devil! Finally… I finally have the strength to get my revenge on that man!"

He was hopping about while shouting like a madman. Sophia's dull eyes looked at that excited figure and smiled weakly.

"…Let's go." Sungchul started to walk away.

"Weren't you going to save her?" Bertelgia asked while following behind him.

"Her death here might be the greatest ending she could hope for. Just so that she could be spared from the hell that would await her from this point on."

Sungchul let out a shallow sigh as he left the room. Meaningless cheers of celebration echoed out from the empty room of the High Devil

—

It was a usual day of training. Sungchul entered a rundown bar to buy ingredients when he overheard a rumor about a new powerful demon that had made an appearance on the front lines of the Demon Realm. He seemed to have appeared in the area under the jurisdiction of the Storm Battlefront. This devil threatening the Dwarven fortifications was powerful, but it was gaining more notoriety for its unusual appearance.

The devil was terrible to behold as it bled from its empty eye sockets formed after it ripped its own eyes out. But it carried the corpse of a beautiful woman tied to its back. They say that this devil seemed to shout some nonsense occasionally as he assaulted the Dwarven walls which people have assumed was the name of the woman hanging behind him.

"…"

Sungchul did not speak regarding this matter. Instead, he bought a bottle of alcohol and returned home.

It's almost over.

Sungchul felt the strong alcohol rumbling in his stomach as he looked toward the skyline of the Demon Realm.

***

Lord Martin Breggas looked on at the Knights prostrating before him with a half-hearted expression. The Knights were bowing before him, trying to appeal to his mercy with a low tone of voice.

"Our frontlines have been obliterated. Most of the Mobile Fortifications have been destroyed, and we have lost countless Knights. Without reinforcements, we might not last much longer."

They were the Knights of the Order of the Iron Blood Knights. It had been quite a long time since the Order of the Iron Blood Knights received concentrated attacks from the Demons. It has long been a tradition among the Demons to halt their offensive during the winter, but they had broken this practice and continued their assault through the winter driving the Order into a corner.

The Order of the Iron Blood Knights had rightfully requested reinforcements and support from Martin Breggas who was in charge of the front lines of the Demon Realm, but for some reason Martin did not send even one crummy soldier to help. It was also becoming increasingly clear by the man's attitude that he didn't intend to send any support. As Lord Breggas did not utter a single word, the Knights clenched their lips and left. The eyes of the Knights who looked back from outside the door were filled with rage and resentment.

When the doors shut, Martin yawned as he picked at his ear. His attendant who was standing beside him carefully drew closer.

"Is it ok to just send them back? We analyze that the Order of the Iron Blood Knights are in a really critical state."

"How critical?" Martin squinted at the earwax that had been stuck to his finger as he asked his question.

"The Order has lost 60% of their military forces. With the exception of their last line of defense at the 'Fortress of the Iron Blood Cross,' every other base is under siege or captured. They will not last once spring arrives."

"Is that so? That's good news. I didn't like their kind from the beginning. Worthless Summoned referring to themselves as an order of knights. It might not be so bad to let them fall given this opportunity?"

Martin drank the milk poured into his cup with a relatively gleeful expression on his face.

"But, Lord Martin, if the Order of the Iron Blood Knights fall, the Demon Army will head to our direction. Not to mention the blame for the fall and destruction of the Order will be on our heads as well."

"Don't worry about that. Wasn't it for this purpose that we poured our hard-earned money to develop our friends over here?"

Martin rose from his seat and stepped towards the window. Beyond the window filled with the blinding rays of the sun, soldiers numbering in the thousands were awaiting orders in neat formations. Soon, a youth dressed in lavish clothes stood on a podium and spoke to the soldiers in a cheery voice. The contents of the speech could not be heard from here, but Martin had a satisfied smile as he looked at the youth's backside.

"If the Order of the Iron Blood Knights falls, we can just have him contain the situation."

Martin had countless illegitimate children. Parlim Dargot, the leader of the militia of Trowyn, the army which Martin had poured his heart and soul over for a long time to create, was one such child. Being the child of a dancer at a bar, Parlim could not use his father's name, but if he were to thwart this demon invasion which put the Iron Blood Knights in peril, then he would be in a position to lay claim as the true heir of Martin Breggas.

"Reinforcements will only be sent once the Order of the Iron Blood Knights falls."

Martin was prepared to do anything for the child of the only woman he had ever loved.

On the other hand, upon hearing this news, the Order of the Iron Blood Knights prepared to use the trump card that they had been holding back until now.

The Leader of the Iron Blood Knights, Sungtek Jo.

He had once been hailed as a great hero and word of his might was spread throughout the North, perhaps even the entire continent. But he was currently diminished to the state of a local feudal lord. Nothing had been going his way and recently, even his own son had met a terrible end in the Summoning Palace, which caused the world to frown upon him. The situations that surrounded him displeased him greatly.

"If you bastards are going to come at me like this, then I also have my own plans."

Sungtek ordered for the guest he had secretly accommodated at the palace to be brought before him. A strange being with the wings of a bat, hooves of a goat, and the head of a human was brought to his audience chamber. Surprisingly, the guest was a demon.

"Have you finally made a decision?" the demon quietly asked in a soothing voice which was pleasing to the ears.

A crease appeared on Sungtek's forehead. It was possible that this decision would destroy all the reputation and renown he had accumulated over the years. However, when he thought about it, did any of those have any value?

The children I sired in Other World have died from the curse and even my little Ahram brought to the Summoning Palace was killed pitifully by the brats of the other bastards. And now even Martin Breggas, that son of a whore who couldn't look me in the eye, wishes for my ruin.

It didn't take long for Sungtek to reach a conclusion. He raised his head and gathered his hands before speaking in a quiet voice to the demon standing in the corner.

"… I will collaborate with your king. However, do not forget to fulfill your end of the bargain."

Eight years ago, the Thirteen Champions of the Continent agreed to prolong the approaching Calamity at the first stage, which seemed the most manageable, and set this plan into motion. A single Champion had opposed obstinately and deserted the group in the process, but the Calamity was managed smoothly over the past eight years, and those in power enjoyed great wealth and prosperity no different than before.

However, the Calamity cannot be stopped. The words "cannot be stopped" actually included the fact that it also cannot be delayed, but the people often thought of these two ideas as separate things. The Calamity that the people mistakenly believed was postponed would continue to grow stronger and stronger until it broke free and was unleashed upon the world even more violently than before.

—

The meteor fell from the sky and critically struck the Deep Sea Demon. Successive meteors fell without any additional Aria. The number of echoes had naturally increased as his Magic Power grew. Sungchul, who was getting close to reaching the value of 500 for Magic Power, gained an additional 2 echoes for every spell that he had cast. In other words, two additional meteors would fall for every single cast.

"Guwaaaaa…"

The Deep Sea Demon could not endure the consecutive blows from the powerful meteor. This meant that Sungchul, who used to beat up the Deep Sea Demon once a week, now had to change his schedule to beating it up once every 2 weeks. If he went any further, he might end up killing the demon.

If it were possible to land a meteor on the Demon King, then seeking him out now wouldn't be a problem, thought Sungchul.

The Meteor's offensive might belonged to highest tier in magic. The greatest problem was with its accuracy. But if it were to hit, it might even be enough to critically injure the Demon King when combined with the echo effects. However, Sungchul did not rush forward.

Intuition is going to hit 500 soon.

Currently, it was sitting at 479. A month and two weeks had passed since he left the Tower of the Devil Worshippers, but he only managed to raise his Intuition by 2. He thankfully had Alchemy to raise it by that much, because otherwise, his growth would have stopped completely. And as a result, he was also about to complete a quest of the Path of the Creationist after a long while.

"More! A bit more!"

Sungchul felt his enormous magic power being drained away as he mightily stirred the cauldron. He could smell a unique scent emanating from Eckheart's Portable Alchemic Cauldron before a blinding light poured out to signify the success of a creation.

[Synthesis Success!]

Sungchul confirmed the message that appeared before his eyes as he held up the new Alchemic item within his cauldron. It was a statue of a duck radiating a golden light. Sungchul had improved from being limited to altering simple characteristics of ingredients to being able to create specific forms using the Alchemic Cauldron.

[Golden Duck]

Level: 4

Grade: B

Attribute: Gold

Type: Everyday Item

Note: Floats when placed in the bath.

"…"

It was a relatively useless item. It radiated with blinding golden light, looked adorable, and floated on water despite the material it was made of, but it didn't have any more significance than a useless trinket. There were too many items in Alchemy that weren't helpful in combat.

Despite this fact, Sungchul continued to pump out items in order to complete Bertelgia's Illustrated Alchemic Collection Journal. He had finally managed to complete everything that Bertelgia had categorized as basic Alchemy. And the rewards were now about to be unveiled.

"Hm Hm. You've done well. You've finally taken a step onto the true path of Creationist from being a human butcher!"

A strange light poured out from Bertelgia's body as she fluttered in the air and enveloped Sungchul's body. Sungchul finally witnessed the long awaited message within its splendor.

[You have followed the great legacy of the Eighth Hero, Eckheart, and succeeded in recreating some of his great inventions.]

[Ordinary Collection Journal Complete!]

Reward:

Magic Power +20

Intuition +20

Eckheart's Collection Notebook

Sungchul immediately brought up his stats.

[Stats]

Strength	999+	Dexterity	853
Vitality	801	Magic Power	494
Intuition	499	Magic Resist	622
Resilience	502	Charisma	18
	Luck	18	

"Mmmm…"

He was 1 short. He was 1 short of hitting 500. As had he managed to raise his Intuition through Alchemy 3 days ago, it would take three weeks minimum and a month maximum of Alchemy to raise it once again.

"How is it? How do you feel taking in the knowledge of the Creationist?" Bertelgia spoke proudly.

"Very unhappy," replied Sungchul.

"W-What? What did you just say?!"

"I didn't mean that. I'm just a bit short on my stats."

Sungchul sighed as he gazed out towards the Demon Realm's sky. Deep regret welled in his heart. If everything had gone according to plan, he would have killed Hesthnius Max today and resolved the first Calamity. His plans had gone awry due to his unexpectedly stunted growth.

Sungchul calmed his turbulent heart and gathered the other reward that had fallen beside his feet. It was a small book which he opened immediately. It was filled with illustrations and microscopic letters written in ink that moved freely in the pages. Sungchul read one of the passages.

[… Ogres of the Foggy Mountain Range sleep on beds of rock. To human eyes, the bed of rock may appear like any other bed of rock, but to Ogres, they have some standards with which they rate these rocks. They rated excellent beds of rock with stars. And the more stars it was rated, the better it was. Upon the great bed of rock, there are…]

Sungchul read up to that point and put the book down. It prattled on pointlessly, but Eckheart's Collection Notebook appeared to be some kind of guide with the locations of rare alchemic ingredients recorded within. The problem was that the era in which Eckheart lived and the current era in which Sungchul lived had a vast gap in time.

"… I can't use this."

There were major differences even in that page he had just read. There were no longer any Ogres living in the Foggy mountains in Sungchul's era. Through frequent subjugation by the humans and enslavement of the orcs, it had been a long time since the Ogre Kingdom had vanished.

Sungchul placed the notebook into his Soul Storage and grabbed the duck before leaving.

"You didn't like Papa's notebook? He might be a worthless person, but his information is real!" Bertelgia followed behind and spoke in a sullen tone, but Sungchul didn't pay them any mind. He arrived at a hot spring that reeked of sulfur. It was a bath that he occasionally visited.

Sungchul tossed away his clothes.

"Oh my God!" exclaimed Bertelgia as she quickly hid herself behind a tree, and when she sneakily peeked from one side, the hardened body of a man veiled by steam came into her sight. The countless scars and burns across his wide back appeared like medals for Sungchul who lived a life of conflict.

Sungchul immersed his body into the hot spring and floated the golden duck that he had just created. The golden duck that had been made entirely of gold surprisingly began to float around Sungchul's vicinity.

"It really does float." An amused smile slipped onto Sungchul's lips. Cries of demons rang out from a distance, souring the mood, but overall, it was a decent bath. Sungchul closed his eyes and let time slip by.

It wasn't clear how much time had passed since that moment, but a muffled explosion could be heard from the southeast side. It was in the direction of the fortifications along the Storm Battlefront. He tried to ignore the noise, but the sound of explosions continued and he could hear the faint sound of drums.

Did a battle break out? Can't be. I didn't notice any activity from the Demon army to the north.

He felt a terrible premonition.

***

Sungchul dressed himself and hurried toward the tallest peak in his vicinity at once. He was able to look over a large area once he climbed the perilous peak known as the Palm Tree Peak, named for its likeness to a palm tree. The dwarven fortress was one of the areas visible from the vantage point.

Sungchul found the dwarven fortress within the mountain range that seemed to unfold endlessly before him without much difficulty. This was because the fortress stood at the base of a column of black smoke rising into the sky.

Suspicion rose within Sungchul's mind. *Were they attacked from the rear?*

The battle was taking place in the Southern and Eastern flanks where the defenses were weaker, instead of the North, which was the front. However, the Southern and Eastern directions were supposed to be protected by their allies. Especially the East, which was the region under the jurisdiction of the Order of the Iron Blood Knights. An assault from that side meant the Order of the Iron Blood Knights had already fallen.

Now that I think about it, I had heard from several sources that the state of the Order of the Iron Blood Knights wasn't good. But still…

The defensive focus of the Storm Battlefront lying deep within this perilous mountain range was incomparably narrower than the Order of the Iron Blood Knights that defended an open field. The fact that the demons were able to attack all the way here meant that aside from the last line of defense of the Order of the Iron Blood Knights, the Fortress of the Iron Blood Cross, all other defensive positions were overrun by the enemy.

"…"

The front lines of the Demon Realm were being shaken, and if they crumbled, humans of Other World would witness true hell.

"What will you do?" Bertelgia asked while looking down on the burning fortress below.

Sungchul pulled out something from his Soul Storage. It wasn't Fal Garaz that he favored, but a discolored and worn-out iron sword. "We're helping the Dwarves."

"Huh? What miracle brought this on? You're actually helping other people?"

"I owe the dwarves a debt."

Before he became the Enemy of the World, Sungchul had maintained an amicable relationship with the dwarves. It was a part of this goodwill that allowed them to share their secret of where Fal Garaz had been hidden. Unfortunately, it was this show of good faith that had been turned against them. The collapse of the entire front line of the Demon Realm was not something Sungchul desired at the moment.

There is a need to maintain the current status quo before the approaching battle against the Seven Heroes. It will be the responsibility of the humans and their allies to restrict the movement of the Seven Heroes.

Sungchul headed toward the burning fortress with the iron sword in hand.

An intense battle was unfolding around the entire fortress. Dwarven artillery rained down fire upon the demon forces, while the Hell Siege Engines of the demons answered back with flames of destruction. The artillery that the dwarves were so proud of remained standing, but the fort walls were crumbling under the assault of the Hell Siege Engines, which allowed the demons to find the opportunity to latch their ladders onto the walls. The Dwarven Axemen desperately tried to chop down the ladders, but the demons positioned below the walls were not going to simply watch it happen. Hundreds of crossbow bolts flew toward the dwarves.

"Guwaaa!"

The dwarves that had been chopping down the ladders were struck by these bolts and fell down the dizzying heights of the castle walls. The devils that were watching the scene felt their morale soar, causing them to shout or howl in cheer. "Press harder!"

Leading the demons was a Balroq with massive wings dressed with a white gold helmet. The devil, which held a whip reminiscent of the Demonic Weapon Cassandra, roamed the skies while commanding his men for battle.

The flames of the Hell Siege Engines continued to roar ceaselessly, and dozens of ladders flew toward the castle walls in response to the siege.

"Stop them! Stop those bastards!"

The Dwarf commander could recognize that this was a critical moment for the battle, but they were outnumbered. The enemy came well prepared and had attacked from an unforeseen direction, and in contrast, the dwarves who had believed their flanks to be secure had only a few soldiers to defend with. And although they were fighting bravely, they could not help but steadily lose the fight.

It was at this moment when a massive magical formation appeared in the sky which was dyed red by the smoke and flames. The sole magic formation that appeared in the black, smoke-filled sky was connected to the great expanse of space beyond this world and interfered with the immeasurable universe to bring forth a fragment of the heaven, ejecting a meteorite. And this meteor landed on the heads of the demons that were densely packed beneath the castle walls.

BOOBOOOM!

It left behind a field of demon corpses in its wake. The core spell of Cosmomancy, Meteor, which had the most destructive might among all branches of magic, was on full display at the northern end of the battlefield.

Oh! Is it reinforcements?

The dwarven eyes that had been driven to despair were now filled with hope as they sought out the Mage. However, what they saw with their eyes wasn't the army they desired, but only a single man standing on top of a steep mountain slope with a ragged coat fluttering in the wind and an iron sword in his hand. There also appeared to be a familiar in the form of a book flapping behind him, but the dwarves didn't really care about that.

Sungchul did not activate the echoes. He wanted to land the most cost-effective blows possible out of consideration for his limitations with mana. Currently, Sungchul could only use Meteor a total of twenty times with his mana pool. Sungchul left Bertelgia to mind the remaining number and inserted himself into battle.

"Nineteen shots left!"

Sungchul took notice of Bertelgia's shout as he turned his sights toward another area in danger to fire his Meteor. The punishment from the heavens dealt a heavy blow to the demons as their ladders and forces were left in shambles. His might was lacking when compared to going wild with Fal Garaz, but to the dwarves watching the scene, it was a refreshing sight; like a nourishing rain from the sky falling on land as dry as bone.

"What is that?! Take out that human!" The Barloq wearing the white gold helmet pointed his finger with a sharp nail in Sungchul's direction as he shouted his order. A portion of the winged demons that had been roaming above the battlefield broke off to head toward Sungchul's direction.

There were six in all. It may appear a small number, but to an average person, this was more than enough for the task. These demons, known as Raptor Gargoyles, were known for their peerless prowess in close quarter combat and also their naturally high vitality which made them highly effective against mages that had comparably terrible endurance.

The Raptor Gargoyles flapped their hideous bat-like wings to overwhelm Sungchul as they brandished their Scythes threateningly.

"Die, human!"

The dwarves looked on with expressions of concern from their fortress wall. In their eyes. Sungchul's life looked to be in peril like a candle before the storm, but when the demons rushed forward, countless streams of light burst out from the man's fingertip causing the demons to be burned away in an instant. The dwarves let out a cheer. It was a scene that was difficult to believe even as they witnessed it. A Cosmomancer, a class known to have notoriously poor melee capabilities, was overcoming Raptor Gargoyles, who were famous for their fearsome strength in close quarters, with what appeared to be simple magic.

The secret was in Sungchul's hidden class.

[Echo – 2]

It would be pitifully lacking to kill the winged demon – raptor gargoyle with a single casting of Glare regardless of the number of times the spell had been empowered. However, what if Echo, which was the basic ability of the legendary class Echo Mage, was combined with Sungchul's superhuman dynamic visual acuity and meticulous precision? The synergy between the three aspects produced a destructive might beyond a mere three castings of glare. The Raptor Gargoyles that were known to be "Nightmares of Close Quarter Combat" fell out of the skies as their weaknesses such as mouth, neck, and eyes were showered with beams of light at the same time.

"Hm Hm. Eighteen shots of Glare used. It's probably a good idea to deduct at least three of the remaining Meteors!"

When Bertelgia began to shout haughtily, Sungchul looked down at the demon forces and spoke in a firm voice. "How many shots remaining?"

"Can't you at least count that much?"

"My mind is getting rusty with age."

"More like you think it's too annoying!"

"…"

"Sixteen shots of Meteors in reserve!"

Sungchul calmed his breathing and looked down at the battlefield once more. There were still countless demon forces awaiting below the castle walls. Even with all sixteen… no, hundreds of shots of Meteor, it would still be difficult to get rid of all of them. Sungchul's sights turned toward the Hell Siege Engines that exuded a fearsome presence in between the demon armies.

If I can destroy those, the capabilities of the demon army would be brought down a peg or two.

Sungchul concentrated his gaze on the Hell Siege Engines that had a form similar to a giant scorpion and began to chant the Aria in his head. He recited the activation phrase in his mind as indescribably complex intricacies of the spell flowed like a song through his consciousness.

Meteor.

Another magical formation appeared in the sky, and a blue meteor fell toward the demon army through the formation. Its target was the Hell Siege Engine. The bluish meteorite landed short of the hell siege engines which were battering away at the walls with greenish flames, but there was no need to recite a second casting. It was enough to simply let the mana continue to flow after the incantation of the spell. Another meteor soon fell toward the same target after the first that had landed near the Hell Siege engine.

[Echo – 1]

The meteor managed to land on top of the Hell Siege Engine. The waist of the giant scorpion snapped like a shrimp before it caused a massive explosion of fearsome green flames.

"Sweet! This is how we do it!" Bertelgia exploded into cheer as she watched the flames shoot up into the sky like fireworks. But the battle was not over yet.

Sungchul had only managed to rid himself of a single siege weapon among three. He immediately turned toward another Hell Siege Engine and began his incantation, but the devils were not going to simply watch it happen.

"Every winged unit go tear that human to shreds!"

It might have been the simplest solution to personally deal with the problem at hand, but the Commanders of the demon army tended to sit back and order around their inferiors. The Barloq commanding the demon forces did not step up, and instead, commanded all of his aerial forces under him toward the Mage on the mountain peak. But before the demons could even reach Sungchul, another meteorite landed right on top of the second hell siege engine.

Hell Siege Engines were infamous for their heavy plating and fire power, but it couldn't withstand an assault of Meteor. Dozens of winged demons put the skies littered with green sparks behind them and charged at Sungchul. The Dwarves who were watching this did not stand by this time.

"Go help that man! He is our savior!"

The fortress surged with life once again and began to spit out terrifying artillery fire with the beating of drums. From ballista to grape shots, a variety of weapons were deployed toward the flying demons, and the demons that were caught within their web of fire were torn apart mid-air. Only a few of them managed to survive the attack.

"Come inside, Bertelgia." Sungchul, after collecting Bertelgia, postured himself as though he was snowboarding and began sliding down the mountain slope. The demons that were led by the Raptor Gargoyles began to dive toward him, but their timing was awry, causing them to miss by a narrow margin, which forced them to ascend once again.

The demons began to gain a better feel for the timing and dove toward Sunghcul once again. Sungchul took a look at his pursuers and struck the ground with his iron sword as they approached. Fragments of rock shot out like buckshot and became embedded in the face and eyes of the pursuing demons.

"Kiiiii!!"

One of the demons that had become a bloody mess flew past Sungchul and tumbled down the mountain. Another demon aimed for the front this time, but Sungchul lifted his finger and used Glare to take care of it. The demon that was struck with the unavoidable beam of light in both of his eyes and mouth began to smoke from his mouth. It died instantly and crashed into a rock that Sungchul passed by.

Sungchul peeked back once again. There were five remaining. However, he didn't notice the presence of any tracking magic, and they were no longer visible from the battlefield as well. Now, he had no reason to hold back.

Sungchul, who had been riding along the steep slope of the mountain, put his foot down on the ground. His rapid descent came to an abrupt stop.

The demons that had been circling Sungchul's vicinity felt suspicious regarding his sudden movements, but they also felt that it was an opportunity and immediately rushed toward him. Unfortunately, the consequences of opposing Sungchul, who had no reason to restrain his strength, were dire. He did not use magic or weapons as he gripped the demons with just his hands and grated their faces against the rocky surface of the mountain. A demon that had lost his comrades tried to escape as it was stricken with fear, but a stone from behind struck the back of his head causing it to pop like a grape.

"Nice shot!" exclaimed Bertelgia.

"…"

After ridding himself of the demons, Sungchul hid his presence this time and stepped back onto the tall peak in stealth. The tide of battle had changed.

When two of the three Hell Siege Engines were destroyed, the dwarven firepower reignited, causing the demons to be pushed back. The final hell siege engine tried to continue on with the assault, but it was focused down and destroyed by the dwarven artillery. The demons were forced to retreat at sunset, leaving behind innumerable corpses.

Sungchul revealed himself to the dwarves who were cleaning the battlefield. They immediately recognized him and began to surround him with cheer.

"We are truly grateful, unknown Mage!"

"If not for you, we'd have truly died out here!"

Sungchul looked at the dwarves surrounding him with a calm expression on his face. Stocky build with bushy beards. Every last one of them looked similar to one another, but thankfully, he didn't find any recognizable faces among them.

"I am a wandering Mage. Call me Ahmuge."

Sungchul introduced himself without reserve.

Chapter 15 – Facing Them Alone

Sungchul was able to meet the commissioned officers in command ranks at the dwarven fortress. Kevan Kemaal's commander of defenses, Kaal Bomba, was among them. Along with a gruff voice with large hands the size of pot lids, the dwarf had bright eyes that lit up like lanterns as he briefed the room of the current situation while gulping down a large mug full of beer.

Bomba himself wasn't quite sure how the demon Army managed to ambush them from the rear, but he knew of recent rumors from the frontlines of the Demon Realm.

"I've heard rumors that the Order of the Iron Blood Knights requested reinforcements from Lord Martin. Not to mention, the Order was already in quite a poor shape from the continued assault from the demon forces all throughout the winter. In any case, the Order of the Iron Blood Knights put aside their pride and asked several times for reinforcements, but the bastard Lord Marquis ignored their plea each time. It was only a matter of time before they fell."

"…"

Sungchul knew all too well what kind of man Martin Breggas truly was. He was certainly a man who did as he liked, but he was not a man so irresponsible to neglect his responsibilities without reason.

Another dwarf opened his mouth. "I suppose the rumors are true after all. The rumor that he decided to use the Iron Blood Knights as sacrificial lambs to elevate a bastard son of his, from a beloved mistress, as his rightful heir."

"That rumor. I'd like to hear more about it," said Sungchul who suddenly showed a bit more interest.

When the man they were indebted to, who had been silent all this time, suddenly spoke up, the attention of the dwarves shifted all at once towards Sungchul. The dwarf who had been speaking took a few more swigs of his drink before speaking again with a belch.

"Martin Breggas looks like a person, but on the inside, he is nothing more than a dog in heat trying to sow his seed into every beauty he lays his eyes on. This disgusting habit allowed him a lot of progeny, but even the Marquis himself probably doesn't know how many bastards he has."

The others began to laugh along and kept up with the banter.

"I've heard that the conservative estimate goes over twenty."

"What's twenty kids? I've heard there are more than a hundred."

Sungchul recalled Sophia Breggas's final smile, she who died so tragically. *Did that kid also come from a mistress?*

He had coincidentally seen the genealogy of the Breggas family upon one of his returns from the Demon Realm. He had seen Elijah's name from the genealogy that recorded everyone from the founder to the current successor of the family name in the seemingly endless branches of the family tree, but he had never seen Sophia's name. For her name to not be recorded on the genealogy meant that she was not formally a part of the family.

"The problem is…" The dwarf who had been speaking suddenly shouted in a loud voice to clear the air. When the rumbling around him began to calm down, he spoke on.

"The problem is that, even among the countless number of progeny, there is a single one that he favors! He loves that child enough to throw away the child he had with his own wife in the Demon Realm."

"Who is that?" asked Sungchul.

"Parlim Dargot. A High Elf. He's the child from a dancer of some renown in Trowyn. There is actually another rumor regarding that bastard."

"Oh?" When Sungchul showed a bit of interest, the dwarf gave a toothy smile and lowered his voice.

"That the progeny that Martin adores so much might not actually be his own… Kehahaha!"

The dwarf seemed to have found the rumor so hilarious that he didn't manage to finish his own story before bursting into laughter. The other dwarfs laughed along in mockery of Martin.

When the laughter bursting from every seam of the hall died down, the storytime continued. But the speaker this time was not a dwarf, but the commander sent by Kevan Kemaal, Kaal Bomba.

"In any case, the rumor is that Martin is trying to make this progeny his heir. The man has no scruples and has already driven his wives and all of his other sons to their death. But even that impudent man thinks it's unreasonable to make a bastard child of a dancer with no basis for the inheritance to become his legal heir. So, he is preparing a sacrificial lamb."

"Are you talking about the Order of the Iron Blood Knights?" asked Sungchul.

Kaal nodded at Sungchul's inquiry. "I'm sure they knew about it too. It was a popular rumor after all. But the Order has no strength. They couldn't even pull their Knight-Captain's son who was summoned from that other world through the Summoning Palace, so is there anything more to be said?"

Sungchul recalled Ahram's wolf-like face as the dwarf was talking.

I'm the one who killed that kid. If I wasn't involved, Ahram would have graduated from the Palace and been accepted into the Order.

Every action has a consequence. Out of the many possible outcomes, there were bound to be a few that were outside of expectations. It appeared that Ahram's death had been the final blow to the Order of the Iron Blood Knights, and a declining house was bound to collapse quickly.

Sungchul tipped his glass as he contemplated the stories he had heard today.

—

The Order of the Iron Blood Knights was a military organization composed of the Summoned, especially those summoned from Korea. The Knights, with the Knight-Captain Sungtek at the head, were nothing more than a band of mercenaries until they positioned themselves within the Demon Realm Frontlines at what was known to be the most dangerous region and fought against powerful devils with their lives on the line.

As the danger grows, so do the rewards. Their struggles looked fruitless, but in reality, the Order experienced massive growth. Starting with the Knight-Captain Sungtek, a few dozen under him quickly exceeded the level of Superhuman, and they began calling themselves Iron Blood. These were the humble beginnings of the Order of the Iron Blood Knights that rose to become one of the three most powerful factions in the entire continent including the northern region. However, the Order that had been on the fast track no longer existed.

Sungtek might have been strong-handed in his formation of the organization, but he showed weakness in his ability to maintain such a massive group. Between schemers such as Martin Breggas, Aquiroa, and the Emperor, his organization was taken advantage of and discarded.

There was news spreading throughout the fortress of the Storm Battlefront that even the final bastion of the Order had been relinquished.

"The Order of the Iron Blood Knights has fallen."

"The Fortress of the Iron Blood Cross was forfeited, and the few that remain have given themselves to Martin Breggas."

"The Eastern Front of the Demon Realm Battlefront is completely abandoned."

"It'll only be a matter of time before the Storm Battlefront is overrun."

Sungchul, who had been staying within the Dwarven Fortress as a guest of honor, could hear all of their gossip. They all contained grim and vital news. As people's concerns seemed to grow heavier, a unit of Wyvern Knights entered the fortress. They delivered the command of Martin Breggas to Kaal Bomba even after returning with all manner of injuries after an attack en-route.

The main force, led personally by Martin Breggas, is moving to strike at the Devil's main force. All subordinate officers that see this news are expected to dispatch all forces except the bare minimum to maintain the line.

So, he ended up moving personally. Martin Breggas, thought Sungchul.

This was the worst crisis since the formation of the Demon Realm Battlefront. There had been several of them, big and small throughout, but there had been none that threatened its total destruction such as now. There was no way for Martin to keep out of the thick of it any longer.

There was news that an army from the Elven Tribal Alliance of Varan-Aran which had been defending the west was now marching east toward the region overseen by the Storm Battlefront. Kaal also decided to send out every unit other than the injured and a few veteran soldiers to the east. Sungchul joined Kaal's army as an honorary mage.

The Dwarven Army sang marching tunes as they held lengthy spears five times their height while heading out to the land of death. There was a marching tune related to Sungchul.

"Fucking Sungchul, Return Fal Garaz, You Son of a Whore, Sungchul the Eunuch, Give Back Fal Garaz, Shit of the World~"

There was even a second verse. This was a widely known truth, but Sungchul was the first entry within the Dwarven Book of Grudges. If Sungchul revealed his identity at the current moment, it would most certainly lead to all the dwarves turning against him.

"Man… you have a lot of enemies. Do you… have any friends?" Bertelgia shook from laughter as she spoke from her pocket.

"…"

Sungchul didn't respond. Instead, he pulled her out of his pocket and tossed her onto the floor.

"Ouch! You're too much! Really!"

The dwarves that saw Bertelgia fly shouted in wonder. The day passed by like this, and they finally arrived at some village. It was already in ruins by the hands of the demons. Sungchul discovered the half-burnt sign of the village within the ashen wreckage. It was written in Korean which he hadn't seen since he arrived to the Other World.

[신 파주]{New Paju}[山]

"…"

Sungchul and the dwarves could smell the faint stench of blood permeating throughout the village as they entered. There was a disgusting construct left behind by the demons who hadn't left a single structure standing. It was a tower of stacked humans. Men and women of all ages seemed to have gone through some atrocious torture before being used as material for the tower while they still held their breath only to die upon it.

Those that died defending the village appeared to have been eaten by the demons. The corpse of a warrior that had been hollowed out of internal organs was left rotting on a dining table.

"…those damned demons." The dwarves had become calloused to the gore, but atrocities performed on civilians were revolting to a different level.

The entire continent will be subjected to this Calamity if the front line of the demon realm is breached. Sungchul resolved himself with this thought as he knew the demons better than anyone else. Humans were food and playthings to the demons, and the two could only be eternally at odds. There was also no need for diplomacy or negotiations with demons.

Kaal Bomba's march had slowed, perhaps due to the pitiful scene of the village.

Sungchul's group managed to see the fluttering flag of Martin Breggas after two days had passed. The military flag with the image of a winged skeleton holding a sword was visible from far away. Under that flag were several hundred other flags, representing roughly thirty thousand soldiers. A diverse army from various battlefronts and from all over the continent had gathered in one location.

The largest and the most central of the forces were the militia of Trowyn lead by Parlim Dargott known as the progeny of Martin Breggas. Sungchul could see that the group was a militia in name only and that they didn't fall behind any of the knight's orders in equipment or number after a single glance.

Parlim Dargott was a handsome man with a confident and charismatic demeanor. He didn't share any resemblance with Martin as the rumors said, but he had a large presence that seemed to draw the eyes of every person near or far. It was a sharp contrast to Elijah who was similarly handsome yet lacked strength and leadership.

Parlim sought out every captain from various regions and introduced himself while discussing his unit's size and role with a confident and concise manner.

"Hmm. That's the rival of the kid that turned into a High Devil? Honestly, this guy's a lot better," said Bertelgia. She was in agreement with Sungchul's opinion.

On the other hand, the Order of the Iron Blood Knights that occupied a corner of the army looked incomparably pathetic. Sungtek, who once wielded the might of one of the top factions of the continent, looked haggard and had little presence as he kept to his little corner of the army with his surviving soldiers. No one showed any respect toward the group.

Those that were aware of the goings-on of the Demon Realm Battlefront sympathized with them, but those that were blind to the situation scorned them as the incompetent Order that relinquished their front causing their current predicament.

Sungtek Cho. Sungchul knew the man personally. The man had been a brave and lively leader of great ability before the Calamity had struck. He was once bolder and more driven than even Sungchul, but Sungchul could see none of the spark of the past in Sungtek's current appearance. All that was left of the man was an aged husk.

So, the Order of the Iron Blood Knights has fallen this far.

There was only one reason for the Order's fall. They had stood against the Calamity. Many had deemed the Calamity as minor and insignificant, but the Order of the Iron Blood Knights had withered away as a result of weathering against it. They were unlikely to stand tall ever again. These were Sungchul's thoughts as he left the area.

Sungchul then looked around to check for anyone familiar. There was only a small minority of people who were aware of Sungchul's current appearance, but if he were to meet any of them, he would be greatly troubled. Thankfully, he didn't find Deckard or anyone from the Penal Unit. This meant that Sungchul could act as Ahmuge Kim for the moment.

Everything should reach a conclusion within a week. If the humans lose this battle, then a third of the population living in the continent will fall prey to the horns and claws of the demons.

Powerful nations such as the Human Empire might be able to withstand the demon invasion, but the minor nations would be helpless against them. The image of the ruined village flashed by Sungchul's eyes.

A shallow sigh escaped his lips. *If my Intuition only managed to get a single point higher.*

As he turned around with regret lingering in his mind, someone grabbed his shoulder. Shock spread through Sungchul's eyes. *I couldn't feel the presence?!*

It was impossible. For someone to have intruded on Sungchul's transcendent senses that is. However, there were several situations in the past where this had happened. Sungchul felt a sense of deja vu as he faced the woman that held his shoulder with a frosty glare.

"Oh, it really was you! Mr. Sungchul." The identity of the woman smiling wide with her teeth showing was none other than Ahmuge.

***

Why did this woman turn up in a place like this? Sungchul didn't show it, but he was quite startled. Sujin Lee the Regressor. They had had a one-of-a-kind meeting during their time in the Summoning Palace, but he felt that she was a dead woman walking, as that was the fate that awaited all Regressors. However, the Sujin that he met now was healthy and overflowing with vitality. The attire she wore wasn't some ragged thing for commoners, but quite a proper gear for adventurers.

"You haven't changed one bit, have you?" Sujin laughed with her eyes as she spoke. It appeared as though she was overjoyed to have met Sungchul.

"…What happened?" Sungchul took a quick look at his surroundings before asking the question. He was especially careful of the dwarves, as the name Sungchul was pretty much considered a taboo among them.

"What do you mean?"

"… Let's move locations." Sungchul led Sujin, who had an air of naivety, to the edge of the barracks. At the end of the encampment, a vast expanse of wasteland could be seen past it where giant grassy tumbleweed rolled by. In this place with little human presence, Sungchul briefly asked Sujin politely about her days after their split. Sujin replied in a hushed voice after putting aside her warm smile.

"I joined the Assassin's Guild."

"The Assassin's Guild…?"

The inexplicably vacant eyes of his former companion, Shamal Rajput, came to his mind.

"How did you enter the Assassin's Guild? Those guys wouldn't have left a Regressor alone."

"I have my ways, but it seems that you are already aware of how Regressors are normally treated," Sujin retorted with a mischievous expression on her face.

"…"

"I was kidding. Anyways, how are things on your end? How did you end up in this hell hole?" Sujin quickly changed topics.

Sungchul firmly pressed upon the thrashing Bertelgia to quiet her before replying with a calm voice. "I am here to participate in the battle that holds the fate of the World at stake."

Another smile appeared on Sujin's lips. "As expected, you came to save the world. It surely is appropriate for the one that shares names with the one who must not be named."

"More importantly, why are you here? Did the Assassin's Guild send you to join this fight?" asked Sungchul.

"Who knows."

"This battlefield should be too much for a Summoned who has not even been around for a year to handle, shouldn't it?"

"I'm not strictly here to fight. It'd be more appropriate to say that I'm here to test my luck." Sujin let out a sigh as she stared off into space.

"To test your luck?"

"That's right. I am being tested whether the future I've seen is correct or not. It turns out that being a Regressor isn't all hugs and kisses."

"Of course. They are beings who destabilize the timeline. They must pay the cost."

The future isn't predetermined. The minor details that the Regressors had seen were bound to be altered. The problem was that the results were often contrary to what the Regressors had hoped for.

When their existence was discovered, the Regressors fell into a state where they were unable to impact the world in any significant way. Of course, nobody knew anything about the Regressors who came before Regression became widely known. Sungchul had a bad impression of Regressors, and he did not trust the futures they had seen. It was for these reasons that Sungchul did not ask anything regarding the future.

Sujin who noticed his disinterest took a step closer to ask the question herself. "Aren't you curious? Don't you want to know what future I'm here to test?"

"Not particularly."

"Try to guess."

It was in this moment that Bertelgia let out another powerful struggle. Sungchul calmed her once again before opening his mouth with his eyes trained on Sujin. "Are you predicting the results of the battle to come?"

Sujin shook her head. "Boo-Boo-"

"What a strange sound effect."

"Regardless of how strange the sound was, you're still wrong."

"Then what are you here to test?"

Sujin took a deep breath and looked over the distance in response to Sungchul's question. Her eyes that had been filled with joy were now filled with dark clouds of concern. She allowed a brief moment to pass before she spoke in a quiet voice followed by a sigh. "He will appear here."

Sungchul's pupils turned toward Sujin, and she continued in a firm voice, "The Enemy of the World. That is the future that I had seen, and the future that will soon come to pass."

Sujin left it at that. She had said that Sungchul would turn into the very Calamity that ends up destroying the world. Sungchul had lightly ignored her words and forgotten about it entirely, but Sujin was testing his resolve once again on their second meeting. It wasn't clear whether this was her intention, but Sungchul couldn't help but feel indescribably uneasy. An uncomfortable silence continued on.

"..."

When Sungchul became silent, Sujin wore an awkward smile before speaking on vaguely. "Well... if it doesn't come to pass, I'll be passed off as a cheat and be eliminated by the Assassin's Guild. I am being watched as a result."

Sujin looked behind her with a fleeting glance. Sungchul could feel the presence as well. It was a faint presence that had been lingering in a single location since a while back. He could feel that presence walking toward them now. It was an unwelcome presence of a familiar person that was approaching him. His face was entirely covered with a dark turban, but nothing could be hidden from Sungchul's eyes.

Is it that assassin that I met back at Airfruit?

It was the final survivor of the Almeira Family of Assassins that had fought against Sungchul during the battle of Airfruit; Kaz Almeira.

The young man who Sungchul had believed that he had split in half was wearing a distinct mantle which covered his entire arm from the shoulder.

I ended up allowing him to live by trying to let him die in agony.

Whatever the reason, it was an opponent Sungchul did not wish to face at this moment. Sungchul kept his back toward the assassin as he walked forward and said, "Let us part here."

Sujin was not quite warmed up to Kaz either. She quietly nodded before whispering under her breath.

"If opportunity strikes, let us meet again. I would like to eat another meal made by your hands. The people from the Assassin's Guild have terrible palates."

"If there is an opportunity."

The two parted in different directions. Both of their faces didn't look well as they walked in their individual direction, but Sungchul's expression was a shade darker.

"…"

The man who had never once doubted himself calmed his turbulent heart as he looked out toward the dry wilderness.

—

The armies of the devils appeared onto the wilderness. It was an overwhelming army that enveloped the horizon in darkness. One scouting party with a wyvern knight at the head took on the danger to gather the general information about the demon army. According to the scouting party, the demon army that was approaching the last line of defense of the Demon Realm frontline was nearing a hundred thousand soldiers in total. It was almost three times the thirty-five thousand soldiers gathered for the Human Allied Coalition, but even then, their morale was at its peak with the desire to drive out the intruding demons in this upcoming battle. It was because they knew that their loss would turn this land into the playground of these demons.

Head Commander Martin Breggas chose the entrance of Trowyn, the Harupaya Ridge, to deploy his army and wait for the demons to arrive. It was an ideal topography that was easy to defend and permit supplies and reinforcements to arrive from the back. However, there was no room for retreat if they lost. There were fertile farmlands, bountiful hamlets, and cities scattered just beyond Harupaya Ridge. If the ridge were to fall, the demon army would flood in like the tide and destroy everything in sight. Despite the fate of half of the continent being staked upon this moment, Martin's thoughts wandered to something completely unrelated.

"The upcoming battle tomorrow shall be the stage for your glamorous debut. You will hold the most important role, so be brave but don't be careless in battle." Martin spoke in a soft voice toward the son that held all of his affection.

"I understand, Lord Marquis."

"I would like it if you could call me father the next time we meet."

"I was thinking the same thing, sir."

Martin gazed proudly at Parlim's dependable back as he left. It was only after Parlim had left that Martin began to stare deeply into the map of the battlefield located at the center of the barracks.

How should I set the stage for Parlim to really shine?

The matter of victory was a problem, but for Martin, the most concerning matter was the part that Parlim would play in the victory. He modified the formation of dispatch countless times and drew out the scene of the battle in his head. After several trial and error, Martin discovered the ideal deployment that would allow Parlim to display his fullest. However, it was only natural to give something up in order to gain what he wanted. He needed the sacrifice of another for his plan to work. It was up to him to choose who that sacrificial lamb would be.

Out of the countless pieces on the map of the battlefield, a single one stuck out in Martin's eyes like magic. A satisfied smile appeared on his lips.

The Order of the Iron Blood Knights seems perfect. They are desperate to restore their name more than anyone else, and the more I consider it, the more ideal it seems. I get to rid myself of the roots of that Order that was a thorn in my side, and I get to make good use of them for a final time.

He chose to dispatch the Order of the Iron Blood Knights toward the right wing where the attack was expected to be the heaviest. The only problem was whether Sungtek would accept his request. People expected Sungtek to refuse, due to his ongoing conflict with Martin. Therefore, Martin had been working on coming up with a pretext to enforce compliance in case Sungtek caused a fuss.

Surprisingly, Sungtek relented to the order without a word in complaint. It was a peaceful resolution that no one had expected. Martin sent praise to Sungtek for the courageous decision along with a meager sum of gold as a gift, using the excuse that it was a bonus reward. That looked to be the end of the situation at hand, but that was when the real problem began.

"We no longer have anything to lose."

Sungtek had a plan prepared in secret. He wore a complacent smile as he looked toward the wilderness to the north where the army of the demons was situated. The demon army was now almost upon them.

—

In some place a short distance away from the battlefield, several individuals were watching from the darkness.

"To give such credit to the words of some Regressor. Did your skills rust after spending so much time in that dark and musky place, Shamal Rajput?"

343

The grating voice of an old woman tore through the stillness and rang out. It was an elderly woman who donned a deep dark blue robe adorned with specks of gold wearing a mask covered in indecipherable letters. The woman with an extraordinary presence was Aquiroa the Executor. She was someone veiled in mystery, exerting great influence in the shadows as a major force of this era as the Second Champion of the Continent. It was difficult to recognize her due to the mask, but it was plenty obvious from her voice and movement that she was anxious. Her gloved emaciated fingers pointed toward a young woman in a corner. "Tell me, Regressor. Is it even true that the Enemy of the World will reveal himself here?"

The woman singled out by the champion was none other than Sujin Lee. She nodded her head and spoke with a firm voice without hesitation. "The Enemy of the World will show up in the battle of Harupaya Ridge."

Hearing her words, Aquiroa snorted in jest.

A man in another corner opened his mouth. "This Regressor predicted the appearance of the Enemy of the World in Airfruit."

It was an indifferent voice without a shred of emotion. The speaker, whose vacant gray eyes seemed to merge seamlessly with the surrounding darkness, was the Fifth Champion of the Continent Shamal Rajput. He was the Leader of the Assassin's Guild whose name was feared by everyone living.

"And, if her prediction matches up once again, we will have justification to believe this Regressor's words," Shamal said and melded back into the shadows.

Executor Aquiroa turned to face Ahmuge. "Then I'll ask this. Will Sungchul be the Calamity that destroys us?"

Sujin nodded in reply.

"That is nonsense. How can someone like Sungchul become a Calamity? I can take care of someone of that caliber all by myself. He was trying to resolve the Calamity, but even though he was cast out, he has yet to take care of one measly Demon King."

Each one of her words stabbed at her like daggers, but Sujin's eyes did not falter as she withstood Aquiroa's forceful words. Sujin looked at her directly in the eyes as she spoke in clear words. "The Sungchul I have seen is no longer human."

"What did you say?"

"He had become some existence in between man and deity."

Aquiroa who had heard this was frightened out of her wits. "You…You're saying he became a Lesser God?!"

The man who was wordlessly standing by a corner with a sword in hand looked in their direction. He was a well-balanced knight with a full suit of armor and a helmet that couldn't be peered into. The world called him the Vagabond King instead of his title as the Third Champion of the Continent.

"Let us just assume Sungchul will actually appear here. What will he do next?" the Vagabond King asked Sujin.

This man… is THAT Vagabond King?

She barely managed to answer as an eerie sensation of her body being stripped naked flooded her senses.

"He kills the Demon King. Without anyone's assistance."

***

"I will not believe those words."

Aquiroa's words were filled with disgust. A chilling light flashed within the dark interior of the Vagabond King's helmet.

"But, what will you do if that Regressor's words turn out to be true?" A soft, but unrefusable words flowed out from within the helmet.

"Shouldn't we take measures?" Shamal replied.

"Measures? Such as?" When the Vagabond King asked, Shamal looked over at Aquiroa the Executor.

She remained silent for a brief moment before stating, "Whether that girl's words are true or not, we must stop Sungchul if he appears here."

"How do you plan on stopping him, Aquiroa?" The Vagabond King spoke while flashing his eyes once again.

Aquiroa fixed her mask and spoke formally in her grating voice with strength behind her words. "As long as the Demon King does not die, the Calamity will be halted at the first level. At a level that can be managed by us. We have seen that my thoughts were in the right during the past eight years. The viability of our plan has already been demonstrated. We must not allow the status quo we've worked so hard to maintain to be shaken, your majesty."

Aquiroa observed strict formality, unlike when she was dealing with Shamal.

The Vagabond King let out a heavy sigh before asking again, "Are you trying to tell me that it is possible to delay the Calamity? And yet some people say that the Calamity cannot be stopped or delayed. What do you have to say about this?"

"Heathens that call themselves the Order of Extinction have said those exact words. However, what do those heathens know? They are fallen people who have scattered and resorted to thieving, prostitution, and begging as they failed to predict their own fates and lost their land and crown. There is no need to take heed to a single utterance of their words." She became a bit excited, but her words continued without faltering and with powerful strength throughout.

"If the honored lady's thoughts are so, then I have nothing more to add," the Vagabond King said and did not open his mouth again.

When the individual she was most careful with had turned silent, Aquiroa got the opportunity to speak her mind without any interruptions. "If Sungchul appears in this area, we'll use everything to take care of him."

"If killing him is impossible?" Shamal suddenly tossed out his question to which Aquiroa let out a soft laughter.

"Not that it would happen, but if that becomes the case, we must at least protect THAT from him."

Sujin felt unease at Aquiroa's tone.

"And that is?" When Shamal followed up with a question, Sujin's unease hit its peak, and Aquiroa's blunt answer confirmed her suspicions.

"Protect him. The Demon King Hesthnius Max."

—

When dawn broke, the full might of the Demon Army that had been veiled in darkness was revealed. The demons had the numbers to envelop the horizon from end to end. The sight of hell siege engines and the gigantic towering monsters were intimidating to behold. The soldiers positioned on top of the hill began to murmur when they saw the grand army of the demons.

"Look over there, it's a variant of Tam Tam! It looks as terrifying as it is described in ancient texts."

"Is that the Hell Siege Engine that is their main weapon of war? It's larger and scarier than I had imagined it."

"There are also juvenile Sea Demons. If the babies are that huge, I can't even grasp how large their adults are."

The soldiers reacted with curiosity rather than fear. The morale of the allied forces commanded by Martin Breggas was so high that it could pierce the clouds. More importantly, an important mission weighed on their shoulders: the sacred mission of protecting one's home and family.

The Army gathered under the banner represented every spare warrior from the front lines of the Demon Realm and its neighboring territories. If Harupaya Ridge were to fall, then not only Trowyn, but the territories of Storm Battlefront and the Elven Tribal Alliance of Varan-Aran which neighbored the ridge would also be in immediate danger. The Elves and Dwarves who had lived on their land for thousands of years burned with a greater sense of duty than the humans.

"Victory or death."

Sungchul had to have heard this phrase being repeated hundreds of times as he roamed about the dwarven barracks.

A steady stream of new updates was brought by the scouts to this location. Currently, the devil that commanded the Demon Army was not the Demon King Hesthnius, but a High Devil below him known as Prontorowa. He was a commander whose rank wasn't particularly high, being ranked 8th, but he was ancient even among the devils. He had lived for tens of thousands of years, so he was said to be a cunning devil well versed in vile black magic and military strategy.

Martin's headquarters had determined that the devil itself was not a strong combatant, but it more than made up for it with abundant experience with commanding large-scale operations, making it an especially tricky enemy to deal with.

Sungchul was lingering around Martin's tent; gathering all of the needed information. *Prontorowa. It looks like he wasn't there during the last attack on the Demon King's Palace.*

If this devil had been there, he couldn't have been here. Sungchul had killed every devil in sight during that assault.

Whatever the case, the good news was that the upcoming battle on Harupaya Ridge seemed to be slightly in favor of the humans. Their numbers were a third of their opposition's, but they held the advantageous terrain along with seasoned troop with high morale. The desires of Martin who stood as their leader were also quite high. His selfish desire to have his favored offspring hoard the merits stood out, but it was undeniable that the man desired victory overall. He personally oversaw various parts of the battle line to inspect the deployment and the state of soldiers and used a pittance from his own pockets to rile up their morale.

The civil militia led by Martin's child also had unexpectedly high combat potential. It didn't quite meet up to the Order of the Iron Blood Knights in their heyday, but they had a number of powerful warriors that could hope to meet up to those standards. If they were placed in the right place at the right time, they had the potential to change the flow of battle in a single moment.

It looks like Ahmuge's prediction won't come to pass.

Ahmuge's predictions were something he let pass through one ear and out the other, but they couldn't be completely ignored. Regressors tend to speak of uncertain futures, but it was undeniable that the future they had seen was one of many that could unfold. Fortunately, if the battle would continue at this rate, then Sungchul would not have to reveal himself here.

Sungchul estimated that the human faction had over a seventy percent chance of victory. Even if they did not win, they would not suffer a defeat, as the demons would have incurred a large enough casualty to make any further invasion impossible. In other words, it meant that he had no reason to step up, whether they won or lost. That is, as long as nothing exceptional happened that could cause the frontline to fall apart.

Sungchul's unit had been dispatched toward the left flank of Harapuya ridge where it was especially dangerous. The dwarves who were skilled in mountain battle formed the main front line of the left flank, and a great many of their famous siege artillery were fielded. And to combat possible assault by air, many units of Elven bowmen were likewise deployed with the Dwarves. Sungchul was planning on giving his all as the guest mage, Ahmuge Kim, during this battle.

It should be enough if I destroy about ten Hell Siege Engines.

Firepower superiority over the left flank should be decided with that amount.

Sungchul had a light heart as he waited for the battle. He utilized the leftover time to practice Alchemy as he had always done in an effort to raise his Intuition and walked up and down the ridge with the dwarves to get familiarized with the nearby terrain.

The day of battle soon approached. A messenger from the demons came to Martin. It was a demand for surrender asking for passage through the region in return for a guarantee from the Demons that the surrounding regions will not be harmed. And as a bonus, the Demons offered to impart their knowledge of magic. Martin refused the offer without hesitation and prepared for battle.

The Commander of each division relayed orders to prepare for battle.

The Defensive Unit of Kaal Bomba that Sungchul was affiliated with began to inspect their weapon and armor before standing along the battle line. Demons nearing a hundred thousand stood before them.

"There is a disgusting amount of them."

"It looks like there are more here than yesterday, or am I just seeing things?"

"It's a good thing that there are more demons to kill."

The dwarves swapped light-hearted jokes as they put the final touches to their oversized crossbows and axes.

The Elven archers stood behind the Dwarven axemen. In contrast to the noisy dwarves, they calmly stood their ground and gauged the strength and direction of the wind with their fingertips. The thundering voice of the Commander rang out in the distance. He was far away and on a different elevation making it difficult to understand what he was saying, but people knew that the voice belonged to the head commander of the allied forces, Martin Breggas.

Martin Breggas, who stood in flashy armor behind the banner of a winged skull, looked over his subordinates and began a speech to raise their spirits. It wasn't clear whether the speech had actually managed to raise their morale, but it at least appeared so on the outside.

The sound of the horn flute of the demons came next.

"Prepare for battle!"

The commands of the non-commissioned officers rang out in every direction with a slight delay.

THUD

The dwarven axes moved in perfect order to form an axe-shield wall.

As expected of veteran soldiers polished through a hundred battles on the Demon Realm Frontlines. It would be impossible for the common demon to break through.

Sungchul turned his gaze to look toward the commander situated below. The central unit that Martin was commanding was mainly composed of humans, and they were the core force of the allied forces made up of powerful mages experienced in battles big and small and veteran mercenaries hired from various regions. Behind Martin was his son, Parlim Dargott. The powerful Trowyn Civil Militia he commanded was holding the ground as reserve forces. The central unit was the most powerful among the entire army.

The most concerning region was the right wing held by the Order of the Iron Blood Knights. They formed a defensive barrier composed of two unique fortresses said to have been made by taking apart ancient artifacts, but the ranks of the Order of the Iron Blood Knights were greatly diminished, and their morale had hit rock bottom. Sungchul held a great deal of suspicion regarding that topic.

Martin's personality was the worst, but he is a man of great ability. Why did that man leave such an important flank to that husk of a group?

The way Sungchul saw it, it was only a matter of time before the Order of the Iron Blood Knights crumbled. They would endure until the end, but that would be just that. A story regarding Martin suddenly appeared in Sungchul's mind.

Could it be? Did that bastard dispatch the Order of the Iron Blood Knights to their graves on purpose?

The blades of the spears held by the civil militia of Trowyn glistened in the sunlight as they stood behind the central unit. It was at this moment that Martin's intentions connected clearly in Sungchul's mind. He could feel a familiar feeling of revulsion in his stomach.

To use them as stepping stones even during a battle with the survival of humanity on the line.

It wasn't only Martin Breggas. Those that held their vested interest in this land with a death grip had made a choice no different than Martin.

Sungchul did not detest avarice or self-interest. Instead, he believed that avarice and self-interest were the driving force of progress. It was just that those with power in Other World exceeded the bounds of greed. They had forsaken their duties and had repeatedly chosen options that benefited them. They didn't care how many died in the process. These were people who would offer up the entire world for their own security.

"…"

Sungchul's hatred of humanity that he had forgotten about began to bubble back up from the depth of his heart. He now had to question whether he should participate in the battle since the ones who would benefit the most from the battle would be Martin and his child. The faces of Sophia, who had been abandoned by her own father, and Elijah, who would live out the rest of his life in eternal suffering, entered his mind.

It was at that moment.

"What are you standing there frozen for, human friend?"

The dwarves including Kaal Bomba had surrounded Sungchul at one point.

"He couldn't be stricken by fear, is he?"

"…"

"Well, there is no way someone of your calibre is scared, but an army of that size is enough to make one freeze, but don't be so concerned."

The dwarves marched forward past Sungchul. "This land is our land and home. We will definitely protect this place with our blood and life."

The reserved elves bowed toward Sungchul and followed after the dwarves. Sound of the horn flutes of the demons rang out toward the skies, and the Hell Siege Engine began to pour out fire. The battle had finally begun.

Sungchul calmed his momentarily turbulent heart as he stood beneath the banner that was fluttering in the strong gale flowing along the top of the mountain's high points.

That's right. I'm not fighting for my own benefit.

Nausea and revulsion still swirled in his mouth, but Sungchul shrugged off those emotions and stepped confidently onto the battlefield.

"Bertelgia."

"Yes!"

"I'll leave the counting of Meteors to you once more."

"Can't you just fight with the hammer?"

"I can't."

Soon, meteors began to fall from the sky and mercilessly struck the Hell Siege Engines spewing green flames. Five of the Hell Siege Engines broke apart in moments due to Sungchul's Meteor.

Cheers echoed from every direction, and the dwarven siege weapons spat out flames in response. The firepower superiority of the left flank was being firmly grasped by the dwarves. Everything was proceeding smoothly.

As Sungchul thought this, there were some unexpected movements from the right flank of the battlefield.

"It is now. My brothers. Let us deal proper punishment toward the traitors that turned their backs on us."

The tip of the spears held by the Order of the Iron Blood Knights toward the direction of the demon army suddenly reversed. They were now faced toward none other than the army commanded by Martin Breggas.

***

Martin Breggas was struck the hardest by the betrayal of the Order of the Iron Blood Knights.

Sungtek Jo, did you finally go mad?

353

Strategies that had been planned out with his heart and soul collapsed in a single moment. Putting aside Parlim's glorious debut, he couldn't even guarantee the victory. Martin trembled as he watched the tide of battle.

The Mobile Fortresses that the Order of the Iron Blood Knights boasted of were busily circling their eight massive legs toward his direction. The cannons that were densely packed onto the front face of the fortress were now facing his way.

"Fire!"

Dozens of cannons fired explosive shots at the same time toward the center unit when the officers shouted out the command. All that remained after the chaotic bombardment were countless corpses and the moaning of the injured.

Then the demon army joined forces with the Order and broke through the right flank to head toward the side face of the center unit at a rapid pace. There was a face that Martin recognized well at the head of the charge.

"Martin Breggas! You fucking mutt! This will be your grave today!"

Knight-Captain of the Order of the Iron Blood Knights, Sungtek Jo. He stood at the head and was charging in this direction with the knights and the demons. Martin's thoughts momentarily went blank as he witnessed this scene. His thought process only managed to resume at the urgent cry of his advisor's voice. "Lord Marquis! A command! Give us a command!"

Martin kept the embarrassment of his momentary lapse in thought to himself before giving out a short command. "We face them. Give the command to the Civil Militia of Trowyn. Tell them to punish those fucking traitors appropriately."

The Civil Militia of Trowyn lead by Parlim Dargott began to move. Their imposing armor and blade shone in the light as they marched toward the traitors.

Sungtek, who noticed this, was livid. "Good! It's the unit led by that son of a bitch's child!"

The spirit of the Order of the Iron Blood Knights burned as if on fire. Sungtek swung his blade as he rode on his large black steed. One young militia member raised his sword confidently to meet Sungtek's blow. The victor was quickly decided after they crossed swords a few times.

"Kuwaaak!" The young militiaman bled out as he fell.

Sungtek snagged the fallen militia's body with a single arm, quickly slit his throat, and raised his body into the air. "This will be the future of you bastards!"

Sungtek held the head that was dripping with blood in the air while the winged devils behind him flew past. They were the Balroqs wielding a flaming whip and sword. The morale of the civil militia plummeted when the very symbol of the demon army's might, the high rank devils, appeared. Their formation broke as they began to scatter.

"Everyone. Everyone, calm yourselves! Please put your faith in me and follow me into battle!"

Parlim calmly tried to reassure his men, but they were a fresh unit without military tradition or history. It would have been different if the battle was in their favor, but their limitations were fully revealed as their current circumstances quickly grew dire. The civil militia ran away as the Balroqs approached with the Order of the Iron Blood Knights. Martin, who saw this spectacle, began to rack his brains with his mouth clenched shut.

I-I think there might be a way to turn this around... but the civil militia that I raised with such painstaking effort might suffer grave losses, and Parlim might not even be able to ascend the ranks. That's not profitable. In any case, this loss wasn't even due to my mistake.

Martin took in the sight of Sungtek letting out a bellow in the distant battlefield with his faded blue eyes. He clenched his hand into a fist.

It can't be helped.

Martin looked around his surroundings and spoke with a pained voice. "We give up Harupaya Ridge."

It was a response that the commanders could not believe. The entirety of the Order of the Iron Blood Knights might have betrayed them, and the civil militia might have fallen, but for the man that held the duty of protecting the Demon Realm Battlefront to renounce that duty once it became disadvantageous was despicable conduct that couldn't be believed even as they witnessed it.

A few commanders who had a stronger sense of duty spoke their honest opinions.

"If you back from here now, even the Lord Marquis' territory will be devastated."

"If we turn away here, the northern territories will fall to the hands of the demons."

"We still hold the advantage on the left flank. There is still an opportunity to turn the tide."

However, Martin wasn't listening. He had no desire to. "If you people want to defend this place so badly, you all are welcome to do so."

He tossed aside the baton prepared by the joint effort of rulers of several nations without a second thought and left the military tent. He shouted toward the advisers following behind him.

"Send word to Parlim Dargott. Keep the unit intact and immediately leave this place!"

He no longer paid any attention to how he looked to the others, but he must have known how disgraceful his act was. He quietly called over his trusted adviser and secretly whispered into his ear, "Immediately head to my residence in Trowyn and grab everything that holds value before escaping South. There will be an airship at the Sky Pier under the name Sophia Breggas, use that for the escape."

Martin's actions were ruthless. He abandoned his duties under the eyes of countless soldiers and commanders and fled south after deserting his own corps. There was no way that the battle would be able to continue after the head commander had acted in this manner.

The central unit that possessed the most powerful military might of the entire allied forces quickly fell. Several commanders that chose to remain behind attempted to consolidate their own forces to stand against the demons and the Order of the Iron Blood Knights, but it was a meaningless resistance.

The demon army quickly overtook central headquarters and tried to take hold of the entire Harupaya Ridge.

"..."

Sungchul watched the tide of battle turn increasingly bleak without a word. However, he was not the only one watching silently. The dwarves and elves who were in high spirits from their victory at the beginning of the battle were also watching the situation in silence.

Any chance of overturning the battle had disappeared when Martin fled. The right flank had betrayed them, and the main forces had fallen. All that remained was the left flank, but they were also fated to be overwhelmed by their enemy.

The commander of the allied forces of the Storm Battlefront that was left in charge of the left flank, Armuk Bakr, sounded the retreat, but no one moved from their posts. They stood resolutely as trees and boulders formed through the ages.

"If we die, we die here."

"Humans may have a place to fall back to, but we have nowhere else to go."

The battle had turned bleak, but it could not break the spirits of the dwarves and elves. They let out a roar as they tempered their fighting spirits and poured out fierce opposition against the demons. The surviving human forces of the central unit soon joined the left wing, but the tipped scale of battle could not be overturned.

The demons leisurely surrounded the allied Dwarven-Elven forces who were entrenched within the tall mountains and began preparation for a final assault. It was at this moment when a monstrous roar rang out from the skies. The people turned to where the sound came from and began to point and shout toward the sky.

"D-dragon!"

"A dragon appeared!"

A massive dragon covered in black scales appeared within the ranks of the demon army. The black dragon was the half-dragon, Kha'nes. The most powerful hermit within the Tower of Recluse.

Now that I was getting ready to do some work, the Demon Realm Battlefront is falling apart. What's up with that?

Kha'nes who had been dispatched to find the cause of the altered Calamity had been procrastinating by exploring popular eateries and arrived late to the Demon Realm Battlefront only to discover that it was crawling with demons. She was attempting to move to someplace without devils and found herself involved in the battle at Harupaya Ridge.

"Where did all those fucking humans go?! Huh?" Kha'nes shouted with a thunderous voice as she struck out with her tail and claw to ruthlessly slice apart the devils who were inferior creatures to her.

"How is it fair that I have to step in because they couldn't even stop a few garbage demons?" bellowed the dragon.

The battle potential of dragons, the most powerful race, was indeed fearsome. Even Balroqs that were terrifying to humans were turned to ash once met with her breath. How would the lesser demons below them fare?

After Kha'nes ripped enough devils apart, she rose back up into the sky to launch another breath attack. Massive demon beasts and Hell Siege Engines melted under the flames. The demons tried to retaliate with their crossbows and catapults, but they could not penetrate through Kha'nes' scales. She was unmatched.

However, even Kha'nes was not invincible.

Oh, my. I'm starting to feel a bit peckish. As a half-dragon, she could turn into a dragon at any time, but there was a time limit.

She felt her reserved strength hitting its limits and retreated from the battlefield.

"Smell you later, devils!"

Kha'nes began to swiftly fly south after having her fill of rampage, leaving behind mountains of devil and war machine remains. Unfortunately, she only managed to cut down a portion of their forces. This was nothing more than a small incident that delayed their assault in their eyes.

After Kha'nes left, the devils consolidated their forces once again and began their advance to wipe out the remnants of the allied forces. The Mobile Fortress that was the dependable bastion of the humans stood at the front of the charge.

It was a literal castle with eight legs attached to it made possible through magical engineering. This free-moving mobile fortress was the greatest asset of the Order of the Iron Blood Knights, displaying oppressive defensive and offensive might.

The mobile fortress absorbed the dwarven artillery fire with its body and moved all the way up to the foot of the mountain before opening fire on the dwarves. Dozens of cannons opened fire onto the dwarven encampment and landed a strong blow against them. The dwarves tried their best to retaliate, but they were vastly outnumbered. Combined with the Hell Siege Engines from the other fronts, the siege units that the dwarves were so proud of were being demolished one by one. Sungchul tried his best by destroying a few of the Hell Siege Engines with his Meteor, but it was impossible to turn the battle with his efforts alone.

When the dwarven artillery was neutralized, the demons began to attack from the skies. The winged demons began their assault en masse, but the Elven archers dropped them from the skies. But because their attention was focused above, the demon army on the ground was no longer impeded in their march toward the mountain.

Dwarves could only helplessly watch as the dark tide of demons that had filled the horizon began to climb toward them as to swallow them whole.

"Looks like this is it."

Several gryphons tore through the demons to escape into the skies. The commanders and VIPs that had to survive were being evacuated. Kaal Bomba readily handed his own gryphon to Sungchul. "Ride this and escape human mage."

"Why would you do this for me?" When Sungchul asked out of surprise, Kaal raised his axe mightily and laughed with a smirk.

"I feel as though you will be a greater help to future battles than I. I have never seen a mage destroy Hell Siege Engines that well!"

He did not look back toward Sungchul before running toward the frontlines. He joined the bloody battle with a roar.

"..."

Sungchul gave a bow toward the dwarf's direction to show his gratitude before hopping onto the gryphon. It gave a sharp cry before it began to flap its massive wings and flew toward the sky. Winged demons attempted to overtake the gryphon, but it easily clawed and pecked its way to the blue sky.

Sungchul could see the battlefield much more easily from up above. The mountain range in which the allied force of dwarves and elves remained was completely surrounded, and the final bastion of the Demon Realm Battlefront that was Harupaya Ridge had been taken. It now looked like nothing could stop the invasion of the demons.

The gryphon that carried Sungchul landed by a lake not far from the battlefield. The commanders and VIPs that had escaped the battlefield were already resting by this lake.

"Damned... That damned..."

Armuk Bakr who had been in charge of the left flank was among them. The man who had managed to earn the trust of the dwarves despite being a human and had climbed to the position of one of the commanding generals of the allied forces was furious as he watched his comrades currently being slaughtered on the mountain range with eyes filled with sorrow. "I'll kill him. Martin Breggas. I vow to at least kill that bastard."

The Omens of Calamity were flapping their massive wings as they leisurely glided above the battlefield. They were a rare sight to see this far back from the front lines. It meant that the Calamity had drawn that much closer to this land.

Sungchul turned to look toward the road. There was an endless procession of refugees on the road stretching south. One of the Omens of Calamity discovered this mass of refugees and descended upon them with its talon flared claws. The helpless refugees were nothing but fodder for the beast of the Demon Realm.

The Omen of Calamity pinned a refugee with its massive claw and tore off the waist of another with its beak in order to swallow him whole.

The refugees hollered and fled, but there was nothing more they could do. The guards tried to fend off the Omen of Calamity, but it only made a few gestures with its wing as to show its annoyance before escaping into the sky.

The sound of a horn flute could be heard from the distant mountain range.

"…"

Sungchul who had been sitting powerless on the rock like the other stragglers suddenly rose from his seat. Armuk who had been cursing Martin Breggas looked over at him. *Huh, who is that guy?*

He had definitely seen that face before. He dug through his memory to the festival in Golden City that was held to welcome the Summoned in order to recall a man with a similar face and attire.

"You. I remember. You were one of the Summoned in Golden City, weren't you?" He acted as though he was familiar with Sungchul as he approached. However, an elegant hammer with a long handle appeared in Sungchul's hands in the next moment. Armuk's jaw dropped the moment he saw the hammer. It was Fal

Garaz. The hammer forged from a fragment of the sky; a divine artifact of the dwarves.

"G-gulp!"

Armuk who had been approaching him amicably fell back in shock.

"…"

Sungchul's indifferent gaze turned in his direction. Armuk felt enough pressure to cause his heart to explode.

Sungchul, with Fal Garaz in hand, walked forward in the direction of the horn flute. Divine strength gathered in his legs. His slow-moving feet suddenly couldn't be seen as he headed toward the battlefield at an unbelievable speed.

BOOM!

Sungchul's godlike figure appeared at the crossroad of Harupaya Ridge; evoking a cloud of dust in his wake.

"Huh?"

The devils over the ridge were already alarmed at his arrival, but they couldn't react to the hammer flying towards them in time.

BAM! WHAM!

One man stepped over two bloodied corpses as he revealed himself to the devils. The devils didn't quite recognize the man's face that held the hammer, but they recognized the hammer and what the man holding this hammer represented.

"D-destroyer!"

That cry instantly spread among the demons. Unprecedented terror filled the eyes of a hundred thousand demons. Sungchul stood alone in the front as he looked down upon them.

"…"

The man called the Destroyer, the Enemy of the World, engaged the hundred thousand demons on the hill. There was only one man standing in their way, but none of the devils dared to meet his challenge so foolishly.

There were a few that were watching this scene from a distance. Each of the gathered that saw the face of the man reflected onto the scrying orb reacted to his presence in their own way. One of them, in particular, was quite shocked.

What in the world... it can't be! Sujin looked in astonishment at the man in the scrying orb, with both her hands covering her mouth.

You are the Enemy of the World?!

***

Sungchul's presence had a different weight than the appearance of Kha'nes the Half-Dragon. The flow of battle instantly changed. The haughty devils that had been preparing for victory instantly reeled back in fear at the appearance of their bane, and the demon army that had been ready to snuff out the Dwarf-Elf allied forces immediately ceased its assault and turned back toward the unexpected appearance of this era's superhuman. Prontorowa, ranked eighth in the Demon Realm, was not pleased with this situation.

"Why are you so scared? Your opponent is a mere human. Do you think it's right for the proud demon race to be terrorized by a mere human?"

The devil that had lived over ten thousand years had yet to see Sungchul personally, and this was why he was able to maintain a cool disposition compared to the other devils. Prontorowa gestured with his emaciated hand and relentlessly gave out orders.

"Send out the Demon Beast unit!"

Massive monsters appeared amongst the demons. A group of mutated Tam Tams stood at the vanguard. These monsters, which were a demonized version of the giant monkey Tam Tam, revealed their bloody teeth and roared.

"Go!"

The low-rank demon soldiers cut the metallic chains that restrained the mutant Tam Tam. The monster first tore apart the tamer that had abused it, then drank his blood before heading in Sungchul's direction.

BOOM!

Followed by a quaking force, the mutant Tam Tam that had landed gathered his hands to strike toward the tiny human standing tall below him. The moment its fists reached Sungchul, Fal Garaz moved with blinding speed. The Tam Tam's skull reacted to the swing of the hammer before its eyes could.

BOOM!

The massive monkey fell backwards with a shattered skull. Sungchul grabbed the leg of the gigantic mutant Tam Tam that was several dozen times larger than him and threw it toward the demons watching the spectacle. The mutant Tam Tam corpse that carried the momentum of his divine strength flew at a low angle before bouncing off the ground and rolling through the demon army.

BOOM! BOOM! BOOM!

The corpse only managed to stop after flattening countless demons along the way.

"W-what is that?"

"Is he human? Is that thing still human?"

The fighting spirit of the devils who had only heard rumors of the Destroyer took a huge blow.

"Push on with numbers! That bastard is a human, so he'll just get tired like that dragon a while ago!"

Prontorowa flinched at Sungchul's display of might, but he still wasn't completely intimidated. He ordered the entire army to move toward Sungchul. The main force that had been attacking the Dwarf-Elf allied force now descended the mountain range and stood in formation before Sungchul. Winged demons of all different kinds gathered below the hovering Omen of Calamity, like a thick black storm cloud covering the sky.

"The Demon King has spoken. The one that kills the Destroyer will be given 2nd rank within the Demon Realm and power to befit that rank! Anyone willing, go take the Destroyer's life and glory shall follow!"

Prontorowa ordered his entire military might toward Sungchul. Excessive rewards managed to abate the terror to a certain degree, and the memory of that dragon that fled in exhaustion after its rampage was still fresh on their minds. As Sungchul was still human, they believed that he too must have a limit and eventually reach a point of exhaustion. Not to mention that their forces had a hundred thousand demons. According to Prontorowa's calculations, he would be able to put an end to Sungchul's legend at the sacrifice of just ten thousand demons.

BUOOOOOH

The devil's horn flute indicating the advance rang out bleakly throughout the entirety of Harupaya Ridge. The demon forces that surrounded Sungchul had begun their assault.

At the front of the charge were the Fallen Trolls, who were smaller than Demonic Beasts but still considerably large. The giants swung clubs as large as a fully grown adult human as they attacked Sungchul. The earth trembled when these massive creatures moved together in a group.

"Hiiii… Why was I chosen by a person like this?"

Bertelgia was letting out shrieks of terror from Sungchul's pocket. On the other hand, Sungchul looked at the approaching trolls with a calm gaze. He raised his foot slightly when they came close.

"…"

Divine strength was instilled into his feet, and the slightly raised foot struck the ground once.

BOOOOOOOOOOM!

A force on a different level than one caused by the drumming of the trolls' feet struck the earth. The ground not only trembled, but also shook violently. The trolls began to lose their footing in the intense tremor that resembled an earthquake. A dark light pierced through their formation like lightning.

BOOM! BOOM! BOOM! BOOM!

One blow for one troll. Fal Garaz's brutal blows popped each of the trolls' heads. Twenty trolls fell to the ground in a matter of moments, but Sungchul was still not satisfied. He entered the military base of the devils who had been holding their breath and watching the battle behind the trolls. He ceaselessly moved Fal Garaz in order to blow away all the nuisance in his way.

BOOM!

Dozens of demons flew away at each strike of the hammer, and that sort of hammering continued at several times per second. The immediate area around Sungchul turned into a no man's land within ten seconds. All that remained were splatters of blood and flesh, but not a single drop was on Sungchul's clothes nor was his breath ragged. He continued looking indifferent as he looked down toward the devils and fixed his grip on his hammer.

"…M-monster!"

"That… is not human."

It was then when the devils realized it. They could not overcome the human standing before their eyes, nor should they try to overcome him. It was not a matter of numbers, but their realization had come much too late.

Sungchul now entered the ranks of the Order of the Iron Blood Knights. He began another round of one-sided slaughter. The mobile fortress that the Order had been so proud of instantly lost half of its legs and sat in a twisted form onto the ground.

Sungchul, after silencing the Order of the Iron Blood Knights, immediately aimed for the Balroqs, Baals, and other such high-rank devils hiding amongst the low-rank ones. He didn't stop at simply killing those devils. He grabbed the horns of Balroqs to pry off their heads and grated the faces of Baals onto the rocky surface of the ground to kill them.

Everywhere Sungchul went, blood was spilled and mountains of corpses were formed. Not even five minutes passed before around ten thousand demons were slaughtered.

"W-what the fuck! Just what is that?"

When Prontorowa the high rank devil had heard the news that Hesthnius Max had thrown away his physical form to escape from Sungchul, he had mocked the Demon King, calling him a coward who lacked the fundamentals of a demon. But little by little he was forced to see differently, until now when Sungchul headed straight for him and completely changed his opinion.

"Are you the head of these devils?"

The human, without a drop of blood on him or breath out of place, stood tall before Prontorowa. When that human looked at him indifferently without any emotion in his eyes, Prontorowa felt a strong compulsion to bend his knee and beg for his life, but his pride as a High Devil stopped him. Instead, he managed to muster up some dignity as he opened his mouth. "T-That's right, you lowly human!"

Sungchul's response to the devil was Fal Garaz. As the hammer rose, Prontorowa tried to call out every magic known to him, but the hammer moved faster than his lips. Fal Garaz's head met Prontorowa's mouth. His jaw bone flew out of his skull, and his tongue that had been bent like a snake was pulled out in its entirety after being caught by the hammer.

"Kuuu...."

The leader of a hundred thousand demons met his end without being able to put up any resistance. Sungchul scraped off the disgusting offal from his hammer and looked toward the devils before raising a serious question. "... Who's next?"

None of the demons dared to meet him. A hundred thousand... no, now a number much lower than that fell back in retreat, leaving behind a single man on an empty battlefield.

—

"Sungchul, that bastard. How did he get that strong? The bastard's strength is on a different level than the Sungchul we knew." Executor Aquiroa spat out profanities as she looked away from the scrying orb.

"…Definitely powerful. Even Kha'nes, who is known as the most powerful recluse, would be no match for him," said Shamal who was of a similar opinion. Currently, no one could stop Sungchul. This gathering of powerful people in an undisclosed location was now coming to a consensus.

"There is now a need to utilize every method known to us to stop that beast."

There was a sense of urgency in Aquiroa's voice. If that monster managed to reach the Demon King, his life would be forfeit and according to the Scripture of Calamity, the Seven Heroes would awaken at the death of the Demon King. Not one, but seven individuals whose strength was known to be equal to or exceeding the Demon King would awaken. The chaos wrought at their hands would be unprecedented. At the very least, that had to be stopped.

Aquiroa and the others each held their own thoughts as they returned to their territories. The only ones now remaining were Shamal Rajput and his subordinates. Shamal looked at the young man assimilated into the shadows with vacant eyes as he spoke. "…How is it, Kaz Almeira? Can you do it?"

Kaz shook his head at Shamal's question. "That is not an opponent I can beat. I feel that it is rather a blessing to have survived an attack of such a man and lived."

Kaz who had been burning with vengeance could feel its flames simmer as he witnessed Sungchul's divine might.

Shamal turned his head toward Sujin. "How about you?"

She couldn't reply to his question for a brief moment. It was difficult for her to accept the identity of the Enemy of the World.

If that man was the Enemy of the World, just what have I done? Why did I not recognize that the man was the Enemy of the World? If it was going to be this way, why did I even bother coming back in time?

Shame had enveloped her heart in darkness. She only managed to regain her senses after Shamal called out her name a second time.

"Ahmuge. I asked for your thoughts."

Sujin finally realized that Shamal was calling out to her, and spoke out in surprise. "I can't handle him yet."

Sujin replied as such, but she was different than Kaz. She looked directly at Shamal as she continued in an unperturbed manner. "However, when the opportunity arises and if I manage to get the strength to pierce his heart, I will be able to put an end to the Calamity that he will bring."

A faint smile rose and left Shamal's lips. He could still remember it clearly. The moment when he had met the woman called Ahmuge. It was at the Castle of the Assassin's Guild, also known as the "Forbidden Palace." An intruder had managed sneak into the sect leader's sleeping quarters located at the center of the castle without being detected.

The woman boldly held a cheap dagger aimed at Shamal Rajput known as the King of all Assassins. Shamal realized Ahmuge's presence only when the end of her cold blade had touched his neck. This accomplishment wasn't brought about by strength nor ability, but rather a privilege that could only be earned by those with the unseen blessings, divine blessings, or similar soul contracts. Shamal could see Ahmuge's usefulness as an assassin in a single glance and lent his ear to her story.

Her future had been different compared to those that crossed through the threshold of time for their own personal benefit. There were some amusing and shocking details within. The particular detail about Sungchul, his old comrade, being the one to bring the end of the world was enough to draw the coldblooded Shamal's interest.

"I came from the future to kill him. The Enemy of the World. Killing that man is the life mission from which I cannot be dissuaded and also the sole reason I have come to live in this foreign world." Ahmuge or Sujin Lee bowed as she spoke with resolve. Shamal nodded and looked toward the north with vacant eyes.

"When the time comes, an opportunity will arrive. However, the time is not now. But do not fret. Your heart's desire will come to pass soon." Shamal disappeared in a puff of smoke after those words.

At the same hour, Sungchul was now situated in the middle of Harupaya Ridge in between two hostile factions. In front of him was the brazen demon army that was still occupying the wilderness, but they didn't dare to attack Sungchul. The problem was the factions situated behind him.

"Enemy of the World! Return Fal Garaz! Only then will we spare your life!"

They were the survivors of the dwarf, elf, and human allied forces that had been fighting alongside him just a moment ago. They spat out every threat and insult they could muster first, then followed up with arrows and catapults.

Sungchul looked at his former comrades attacking him with disinterest. A single arrow split his hair and stuck onto the ground.

"…"

He knew that it would end this way, and that was why he was hesitant. Hesitant to help his fellow fighters that were fighting with him under the same banner.

"This is too much. Really. Why are they acting like this? Even after you saved them?" Bertelgia asked, her angry voice filled with frustration. "Why are they doing this to you?"

It was then that a massive artillery shot, fired from the dwarven camp, flew past Sungchul and caused a large explosion. When the explosion subsided, Sungchul was visible again without so much as a scratch on his clothing.

Sungchul raised Fal Garaz high into the air and struck the ground. Powerful quakes shook the earth, and the artillery placed on the unsteady ground fell over, causing a massive explosion.

The dwarf-elf allied forces were scared stiff by his actions and retreated.

Sungchul who had managed to shut them up looked toward the demon army still stationed within the wilderness as he stood his ground at the peak of Harupaya Ridge. The wind blowing down from the mountain rustled his clothing and hair gently as it blew past.

Once silence fell over the battlefield, Sungchul looked down toward it and spoke in a firm voice. "This is my fate."

Chapter 16 – Followers of Calamity

Animosity against the Enemy of the World was universal, and no one would openly dare refute it. The clergymen attributed all sorts of evil to the Enemy of the World during their sermons and denounced him while wanted posters of him with an astronomical figure as a bounty were stuck in prominent places in plazas.

There were efforts in libraries to belittle his achievements. Every one of his heroic acts was erased, and misdeeds were added to his resume in fearsome amounts overnight. Statues of Sungchul that had been erected in places throughout the Human Empire were torn down and destroyed. Those that weren't already aware of him naturally concluded this man known as the Enemy of the World was a dangerous man capable of heinous acts through literature and word of mouth.

However, there were a rare few that questioned this oppressive opinion about the Enemy of the World. "Is what we're doing really justified?"

Kaal Bomba was watching this man who stood at the peak of Harupaya Ridge creating a divide between the human and demon armies with eyes filled with complicated emotions.

"Regardless of what anyone says, didn't the Enemy of the World fight alongside us and save us from disaster twice?"

He could still vividly recall the reverberation of the horn flute that swept up from below like a fierce wave carrying a powerful wind along the slope. If Sungchul hadn't appeared precisely when he did, Kaal and his comrades would have been killed and forgotten. Kaal could understand his comrades that were aiming their siege weapons at the man while pouring out profanities, and yet he was also filled with doubt.

"A dwarven grudge is deeper than the rivers and the seas, but does this mean our grudge is more important than our gratitude towards our savior? This is my question."

Unfortunately, the other dwarves did not see things his way.

"I don't know what he was thinking while saving us, but just look at what's in that bastard's hand. He is holding the divine tool gifted to us by our God with his filthy human hands and dirtying it with filthy devil blood. He has committed the gravest of sin against us and made mockery of our people."

"Rightly so! This is an insult that cannot be overlooked by any dwarf."

Their hatred toward Sungchul could not be diminished. As long as Sungchul refused to return Fal Garaz... or even if he did, their intention to never forgive his actions was clear. Dwarven stubbornness was often compared to that of stone. Regardless of how much time has passed or how strong of a force tries to bend their will, this hatred would not fade.

Kaal shut his mouth as he knew all too well that his friends would not change their minds so easily. Behind the dwarves who were openly showing hostility, armies big and small were taking up positions on the hill. It was a military unit that was gathered by each nation urgently to respond to the loss at Harupaya Ridge and the appearance of the Enemy of the World.

"..."

Sungchul watched without emotion as human reinforcements gathered upon the hill where the biting winds blew.

Martin Breggas had forfeited his duties, and the Order of the Iron Blood Knights now waves the flag of rebellion. It might have been odder if the feudal lords hadn't responded urgently.

The majority of the reinforcements that had been quickly gathered were mercenaries. Lords of every small nation located behind the Demon Realm battlefront had expended all efforts in order to form this mercenary company. Sungchul didn't care if the force was composed of mercenaries or standing armies.

He turned his head to look north. The demon army had suffered greatly because of Sungchul and lost a lot of vigor, but the grand demon army that was positioned in the plains still had numbers nearing a hundred thousand. They had their feet tied due to a single person, but as soon as Sungchul left, they were prepared to move south once again.

There was only one reason that the demon army was showing such leisure. It was because of the attitude that the humans and its allies had towards Sungchul; the Humans launched sporadic assaults against Sungchul while the Devils watched.

Sungchul's response to this had been passive, but it gave assurance to the devils. Sungchul was also an enemy of the humans, and that meant he might not side with the humans and simply depart from Harupaya Ridge. They might have lost their commander and a large number of their high-grade devils, but they weren't willing to give up on this rare opportunity.

"How long are you going to stay here?" Bertelgia spoke with a heavy sigh as though she was fed up.

"I'm staying until the human army and their allies gather a powerful enough force to stand against them." Sungchul looked south through squinted eyes. The numbers were growing with the arrival of large and small mercenary companies, but it was still an insufficient number to stop the demons.

He would probably have to wait at least two more days for the humans to be able to defend themselves. Sungchul briefly reflected on this, leaned on a nearby rock, and closed his eyes.

"So frustrating! You're going to protect those ungrateful idiots who are repaying your help with malice? If it was me, I'd have been long gone. See what they can do without me!"

"There's no benefit for me if this place is broken through," said Sungchul as he picked up a single pebble and tossed it into the air.

PIK! PIK!

Drops of blood fell from the path the pebble had flown by, and the remains of an eyeball fell to the ground like a deflated balloon. It was an Observer's Eye sent by a mage of the human faction. It was one summoned with high-grade summoning techniques on a different level than what could be found back at the Summoning Palace, but to Sungchul it was just a plaything to pass the time.

"To get rid of the Seven Heroes quickly, it is advantageous to maintain the current strategic state in many different aspects. If by chance the Seven Heroes arrive in a land where humans have been exterminated, it'll make things more complicated."

"But still, I don't like it. Especially those dwarves! They're calling you a son of a bitch! Just 'cause you stole a hammer!"

"It's because this hammer isn't ordinary."

He had now held the hilltop for two days and had begun to feel peckish. He had filled his belly so far with water and date palms, so Sungchul decided to cook for himself before the watchful eyes of a hundred thousand demons.

There wasn't anything particularly edible in the area; just the colorless, odorless, and tasteless mushroom that he didn't know the name for. Sungchul held a head-sized stone and looked toward the Omen of Calamity soaring through the air. He waited patiently until the Omen was at the nearest point to him and threw the rock. It flew in a straight line like a beam of light, tore through the Omen's beak, and smashed its skull causing the massive bird to crash toward the ground. Sungchul butchered the fallen Omen of Calamity with a blade and inspected the state of its meat.

"… This is not something anyone should eat."

It was something he put effort into hunting, but he left it behind without a second thought. Instead, he dug through his Soul Storage and pulled something out. It was noodles fried with oil and dehydrogenated soup. It was something called "instant ramen" back in Sungchul's world. Strictly speaking, it wasn't instant ramen. There was no ingredient that hadn't been carefully prepared by Sungchul's hands within the homemade instant noodle.

Sungchul took one of the helmets rolling around and used it as a canteen by carefully washing it with water before boiling some water within it. Once the water began to boil, he added a soup base he had sealed inside of a tin container and added noodles that had been fried in oil into the water. All that was left was to watch it boil.

Sungchul didn't use any additional additives in his ramen. He followed the principle that the true flavor of the ramen would come alive as long as he stuck to the standard ingredients.

"Mmm." His stomach, which had been filled with nothing but hard palm dates for the past few days, began to rumble when he breathed in the aroma of his cooking. Sungchul pulled out some chopsticks and began to stir the ramen boiling in his helmet as he took in the aroma. It was at this moment that he could feel an unfamiliar presence close by. It was an intruder.

"…"

Sungchul glared as his eyes shifted toward the direction where he felt the presence. He couldn't see anything with his naked eyes, but his Soul Contract – Eye of Truth activated automatically to see the single human figure beyond what his eyes were capable of.

It was an individual who cloaked her body with an unconventional invisibility magic. A young woman draped in a thick robe. Her yellow pupils that held a persistent light resembled one from a reptile. Curiosity rose in Sungchul's eyes. *Isn't she that dragon that appeared two days ago on the battlefield?*

The one approaching Sungchul was none other than Kha'nes from the Tower of Recluse.

Is he the man known as the Enemy of the World? Quite plain. Not to mention his clothes are pretty much just rags. She did not even imagine that Sungchul had already discovered her. She had not hidden herself through ordinary magic, but the highest-grade magic of the dragons known as Dragon-tongue. She did not think a mere human would be able to see her at all.

However, she did not have a chance to witness Sungchul's fight herself. She had been at some nameless lake in Trowyn sprawled onto a sandy beach while Sungchul was massacring the devils. All because she had overexerted herself from being in Dragon form for so long.

She had heard that Sungchul managed to defeat the demons by himself but to simply accept the rumors of his exploits would be exceedingly unrealistic. Seeing is believing. It was all for this reason that Kha'nes had decided to discreetly investigate this man known as the Enemy of the World, but a strange aroma tickled the tip of her nose as she took a few steps closer.

Huh? I can smell something delicious.

Sungchul was boiling something on the fire. A red soup was boiling inside a helmet, and she could see some white flour-based noodles dancing within it. It was an aroma that she had never smelled before coming from the food she had never seen before.

"…"

As Kha'nes didn't seem to take any further actions, Sungchul took a mouthful of ramen to his lips.

SLURP.

The chewy noodles steeped in the salty soup was sucked in through Sungchul's lips. It wasn't all that bad by Sungchul's standards. Accompanied by hunger, which was the greatest side dish, at the top of a mountain with biting wind, it worked his appetite to a degree he had never felt before.

[The Score of this Recipe is… 57 points!]

Even this mysterious person that had judged Korean cuisine so harshly decided to give a relatively decent score for Sungchul's homemade ramen.

Of course. It was stock made from the highest grade of chicken fit for serving the emperor and mixed with 32 different spices to make the soup.

Sungchul continued his meal regardless of whether Kha'nes observed him or not.

"Over a hundred thousand demons are watching, but I guess food still crawls down your gullet just fine?" Bertelgia mocked him, but Sungchul didn't hear any of it. This ramen that he had prepared after so long was truly an exquisite dish. If there was a single flaw, it was that there was no Kimchi to accompany it. It goes without saying that Kha'nes who was watching secretly was starting to drool.

Gulp. Her stomach began to rumble as she watched Sungchul eat this strange dish that she had never seen before with such enthusiasm.

Now that I think about it, I haven't eaten a proper meal since I took on Dragon form.

She had eaten two warhorses in her state as a Dragon, but Kha'nes didn't remember this fact. As she was drawn by this strange aroma from this foreign food, she unknowingly took a step closer to Sungchul.

"I know you're there."

When Kha'nes approached within ten meters, Sungchul stopped his chopsticks and looked toward her to let out a sharp remark.

He saw through my Dragon-tongue magic?! How can that be? He must have good instincts! Kha'nes wore a bitter smile as she pulled off the magical veil that covered her body. The young woman with the eyes of a dragon wearing a thick robe appeared before Sungchul. Bertelgia, who had been complaining, quickly retreated into Sungchul's pocket at the sudden appearance of this monstrous person.

"Hey there, human." Kha'nes held up her palm as she threw out a friendly greeting.

"They call you the Enemy of the World?"

***

"What's your business with me?"

Sungchul spoke out abruptly while continuing to slurp down his noodles.

"I just came to see what you looked like. I was curious as to how the most infamous person in the world would look."

Kha'nes walked up casually and sat down across from him. Sungchul did not mind her at all. He didn't feel any hostility from her, and she would need to transform before she could do any meaningful harm to him.

Kha'nes continued to observe him from close by.

He looks like an average human on the outside. Even his clothes are pretty ragged. I thought the thing in his pocket was a person, but I guess her outer form is a book. His stats also... I guess he's wearing the Deceiver's Veil?

She couldn't know his exact strength, but it was clear that Sungchul was not someone to take lightly.

I might have to fight against the Avian King, so it might not be a good idea to waste my strength on someone of this caliber.

Kha'nes decided not to engage Sungchul in her mind. Sungchul continued to eat as Kha'nes watched.

Her voice could be heard in the midst of his meal. "You don't have to eat so fast. I didn't come here to fight."

Kha'nes' attention shifted away from Sungchul to his food. "What kind of recipe is this? This aroma is foreign to me."

"It's just normal food." Sungchul gulped down the rest of his noodles and began eating the soup with a spoon.

"Mm." He judged that the taste was decent, and began to slurp down the soup from the helmet.

Kha'nes who was watching this felt drool unwittingly gather in her mouth. "Hey," she called out to Sungchul.

"What?"

When Sungchul responded curtly, Kha'nes didn't hesitate and asked her question in a lively voice, "Can I have a taste?"

"..."

Sungchul silently downed the rest of the soup.

"That's going too far!" Kha'nes pouted out of annoyance, but as she did, Sungchul held something out toward her. On closer inspection, it was some fried noodles and a glass bottle filled with an unknown powder.

"If you want some, cook it yourself. It's not my hobby to cook ramen for women I don't know."

He said as such before quietly opening up his coat. A golden gleam hidden within the coat blinded Kha'nes' eyes. Her jaw dropped.

No way... that's the Insignia of a High-class Chef?! And isn't that a Gold Class as well?!

It had been three hundred years since she had last met a High-class Chef that managed to reach the Gold class. It was already hard enough in this world to meet a High-class Chef, not to mention one of Gold class, so to meet a chef of this caliber was something of a miracle. Kha'nes could feel her apathetic dragon heart beginning to pound with excitement as she looked back and forth between the instant fried noodles and the soup powder.

This looks like a type of military rations. But I haven't seen this preservation method before. Taking noodles, an ingredient not usually found in preserved food, and frying it in oil to make it last longer is very innovative.

She broke off an end of the instant fried noodles and placed it in her mouth. She could taste the crunchiness and the flavor of oil combined with the savory flour-based noodles in her mouth.

"This is fried with bean oil?" Kha'nes directed her comment toward Sungchul.

"That's correct."

Impressive, Sungchul thought, as he paid close attention to Kha'nes's behavior. Kha'nes was investigating the soup powder inside the glass bottle at this moment. She dabbed an end of a finger onto the powder and made complicated expressions as she fell into deep thought while tasting it.

"Hmm, this is stock made from ground chicken bones with red pepper, garlic, ginger, among other things and made into a powder."

It was incredibly accurate if not for a few missing ingredients. Sungchul acknowledged that the half-dragon in front of him possessed an incredibly sensitive palate.

"Wait." When Kha'nes was about to begin cooking, he added the proper amount of water into the helmet himself. "I'll do it. It's not hard."

Everything changed as he realized the person in front of him knew proper food. It also appeared that Kha'nes knew the implications of the broach that Sungchul wore on him. Even though it was a simple dish, Sungchul did not want others to poorly judge the taste of his food.

"Oh my, how friendly." Kha'nes smiled lightly with her eyes as she observed him cooking. Ramen cooking couldn't really be improved upon, and there wasn't much work involved. He waited for the water to boil, dropped in the noodle and soup powder, and gave it a few swirls in between. Sungchul held out the finished dish to Kha'nes after four minutes.

"Try it."

Kha'nes revealed a huge smile as she pulled out the fork from within her clothes before digging in. Firm noodles that had been properly boiled were slurped through her lips. A flash of interest passed through her lizard-like eyes. "This dish is tasty!"

"Of course." Sungchul turned his back toward her with his arms crossed. Kha'nes gulped down the entire bowl of ramen in a frenzy while carefully blowing on it.

"That was a great meal, Enemy of the World!" Kha'nes patted her belly while expressing her gratitude.

Sungchul peeked at her through the corner of his eyes, and he could see that she was extremely satisfied. He could feel his pride soaking into his heart as he turned back toward her. "If you have no further business, I would appreciate it if you left this place."

"I got it. I was about to leave anyways."

"..."

"Aren't you curious about my business?" Kha'nes spoke subtly while looking at his back.

What a talkative dragon, thought Sungchul.

Some dragons would not open their mouth once in a thousand years, but there are those who would blather on throughout the same thousand years. Kha'nes appeared to be of the latter type.

"In truth, I was planning on heading north. There is a root of Calamity that isn't well known yet," continued Kha'nes.

"A root of Calamity?" Sungchul showed interest.

"That's right. A new Calamity was recorded within the Scripture of Calamity before it disappeared."

"Is that even possible?"

"Not normally, but if humans keep trying to forcefully stop the progression of Calamity like now, there is bound to be background noise from time to time. The calamity that had appeared momentarily might have been a consequence of that"

"May I know which Calamity that was?" asked Sungchul.

Kha'nes briefly considered Sungchul's request before she opened her mouth to speak in a serious manner that was unlike her.

"The Final King. It is a Calamity regarding the Avian King with black wings."

"Ah, that one."

Her revelation took the wind out of his sails as the Calamity had already been resolved by his own hands. Sungchul's disappointment was soon revealed on his face. Kha'nes felt perplexed at his reaction and hastily threw out a retort.

"Eh? Why are you making that face? Aren't you interested? It's the Calamity of the Avian King!"

"Sorry, but it wasn't something I wanted to hear about. It seems like I've taken away too much of your time, so shouldn't you get going already?" Sungchul coldly chased her away.

Kha'nes revealed more information with a hurt expression on her face, but none of it could evoke Sungchul's interest.

The half-dragon Kha'nes had to climb down from the hill after being treated to a bowl of ramen. "Visit the Tower of Recluse some time. I'll give you a good surprise if you cook some good food for me."

"I'll keep that in mind."

He had been planning on visiting the Tower of Recluse in a day or two regardless. He wanted to see the change on the Scripture of Calamity himself after eliminating the Demon King Hesthnius.

After the noisy Kha'nes had departed, silence returned to the peak of Harupaya Ridge. Sungchul let the time pass while sitting by the fire.

—

It was the fourth day since Sungchul had situated himself on Harupaya Ridge. He could sense an unusual number of Observer's Eyes on him since very late last night. As morning approached, a group of mages had moved to someplace not far away through Teleportation. Sungchul watched the approach of these unfamiliar mages with an indifferent gaze from his seat.

The mages were wary of Sungchul and approached him carefully. When they finally reached him, they showed him proper respect by speaking in a lower register. "Lord of Heracles, I greet the Destroyer."

Sungchul could immediately sense that the mages had approached him with ill intentions.

"What do you want?" he urged the mages with a voice mixed with revulsion.

"It might be more appropriate to introduce ourselves before we get down to business. We are a part of the Followers of Calamity, who you detest so much."

The Demonic Weapon Cassandra appeared in Sungchul's hand. "Get lost."

The mages trembled slightly at the sight of the fiery whip in Sungchul's grip, but they pressed on despite their fears. "We have only come here to deliver a message from a certain person."

"What? A certain person? Speak plainly."

Cassandra moved about like an angry snake and struck a nearby boulder. The entire boulder shattered at the moment of impact and rolled off the hill in pieces.

One of the mages visibly wavered as though the tension had overwhelmed him. Among them a person who appeared to be the eldest broke the silence with his head still bowed.

"Our master, The One Who Guides the Calamity, wishes to meet you personally."

The One Who Guides the Calamity. It was a title Sungchul had never heard before, but he had heard from Elijah earlier that the Followers of Calamity now had a leader.

The person mentioned by Elijah and this guy, are they one and the same?

The face of a single woman passed by Sungchul's memories. It was the face of a blonde woman with a pale skin as white as snow and dreamlike eyes that appeared and faded like smoke.

Vestiare.

Sungchul glared at the mages with eyes filled with hostility. The mages didn't dare to meet his gaze.

"Why is that woman looking to meet me?"

"W-we cannot dare to pretend that we understand that one's intentions. We only wish to say that that one wishes to help you. We only hope that you don't attack her on sight..." The mage didn't even manage to finish his thoughts when the Demonic Weapon Cassandra had split them all in half.

SRRKT.

The halves of every corpse rolled off the hill. He felt the metallic stench of blood brush past his nose as he turned around.

"Why don't you start revealing yourself?"

The One that Guides the Calamity was already here. A blonde woman in a white robe appeared from behind a boulder like a mirage. The Seventh Hero, Vestiare.

The Calamity-to-come revealed a cruel smile as she stepped toward Sungchul.

"As expected, you have good senses." Vestiare spoke with a soft smile on her face.

"Looking for an early grave?"

"You could see it that way." A magical formation appeared at the tip of her finger, and a single scroll appeared. This unusual scroll had a mixture of crimson and dark coloration. The scroll lifted itself into the air and floated toward Sungchul.

"I've heard you have been having much difficulty getting rid of the Demon King. You will be able to rid yourself of that problem much more quickly with this."

Sungchul grabbed the scroll Vestiare had handed over, and when he did, information about the scroll appeared in his eyes.

[Scroll of Harmageddon]
Grade: Epic
Type: Scroll
Effect: Casts the Destructive Magic "Harmageddon"
Note: It immediately unleashes the most powerful destructive magic, "Harmageddon ."

Sungchul's eyes twitched. *Harmageddon? Isn't that an 8ᵗʰ circle magic? I've heard of its name, but I never got to see it in person.*

It was unprecedented territory unexplored by any School of Magic. This kind of fortune was so simply handed to Sungchul.

"One receives greater harm from magical attacks in ethereal form. This means that it's not strictly necessary to use Harmageddon, but isn't there nothing better to make sure the job is done right?" Vestiare spoke in a dream-like voice.

Sungchul's hand that held the scroll trembled slightly as he asked, "Why are you giving me this?"

Vestiare held a faint smile at Sungchul's question. "Because we can only step up when the Demon King falls."

***

The Floating Palace. It was the dwelling of the Emperor and the heart of the most powerful nation within the continent, the Human Empire. A special guest had been invited to the Floating Palace by the Emperor and been granted audience.

"Speak, Regressor."

The Emperor who sat on a throne made of gold spoke in a low voice, and the young woman who was prostrated before him finally raised her head. Her identity was none other than Sujin Lee. She took care in speaking to the first among the Champions of the Continent and the one most deserving of the title of "The most powerful man in the Continent."

"That's right, your highness. Sungchul will take care of the Demon King all by himself after revealing himself to the world. This is the future I have seen with my own eyes."

"How did Sungchul kill the Demon King?" asked the Emperor.

It was rare for the Emperor to inquire about the details. For a man who was the head of an imperial hegemony which was in control of the continent, he was only given vague reports on the situation. But he asked about such a seemingly negligible detail nonetheless.

Sujin felt the Emperor's curiosity weighing on her body like countless tons of weight, but she calmly proceeded to answer him. "I do not know, as I wasn't able to see it myself."

"Is that so?" A brief look of disappointment flashed across his eyes.

Sujin spoke again. "However, according to my companions, an explosion on a scale never witnessed before took place. They say a massive explosion comparable to the atomic explosion in the world of the Summoned enveloped the surrounding area."

"Is it magic? I can't imagine that Sungchul brought a nuke with him. Well… more importantly, that kind of intricate device would become unusable due to the curse."

"It becomes recorded historically as magic, but the important part is the aftermath."

"Isn't the result that the Demon King is killed?"

Sujin firmly shook her head at the Emperor's question. "The Enemy of the World also becomes swept up in the explosion and is left in a critical state."

"Hoh." A strange light flashed across the Emperor's eyes. Sujin nodded and spoke in a stern voice as though she had understood his thoughts.

"If we had pushed back against the Enemy of the World a little harder, the future I have seen might have been avoided."

Sujin hadn't seen it directly, but every one of her period spoke of the same thing; that moment was the final opportunity to kill the Enemy of the World. If they had a few more soldiers with a few more talented fighters, they might have been able to squeeze the life out of Sungchul's throat.

The Emperor looked at Sujin. There wasn't a single mark of deceit in her eyes.

The first priority is to keep the Demon King breathing, but if that becomes impossible, it might not be a bad option to eliminate the guy who might become a threat.

Once the decision was made, the Emperor rose from his throne. He gestured with his arm to command the generals bowing toward him in the vicinity.

"Sortie every deployable unit!"

The Generals of the Human Empire let out a shout at his command before rushing out in perfect order. It was a display of power befitting the strongest nation. Fleets of airships, the pride of the Human Empire, soon took to the air around the Floating Palace.

"We will deploy five fleets. The direction is north-northwest. The target is the Enemy of the World."

The noses of the airships that had lifted into the air faced north-northwest. The powerful sound of the marching horn rang out in the entire area around the palace, and the Emperor ordered an attendant to hand Sujin some particular items: a single sword embedded with a red ruby and a single glass bottle filled with some black liquid. The Emperor watched Sujin put the items away while he spoke.

387

"I've been told that you have a unique ability. The sword might not be anything special, but it has a legendary sharpness, and this glass bottle contains poison of a legendary strength." The intention behind his words was clear.

"When the opportunity arrives, kill my old friend."

–

"Brilliant reasoning."

Sungchul allowed himself a faint smile as he turned around, tucking the scroll away. His figure suddenly disappeared from Vestiare's sight.

Grab!

A rough grip clenched down onto Vestiare's neck. He gave no time for her to reflect on the situation. Sungchul applied more pressure onto the hand holding her neck and it snapped like a flower. A pale apparition briefly appeared above Vestiare's body before disappearing again. It was only then that Sungchul realized that it wasn't Vestiare's true body.

This is also an illusion. She's playing a clever trick that's difficult to see through at a glance with the Eye of Truth.

Her consciousness had taken hold of another's living body as a vessel. The fog-like aura that was emanating from the entire body and her appearance that was still beautiful even beneath it made it hard to distinguish the truth. The woman whose neck had been snapped by Sungchul was a different woman. He didn't recognize her face, but it would have been one of the Followers of Calamity.

Sungchul threw the corpse onto the ground and gazed at the illusion that had pulled away from the corpse with disinterest.

"I knew it'd turn out this way." Vestiare's illusion spoke with a smile.

"But you'll end up moving according to our will."

"Me? Move to your will?" mocked Sungchul.

Vestiare's illusion laughed coquettishly as she floated up into the air. "I know you're diligently learning magic, but how much have you progressed in only a year's worth of time? At the most, you'd only have reached the level of a beginner mage. The road of magic is a difficult and winding path."

"..."

"Sadly for you, there isn't much time left for the humans. They haven't yet realized that delaying the Calamity isn't a solution."

"You say some interesting things." It was something he had heard many times before, but Sungchul pretended it was new information.

Vestiare's illusion began her tale as though she was dreaming. "The world is crumbling. The tide of Calamity is crashing oppressively onto levees built by the humans. The foolish humans believe that it might be possible to buy time by plugging up the levee, but leaks will spring from all over until the flood of Calamity drowns the continent in death and anguish."

"But, there hasn't been any incident in eight years. The way I see it, there's still plenty of time left." Sungchul made an immediate judgement. He decided that Vestiare and the other Seven Heroes weren't aware of his movements. They seemed to only know that he had overcome a magic-related objective of the Seven Heroes and other details that became widely known when he revealed himself to the world. There had been many opportunities for Vestiare to appear before him if she had seen through his movements, but she had shown herself at Harupaya Ridge four days after he had shown himself. It was only after the news had spread across the world that she had appeared.

It was a good thing that I adjusted the Deceiver's Veil after I met with Kha'nes. These bastards don't know much about me yet.

She didn't even seem to know that Sungchul had acquired Meteor. Their ability to gather information was sub-par. Sungchul figured all of this out while he stared her down. Vestiare had a mystical expression on her face as though she still believed that she had all the information at hand.

"That scroll is my gift to you. Please hurry up and kill the Demon King. If you don't, even I can't say how the Calamity will change."

Sungchul looked at the scroll in his hand that contained some sinister power. It reeked. It reeked with a fetid rotting stench. If Sungchul had not obtained Magic Power, this might have been the sole, irrefutable offer. However, he had other options available to him.

"This scroll looks like a trap." Sungchul stared her down as he spoke. It was obvious, but her expression remained unchanged as she withstood his accusation.

"Every rose is bound to have thorns. To use it or not is up to you."

"I see." Sungchul threw the scroll onto the ground.

Vestiare's lips twitched slightly. "You can't take care of the Demon King without it."

"Is that so?" Sungchul glanced at the scroll without a shred of interest before answering unemotionally. "I want to raise my Intuition."

The wind blowing up the mountain ridge ruffled Sungchul's hair and clothes as it blew past. On the other hand, Vestiare's appearance was unaffected.

"The scroll doesn't require Intuition," she replied.

"No, this is my personal desire apart from the scroll. It's been quite fun dabbling in magic recently."

Vestiare wasn't fully aware of Sungchul's current situation, but when Sungchul brought up the topic in a cunning way, a warning light flashed across her eyes.

"Are you perhaps attempting to get rid of the Demon King by learning magic?"

"I'm just the type of person to stick to stat points, personally. I only feel good if I manage to raise it, even by a single point. In any case, I could consider using it if there was some quest."

This was a battle that Vestiare could not win from the very beginning. It might have worked if she had approached him with the offer earlier, but her window of opportunity had already passed.

"I don't make bad offers." Sungchul was planning on taking his time to deal with the Demon King, even if it took another month or so.

This man... just what is he planning? Vestiare fell into deep thought trying to decipher his intentions. *Could it be that he already has the magic power to kill the Demon King?*

She could not see through Sungchul's stats because of his Soul Contract – Deceiver's Veil, but Sungchul shouldn't be at that level yet. If Sungchul had, the Demon King would have long since departed from the land of the living.

Another possibility was that this was an old-fashioned bluff. Vestiare had seen plenty of men trying to pull a fast one. *But, I can't lower my guard just because this man is bluffing. I can't know if this man has already attained the magic power to kill the Demon King somehow.*

Vestiare held a smile once again after organizing her thoughts. "You're saying that you'll be satisfied with a quest that can raise Intuition, correct?"

Sungchul nodded. Vestiare then chanted a spell with a hushed voice that formed countless magic formations around her entire body.

Sungchul could see that these weren't ordinary magic formations, but communications or an urgent request to a god.

Is she making a quest?

It usually took a great deal of time and dedication for a human to make a quest. It was because they were creatures far apart from gods, but Vestiare, who had become a Calamity herself, seemed to have little difficulty in making a request of a god. When the countless magic formations around her body had disappeared, Vestiare held a faint smile as she pointed below her own feet. There was an image resembling her own face below her feet. When

Sungchul laid his hand on the image, bright letters appeared in his eyes.

[Admiration of Beauty – To draw 33 portraits of Vestiare who is the most beautiful in the world.

Reward – +1 Intuition, Vestiare's portrait drawn on Jewel Papyrus]

The quest contents were one thing, but the rewards were also quite something. It only raised a single point of Intuition as he mentioned earlier even though it was possible for Vestiare to raise it by more than 10 points at a single time. The worthless portrait was just tossed in there.

Sungchul burst out laughing, and Vestiare watched him with leisure as she casually spoke again. "I made the quest as you requested. You aren't someone that doesn't keep their word, are you?"

"My, you've made a shit of a quest." Sungchul held a bitter smile and picked up the scroll that had fallen to the floor.

"I'll be waiting then." Vestiare flashed a captivating smile toward Sungchul and disappeared like smoke. Sungchul looked around the vicinity where she disappeared. Other than the gazes of devils in the distance, he couldn't feel any presence of magic.

"Bertelgia."

Maybe from holding his expression for too long, he could feel a slight cramp on his lips.

"Hm? Why are you calling?"

"It's time to learn drawing."

Vestiare would never be able to imagine that that one Intuition point was exactly what Sungchul needed; nothing in this world that is worth having comes easy. Clouds in the southern skies rumbled as massive magic formations began to appear. Sungchul who had been sloppily drawing pictures of Vestiare looked toward the southern skies. Dozens of Airships had popped out from the magic formation. The Golden Flag of the Sun flapped high in the air. The main fleet of the Human Empire made its appearance on Harupaya Ridge.

Chapter 17 – Bid for Redemption

A single man was laughing in a rumbling voice in an airship with his hair waving in the wind.

"Kekeke."

He was Admiral of the 4th Fleet of the Human Empire Minamoto Daisuke. He had risen to his current position after accumulating unclear accomplishments that remain a topic of controversy to this day.

He calls himself a tactician, but when he introduces himself, he shares that his success is because he had read through so many books on warfare that his head is filled with the *Three Strategies of Huang Shigong*[2] and his gut with the ability to respond to anything. However, his strategies were one-dimensional and distasteful, and more than anything, they resulted in large casualties. If there was anything else of note, it was that he was a Summoned. He was summoned from Japan, as could be guessed from his name, but whether he was Japanese or not was a topic of debate. According to a Summoned from Japan that had spoken to him, all of Minamoto's conversation is limited to "Yosh!" and "Hai!"

Regardless of all of these bad rumors about him, Minamoto was a truly powerful swordsman. With his hip-length hair flying wildly in the wind combined with his shouts befitting that of a madman while swinging his katana, he looked like the incarnate of an Evil Yasha itself. He was a figure that had brought terror to both enemies and allies alike. This Minamoto arrived at the peak of Harupaya Ridge undertaking the weighty mission of subjugating the Enemy of the World. He held a cylindrical scope to his eye as he observed Sungchul and began to mutter under his breath.

"Mm. To be able to sit on the peak by himself while confronting a massive army. Isn't this the 'Empty Fort Strategy' by Zhuge Liang[3]?"

His strategist mind began to work overtime, but his concentration didn't last very long. The overseer of the subjugation of the Enemy of the World, Dimitri Medioff, had summoned each fleet commander to the deck of his flagship, Andragoras. Minamoto was displeased, but he had no choice but to obey.

Minamoto kept grumbling as he stepped onto the miniature ferry to board the deck of Andragoras. The other fleet commanders were also gathered on the deck for a strategy meeting. The head of the meeting, Dimitri, looked at each commander in the eye as he spoke in a serious manner.

"According to the reports, the strength of the Enemy of the World well exceeds our expectations. I don't need to reiterate what kind of strength is capable of driving away a hundred thousand demons alone. So, we will need to seek out a method to oppose the Enemy of the World with the utmost seriousness."

Dimitri looked at each of the commanders after his speech. They all kept their silence. None of them was able to come up with a good solution. Their opponent was a monster among monsters that had walked up to an army of a hundred thousand demons as leisurely as one walks into one's home and had struck down their commander. Dimitri's gaze shifted over to Minamoto, who was the last to arrive. Minamoto was filled with anticipation as he was prepared to relay some kind of plan he had just come up with and mulled how to express it. But Dimitri tactfully avoided locking eyes. Unfortunately, Minamoto wasn't one to be so easily discouraged.

"Head Commander, I have a good idea."

Dimitri briefly let his emotions show on his face. *What kind of stupid thing does this crazy bastard have to say this time?*

Dimitri didn't wish to open the floor to him, but Minamoto was still one of the fleet commanders. Dimitri let out a sigh as he spoke bluntly. "Say your piece."

"The way I see it, Sungchul is using the 'Empty Fort Strategy.'"

"I see. That's a brilliant opinion." Dimitri spoke drily while applauding before he turned away.

"But, I wasn't quite done yet?"

"Ah, you had more to say? Looks like I made a mistake." Dimitri's face continued to broadcast that he didn't wish to hear any more of what the man had to say, but none of those signals entered Minamoto's eyes.

"The only method to avoid getting caught by the 'Empty Fort Strategy' is to rush him down without giving him any moment of breath."

Dimitri started a conversation with the other commanders, played around, and even closed his eyes pretending to sleep while Minamoto spoke, but Minamoto's speech continued on regardless. When Dimitri's patience had reached its limits, a senior adjunct walked in like a miracle.

"Reporting!"

"What happened?" Dimitri greeted the adjunct brightly, but Minamoto seemed to be muttering something or the other while this occurred.

He quickly made some distance from Minamoto with rapid steps while gesturing the adjunct to speak.

"The Enemy of the World is gone!"

"What?" Dimitri immediately moved portside and observed the spot where Sungchul had been with a scope. He was gone. Sungchul, who had been lingering around like a caged animal in a zoo, had simply disappeared.

"The time to attack is now! Commander Medioff!" Minamoto approached closer and continued to speak his nonsense.

Dimitri sighed as he pointed to the peak of the ridge on the portside with his finger. "Go by yourself then. No one will stop you."

Minamoto only now discovered that Sungchul was no longer there. His brain immediately began to toss around millions of strategies of war that he had only read about in his books. "This… is Sungchul's trap! We must not pursue!"

—

A rocky valley filled with strange and bizarrely shaped rocks.

Sungchul, who was in some clearing hidden by rocks and its shadows, was focusing intensely on creating portraits. The topic was Vestiare's visage, but Sungchul had no experience in art. He tried to copy the sample drawing left behind by Vestiare, but in the end, they all became some form of abstract art.

"Goddamn it!"

Sungchul threw down the abstract art that even he himself couldn't identify and laid back onto the stone. As he prepared to take a breather, Bertelgia popped out of his pocket.

"Is the Demon Realm Frontline safe now?"

Sungchul, who had been staring up at the ashen sky through the crevice in the rock, shifted his head slightly and nodded.

"It is the main fleet of the Human Empire; the self-proclaimed protectors of Humanity and its allies. They might have put up all kinds of excuses to delay deploying their troops, but as they have made an appearance in the Demon Realm now, they shouldn't just turn back when they can clearly see the danger with their own eyes."

The only reason that Sungchul decided to move locations was because he could see that the balance between the humans and the demons had been restored. There was no more reason for him to act as a human barrier. Sungchul had made a quick decision and made himself scarce. However, a bigger obstacle stood before him. Sungchul watched Vestiare's portrait which he had laid on top of a rock with tired eyes.

"That damned woman. She gave me one bitch of a quest."

No matter how much he drew, he could not produce even one decent portrait. Not a single one of them had been accepted, and Sungchul had to draw a total of 33. His future looked bleak.

"You're so good at cooking and alchemy, but it looks like your artistic ability is quite terrible." Bertelgia peeked over at Sungchul's half-finished sketch of Vestiare which more closely resembled a goblin.

"..."

Sungchul did not speak any further. He stared blankly at the passing clouds through the crack between the rocks. After much time had passed by in this way, he heard the sound of paper rustling in the breeze. Sungchul, who had been resting with his eyes closed, turned his head and cracked his eyes open. A faint smile appeared on his lips.

Bertelgia was sketching something. She had placed a pencil between her two pages and held the drawing paper with a rock while she was scrawling something busily onto the page.

It looks like a kid playing with a crayon, thought Sungchul. He suddenly stood up from his seat and stole a peek at what Bertelgia was doing. His eyes soon grew wide from shock.

'T-this is…?!'

A detailed sketch that could not be compared to what Sungchul had drawn before was on the page.

"Ah, you're up?"

Bertelgia delicately moved her body to allow for the subtle pencil work that drew Vestiare's ruffled hair. It was a technique that Sungchul could never perform in this lifetime or the next. He waited for her to finish her drawing with his mouth shut.

The sketch was soon completed.

"Ta-da!"

Bertelgia rose high into the air to admire her work, but it appeared as though she wasn't pleased with it.

"Hmm. The proportions don't look quite right. I must have lost my edge since it's been so long."

Bertelgia pushed away the rock which held the paper with her body and let it be carried off with the wind. A forceful hand roughly grabbed the flying page.

"…"

It was Sungchul. *As expected, her skills aren't normal.*

"What are you doing with that drawing? I was just playing, don't look at it! It's not even well made." Bertelgia tried to object with a pouty voice, but Sungchul did not relent and held the sketch in front of Vestiare's portrait. Her artwork disappeared as glittering letters appeared in his eyes when he did so.

[You did well. What did you feel while you were drawing me? Progress: 1/33]

The quest had accepted the drawing.

This was an unexpected boon.

If Vestiare had put some effort into it, the quest would have been set up to only accept Sungchul's drawings, but it had been a hastily-made quest. It might have been too bothersome for even Vestiare to put together a complex formation for a quest she made out of spite which granted a single point of Intuition. It required a lot of effort in order to check the trace of the soul within an object, such as embedding a familiar within the quest to verify the maker of the object.

That woman must not have imagined that there was a person willing to draw the pictures for me.

Whatever the reason was, the solution to the problem that had been plaguing him for half of the day appeared to have been found.

"Bertelgia." Sungchul spoke with a composed voice.

Bertelgia felt a premonition and replied with a trembling voice as she tensed her body. "Hm…?"

"It looks like it's finally time for you to earn your keep."

"Huh? I don't have any expenses. I'm a Living Book, as you can clearly see."

"Then you'll have to pay fees for babysitting."

"Who's taking care of who?!" Bertelgia strongly tried to refuse him, but Sungchul's will could not be broken. She soon became Sungchul's art slave.

"Don't even think about slacking before another thirty-two portraits."

"You're too much…" Bertelgia let out a pitiful voice as she drew.

Sungchul comfortably lay on a boulder as he spoke. "Don't fret. I always pay my debts. I'll do you one favor afterwards."

"For real? My memory is wicked good, so don't go denying it later."

Bertelgia went as far as to record Sungchul's promise onto her pages.

[5th Era. Sun of the Thirty-Ninth Blue Dragon. Moon of the Cloud Witch. Eighteenth Day. Sungchul promised to perform a single favor.]

"Since you're making a promise, why not go as far as forming an oath?" Bertelgia who had recorded Sungchul's promise with the time and date onto a corner of her page tossed out a question.

"If you're talking about an oath, I'm already bounded by such a thing." Sungchul pointed toward his chest while speaking.

"Really? With who?"

"Can't say. Anyways, I'll keep my promise, so finish the drawings."

"Ok. OK! I'll draw it!"

Scribble, Scribble.

Bertelgia began to draw Vestiare's portrait onto the drawing paper once again. As Vestiare's beautiful visage was being recreated one by one, Bertelgia spoke up again. "This woman. She looks a lot like my mama."

"Really? You're not trying to say that you're Vestiare's daughter or something, are you?"

"My mama is a human. This woman is a High Elf. How can she be my mother when her race is completely different?"

"…"

"Papa must have really liked this woman."

"Is that right?"

"Yea. Papa followed around the Seven Heroes and adventured with them when he was younger. Demon Realm, Sea of Trees, Subterranean World, Land of the Dead, Floating Archipelago, etc. Here and there."

"Is that why he called himself the Eighth Hero?"

"That might be why, but the Seven Heroes never considered him as one of them. They treated him like some toolbox that spat out convenient tools."

"That's quite pitiful." Sungchul recalled Eckheart's quest that had strongly emphasized the name Eighth Hero.

How pitiful to have been denied camaraderie even though they fought the same enemies.

Judging by Bertelgia's words, they appeared to have known each other for decades, and yet it looked like he wasn't considered a comrade.

"Here. All done," Bertelgia said blandly as she took her pencil off of the page and floated into the air. Vestiare's portrait whose eyes were looking dreamily toward the front was left in her place. Bertelgia then peeked over at her own drawing while circling in the air as she spoke. "In any case, my mama was prettier."

Sungchul held a faint smile as he collected the picture and placed it on top of the sample. The picture melted away as snow does leaving only bright letters in front of his eyes.

[Have you now grown accustomed to my appearance? Don't fall for me too deeply. If you set your standards too high, you might never marry! / Progress 2/33]

"… talking full of shit."

Sungchul had wanted to kill Sajators first out of the Seven Heroes, but he deeply considered revising his plans. However, even those thoughts quickly grew cold. A strange thought entered his mind within that brief serenity. How long had it been since he left a task meant for him to another? Eight years? No, at least ten years must have passed. Bertelgia, who had grown into a trustworthy companion since the day they met, was busily moving her body while drawing a portrait.

Scribble Scribble.

The sound of the pencil scribbling through the page was the only sound present beside the blowing wind. Sungchul felt the flow of time with both his eyes closed. Faces of countless people and sceneries flashed in his mind leaving their traces. The voice of an energetic girl could be heard in the darkness.

"Ah, this slave is the head of the rebel force claiming to have come from another world? Huh? Not the head, but the right-hand man? In any case, he's not my type. Do you even have any strength behind those thin arms?"

The moment he recalled that particular voice, he felt a lingering pain like a dagger digging deep into his chest. His breath immediately got caught in his throat, and his breathing grew ragged. The pencil used to trace the lines on the page stopped moving.

"Did you see a ghost in your dreams?" Bertelgia asked bluntly.

"No." Sungchul took a deep breath and shook his head.

"It's nothing." He said as such, but his heart was still pounding rapidly in his chest, and the Cross of Oath embedded inside his chest was radiating a pure light within the stirring of his thick blood.

***

Murmurs of dissent rippled through the Allied Fleet of the Human Empire that had organized at the peak of Harupaya Ridge. The source of this discontent was the Head Commander of the fleet, Dimitri Medioff. He had positioned three fleets on the peak in order to keep the Demon Army in check while the rest of the army was ordered to pursue Sungchul, but a completely unexpected person was nominated to lead the pursuit.

The one who was handed the command was the next most hated man beside the Enemy of the World. That man was none other than Martin Breggas; the coward who had abandoned the Demon Realm Frontlines without a second thought despite his role as the head commander.

The men whispered behind Dimitri's back that he was suffering from diplomacy fever. But no one dared to openly oppose his decisions.

"All of this is the will of the Great Emperor."

It was because the Emperor himself had issued this order. Martin had fiercely lobbied on this front. He begged for cooperation from the Human Empire by offering an enormous tribute, economic rights, and absolute obedience in the next year's world council meeting.

Martin desired only one thing: to restore his name. As a lord who had thrown aside all of his subordinates and territory alike, he needed a victory large enough to wash away his sins. The subjugation of the Enemy of the World was his sole chance to clean the slate.

He had but a single concern. According to rumors, Sungchul had become some Transcendent powerhouse. All those who had witnessed him fight spoke the same thing: that the Enemy of the World was a Transcende…no, he had become something more.

But Martin had never seen Sungchul fight with his own eyes. "I can't deny that Sungchul has grown stronger to a certain extent, but that man is still human. Mortals aren't perfect; he must have a weakness."

Martin led two fleets of the Human Empire by sky and the Militia of Trowyn along with few elite veteran soldiers by land as he headed north-east to pursue Sungchul. He had expertly narrowed down the possible locations where Sungchul could be hiding thanks to his knowledge of the surrounding area as the Commander-in-Chief of the Frontline of the Demon Realm and quickly began the search.

Sungchul, who was taking a rare break, soon confronted the pursuers. The roar of a flying Wyvern tore through the sky. Dozens of Wyvern Knights flew past the crack in the rock through which he watched the sky. The pursuers had also managed to reach him by land.

"He couldn't have gotten much further! Don't leave a single stone unturned in this area and find him."

Elven rangers led by three-horned deer went through the area like a comb.

"Mm. No matter how you see it, I don't think this is the time to be drawing pictures?" Bertelgia stopped working.

Sungchul also had the same thought. "They're being such a bother."

However, he didn't intend to kill them. They were mere pawns following the will of those in power, and it wasn't Sungchul's way to kill the innocent, unlike those in evil organizations such as the Followers of Calamity.

Sungchul lifted his body up from the rock and gestured toward Bertelgia. "Let's go."

"Where to?"

"Northeast."

Sungchul was thinking of heading to the Storm Battlefront. The Great Forest Belt of the Varan-Aran Tribal Alliance was the best for hiding, but it might not prove to be so great once the Elves, who are familiar with the forest like the back of their hand, begin to track him. Sungchul, who had decided on his destination, stepped forth without a second thought.

—

The scene of a familiar mountain range opened before his eyes. Below, the dwarven encampment caught the last few rays of light from the sunset, making it glitter with a mysterious and profound light. This was the area supervising the Storm Battlefront. It was an extremely rough mountainous region referred to as "the source of all mountains."

Sungchul had made camp at various points along this area. It was the only option left to the man driven away under the label of Enemy of the World. He headed toward one of the camps he had prepared in the past. It was located on the edge of the mountain cliff that overlooked a fortress named Archon Crack. It was a dark and damp place due to the unique geological shape of the mountain that didn't even allow a single hour of sunlight to reach the ground.

Sungchul had dug a cave into this shady spot and made a storage for fermented food. The cave was packed to the brim with Jeotgal[4] made with salted oysters that come into season during the fall and salted fish of various species caught all throughout the Demon Realm that he had prepared with a sense of experimentation.

Sungchul started a fire and prepared food when the sun started to set. He stuck a finger into one of the pots filled with brine on the shelves as he was cooking rice and was instantly immersed in its exquisite flavor. Bertelgia was sitting under the dim light of an oil lamp still drawing portraits of Vestiare. She had managed to complete only five till now at a rate of one per hour. Bertelgia also took a break between each drawing that lasted thirty minutes to an hour making it so that she only drew a single portrait every two hours realistically and additionally threw a tantrum saying that she couldn't draw more than four pages a day.

Sungchul didn't rush her. He was well aware that it would be much faster to gain the Intuition by simply waiting for quest completion through the paintings.

I waited eight years. It's a drop in the well to wait a week more. Sungchul affirmed these thoughts as he stuffed a spoonful of rice with some of the Jeotgal. The warm and fluffy flavor of the rice and the salty deliciousness of the Jeotgal stirred his salivary glands as well as his taste buds.

[The score of this dish is... 5 points!]

The judgement of the Chef Class was harsh, but what could he do? Sungchul cleaned out his bowl of rice with a satisfied smile on his face. But while he was eating, he discovered a small but important change in the scenery that he was observing. The Dwarven fortress that should be lit brightly with torches and lamps was still steeped in darkness.

Was the fortress taken?

The recent assault by the Demon Army had caused the state of the Demon Realm Frontline to become unstable on an unprecedented level. It was at a point where the disappearance of a small fortress or two wouldn't seem strange.

The next day, Sungchul turned in the seventh portrait for the quest and headed toward the direction of the fortress in the spirit of exploration. Bertelgia who had just completed a drawing joined in on the momentary rest.

As Sungchul expected, not a single dwarf could be found within Archon Crack. He discovered that the outer walls of the fortress had suffered severe damage from magic and material attacks and found several corpses with the scraps of numbered clothing usually seen on the members of the Penal Unit deeper into the fortress. But, there were too few of them. It appeared as though the majority of the dwarves who had been defending the fortress had managed to escape.

They escaped quite cleanly despite being attacked by demons.

Sungchul entered the fortress as though it was his own home and headed toward the underground storage. The underground storage was where the Dark Beer brewed by the dwarves were stored. He had stolen a few of these oak barrels whenever he felt thirsty. Thankfully, no dwarf had managed to discover him, so this thievery was not added to the Dwarven Book of Grudges.

Sungchul felt an uncomfortable presence when he exited the fortress with the Dark Beer in tow. The unique damp aura of the devils was spread thickly in his surroundings. The way that this aura made even the air stale was outside of the norm.

It looks like this isn't an ordinary devil. Maybe a Devil Lord or one on par with a High Devil has shown up.

High Devils and Devil Lords were often lumped together when assessing powerful demons, but strictly speaking, that wasn't correct. High Devils were those with stats that surpassed what the humans referred to as "Transcendent" or "Superhuman" thresholds, and among them, the ones that held territory were further separated into Devil Lords. No matter how strong a devil became, without land they would simply be referred to as a High Devil, whereas even a weaker devil with land was titled a Devil Lord. However, in order to become one of the lords of the "72 Seats of Power" in the Demon world, a great deal of strength was absolutely necessary.

Among the hundreds of High Devils, only those within the 72nd ranking could hold lordship over a territory within the Demon Realm, and only one that managed to subjugate all of the seventy-two Devil Lords was able to become the sole ruler of the Demons known as the Demon King. However, Sungchul was someone who stood over even above their King, and thus this distinction held no meaning. Whether it was a High Devil or the Devil Lord, they would all be removed from this world with a swing of his hammer.

Sungchul took in the presence of this powerful devil and walked over to the direction of the source while holding the oak barrel with leisure; boldly making his presence known. Soon, an ominous shadow loomed over the fortification as a demon revealed itself before Sungchul. Sungchul's eyes wavered the moment he saw the devil.

That guy is…?

His appearance had changed drastically, making it hard to recognize him, but there was no doubt. The massive devil that loitered before the crumbling walls of the castle was someone Sungchul already knew.

Elijah Breggas.

He had heard it through rumors. It was the story of an eyeless devil that had been attacking a Dwarven fortress. It was said that he shrieked an odd noise while carrying the body of a beautiful woman on his back.

So he was in this kind of place.

Elijah had yet to feel Sungchul's presence, so Sungchul observed him from a shadow drawn by a castle wall. The youthful air from his adolescent form could be found no longer. Instead, he had the figure of an angry devil whose torso was four meters on its own, and the eye sockets that he had emptied himself were filled with a darkness that was discomforting to behold. His back held a corpse of a woman tied down in metal chains. Her face was covered by her hair, but looking at the virtuous attire of a female knight on the corpse, it wasn't difficult to guess that it was the body of Sophia Breggas.

"That Devil. It's that one sibling, isn't it?" Bertelgia must have figured out the identity of the devil after seeing Sophia's corpse.

Elijah was busily stacking rocks onto the collapsed wall with his massive arms.

The Devil spoke. "Sophia. Look at this! Our castle is being completed. Once the castle walls are repaired a bit more, we'll be able to hold land without the help of that man!"

The corpse of Sophia that hung behind him did not respond. It swung limply from side to side along with the Devil's movement, but Elijah continued to speak with an excited voice for some reason. "This is where it all begins. Starting from this castle, I'll take over every castle in this area one by one. Then I'll give you a castle too. We'll make a country, just the two of us! What kind of country? I'm still thinking on it. I like the Human Empire that the Summoned have created, but I also really like the Hegemony the evil 'Holy Rutheginea Kingdom' once held."

The eyeless Devil that had been stacking stones stood dumbly and scratched his head while making a grotesque smile before speaking. "Regardless, whatever country I make will be better than that man's."

Sungchul who had been watching from a distance realized that Elijah's mind had been completely devoured by the devil's flesh. He hoisted the oak barrel filled with the Dark Beer and silently left the fortress.

As he climbed the mountain road leading toward his camp, Bertelgia popped out to speak. "Was it Sophia? That girl... she's so pitiful."

"..."

Bertelgia poked his shoulder with one of her corners when he didn't say a word. "Couldn't you have just saved her? So terrible!"

"Dying was the best recourse for her." Sungchul spoke in a firm voice.

There are times when reality is much harsher than death.

It was at that moment when his eyes caught sight of something he wasn't too pleased to see. Toward the southwestern sky, the fleet of the Human Empire pierced through the inky clouds. They were the ones pursuing him. There was also an army holding a flag with a winged skull marching below them. Sungchul who was watching them approach with indifferent eyes discovered a single figure among them and clicked his tongue.

"It is most likely that the Enemy of the World has hidden himself here. Regardless of the number of days or nights it takes, turn over every rock and search every cave. Our labor shall soon be rewarded."

The one who was making the speech toward the marching army at the lead was none other than the father that the Breggas siblings hated so dearly, the Lord Marquis Martin Breggas.

He gazed at the distant fortress of the Dwarves and led his army toward it, unaware of what was waiting ahead.

***

SCRITCH SCRITCH

Regardless of the situation at the Storm Battlefront, Bertelgia's pencil was busy with her portrait on a sketchpad. Sungchul stood on the mountainside with fierce winds watching the situation unfold below him.

Martin, as befitting someone who was born and raised on the battlefield, sent a small number of patrols toward the fortress first to gauge any potential dangers ahead. The five-member patrols composed of Dwarves and Elves entered the fortress, and two of them ran outside in a panic after ten minutes. They ran, soaked in blood, toward Martin Breggas with an urgent message. Their message didn't reach Sungchul's ears, but he could roughly guess what they had to say. They had met him: Elijah Breggas who had become a High Devil.

As Martin was preparing his entire army for battle, he also sent a signal to the Human Empire fleet waiting in the sky. The fleet made some distance from the fortress. If the precious airships happened to fall by chance through this High Devil's magic, the cornered Martin's already miniscule chances of success would diminish even further. Martin was planning on using the forces he had on hand to face the High Devil hiding within the fortress. However, there was something bothering him.

There is no way a High Devil is moving alone here. Devils are prone to forming packs, and it is common knowledge that they gather more subjects as they become more powerful. If this Devil is at the rank of High Devil, he would have at least a thousand to ten thousand followers.

As his thoughts trailed on, his hesitation grew longer. The people around him carefully urged him to come to a decision. Despite this, Martin decided to inspect the vicinity once more with the patrols he had with him. It was in this process that a Dragon Knight discovered Sungchul accidentally. He was caught up in turbulence causing him to fall behind from his group, allowing him to catch sight of Sungchul hidden among the strange rock formations.

Sungchul was standing outside as he noticed the flight path of the Dragon Knights and never imagined that they would be able to see him, only to be discovered by this convergence of coincidences. Fortunately, it wasn't as though Martin could strike at Sungchul, whether he knew Sungchul's location or not. To move his main force, the Civil Militia of Trowyn, toward the mountainside that Sungchul was in, they would have to go through the fortress that was impeding their path across the rugged valley, Archon Crack. However, there was an unknown devil holding his ground within the fortress.

Martin was now in a troublesome situation where he would have to get rid of the High Devil first before he could get a chance at taking down Sungchul. It might have been a monumentally easier task if they were on an open field, but to take care of a High Devil in the cloistered fortress was incredibly difficult. It might have been the best option for Martin himself to step up for the job, but Martin was not the type of person that would face this level of danger.

It wasn't an option to utilize the Air Fleet of the Human Empire. It was also problematic to lose soldiers from the Human Empire's forces, but it was unacceptable for Martin to have the credit taken away from him. It was for this purpose that he did not alert the fleet that he had discovered Sungchul.

It's a miracle that the leader of the dispatched forces is an idiot.

The one in command of the dispatched forces was none other than Minamoto Daisuke who was known as a fool. He had thought that Dmitri Medioff had left him in charge of the dispatched forces as a recognition of his abilities, but in truth, he was being sent away as a nuisance. Minamoto was sharpening his beloved weapon – Yodo Kamaitachi which was an imitation of the Japanese Katana on top of the deck while waiting for his bout with the Enemy of the World.

"Just you wait, Yodo Kamaitachi. Soon… you'll be feasting on the blood of that fucking bastard, Sungchul! Kekeke…" Minamoto's eyes, which were burning with madness, were fixated onto a single scene that occurred more than ten years ago. A battlefield filled with bodies. Blazing sky. Warriors tempering their breath in preparation for the final battle.

"I'll settle the score for what happened at La Grange…!" Minamoto's entire body was burning with passion, but he wasn't aware that Sungchul was right under his nose.

Martin let out a sigh of relief only after confirming that the fleet led by Minamoto had shown no sign of movement. "It looks like God hasn't forsaken me yet. Seeing as I got picked an idiot to accompany me among all those other admirals, but the real problem starts here."

Martin stared at the sheer cliff that Sungchul was situated in with his blue-gray eyes. Sungchul was fully aware he was discovered, yet chose not to move from his spot. The reality was that in order to attack Sungchul, Martin would have to take on the High Devil lurking inside the fortress, Archon Crack.

Minamoto was a Summoned who had arrived in this world at a similar time, but the difference between their potential was like the difference between the heavens and the earth itself. Sungchul had even gone as far as lying on a flat rock to comfortably spectate the spectacle unfolding on this side. Martin couldn't see what Sungchul's facial expression was like, but he predicted that Sungchul was likely smiling, fully aware of what Martin was doing and what the consequences were. Martin felt like shit.

Sungchul… that bastard…!!

He immediately sent another message to the Human Empire fleet, advising them to distance themselves a bit further. It was another small miracle that Minamoto hadn't detected anything despite the fact that Sungchul had now revealed himself publicly. Minamoto acquiesced Martin's report and moved the fleet to an open space very far away.

"…"

Sungchul watched the entire scene, amused.

"Shouldn't we start running again? We've been discovered here, right?"

Bertelgia had completed another picture and clasped it between her pages as she presented it. "It's the tenth page with this one!"

Sungchul brought the drawing to the original portrait to turn it in and scattered the detailed message that appeared in front of his eyes with the wave of his hand before speaking calmly. "Martin has to cross through that fortress in order to meet me here, meaning he will face his karmic punishment in the process. And…"

Sungchul's eyes turned beyond the mountains big and small to the dust cloud lingering there. There was a figure of a fortress with eight legs looming between the dust clouds. It was the Mobile Fortress of the Order of the Iron Blood Knights. The Order who had become subordinates of the devils were heading in this direction. Their objective was clear.

"… It seems like there is more than one karmic retribution waiting for him."

The Lord Marquis' fortune of having discovered Sungchul had turned to poison. He was stuck hesitating between a High Devil that stood in his path and the Order of the Iron Blood Knights coming from the side without having made a decision. He wanted to retreat, but then he would lose Sungchul, who he had worked so hard to find. To stay meant committing to a meaningless battle against the Order of the Iron Blood Knights.

"Should we request aid from Admiral Minamoto?"

A young adjunct lacking tact suddenly spoke. Martin's face grew stiff. Displeasure permeated the surrounding air making the atmosphere heavy and suffocating. Martin pointed toward that tactless adjunct in that heavy silence. "I'll give you a small number of men. Go into the fortress and lure the High Devil out."

"Sir…?" The adjunct was the child of a reputable family within Trowyn. His placement in the position that was beyond his age and ability was all because of his parents who sponsored Martin, but such realities were just sentiments currently.

"Go immediately, and carry out the order. Or you can choose to die here by my hands instead."

Martin reached toward the hilt of his blade while giving a murderous glare. The young adjunct who believed that he would make it out of this at the very least ran out of the tent in a panic. A suicidal bait tactic was formulated under the gaze of thousands of soldiers. The young adjunct entered the dark fortress with a small number of men with a pale face. It didn't take long before an unrecognizable piece of meat was spat out through the dark hole.

The soldiers could hear the sound of chains in that darkness, and two sunken lights lingering from within.

"This is our castle. Those who trespass our castle will not be forgiven."

The High Devil's voice rang out in the darkness. The voice was clearly transmitted into Martin's ears as well. He felt goosebumps breaking out all over his body. It was because the voice was remarkably similar to a voice he was very familiar with.

It couldn't be... It can't be!

He found himself approaching the entrance of the fortress before he realized it.

"Lord Marquis! It is dangerous to enter alone!"

Martin snapped awake and retreated from the entrance when the adjuncts around him stopped him.

"It's fine, whether it's a torch or magic. Bring everything that can illuminate the darkness and follow me."

Martin entered the fortress accompanied by dozens of warriors and mages. Normally, he would never do this, but the voice he had heard was compelling enough for him to enter the perilous darkness.

The Devil's rough breathing and the sound of metallic chains grew closer. The knight at the vanguard who held a roaring torch was suddenly swallowed up by something in the darkness and disappeared.

"Prepare for battle! Prepare for battle!"

The soldiers formed a circular formation with Martin Breggas in the center in an effort to protect their lord from the worst-case scenario. A massive figure could be seen beyond the torches and magic lights that lit the surroundings. The sound of saliva being swallowed could be heard from various places. It was the High Devil.

Martin held his hand on the hilt of his blade and observed the dark figure with his breath held. The Devil finally revealed itself under the firelight. A brawny arm wrapped in crimson light and

414

clothing that had been torn away came into sight first. Martin's eyes were locked onto the fluttering scraps of clothing. On the corner of the clothing, there was a patch with an image of a winged skull on a black background stitched onto it. Martin who caught sight of this felt a sinking feeling that continued without end.

That can't be. That kid… is dead. In the Demon Realm.

Aaron Genghis, the vice-captain of the Penal Unit, who was in charge of Elijah's murder, had left the Demon Realm Battlefront as though he was fleeing from something, but it was undeniable that Elijah had crossed into the Demon Realm. That place wasn't something that just anyone could survive.

The High Devil took a step closer and his face veiled under the darkness was revealed. The hideous face with its eyes carved out was looking towards Martin's direction expressionlessly.

"Another intruder? Who dares trespass my domain!" The High Devil spoke with a calm and grounded demeanor ill-fitting his grotesque appearance.

"Lord Marquis." Parlim Dargott carefully broached the topic with Martin. He had also sensed it.

Martin pulled his blade and spoke calmly toward the son he loved the most. "You. Head outside."

"But…!"

"Head outside and prepare for the movements of the Order of the Iron Blood Knights who are approaching from the north."

Martin spoke resolutely. After confirming that Parlim had left the fortress with a small number of men, he moved forward.

"Who are you?" His voice was weak and trembling, different than usual.

"Me?" The High Devil tilted his head toward where the sound originated. The metal chain wrapped around his shoulder and waist shook as he moved. Martin could see what appeared to be the hair of a woman beyond the metal chains. It was a familiar blonde. The face of the blushing woman on the farm who lowered her head toward him when he inspected the farmlands suddenly flashed across his eyes.

"Are you referring to me?" The Devil spoke again.

Martin nodded.

The Devil's mouth slowly opened, and he spoke the words he had expected yet could not accept. "I am Elijah Breggas, and this is my most beloved and reliable sister, Sophia Breggas."

The Devil turned his back, and Sophia's limbs and head shook like a doll as she hung on his back.

Martin's eyes flared up. "K-kuh."

Soon, his arms and legs trembled and a strange sound burst forth.

CLANK.

The blade in his hand fell on the ground. His body collapsed and had to be supported by his subordinates.

"Who are you? I have definitely seen you before. I have certainly heard your voice before. I can't see you right now because I have no eyes." Elijah reached out with his hand and scratched his head. When the Devil's nails scratched his head that was covered in crimson fur, skin flakes like rock salt with a pungent stench fell off.

"Kkkkuuu…." Martin discovered that he could speak no more. A reality harsher than death had stolen his speech. His heart felt taut, and his mind unfocused. He felt as though he would die if he gazed upon this creature even a second longer. His hand gestured for him to be dragged away from this place, and his soldiers supported him in leaving the fortress.

"Who are you? Why do you leave without a reply?" The High Devil followed in pursuit.

The soldiers stood their ground, but they were crushed under the High Devil's toenails and turned to meat. It was only through great sacrifice that Martin was able to walk out of the fortress alive.

"Kkku… kkuuuuu…!" Martin, who was now heading toward his tent, borrowing the shoulders of his men, had already died in some sense.

"…"

Sungchul was watching this scene unfold with an indifferent gaze.

—

Three days passed.

"Tada! How is it? The new technique from Miss Bertelgia?"

Bertelgia who had been forcibly conscripted into labor for many hours now had come up with a new technique as though to prove that she was a clever child. The new method wasn't to draw the face, eyes, nose, and mouth using her hand like a human, but to take her form into consideration and draw the portrait in its entirety from top to bottom and left to right. She didn't realize it herself, but her movements were reminiscent of a printer.

"With this, it's the twenty-sixth page."

Sungchul turned in the new picture on top of the original and continued to observe below. Ominous clouds of war were drawing in as the Mobile Fortress of the Order of the Iron Blood Knights stood tall behind Martin's base where he had holed himself in after receiving the trauma. Both sides were waiting with bated breath and were about to commit to battle soon.

Sungchul looked over at Bertelgia and asked, "How much longer do you think you'll need?"

"With the new Bertelgia's expression technique, maybe two hours?"

"It might be ok to take it slow."

Sungchul chewed on dried date palm and watched the scene below his feet unfold. The Iron Blood Knights that held the brand of the Devils on their forehead were making a formation under the Mobile Fortress while roaring in anger.

"Death to the traitor, Martin Breggas!"

"We repay what is owed!"

"Hey, Breggas! We'll make you regret underestimating us!"

Martin's bid for redemption was going awry in the worst way imaginable.

Chapter 18 – Debt of Punishment

The battle began with bombardment from the Mobile Fortress that the Order of the Iron Blood Knights was so proud of. The cannons lined on top of the moving castle's walls fired all manner of artillery at Martin Breggas' camp.

There was a secret technique solemnly guarded by the Order of the Iron Blood Knights hidden within their cannonballs. It was a method to store a time-delayed scroll within the explosive.

Utilizing this method, the Iron Blood cannonball made the first impact when it fell, then a secondary impact after the scroll activated, allowing for a devastating advantage. Of course, the might of the second impact was completely dependent on the strength of the spell held within the scroll.

During the height of their power, the Iron Blood Knights were able to employ a great number of mages who provided them with a large number of scrolls. However, as the Order declined their technique had all but disappeared. But thanks to the alliance with the Devils, the Order was able to boast firepower far stronger than they had ever fielded before.

BOOM BOOM BOOM!!

A tornado made of fire emerged from where a bomb had landed and began to burn everything in its vicinity. An explosion powerful enough to cause a small quake burst forth from one of the shells, and another shell exploded in a burst of frost followed by a blast of icy shrapnel sharp enough to mercilessly tear apart every human in its vicinity. Every single one of the artillery shells contained powerful scrolls that sealed devastating magic of the Devils. The average ranged from 4th grade to 5th grade. Some even had destructive magic that reached 6th grade.

"How does it taste? Dogs of the Marquis!"

"Did you think that it would be so easy to steal what the Order of Iron Blood Knights had spilled sweats of blood to attain?"

"You will soon face a storm!"

Just the bombardment from the Order of the Iron Blood Knights was enough to drive Martin's forces into chaos. Martin, who had been tending to his trauma within his tent, realized that the situation was quite dire and returned to the field.

He looked haggard and ill as he had been refusing food and drink for the past three days, but he was a battle-hardened warrior. He immediately gathered a healer and a witch and requested a stimulant, and they each brought one made from their own recipe. Martin tested both stimulants and selected the witch's.

"The side-effects will occur after a day." The witch blinked in hesitation as she spoke.

"Doesn't matter." He downed two bottles of the stimulant and headed toward the chaotic one-sided battle.

"Lord Marquis!" Parlim Dargott was putting forth his best effort in commanding the frontline. His attire was already covered in dust, and his forehead was spotted with beads of sweat.

Martin brushed that sweat off his child with his hand and spoke with a magnanimous expression on his face. "You've done well. I will take over from here. You will handle the threats at the rear."

"Understood." Parlim spoke with a wide smile, but he hesitated at the last moment.

Martin patted his shoulder and spoke softly. "From this point forward, you may call me Father. Don't fear the gaze of others any longer."

Parlim's expression, which had become dark, turned bright once again. It was a refreshing smile that would turn the hearts of men and women alike.

I chose correctly. Martin gathered his thoughts and headed toward battle. His adjuncts were waiting for him.

"Lord Marquis!"

"You've arrived?"

Regardless of what anyone said, Martin Breggas was the head commander of the Demon Realm Frontlines. His reputation had been blemished by his recent choice on the battlefield, but he had mediated the elves, dwarves, and the summoned, each with strong individualities, and defended and stabilized the safety of the Demon Realm Frontlines like an iron cage for the past eight years. That was not a task that just anyone could perform.

"Send an immediate transmission to Admiral Minamoto. We are currently in battle and in need of reinforcements." He had nothing more to lose, and so he did not act on his greed. Martin felt unencumbered.

My ambitions led me to this point, but that ambition has now burned me whole. I will no longer adhere to such ambitions. I will retire once this battle ends.

Martin muttered to himself as though he was making a promise before steadying the wavering battleline. Minamoto Daisuke of the Human Empire arrived in a timely manner. He charged forward into the Order's front lines ignoring the barrage of artillery pouring out from the fleet.

"Kiiiyyyyott!"

Yodo Kamaitachi was pulled from its scabbard. The blade, red like blood, poured out a thick aura of hostility.

"I am unbreakable...!" Minamoto was steeped in madness as he began to perform the dance of death; whatever his blade touched met a bloody end. In the face of Minamoto's oppressive performance, the Order suffered helplessly. Sungchul's eyes grew cold as he watched the scene unfold from a distance.

Taeksu Kim. He ended up bestowing a position to this bastard.

Before the formation of the Human Empire, it was the era of the Kingdom of Rutheginea. It was a dark time where those in power ruled with absolute authority while those below fell into defeat and corruption. The Summoned swore to end this era and stood against the great evil as one, but the Holy Kingdom of Rutheginea was powerful, and the Summoned had to endure a tiring battle. Traitors appeared in the process. Taeksu Kim, the man known currently as Minamoto Daisuke, was a vile traitor who had sold out his comrade Summoned for his own benefit.

"Here, take it."

Bertelgia snapped Sungchul awake from reminiscing about the past. She had stuffed several pages of drawings in between her pages and carried them over. He realized that it contained six pages when he received it.

"Huh? This soon?"

It was a speed that was hard to believe even if with proof. Bertelgia allowed herself to swagger as she boasted. "Ahem! It's the might of the new expression technique developed by the one and only Ms. Bertelgia. I calmly looked at myself and realized that my current form wasn't human anymore, so is there any need to keep drawing like one? It was from this line of questioning that it hit me. I was able to record memory itself differently from humans and those records…"

Her rambling grew long. Sungchul closed his ears in the middle of her rant and began to place the pictures that appeared to have been copied from a printer on top of the original portrait one by one. All six of the images seemed to melt away before his eyes, each leaving behind their own message. Sungchul didn't read any of them.

I remember there was a saying that getting older means you don't have to see or do things you don't want to see or do.

"I think I can finish the last picture in under an hour! With Ms. Bertelgia's superior expression technique that is."

"Brilliant, Bertelgia." Sungchul who was averse to compliments unexpectedly threw out a word of praise toward her.

Bertelgia grew even more elated and began to float into the air before shooting down toward the next drawing paper. "Let's quickly get this over with and get out of this battlefield. I'm so sick of this war!"

It appeared that there was another reason why Bertelgia was rushing. Sungchul nodded and turned his gaze toward the battlefield.

The Order of the Iron Blood Knights that had been ruthlessly pressuring Martin was surrounded and was being slaughtered from both sides. Veteran soldiers led by Martin formed a barrier like an iron wall to hold down the Order, and the ground forces led by Minamoto swept in from the rear. Meanwhile, the airships, the symbol of the Human Empire, continued their artillery fire to demolish the Mobile Fortresses.

The battle was about to reach its conclusion. It looked as though Martin would force his way through the fortress to reach this side, but the portraits were already mostly finished. The situation had been delayed long enough that Primordial light was inches away from Sungchul's grasp. However, something unexpected occurred on the battlefield. A massive being appeared in the rear of Martin's soldiers. It was none other than Elijah Breggas.

"Who dares be so foolhardy as to fight upon my land?!" Elijah, who had been lurking within the fortress, shouted with a youthful voice unsuited for his appearance before leaping into the rear of the weakened Civil Militia of Trowyn. When the mighty Devil entered the fray, a catastrophe unfolded in the rear which was composed of only healers, mages with non-combat specialties, and the injured with the exception of the small amount of guards stationed at the entrance. The support units and the injured were helplessly torn apart by the Devil's claws as there were only a handful of guards to defend them. The small number of mages that were present attempted to fight Elijah with their pitiful combat magic, but it only served to anger him further.

"Our Master has fallen-yeyo!"

"Our family has been ruined-yeyo!"

Around the corpses of the mages that were pitifully torn apart, the homunculi were busy making a fuss. On the other side, the news of Elijah's appearance reached the ears of Martin who was on the cusp of victory.

"What? He left the fortress?"

Martin's eyes trembled visibly, but he didn't feel as much shock as he did before. He calmly spoke. "I'll go. Pull a portion of the veteran soldiers to stop him."

"There is word that Sir Dargott is already heading toward that direction."

"Parlim is? No, don't send him. Send a message to have him immediately turn around."

At that moment, a blood-curdling roar like that of a lion was heard from ahead and a single knight charged as he headed in this direction. Martin could recognize that face even from a distance. It was the Knight-Captain of the Order of the Iron Blood Knights, Sungtek Cho.

It was the final throes of one of the most powerful man of this era now etched with the brand of the Devils. Martin personally swung his blade to face him.

CLANG!

Sword met sword. Sungtek's eyes were filled with deep-seated grudge as he shot fiercely toward Martin's face. "Martin Breggas! You son of a whore! Even if I die, I have to see you fall. Koreans have a saying, 'I'll take you down with me.'"

"Sorry, but I have no intention of dying here," shot back Martin.

A fierce battle took place between the Lord Marquis and the Knight-Captain of the Iron Blood Knights. Sungtek had a greater zeal for the fight, but the one with higher overall stats was Martin Breggas. The victor of the battle was soon decided after a few critical clashes.

"Kekeke…" Sungtek leaked out a rumbling laughter before grabbing hold of where his right arm used to be with his left. Red blood poured out from where his limb was cut away.

"Rest in peace," said Martin as he looked off into some faraway place before inflicting the final blow. The blade pierced Sungtek's heart in a single breath and his body quivered once. Suddenly, Sungtek's left arm grabbed hold of the blade that had pierced his heart and pulled his torso toward Martin.

"Hey, Marquis." Sungtek spoke with blood pouring from his mouth.

Martin only looked at him with contempt and didn't respond.

"Look behind you." Sungtek smirked before dropping his gaze and muttering under a hushed voice.

"Experience it for yourself, what it's like to lose a beloved child of yours…" Sungtek stopped breathing.

Martin who was caught in an ominous premonition peeled Sungtek's corpse from his blade and immediately turned around. He saw his son, Parlim Dargott, being grabbed by his other son, Elijah Breggas, and torn in half.

"Noooo!!"

Sungchul let out a sigh as he heard the desolate scream that could be heard in the distance.

No better example of karma.

Martin Breggas was done for. When one's spirit falls, the body is soon to follow. It was unlikely that he would ever stand again.

"Bertelgia," Sungchul called out to her.

Bertelgia who was hurriedly printing her drawing paused her work and answered him, "Yea?"

"How much longer do you think it'll take?"

"About ten minutes?"

"Sounds good. Keep at it."

"What are you planning?"

"I'm going to go down there for a bit."

The traitor who had taken the identity of Minamoto was now attacking Elijah. The one who had turned himself into a High Devil was not to be a target of empathy, but Sungchul was still concerned about the corpse of the pitiful woman hanging on his back. He also had another objective.

Taeksu. He foolishly showed himself to me once again.

Sungchul descended the mountain slope while recalling the faces of his comrades who had died by the hands of the traitor. He appeared like a force of nature when seen from a distance.

***

"Puhahahaha! Is this it, Devil?" Minamoto's combat prowess went beyond the rumors. He was not only holding his own against a High Devil known to be as powerful as a Transcendent but even pushing him back.

"Ow! It hurts! Stop it!" Elijah was being pushed back one-sidedly despite wielding the power of a High Devil.

There were largely two reasons for this: First was the difference in skill. As a seasoned fighter, Minamoto had seen through Elijah's powerful yet simple attack pattern and negated every move he was making by keeping one step ahead; the follow-up counter-attack that came after was just a bonus. Another reason was simply that Minamoto was powerful. He had used just one arm to block the heavy swing of Elijah's clawed attack.

Elijah flailed about desperately with all his effort, but Minamoto did not retreat a single step. Instead, he was scolding the Devil by shaking a single finger side to side.

"I am unbreakable. This sort of attack does not work on me."

It was an unbelievable sight, for a mere admiral of the Human Empire's Fleet who did not even manage to enter the lowest seat of the Thirteen Champions of the Continent to display such strength. Minamoto was performing a feat that was believed to be impossible with the exception of the Emperor of the Human Empire, Aquiroa the Executor, and Shamal Rajput, the head of the Assassin's Guild. The soldiers who were watching the spectacle broke out into a cheer.

"My God... to stand toe to toe with a High Devil in terms of strength, Admiral Minamoto; he's amazing."

"Is this the strength of the man who was promoted by the Emperor because of his combat prowess?"

"It looks like the rumors that even the Enemy of the World was wary and envious of his skill weren't just hot air."

425

Minamoto did not outwardly appear to be reacting to the sound of praise coming from behind him, but he was burning with passion on the inside.

Kekeke... more. Praise me more. Sing of my praises a bit louder!

To the Summoned, the mass summoning was a tragedy on its own, but to some, it was a gift. This was especially true for people like Taeksu Kim or Minamoto Daisuke who had no outlook in life. Minamoto was a target of group bullying before the word "izime"[5] was adopted to Korean, and he had been a shut-in recluse long before the word "hikikomori"[6] was coined. The Other World was like heaven that overflowed with milk and honey. Anyone could obtain overwhelming power through a bit of luck, regardless of the actual effort involved.

A smile formed on Minamoto's lips. He was assured of victory.

This Devil. He's weaker than me. I might not have been able to beat him before, but the Forbidden Technique sure is great!

He allowed the sinister energy he had obtained via betrayal to run rampant inside of his body. The destructive power that he himself had no means to restrain filled every cell of his being.

"I am a High Devil! How dare a mere human stand against a High Devil! This doesn't make any sense! Why do you think I have become a High Devil?!"

Elijah began to reek of vile Demon Aura as he rushed forth. It was a charge that held enough power and speed to make even the most grizzled knights, who often boasted about having being trained in the battlefield, reel back in fear.

However, Minamoto evaded Elijah's charge with light movements like that of a bullfighter. He recalled one of the scenes from pro wrestling that he saw at a young age as he dodged. The most popular figure on that show broadcast by the American military: the muscled man in the yellow underwear. As an apostle of justice, the patterns of his matches were all the same. His repertoire was to be beaten up by the evil heel[7] until he was awoken by the cheer of the crowd to some monstrous strength that allowed him to overwhelm his villain in a single move. It was simple but always evoked a thunderous applause.

A cruel smile formed on Minamoto's lips. *I'll strike back hard after playing with you for a little bit.*

He was planning on using this opportunity to show his true worth to not only the members of his fleet, but also to the soldiers of the front lines of the Demon World and correct his recently declining evaluation.

Thirteen Champions of the Continent? Don't make me laugh. The fact that I'm not on that list means that the list is worthless!

He delayed the fight as he continued to block or barely evade Elijah's relentless assault. Until the moment when people began to chant his name.

As Elijah began to gather his breath and prepare for his next attack, the cheer of the crowd fell into Minamoto's ears.

"Human! You must get up-yeyo!"

"You must defeat that demon-yeyo!"

The words of cheer that he had been waiting for had arrived. Minamoto smiled as he recalled the man in yellow underwear that stood on the post of the ring in the crowd's adoration.

"Now! You must get up-yeyo!"

However, the voices were strange. Minamoto quickly looked around him.

Huh? It's just Homunculi all over?!

There was a crowd of homunculi. Each one of them had a hideous appearance as their limbs were torn off, clothes ripped away, or their hair singed off. They looked to be the group of homunculi that were used by the mages who had met their ends in the hands of Elijah Breggas when he ran rampant here.

The cheer of the homunculi grew more intense as Minamoto turned to look at them.

"You must get up! Stand up and get rid of the evil Devil-yeyo!"

It was then that Elijah headed toward him with the sound of metallic chains clanking. Minamoto did not hold back any longer.

He put his strength behind the hand that held Yodo Kamaitachi and sliced through the High Devil rushing toward him with a single swing. It appeared as though a fog of blood had sprayed around Kamaitachi like a sprinkler before Elijah was felled like a giant tree.

"I-it can't be true… I-I am a High Devil…"

Elijah wasn't quite dead yet. He had just received a mortal blow that kept him on the floor, gasping for breath. The metal chain wrapped around his back had also been cut, freeing the corpse of the woman, which slid to the floor. A cheer broke out.

This time it was not just the homunculi, but also the soldiers in the rear, but Minamoto could only hear the loud and annoying sound of the homunculi cheering. He walked toward the homunculi with heavy steps.

"We're really grateful-yeyo!"

"Admiral Minamoto is our hero-yeyo!"

The homunculi put on a grotesque smile as they praised him. Minamoto suddenly lifted one up before throwing it back toward the floor.

PIK!

The homunculus was smashed onto the floor turning into a bloody mess.

"To receive praise from this half-made trash. I can't bear it! I won't let anyone who was watching live!"

Yodo Kamaitachi danced once again. The homunculi's heads and limbs flew dizzyingly in the air as bright red blood splattered in every direction. No one could stop him who was dyed in madness. His blade that had soaked his immediate surroundings in blood swung violently in the air seeking its next opponent. Elijah Breggas became its next target as the closest being around.

"I received this humiliation because of this trash-like Devil."

However, Elijah's movements were strange. The High Devil, which had been gasping for breath after the mortal blow, was now stretching his hand in an attempt to reach something.

Minamoto's eyes moved and soon discovered what he sought. There was a corpse of a young woman tied in metal chains in the direction of the High Devil's outstretched hand.

"S…sophia…"

Minamoto's face grew ugly. "Is the so-called High Devil playing with a human corpse like a doll? Not only are you weak and repulsive, you are also perverted."

Yodo Kamaitachi's tip was pointed toward Sophia's corpse. "I will slice up this rotten corpse and feed it to the dogs!"

The blade exploded into a fog of blood and split the air. Just when the sword dyed in an evil aura was about to touch the corpse…

CLANK.

Something stopped the blade. Minamoto's eyes grew wide. *W-what is this?!*

There weren't many people who could stop him. The only ones he expected to be able to block his attack with such ease were the higher ranked Devil Lords, and those with the title of "Transcendent" within the human alliance. But the face that stood before him was someone he could have never expected.

K-kim Sungchul?!

He had not been told that Sungchul was here. His panic-stricken face turned toward the distant Martin Breggas. Martin, who was now kneeling over his son's torn corpse with a distant expression on his face, was lost in many ways.

The man who had stopped the sword smirked while Minamoto still stood in shock.

"Yo, Taeksu Kim."

"E-enemy of the World!"

The atmosphere of the entire battlefield shifted with the presence of a single person. The fleet of the Human Empire who had been carpet bombing, the Civil Militia of Trowyn who had been sweeping up the remnants of the enemy army, the main forces on the ground, and even the Order of the Iron Blood Knights who had been surrounded and waiting for death were wholly focused on the appearance of this one man.

Silence that couldn't have been imagined moments ago fell onto the battlefield. Minamoto pulled his Yodo Kamaitachi away from Fal Garaz, which stood in its path, and retreated.

"It's been a while." Sungchul spoke with a bright smile. His smile picked away at a scar deep inside Minamoto… no, Taeksu's mind. Fifteen years ago, on the plains of La Grange, the humiliation of the time when he had been helplessly tied up without being able to do anything despite being much stronger than Sungchul appeared in his mind.

It's different now. My strength has grown since then, and I have techniques and experience that I didn't possess back then.

Despite the fact that Sungchul's infamy had swept across the world, Minamoto, with his sinister secret, believed that Sungchul's reputation was nothing but hogwash.

I'll kill you and place my name as the First Champion of the 13 Champions of the Continent. No, wouldn't First Champion be too much? Since the one who gave me power is also on the list.

Minamoto smirked. He had become panicked momentarily, but courage stemming from self-confidence quickly sprang forth.

"Yodo Kamaitachi, Blood Fiend Technique! You're a dead man!" Minamoto stood boldly before Sungchul and swung his katana. A fog of blood quickly began to spread from the blade's body. It was the same blade that had cleaved through Elijah in a single slice.

However, Sungchul only looked at Minamoto with apathetic eyes.

Minamoto slowly began to move. It was at this moment that the voice of a young girl rang out from above Sungchul's head.

"All done!" A single book was gliding straight toward Sungchul's head from the sharp mountain slope. Sungchul collected the falling book.

"I told you to wait."

"It was scary waiting by myself!"

He smiled bitterly as to say "it can't be helped" and pulled out the single drawing held between the pages of the book. It contained the image of a beautiful woman.

Minamoto's face grew red.

Why... that's my ideal woman!

Sungchul pulled out the drawing, indifferent whether Minamoto looked or not, and placed it onto another portrait. The final drawing turned into fragments of light and disappeared leaving behind a single message in Sungchul's eyes.

[How was it? It couldn't be that you've fallen for me now, right? It doesn't matter if you did. We can never be.]

Basic Reward:
1. Intuition +1
2. Portrait of Vestiare drawn on Jewel Papyrus

Sungchul immediately threw the portrait of Vestiare drawn on Jewel Papyrus onto the ground without hesitation. Minamoto ran over to the ground to pick up the portrait as quick as lightning.

"Oooh...! Sugoi!"

Sungchul checked his changed stats while Minamoto was preoccupied with the portrait.

Intuition – 500

A smile rose on Sungchul's lips, then...

BAM!

A fearsome strike that couldn't be seen struck Minamoto's abdomen.

"Degayasu!" Minamoto let out an eerie scream and collapsed onto the floor.

Sungchul took a sweep at the gazes of the soldiers filled with awe and fear before heading off. Martin had become a shell of a man, and Minamoto was dead. There was no one left to stop his path.

While he was thinking so, Minamoto's body, which lay on the ground, began to squirm. "Go... no further! Sungchul!"

Sungchul could now see it. The evil energy that surrounded Minamoto's entire body. This thing that could be described as a black fog, or maybe mucus, was now popping Minamoto onto his feet.

"..."

He watched Minamoto who was now heading in his direction with a katana in hand with callous indifference.

***

It was a skill that Sungchul did not recognize. One thing that Sungchul could see was that the strength that had delayed Taeksu's death and held him up was not one of his own but from an external source. Sungchul thought of a possibility.

Is it a Soul Contract?

A Soul Contract is, as the name indicates, a blessing created by a God or a Lesser God which is then etched into the user's soul. The blessings were frequently difficult to obtain, but when obtained, it would grant the user a great power. The Eye of Truth and Soul Storage which were commonly used were also power granted by Soul Contracts.

Souls often possessed metaphysical properties which were known to be impossible to understand by humans, but at least in the realm of Soul Contracts, a difference in the size of souls existed. This was the number of contracts a person can hold.

Empty regions where a contract can be held in the soul were known as Slots. The average person would only have a single slot, if at all. The higher the stats and the higher the number of lives one has influence over, the more the number of slots become available. Those extraordinary ones commonly referred to as Superhuman held three slots. The Transcendents were known to hold between four to five slots. However, Sungchul held six slots.

Every one of the Soul Contracts was a precious thing that was difficult to obtain and only found through the harshest of trials. Among them, these three were the most important:

First, Soul Harvester. A legend-tier Soul Contract that restores one's vitality by the amount of damage inflicted. It was this ability which restored his strength after he killed his enemies that allowed him to become the immortal figure when standing against armies.

Second, Thunder Shield. Another legend-tier Soul Contract which had the fearsome effect of reducing all magical damage by half and also granted immunity to all mental attacks below legend rank. Seeing as the only beings capable of utilizing mental attacks above legend rank were god-level beings, it wouldn't be an exaggeration to say that there was no person in the world capable of harming Sungchul through a mental attack.

Third, Eye of Truth. It was the most commonly used legend-tier Soul Contract that negated all illusory magic below epic rank, and it also allowed him to inspect all items, cursed items, and skills. It couldn't be more emphasized how necessary this skill was for Sungchul who had made the vast majority of the world his enemy.

It was to acquire these three Soul Contracts that Sungchul had traversed the world discreetly, having to pass trials with his life, and sometimes his soul, at stake. He had to overcome mortal risk many times and met face to face with horrendous pain and despair which cannot be fully put into words. It was only after such trials that he was able to gather the Soul Contracts known as the 3 Divine Skills and etch them into his own soul.

The change that was happening to Minamoto's body seemed to be due to some form of a powerful Soul Contract, although it wasn't at the level of Sungchul's.

"Kekeke… Strong. For just a fucking highschool graduate piece of shit…"

CRRICK CRACK.

The sound of his broken spine assembling itself could be heard. Sungchul looked into Minamoto's eyes. His body was being repaired, but his mind was wandering some otherworldly place. Minamoto was gasping for breath while uttering something akin to talking in his sleep.

"What? Enemy of the World? Some overhyped bitch… I know what you were before you came here. Some fucking uneducated laborer whose only accomplishment in life is being fourteen days late out of service because you were rotting in some prison? Not just you, but that Emperor William Quinton Marlboro. I even know that he's some whore's son."

Minamoto began to snicker to himself as though it was something hilarious.

"For the son of some prostitute working the pole at some strip bar to be Emperor! Ehehehe! They say there's nothing like the seed of royalty, but this isn't proper, is it?"

"…"

Sungchul didn't say anything to this. It was because Minamoto's rant was not too far from the truth. He could still remember it. It was on some festive autumn night with a bright full moon. The Summoned who had been brought into Other World had a solemn moment by the crackling fireside where they talked about their previous lives. The man who became an Emperor, the man who became an assassin, and those who had been killed or had returned to their own world were looking off at some distant place with longing eyes as they told their stories. Taeksu might have been there, although Sungchul didn't recall whether Taeksu had been there or not.

Taeksu had been an inconspicuous person at the time without the courage to speak nor the talent to stand out. However, Sungchul had a single question for Minamoto now that it had reached this point.

"Why did the Emperor bring you in?"

On the surface, it might be easy enough to say that Taeksu was another Summoned with powerful combat potential which had swayed the Emperor. Sungchul had also believed those words at the time. No, he just didn't suspect them.

When he was the Emperor's sword, it had never even occurred to him that it was possible to doubt the Emperor. But, he could now ask those questions.

"I'll ask again. Why did the Emperor bring you in?"

"Don't you already know?" Minamoto smirked as he put on a little dance. "I know something you don't. A truth that that arrogant Emperor will never tell the likes of you."

"Is that right?"

"Yep. Of course, I have no obligation to tell you anything. But since we've known each other for so long, I'll let you in on something fun." Minamoto put on a smug smile before whispering to Sungchul in his silence, "The Wandering King had the military power to beat you all in that fight."

"The Wandering King did?"

"Yep. The proof is me. The Great Minamoto Daisuke who has been reborn through the Forbidden Technique. Kekeke!"

An evil aura poured out from Minamoto's eyes. It was the same presence that had raised him from the dead.

Sungchul dug through his past experiences for something similar to this evil aura, but he found no such luck. The closest thing to this aura was the damp and sticky aura of the Ancient God.

"Yodo Kamaitachi!" Minamoto who was swallowed by the evil aura began to exude a blood-colored fog as he headed toward Sungchul with the appearance of the Demon Yasha.

"I am Unbreakable… Unbre…!"

However, the difference in strength between the two was clear. Minamoto's figure scattered like dust as soon as Fal Garaz moved.

"Unbreeeee…!!!"

It was the result of putting some strength behind the swing. The Soul Contract or whatever it may be tried to grab on to Minamoto's scattered flesh, but it eventually scattered with it.

I don't care about your secret.

He was already sick of these dirty schemes. No matter what anyone had planned, it was enough to crush them with Fal Garaz. He had obtained this godly strength for this purpose.

"..."

Sungchul turned his head to one side and saw Elijah Breggas who was still gulping for breath as he lay on his side. Sungchul then turned toward the other side. Martin Breggas who looked to have been hollowed out was kneeling there. Sungchul picked up the female corpse that lay between the two, which was slightly closer to Elijah's side.

A long time had passed since she had died, but Sophia Breggas' appearance looked unchanged from when she lived. He went through the carefully placed magic on Sophia's body with the Eye of Truth.

"W-where is this?" Elijah said. "I can't see anything. It hurts... It's cold..." His life was hanging by a thread. It was Minamoto's handiwork. Minamoto had made it so that the Devil would die in pain and despair as slowly as possible.

Sungchul left Elijah and moved on. He could hear Elijah's voice from behind him.

"Father... Where are you?" Elijah's extended hand desperately sought out his father who no longer existed. Martin, who was the source of all this trouble, had lost his life at some point and was quickly growing cold. It was a senseless and pitiful end for the fortunate adventurer who had risen to the rank of the Sixth Champion of the Continent.

Sungchul abruptly walked forth with Sophia's corpse in hand. There were thousands of soldiers on the battlefield, but no one could think of following him.

—

A stone grave was crudely made on top of a sunny hill. Bertelgia had brought a white flower from some place between her pages and offered it to the grave as she said, "To escape this cruel world into the embrace of a warm god!"

Sungchul read a book while leaning on a rock. It was the secret tome of Cosmomancy, Primordial Light, which he had obtained through incredible effort in Airfruit. An endless horizon and incomprehensible shapes and words opened up before his eyes when he opened the book, and all of it began to organize itself in some recognizable form.

Is this the Primordial Light? It truly possesses a difficult and incomprehensible nature that's hard to describe.

Intuition of 500 was not something everyone could achieve. Even in the greatest of Magical Academies, there might be one or two people that might ever reach this peak. It was a level where they would easily receive the title of Great Scholar. This Intuition that Sungchul had achieved was now whispering to him the story of this world's secret, which a human mind could never hope to understand. After a long and seemingly boring story which he was strangely captivated by, Sungchul sensed; the origin of life before him was filled with unfathomably endless light.

Is this... Primordial Light?

In this blinding brilliance, Sungchul could feel some new strength budding inside his body.

[You have read through the Final Secret Tome of Cosmomancy "Primordial Light – Punishment"]

[You're overflowing with the knowledge of the Skies and Cosmos.]

Reward: Magic "Star Light"

"What are you doing? Why aren't you in silent prayer?" Bertelgia had approached Sungchul's back and began to peck him with one of her corners. In the past, this was something Bertelgia would never have dared to do, but as she drew Vestiare's portraits, she had gained a bit more confidence and a higher position in Sungchul's eyes. Sungchul grabbed the persistent Bertelgia and stuffed her into his pocket before looking toward the northern skies. The thick dark storm cloud that had always loomed over the Demon Realm was projecting an eerie red lightning. Sungchul lifted his finger and pointed toward the northern sky. But then he instinctively sensed that his finger wouldn't be enough.

It's different than Glare.

He had felt it to be uncomfortable even as he cast Meteor, and this was Primordial Light, which was the greatest magic of Cosmomancy. Sungchul pulled a single staff from his Soul Storage. It was an oak staff that looked worn as it had been passed through many hands. Sungchul looked at the staff for a while after grabbing it.

To be using this old thing. His apathetic eyes were suddenly filled with nostalgia.

"Sniff sniff!" Bertelgia showed interest in this staff she had never seen before.

"It smells like a woman? Whose is it?"

"… None of your business." Sungchul stuffed her deep into his pocket before pointing the staff toward the northern sky. A complex magical formation appeared around the staff and him. A decently long aria, though shorter than Meteor, Sungchul thought when the invocation that filled his inner consciousness was spat out in his mind.

"Star Light."

A magical formation brightly opened up at the end of the staff like a mechanical gear. At the same time, a massive pillar of light poured out from the end of the formation. A massive pillar of pure light that couldn't even be compared to Glare. The pillar split the air and struck the storm looming in the northern sky. When the pillar of light faded, a noticeable gap had formed in that storm cloud. It was the flight path of the greatest magic of Cosmomancy, Star Light.

Sungchul felt a joy that he hadn't felt in a long time within that empty feeling when half of his entire mana poured out.

I can do it with this!

There was no need to test this out on the Deep Sea Demon. Primordial Light was the real deal, and it would be the best solution.

"Woah... that's your magic? I thought I was looking at one of the Seven Heroes' magic," said Bertelgia.

It might have been because of the afterblast caused by Primordial Light. When the air that had been pushed out by the pillar of light flooded back, it came like a strong current that swallowed everything up.

"Eek!"

The moment Bertelgia let out her sharp scream, Sungchul grabbed the flower. He offered the flower to Sophia's grave and secured it between the rocks before heading north toward the storm cloud that he had split in half.

Chapter 19 – Heading to the Demon King's Palace

"The Enemy of the World reappeared on the Demon Realm Frontlines."

"The Enemy of the World one-sidedly killed Admiral Minamoto Daisuke of the Human Empire and disappeared with ease."

"Lord Marquis Martin Breggas died suddenly, and now there is no one left to defend the Demon Realm Frontlines."

Urgent messages of events unfolding within the Demon Realm Frontlines were spreading throughout the world. The news even reached the shoddy saloons of Trowyn. A sole adventurer who had been tipping mugs of beer into her mouth in a corner inside the saloon took off the rag around her head as if from frustration.

Her tidily organized hair and her brown eyes filled with soft but powerful resolution were revealed.

Sujin Lee. Her name had been spread as Ahmuge among the upper echelon of this world.

The saloon was rowdy with debates and disputes over the news about the Enemy of the World and the northern frontier. One thing that was certain was that the Enemy of the World, Sungchul Kim, had appeared for the second time. There was also another unconfirmed rumor that a beam of light, which appeared like the spear of god, had split the dark clouds looming in the north.

Ahmuge looked at her lightly shaking mug of beer with eyes filled with distrust. "Why is this happening? The moment he was supposed to reveal himself again was right after the great army of demons was repelled."

She may not know much else, but one thing was for sure: everything was becoming slightly misaligned from the future she had seen.

—

There were only a few that hadn't heard of the name Aquiroa the Executor. Known as one of three Transcendants as well as the Second Champion of the Continent, Aquiroa the Executor of the

World Council was the lord of the mystical and veiled Floating Isles and hailed as a powerful mage hero who had lent her strength to the Emperor William Quinton Marlboro in toppling the evil Rutheginea Kingdom. However, it was rare for anyone to know what kind of person Aquiroa actually was. There was little else recorded about her other than the plain facts that she was old, originated from the Floating Isles, and that she was a powerful mage. Not a single thing about her actual age, her history during her formative years, nor her family situation was known.

Among the Thirteen Champions of the Continent who had each established themselves as powerful heroes, she was like a ghost made up of secrets. That Aquiroa was now entering a hallway veiled in darkness to enter a room filled with stillness.

It was a shabby room adorned with no windows nor any furniture other than a straw mat bed. There was a single man sitting on this bed. Aquiroa carefully spoke to him.

"Your Majesty. It might be difficult to hold off any longer. Judging by his oppressive strength, he seemed to have already met with an existence one should never meet."

Aquiroa bowed in the direction of the man sitting in the dark. Her humble bow was not for the Emperor of the Human Empire that ruled over this world, the king of the Ancient Kingdom that existed for over ten thousand years, nor the heads of Elves or Dwarves that held high pride. There was but one person. It was none other than the crownless king, the Third Champion of the Continent, who was commonly known as the Wandering King.

"… is that so?"

He used to go by another name in the past: The Neglectful King, Kromgard. He was the final ruler of the Holy Kingdom of Rutheginea that had reigned over the majority of the continent before the Human Empire. He had been praised as a genius mage of a rare kind, as a possessor of three magical fingerprints, and a swordsman of unending potential as a child, but he lost interest in

441

all things at some point and shut himself away in his room, focusing all of his attention on mundane tasks.

Nobles began to exercise acts of exploitation and oppression to sate their greed as he turned away from governing which ignited the embers of rebellion across the land. A single man led the rebel army: the Summoned known as William Quinton Marlboro.

The rebel army boldly bypassed countless fortifications and positions and forced their way right up to the vicinity of the Kingdom's capital – La Grange. They had bet the fate of the continent on a single battle.

When faced with the final battle, King Kromgard surrendered and gave up the crown to the rebel army. It was an unexpected decision by the Neglectful King. He was exempt from responsibility and made a free man in return.

What he did after that day was not known, but other than receiving the title of the Third Champion of the Continent upon the assembly of the Thirteen Champions, he was known to wander the world by himself without kingdom or subjects. The world had given such a man the nickname of the Wandering King.

"…"

A helmet that couldn't be peered into. Massive armor that covered his entire body. A white undyed cloth mantle that had slightly yellowed. These were the symbols that now represented the Wandering King.

"There might be a need for me to step in personally." Aquiroa bowed her head toward the Wandering King once again. There was someone resembling a man standing behind her. The strange creature that was too transparent and lanky to be called human was standing half covered in darkness while silently blinking with its large and stretched out oval-shaped eyes. There was something dark within its large eyes that was pulsating while exuding an uneasy aura.

The dark interior of the Wandering King's helm flashed with interest. "Is it finally complete? My true soldiers?"

His vision was focused on the monstrous figure standing behind her.

"I am ashamed, and it is with the deepest of regrets to inform you that we are still not at the final stage yet. However, they might be able to shackle a certain young man who has one-sidedly focused his growth on his physical stats."

"A shackle…"

The face of a skinny young man tied in metal chains and shackles grazed past the Wandering King's eyes, then the face of the woman who stood in front of the man in tears begging for his life bubbled up as well.

I should have killed the bastard then.

However, the past was the past. Only God can tell how the wheel of fate would turn. The Wandering King broke away from his brief moment in thought and looked toward Aquiroa. "… What will you do?"

"I will personally head toward the Demon Realm, leading the fleet under your majesty's banner."

He nodded at her resolute request. "We need more time than expected. We must complete our objective before the Calamity that we can't handle destroys everything."

"I shall carry out thy will!"

The Wandering King melted into the darkness. Aquiroa turned around as well and headed forward in haste.

Sungchul Kim. I can't let an idiot like you ruin our plans.

A blue flame danced beneath the mask.

—

"…"

The Entrance of the Demon Realm.

A Deep Sea Demon was trembling in a fetal position behind Sungchul. Its intelligence was low, but whatever that had occurred here was enough to stamp fear into what little intelligence there was.

Sungchul left the Deep Sea Demon alone and headed deeper into the Demon Realm. There were dozens of airships floating at the end of the passageway which was the entrance of the Demon Realm. It was the fleet of the Human Empire.

"Enemy of the World! You shall not pass."

Below them were the last scraps of soldiers left on the Demon Realm Frontlines who had formed a ground force from a hodgepodge of different races.

"Return Fal Garaz! You thieving rat!"

Several of the dwarves began to spit out profanities in bellowing voices. This was the reply the World gave as Sungchul decided to stand against the Calamities.

Sungchul looked over at these people that stood before him with disinterest.

"Phew. Don't they ever get tired of this?" Bertelgia let out a sigh as though she had already grown accustomed to this scene. Sungchul, on the other hand, was deep in thought.

Strange. They managed to gather such a force after breaking through the Deep Sea Demon.

However, there was no sign of battle around the previous Deep Sea Demon. There was not a single corpse to be found. Deep Sea Demons were nothing but rabid mutts before Sungchul, but they were usually not an enemy to be trifled with. They held the title of Gatekeeper of the Demon Realm.

As one had crushed the Crusaders of Salvation, these Deep Sea Demons could pulverize any army with their massive physique, fearsome strength, and most of all, their unbelievable vitality. Their ability to bypass such a Deep Sea Demon with no casualties brought up a single possibility.

Did they collaborate with the Demons?

It was completely within the realm possibility for the ruling elite. They would do anything for their own benefit. Martin Breggas, who had sacrificed the entirety of the Order of the Iron Blood Knights for the sake of making his son, a hero was a prime example.

Sungchul wanted to put it to the test. He looked up at the airships in the sky. A large airship that was uniquely adorned with flashy decorations caught his eyes.

Is that their flagship?

He checked the flag fluttering on top of the airship. The golden sun symbolizing the Human Empire with a hand grasping lightning was clearly on display on the fluttering flag. It belonged to Overseer Dmitri Medioff of the Human Empire.

I think his flagship was the Vanguard.

The ship that Sungchul recalled was destroyed during the exchange with the demons during the Airfruit fiasco. Currently, Dmitri was aboard the Androgoras, one of the new models of destroyers.

It's fine either way.

Sungchul had no ability to fly. However, he did know of a method to board a flying airship, and had the ability to put that plan into action.

Dmitri Medioff is my only target.

Demonic Weapon Cassandra was pulled out of the Soul Storage after so long. Sungchul held Cassandra and rushed toward the ground forces that stood against him. Elven archers and Dwarven artillery shells poured down like rain.

Cassandra whipped about like a living snake toward the flying projectiles and destroyed them. Due to the unimaginable tensile force it had, it not only deflected everything it touched, but it also reduced them to dust. Sungchul came within thirty meters of the ground forces.

"Spears to the front!"

Dwarven spearmen lined their lengthy spears five times their height toward Sungchul.

STOMP

Short but sturdy military boots kicked the ground to take root where they stood. However, none of the Dwarves believed that their defensive formation would have any effect on Sungchul. Their expectations turned to reality.

Sungchul grabbed the spears that were pointed toward him with his hand and used his strength to quickly leap over the Dwarven formation.

"How dare you!"

"Die!"

Human knights and swordsmen swung their swords and maces and leaped toward him. Sungchul gripped the collar of one of the knights wearing light armor to deflect the oncoming attacks before looking toward the sky. His eyes caught sight of something. It was the hot air balloon assigned to every airship.

In between battles, airships used these hot air balloons to exchange supplies and men with the ground forces. The airship itself could descend, but it would be risking dangers such as an ambush or sudden gusts of wind that might take down the ship. Because losing such expensive airships would be a heavy loss to the national treasury of the Human Empire, they decided to use these hot air balloons on each of the airships. One of these logistics hot air balloons was nearby.

SKKRRT!

Demonic Weapon Cassandra wrapped around the rope hanging below one of them. As expressions of terror spread across the soldiers aboard the hot air balloon, the entire balloon shook and was slowly being dragged below.

Sungchul put strength behind the arm holding Cassandra and leaped on.

"Cut the rope! Immediately!"

However, a black figure had already boarded the balloon before anyone could finish the order. A forceful hand grabbed the soldiers on board and threw them below. The soldiers squirmed in the mud when they touched the ground. They wouldn't have died even if it had been on hard ground. They were trained soldiers of the Human Empire.

Now that he had hijacked the balloon, Sungchul cut the rope connecting it to the ground and began to ascend. Countless arrows and ballista shots shot up from the ground aimed at Sungchul, but they couldn't pierce through the curtain of might formed by Cassandra.

The news that Sungchul had boarded the balloon immediately spread to the airships. High-speed airships capable of much greater maneuverability opened their gunports and aimed toward the balloon Sungchul was riding.

"Fire!"

Several cannon shots fired together tore through the balloon and the torn balloon helplessly fell toward the ground, but Sungchul, who had been aboard, was nowhere to be found. Sungchul had already leaped toward the nearest airship once he had reached an appropriate height. His leap filled with god-like strength had placed him onto a certain airship's deck.

BOOM!

The monster of this era wielding Fal Garaz had boarded the ship. Everyone on board with the exception of the captain wearing a particularly tall hat wore terror across their face.

"…"

Sungchul briskly moved toward the bridge and uttered a single word, "Scram."

Roughly a dozen crew members jumped out of the bridge in a panic. Sungchul grabbed the key and turned the direction of the ship. His destination was the massive airship Androgoras that lied straight ahead.

Other airships were aware that Sungchul took over one of their ships and fired upon him, but it was already too late to stop him. Sungchul leaped off once he made it to an appropriate distance. It was a leap powerful enough to make the boat's hull groan and buckle.

BOOM!

Rather than a bird, Sungchul flew like a meteor and landed on the deck of Androgoras, and he looked at the man who was staring at him with eyes filled with terror to ask a simple question. "Do you remember me, Dmitri Medioff?"

"W-who?" Dmitri didn't recognize the face, but he immediately knew who Sungchul was when he noticed the hammer in Sungchul's hand.

Mommy…

***

"S-stop him."

Swordsmen of the Empire wearing flashy uniforms were rushing in to attack Sungchul with their shiny blades in hand. However, they were laid flat onto the deck when Cassandra split the air like a fly struck down by a fly swatter. Sungchul proceeded as he walked onto the bridge of the flagship Androgoras without interference.

Dimitri sought out escape routes, but it was more difficult to escape Sungchul than it was to take one's own life.

"Hey, Commander," greeted Dmitri.

Sungchul stood before him as though by fate. Sungchul didn't look happy nor upset; he instead inspected Dimitri with his indifferent eyes.

"Did you join hands with the Demon King?" Sungchul asked bluntly. His question was extremely simple and to the point.

Dmitri's eyes trembled ceaselessly. He eventually organized his chaotic thoughts and began to speak. "If… you're talking about a-alliances, that's not true. We only… out of immediate necessity…"

As he continued to stumble through his explanation, he felt something hard and cold touch his neck. It was Fal Garaz. The head of Fal Garaz had been brought to his neck.

"Briefly."

Sungchul's intentions were clear. It was a threat against his life if he continued to speak nonsense. Sophistry: capital punishment.

Long winded speeches: capital punishment. Twisting word games: capital punishment. Just when Dimitri was prepared to work his silver tongue, he had become like a rat trapped in a corner.

"W-we came to an agreement." Dmitri swallowed deeply before he caved in and gave out the information.

"What kind of agreement?"

"T-to stop you from reaching the Demon King…"

"I see." Sungchul, who had heard all that he wanted to hear, lowered Fal Garaz and turned back. He didn't have any particular grievances with Dmitri anyways. The man that he had seen in Golden City was arrogant and full of himself, but in reality, Dmitri was quite the loyal hunting dog for those elite few. He was nothing more and nothing less.

"What will you do now?" Bertelgia brought up the question.

"I'll just walk the path I was walking before." He walked to the head of the ship. Dmitri who had just been brought back from the brink of death was rubbing his own neck while looking at Sungchul's back with a dumbfounded expression. Sungchul looked back as he arrived at the head of the ship and spoke in a clear voice.

"I'll kill you for real if you follow me."

Dmitri recoiled back and kept nodding his head. It was at this moment when the mission of the five fleets of the Human Empire, which had been deployed to the Demon Realm for the purpose of stopping Sungchul, ended in failure.

—

Now, the only human remaining in the Demon Realm was Sungchul. A colorful light of unknown origins lit up the dark skies beyond the endless wasteland in a mysterious light, and beyond the distant skies, some lonely screams could be heard spontaneously from time to time. A sulphuric stench clung to the tip of the nose like a shadow. That fading sulfuric stench indicated that they had entered into Demon Realm proper.

It meant that all of the one-sided ambushes he had experienced, and all those encounters that felt accidents would now become more organized. However, the divine items held in Sungchul's hand worked to repel the ambush from the Demon Army. The Devil Lord leading an army noticed Fal Garaz in Sungchul's hand and turned back to his castle as though his ass was on fire, shutting himself in.

Sungchul, who was well versed in Devil psychology, knew fully that the reason for their abrupt escape was partially due to their fear of him, but it was also to avoid taking too many losses and giving an advantage to rival demon armies. Devils were creatures of self-interest. If virtues like compassion, sympathy, respect, and trust for others were to be purged from a human mind, it would leave something not too different from a demon's.

Storm clouds and sulfur. The skies of the Demon Realm enveloped in fog had no separate night and day. Sungchul walked at a pace that wasn't too fast or too slow toward the Demon King's Palace. The reason for his reasonable pace was to prepare for any potential ambush. Even worms squirm when stepped on, and a rat trapped in a corner is bound to bite the cat.

Sungchul discovered something as he was walking the wasteland. There were bamboo-like objects sticking out of the dark earth like grass. There was so much of it that it wouldn't have been an exaggeration to call it a field of green. However, grass doesn't grow on the surface of the Demon Realm, except for between some rocks or in underground caverns.

Sungchul pulled out the Demon Weapon Cassandra and powerfully struck a part of the tube. When the whip made contact, the air itself seemed to tense for a moment before a bright burst of light went off, followed by a powerful explosion. That single explosion might not have affected Sungchul in the least, but it wouldn't have been the case if the number of explosions grew. The green field that seemed to extend out to the horizon quickly disappeared in a chain of explosions. The dark earth turned bright like the day, and the world itself seemed to tremble for a few minutes.

"Uwah... There wouldn't be any piece left of me if I was standing there." Bertelgia spoke in a shocked voice.

"..."

Sungchul wouldn't have died, but Bertelgia might have been caught up in the explosion. He didn't utter that fact.

When the explosion subsided, Sungchul began to walk the changed landscape full of craters.

"Why are you trying to stand against the Calamity?" Bertelgia suddenly asked in the midst of their walk. It was a topic that hadn't been discussed before, as her goal had always been to lead Sungchul down the path of a Creationist, but now that they were finally drawing close to the elimination of the Demon King, she grew curious.

"Are you perhaps trying to be a hero? Trying to save the world like the Seven Heroes?"

Because Bertelgia was annoying Sungchul from the side, Sungchul replied in a calm manner, "I'm not a hero."

She tried to get a few more words in, but she couldn't. Sungchul's eyes and face grew so different than before that he was now exuding a dangerous atmosphere. It wasn't until long after that Sungchul was no longer stiff. He looked toward the massive black rock mountain looming in the darkness. As he drew closer, the lower portion that was hidden by the horizon slowly revealed itself. The base of the mountain was carved out like the face of a Devil with two eyes and a mouth spewing red fire. It was the only Wonder carved into the drab and monotonous Demon Realm. Pandemonium. The Demon King resided here.

Sungchul spoke as he moved toward the Demon King's Palace. "It is to unravel the Curse of Extinction."

"Hm?" She tilted her head at the sudden response.

"Didn't you ask before? About the reason I'm facing off against the Calamity."

"Oh... that? You didn't look happy about it... so I was just going to leave it be."

"I'm telling you so that you can keep it in mind." Sungchul said as such before picking up his pace. His slow pace grew faster until he broke into a run. The scenery around him blew past quickly with the wind. However, the distant palace of the Demon King did not appear to be getting any closer. It was because of the massive distance between him and the palace.

The mountain into which the flaming face was carved was simply massive. Even if all the mountains of a nation were stacked on top of one another they still wouldn't match its size, and the flames that was spewed out intermittently reached the clouds. Each time it happened, the clouds fired a crimson lightning bolt and sprayed a shower of water towards the ground, but the gigantic flames devoured the water before it even hit the ground.

Sungchul entered that thirsty land upon which rain never stopped. In front of him stood a mob of countless demons. It wasn't the opportunistic soldiers of the Devil Lords but the army of the Demon King, Hesthnius Max.

"…"

Sungchul looked toward them with indifference. Perhaps because he had already killed everyone with a reputation to their name in the previous expedition, there was no one here that appeared particularly strong.

I'll end this as quickly as possible.

Sungchul made this promise to himself as he stepped forward. When that small, but significant step touched the ground, a magic formation appeared above the demon forces. Sungchul quickly recognized that the extremely intricate magic formation was for a long-distance teleportation spell. He also knew that this wasn't a magic technique of the Demons, but one from the humans. On the other side of the magic formation was an airship with an elegant white body.

Sungchul's eyes twitched.

That's Procrustes. Isn't that Aquiroa's flagship?

The Second Champion of the Continent, Executor Aquiroa. The one responsible for turning the twelve champions away from the face of Pandemonium eight years ago dared to show herself before Sungchul. A corner of Sungchul's eyes ignited with flames of rage.

You are the one person I want to kill no matter what.

Sungchul recalled the face of a girl who had fallen asleep, who had become like a tree. Her always-soft and blushed skin became hardened like a bark of wood, and the surface was covered in white fungus as if covered in snow.

"Brazen." Sungchul spoke as though spitting the words from his lips. It was filled with emotion that couldn't be witnessed before. Bertelgia could feel, from her pocket, that his heart was beating differently than it had before. The pure white airship came out of the magic formation and stopped over the head of the Demons. An old woman wearing a robe and a mask engraved with undecipherable letters stood above the airship.

"Sungchul! Don't you know what kind of foolish thing you are attempting right now?!" Aquiroa spoke like she was scolding a child. "It's still not too late. Stop this foolish task and return. If you do so, I'll not only spare your life, but also consider restoring your name."

At that moment, the earth let out an earsplitting cry. Fal Garaz had struck its surface.

The demons standing in formation fell into chaos before the unexpected quakes. One of the devils pointed toward Sungchul's direction. "L-look over there!"

In the direction of that devil's finger was Sungchul holding a boulder that was the size of a house.

"…"

Sungchul lightly lifted that boulder and struck it in the air with Fal Garaz. That massive boulder flew like a baseball and critically struck the pure white airship.

BOOM!

The head of the ship began to tilt to the side with that single blow, and cracks began to form all over. Aquiroa who had been standing on the airship in high spirits began to waver from the blow.

"You dumb bastard! You haven't changed!" Aquiroa raised her hand, and two strange human-like figures appeared instantaneously behind her.

"Go! My soldiers! Restrain that foolish man from committing his foolish act!"

The two figures simply leaped down from the airship and hurtled their bodies toward Sungchul. Sungchul watched the mysterious beings flying toward him.

What are those?

They were creatures that his collection of experiences and knowledge honed through countless battles didn't recognize. However, there was no rule that he had to cut them any slack because he didn't recognize them. Sungchul struck the ground with his hammer and caused countless rock fragments to fly over to the strange creatures. It might be considered a light attack, but with the god-like strength instilled within the rock fragments, they had the power to turn any living creature to rags. The fragments hit their mark, but something strange occurred as the fragments struck them. The fragments had simply pierced through their half-transparent bodies.

Sungchul's eyes twitched. *Are they a type of Slime?*

Aquiroa, who saw this scene, began to snicker. *Kekeke... You were just some dumb worthless warrior. A failure who couldn't walk the long tradition of combining sword and magic. You might have grown one aspect to an extraordinary degree, but how are you so unaware that your weakness is so glaring?*

The creatures that she had created possessed both malleability and durability that exceeded that of a Slime's. Unless it was a particularly sharp sword of great value, it possessed perfect tolerance against blunt weapons that transmitted blunt force.

However, there had been one other who had the same line of thinking; the demon ranked second among the devils of the Demon Realm, Kant Emile. He had discarded his flesh and had become a Slime in an attempt to stop Sungchul's attack. However, that level of wit was turned to dust before Sungchul's oppressive strength.

WHAM!

Sungchul knocked away the persistent enemies with his hammer. It wasn't even multiple hits. Just a single blow. In that single blow, the strange creatures literally exploded. The superior fluidity and regenerative power that it boasted had no meaning in front of Sungchul.

Aquiroa's body momentarily stiffened. *That doesn't make any sense…! It was able to endure a blow from a 700-strength level during testing…?!*

She was unaware of the true extent of Sungchul's power.

Sungchul, who had eliminated the creatures, lifted a boulder once again. The target was Aquiroa's flagship, Procrustes.

Aquiroa realized his intention and began to shout with her arms waving in the air in a panic. "Sungchul! I have something to say! It's very important."

"What could you possibly have to say now?" Sungchul made the boulder fly with Fal Garaz. The pure white airship began to shake visibly as it groaned, and one of its masts fell away as it broke.

Aquiroa spoke again up on the chaotic deck. "I know why you're disappointed. Aren't you disappointed because we chose to simply delay the Calamity?"

"You know very well."

"We weren't trying to delay it! We were preparing another method!"

"Why are you telling me this now?"

"Because you were a nobody back then. Truthfully, weren't you at the point where you wouldn't have even gotten into the Thirteen Champions of the Continent if not for the Emperor's backing? We didn't want to share this information with someone like that!"

"Are you saying that you have a method now?" Sungchul shot a cynical gaze toward Aquiroa.

She felt revulsion shooting up from the tip of her toes as she nodded.

"Speak. Of that method." Sungchul spoke bluntly.

"I can't say."

"Oh, really?" Sungchul put on a bitter smile as he lowered his hammer.

Aquiroa who noticed this mustered up the courage to speak again. "And we will need a bit more time."

It was a slip of the tongue. Something that shouldn't have been said. Sungchul's eyes spat out rays of hostility that caused goosebumps. Aquiroa visibly stumbled as she tried to recoup her mistake.

"Wait! It's just a little bit longer. It'll be complete in just a little more time. All we need now is time. Time!"

"Do you truly believe that you can delay the Calamity? Even if it could be delayed, how much more sacrifice can you justify? Until everyone except you lot is killed?"

Aquiroa could determine that negotiations had drawn to a close by Sungchul's calm expression. She began to wave her two fists like mad as she screamed with her grating voice.

"Why do you go that far! Sungchul Kim! That child you're trying to save isn't even of your blood!"

Upon hearing this, Sungchul lowered his head to look into his pocket and spoke calmly. "Bertelgia."

"Yeah?"

"Go into the Storage for a bit."

When Bertelgia hesitated, Sungchul spoke in an uncharacteristically soft and gentle manner. "It won't take that long."

Chapter 20 – Hesthnius Max

BOOM! BOOM!

The Earth became like artillery shells bombarding the hull of the airship in white. The beautiful body of the vessel that had been held in great admiration was now trembling and tilting under this merciless barrage.

"Hurry up and initiate Teleportation! Hurry!"

The Dimensional Mages who gathered in a circular formation at the center of the airship began the incantations, but a large-scale teleportation was no easy feat. The rocks shook the airship aggressively as the outline of the magic formation was drawn, and the mages had to stop their aria every time.

BOOM! BOOM!

Two consecutive rocks critically struck the stern of the ship. The body of the ship, which had already begun to tilt, finally lost its balance and began to fall. The marble deck of the ship began to collapse like dominoes, and the people on top of the deck were swept away as the riggings hung below the mast became terrifying murder weapons assaulting them.

Aquiroa who sat at the front of the sinking airship did not move in the slightest; only staring intently at Sungchul who was pouring attack after attack toward her.

A worthless Summoned like you dares…

None of it had felt quite real yet. The reality that that human with no background was causing her to suffer so…

"Miss Aquiroa! We must retreat. The ship is falling!"

The captain came up behind her and spoke desperately. Aquiroa finally managed to snap back to her senses and nodded before turning back.

Chaos was unfolding upon the deck. What had struck Aquiroa the deepest was the final moments of the Dimensional Mages. The Dimensional Mages who had gathered in a circle to chant their aria were killed as they were strung up like marionettes on the riggings that had turned deadly.

It looks like it'll be difficult to salvage the ship. Since it's come to this, I need to secure my own escape.

She instantly teleported following a short aria. Being adept in magic, she immediately began casting another aria after her instantaneous movement, and she appeared as if she was walking in mid-air. There was no way that Sungchul would leave her to finish her plans. He predicted her actions and fired off a rock.

"Insolence!" Aquiroa pulled out two staves and began to swing them violently. When she did, a powerful explosion burst out before her causing the flying rock to be obliterated into pieces. Thin fragments were flying around her vicinity, but the magic barrier that had been cast around her protected her from them.

Sungchul did not rush. He put down the rock in his hand and began to walk toward her direction. The slow walk turned into a run, and the run soon turned into a full-on sprint. He who had become a gust of wind pierced through thousands of demons and ran in the direction she was fleeing.

Aquiroa felt a chill from the back of her head and soon discovered that Sungchul was hot on her heels.

"This monster!"

Different spells were cast from each staff. One staff formed an ice wall to block Sungchul's path, and the other borrowed the energy from the abundant power of lightning in her surroundings to strike down the target.

BOOM! CRACK!

Following a flash of light, a single strand of lightning flew toward Sungchul's direction. Sungchul lifted Fal Garaz as the lightning was about to strike him. The hammer, forged from fragments of the sky, absorbed the lightning and struck the ice wall in its path. A sound greater than thunder resounded before the ice wall was shattered to pieces, and Sungchul stepped through it like a leaping beast.

Aquiroa turned pale and quickly tried to formulate her next plan, but Sungchul's hand had already gripped onto her collar.

"You've always looked down on me," said Sungchul.

"A-a mere Summoned…"

"Now it's my turn to look down on you."

Grasping her by the collar, Sungchul threw her to the ground.

"F-fly!"

Aquiroa tried to form magic wings on her back in order to resist, but the momentum building into her body was not something a rushed magic could dare withstand. She flew toward the place where the demons were gathered like a comet and spun a bit like a wheel before coming to a stop.

"U-ugh…"

A portion of her mask broke, and between the shattered pieces, a stubborn red pupil was revealed.

Sungchul sat beside her like an angel of death.

"Is this all?" He subtly taunted her.

Aquiroa gritted her teeth and poured every magic she knew toward Sungchul, but none of it managed to deal any significant damage to him. Sungchul only evaded her assault or smashed through it like a cat toying with its prey, negating all of her actions.

"Is this all the almighty Executor is capable of?" Sungchul spoke without a single ragged breath nor damage to his clothing. His figure reflected in Aquiroa's eyes appeared to be a massive, insurmountable wall. The shadow of despair began to finally loom over the eye peeking through the shattered portion of her mask.

Sungchul slowly lifted Fal Garaz. "Now, let's put an end to this boring villain act."

"Wait! I still have something to say! I-I… am nothing more than a servant!"

"…"

"I am not really the one that has been planning all this. I am simply acting according to the orders of the King of Kromgard."

"The Wandering King…?"

The image of the pallid and lethargic man suddenly appeared in Sungchul's mind. Sungchul had no ill will toward the man. In fact, most of the generals in the anti-Rutheginea rebellion army had more or less a favorable impression of him. No one could know for sure the amount of blood that would have been spilled if the Wandering King had not voluntarily relinquished his crown. Not only that, but Sungchul had also had his life spared by the order of the Wandering King.

It was true that Sungchul had only been begrudgingly given a more lenient punishment because the one giving the sentence had been annoyed by someone's persistent pleading.

"And nothing will change if you kill me anyways. Aquiroa is not an individual but many. There will be another Aquiroa to replace me from the Floating Archipelago. So, show a bit of mercy on this old woman."

While Aquiroa continued to speak Sungchul lightly closed his eyes and appeared to be in thought. He then turned around. "I will speak of this directly to the Wandering King."

What Sungchul desired was very clear. Irrepressible anger and fear were revealed in Aquiroa's eyes underneath her mask.

"Beat it." Sungchul left her where she stood and walked on.

Aquiroa continued to hesitate until her eyes held unspeakable hostility. Magic formations began to appear all throughout her body.

How dare you utter those disrespectful words. I won't let you live.

She was invoking the most destructive magic known to her – Thunder Breaker. It was the final magic of the Seventh Circle in the School of Wind that no longer existed. Her effort to perform magic not belonging to her own Magical Fingerprint caused blue lines to streak across her unsightly face in geometric shapes. Artificial Magic Fingerprint. It was a long forgotten antiquated ancient technique, but all of Aquiroa's actions were within Sungchul's predictions.

"As expected, every hunting dog seems to act in the same way." Sungchul turned around while Aquiroa was completing her aria. He had seen Aquiroa's Thunder Breaker in the past. Ironically, it had also been in front of the Castle of the Demon King. She had used the magic to display her might as the Second Champion of the Continent, but its current form after such a long time was simply full of weaknesses.

A l-little more! Aquiroa's exposed face glowed brightly with blue vein-like Magical Fingerprint, and her eyes, which were full of magic formations, flew wide open.

Sungchul drew closer as he spoke. "Once you threaten to inform their owners that they've shat on the ground, they always seem to react like this."

"W-wait!" Aquiroa hurriedly tried to say something, but Sungchul was beyond forgiveness.

WHAM!

Fal Garaz slammed down onto the Executor, who was now glowing brilliantly with magic. Her corpse was squashed with her body still wrapped around by magic formations.

"I'm a much scarier man than your master." He glared with an apathetic look at the corpse that was disfigured beyond recognition and let out a shallow sigh. A dark aura spread upwards from the corpse, and it forced Aquiroa, who had been turned to rags, to her feet. However, as her upper body had been reduced to a puddle of blood it could not be reborn, so this unknown dark aura could only maintain her clothing to the state it was when she was alive before flying away into the sky.

Sungchul could feel that this aura was similar to the one that Minamoto had reeked of.

Is it some different kind of strength than a Soul Contract?

Unfortunately, this wasn't the most urgent issue. Sungchul turned his head to look at the Royal Palace of the Demon King. There were innumerable demons guarding the front. He proceeded as he headed out alone.

The demons let out a furious roar as they poured onto him like a tidal wave. Sungchul silently marched forth, leaving behind mountains of corpses and rivers of blood in his way. Any devil worth mentioning was steadily killed as he continued while the other demons were now at the point where they turned tail to escape in a panic.

All that now stood in his path was the front gate of the Demon King's Palace that had the form of a fearsome Devil. He had no key, and it didn't appear that it would be opened for him, but the answer was somewhere nearby. The heavy steel gate was broken open.

The blood-colored rug laid out between the colonnade carved directly from the rock wall wrapped in darkness continued on into the darkness. Sungchul silently walked forward.

The devils continued to ambush him from between the pillars. A devil that spat poison. A devil that poured out curses. The types of devils were diverse, but the results were the same. Every time the assassins leaped in, Sungchul's hammer caused more casualties.

Soon, the end of the carpet came to view. At the end of the dull but decadent space with purple colored flames burning in lamps was a gigantic throne. A massive corpse that was very familiar to Sungchul was sitting in a proud posture on the throne. It didn't look much different since his death. Sungchul could see that several smaller minor demons were busy scurrying about performing a form of embalming process around the corpse of the Demon King. The King of the Demons was watching its own corpse being embalmed in a pale form beside it.

"You've come for me again. Not once, but twice. Well, should we say three times in total to be technical? It's not only surprising, but it's also almost endearing." Demon King Hesthnius Max didn't appear all that surprised at seeing Sungchul here. Instead, he had a relatively leisurely smile as though he was greeting an old friend with both arms open to meet him.

"Have you familiarized yourself with some magic? Even if you were some genius in magic, isn't it too brash to come so soon before

463

even a year had passed? It's not like you're coming here to show off your strength."

Hesthnius' voice and pale face showed confidence. Confidence that was rooted in his assurance that Sungchul would never be able to harm him.

"But, you're still quite a foolish human. You would stubbornly choose to rush in by yourself in order to resolve the Calamity despite all the hate you receive from the other humans. Recently, I have been researching human slang, and have happened to come across the word 'subsisting'. Immediately, your face came to mind."

"..."

Sungchul did not respond. Instead, he pulled out a single scroll. It was the Harmageddon scroll he had received from Vestiare. Hesthunius' eyes grew wide.

"T-that is…?!"

A powerful mage at the caliber of Hesthnius could recognize such a powerful spell at first glance. The destructive aura that eerily flowed around the unsettling scroll made the Demon King's eyes dizzy.

Seventh Circle… No, is it a scroll containing an Eighth Circle spell? Where did he… This shouldn't be possible with human techniques!

All sign of leisure vanished from the Demon King's face.

"Could it be… the Seven Heroes? Did those bastards coerce you with that?"

"How did you know that?" Sungchul spoke with a faint smile lingering on his lips.

"You can tell when one becomes a Calamity. Those bastards next in line are aching to be released in this world even a second faster. You know why?"

"..."

"It's because we're all tied together on a single string. According to the Divine Authority that is referred to as a Calamity, that is."

Hesthnius said this in an audibly pleasing tone while being wary of Sungchul's mood. As far as he could see, Sungchul didn't seem to have any intention to fight immediately. There was room for negotiation. The tactful Demon King continued to wag his silver tongue.

"However, it's a fool's errand to trust those Seven Heroes. An errand for true fools indeed. Do you know what their true objective is?"

"Fair reward." What Sungchul had said wasn't far from the few records that remained of those times long past. According to legend, the Seven Heroes sought out compensation after they saved the world from the Calamity, but the world that they saved did not grant them the prize they demanded. The Seven Heroes bitterly removed themselves from history. They vowed to get what they were owed.

The Demon King shook his head. "Wrong. They only want one thing," and he smirked as he continued, "the death of all mankind, and the subsequent end of an era."

"So drastic."

"That's right. It is drastic. Especially compared to the good-natured Devils." The Demon King's hands waved rhythmically in the air like the baton of an orchestral conductor, and when he did so, an illusion of a man appeared between Sungchul and him. It was a man veiled in a bandana who radiated a mystical aura while he carried a two-handed sword the size of a small boy.

The Demon King spoke again. "You might not know, as it must have been about 20 years ago. There was another who challenged me by his lonesome. He was very powerful."

Sungchul looked at the illusion created by the Demon King once again.

"At that time, I told him the same story that I'm telling you now. I told him what would happen once I died, and what kind of pitiful end would befall the fragile mortals."

"And in the end?"

The Demon King's story caught Sungchul's interest, and the Demon King smirked as he continued his story. "He simply returned right then and there. Why? Because I was speaking the truth."

"Who is this man that you're speaking of?" As Sungchul continued to show interest, the Demon King smiled a smug smile in his heart as he hatched his scheme.

"I could reveal his identity if you want, but nothing comes for free. Hand over the scroll."

"This?" Sungchul shook the Harmageddon scroll in front of him.

"That's right. Hand that over, and in one year's time I shall reveal his identity to you."

It was complete nonsense. Laughter exploded out of Sungchul's mouth. *All these devils are the same.*

Sungchul pretended to fall into thought and turned around.

THUD

The scroll fell to the floor, and the Demon King's eyes shined bright. *Kekeke.... Got him.*

He cried out in triumph in his mind as he thought, *Once a year passes, my new strengthened form will be born. Once that's complete, I won't suffer so easily to this monster as I have in the past at the very least.*

He confirmed in his mind that Sungchul had fallen for his scheme, but the one who had been truly fooled was him.

Sungchul was muttering something with his back turned. Not something he had memorized, but a chant that had been accepted into his very being. Sungchul's consciousness was getting a crystal-clear visitation of the ever-blinding Primordial light's memories that he had had a glimpse of once upon a time. The only source of light in the endless vastness of space, it alone shined and bathed the universe with luminescence; giving birth to or bringing an end to life with its light. Sungchul's aria began in earnest.

"Hey, Destroyer. M-mind if I ask what you're doing over there?" Hesthnius Max detected the terrifying magical aura rising from Sungchul's body much too late. A complex magical formation bloomed around Sungchul, whose back was still turned, like a flower. The Demon King quickly caught on that the magic in question was one from the school of Cosmomancy.

I-is he planning on using Meteor?! When did the bastard learn that?

Sungchul turned around and scattered whatever he held in his hand toward the Demon King. It was some powder radiating in black. It was a black crystal formed from Alchemy. It wasn't of the highest quality, but the area covered by the black crystal would greatly enhance the potency of Sungchul's spells.

"L-let's not do this!" The Demon King waved his hands frantically as he backed off. But in spite of what he said, he began to scan the sky.

Something like a meteor only needs to be dodged.

Unfortunately, Sungchul wasn't preparing Meteor. He was about to complete his aria while staring directly at the Demon King. Sungchul could feel the endless energy of a star within his body.

An old staff appeared from his Soul Storage. The moment Sungchul gripped the staff, he had a brief moment of nostalgia, and then the aria was complete. He then pointed the staff toward the Demon King while holding Fal Garaz in the other hand.

Star Light.

The moment the activation word was spoken in his mind, a large beam of light was fired from the end of his staff.

"F-force Reversal!!!"

The beam of light enveloped the ethereal Demon King whole. His ethereal body began to burn. No, "disintegrate" would be the more apt term. Star Light destroyed over half of the Demon King's form, but the target was the Devil of Devils that reigned over all Demons.

"ARRRRRRGH!!! RRRRRGH!!!"

He endured the single cast of Star Light in the end.

"I can't die... Do you know how I rose to this spot?!" A powerful will to survive unlike any other burned brightly in the Demon King's eyes. He performed recovery magic even in the midst of being disintegrated to reconstruct his ethereal form and prevent it from being torn apart. However, his opponent was not an ordinary mage.

[Echo x1]

As the first beam of light was beginning to fade, another beam of light poured out from the staff and overwhelmed the Demon King that was already in the middle of being torn apart. Taking two hits of Starlight was a bit much, even for the Demon King.

"K....KYAAAAAAK!!!!"

The rate of his recovery could no longer keep up with the rate of destruction, and the Demon King was eventually eradicated by the light. He was erased without even a chance to make an explicative.

"..."

Sungchul was overcome with extreme lethargy and dizziness after the light faded. All of the mana within him had been sucked away as he cast Star Light, a 7th circle magic, and its echo. Sungchul pulled Bertelgia from his Soul Storage.

"You said it'd be quick!" Bertelgia who had been stabbing herself into Sungchul with the corner of her covers stopped to take a look at her surroundings and asked in a daze, "Huh? Where's this?"

Sungchul pointed toward the corpse of the Demon King seated on the massive throne and answered her question, "It's the Demon King's Palace."

"H-hiiii...! Really? And the Demon King? Is... is he dead?"

Sungchul nodded in reply. In the next moment, the Demon King's corpse began to turn to dust. As the ethereal form had been destroyed, the physical form that was bound to it was being erased as well.

Finally, the First Calamity is resolved.

There was a rare hint of sentiment lingering in Sungchul's eyes. However, he was struck by a powerful force that caught his breath in his throat. Something was beginning to unfold. Bright letters soon filled Sungchul's sight.

[You have resolved the First Calamity.]

[You have obtained the Blessing "One who stands against Calamity."]

[The gazes of gods have turned toward you.]

Reward:

1. Blessing "One who stands against Calamity"
2. Fragment of Calamity

Something fell in front of Sungchul. It was a flat piece of rock that reflected a deep green light and gave off a cold feeling. It looked like something of no value at first glance, but Sungchul could not take his eyes off of the piece of rock. His hand reached toward the rock unconsciously. The fragment felt rough to the touch and was cold as ice. It was no ordinary object.

Sungchul tried to inspect the object, but his Eye of Truth did not work on the object.

Does that mean it exceeds Legend grade? That might mean this fragment's grade is Mythic.

Putting it into his Storage appeared to be the right move for now, but his Soul Storage could not accept the fragment. As the fragment wasn't able to enter the Storage, it fell to the ground. Surprise crossed Sungchul's eyes. *I seem to have gotten my hands on something unbelievable.*

However, the surprise didn't end there. Something like a black smoke began to rise from the Demon King's corpse. It was no simple smoke. Each individual particle that formed the smoke was filled with an evil aura composed of malice and futility.

Sungchul had seen nothing like it before. He had seen something similar when he killed Minamoto and Aquiroa, but it couldn't be compared with the gigantic smoke interspersed with pure malice that appeared before him now. Sungchul did not know what it was, but he could make a guess.

I-is that… the power that drives the Calamity?

The moment he had internalized that truth, black words obstructed his sight.

[Witness of Calamity]

[You have seen the true essence of Calamity.]

[You who have seen the authority of god have taken a step into the secret of the World.]

[The rewards for being a witness correspond to Intuition.]

Reward:
Magic Power +88
Intuition +88
Magic Resistance +88

He had gained an incredible boon in stats simply by witnessing the flow of Calamity. Sungchul felt like he could understand why the Followers of Calamity wanted the progression of Calamity so desperately.

"What… in the world. These stats… why are they giving so much?" Bertelgia must have seen a similar message. Watching the progression of Calamity was such an event. Simply witnessing it meant receiving a portion of a god's authority. Mages didn't simply become Followers of Calamity out of madness.

The black smoke reconstructed itself to a spherical form near the ceiling and then appeared to move about freely for a while. Soon, the black sphere left the Demon King's Palace as though it had its own will.

Sungchul hurried after the black sphere. However, a look of shock spread across his eyes the moment he stepped out of the Palace.

"?!"

Every last one of the tens of thousands of demonic forces that had been assembled in the vicinity of the Demon King's Palace had perished.

How did this happen?

Sungchul had killed some of them with his own hands, but the vast majority of them had been still alive. However, every single last one of them was now dead. The black sphere was draining the corpses of each demon of the dark and evil aura. Each one of them to the last drop.

Sungchul could only stand and watch this scene unfold. The moment he thought to do something against the sphere, the thought evaporated like ethanol. The inexplicable exhaustion and lethargy were restraining him. A single thought lingered in his mind instead.

As he was restrained by the chains of exhaustion, the black sphere had drained the dark aura from the countless demons to expand to a massive size. It had been the size of an adult's head originally, but now it was the size of a castle. The sphere that had now drained the essence of every demon to its heart's content rose high into the sky before splitting into seven pieces and flying southerly at high speeds. Sungchul could determine what that had meant.

The Seven Heroes. Is this the start of their Calamity?

As to support that theory, whispers that seemed to come from right beside him dug into his ears.

"Don't get cocky 'cause you took care of that Demon King."

"Let's face off fair and square! Delightful warrior!"

"Such a liar. To not use that scroll. But it doesn't change anything."

"… Don't like."

"Kekeke… I wonder how your soul tastes?"

"Just you wait, you dimwit."

"…"

They were the voices of the Seven Heroes. Their voices grew distant until they faded away completely leaving behind their dry laughter.

"…"

471

Sungchul looked toward the direction that the black fragments had flown with indifferent eyes as he tightened his grip on Fal Garaz

—

Tower of Recluse.

There was an incident at the holiest fortification in charge of the storage and protection of the Scripture of Calamity. The caretakers observed that the first prophecy written on the scripture, the prophecy pertaining to the Demon King, disappeared as if it had gone up in flames, and alerted the one in charge of the Tower, Porphyrius. Porphyrius's eyes were in shock as he looked at the Scripture of Calamity.

"Something unthinkable occurred. The First Calamity... has come to an end!"

The next prophecy after the now-burnt Demon King prophecy was reported to have absorbed a dark and ominous smoke-like aura the following day.

The prophecy that had now been set in motion by the power of Calamity read as follows:

[The betrayed, the false heroes of the past who then left a prophecy, shall return to the land. They shall demand what they were denied, what was rightfully theirs. The world shall know when seven ominous stars shine in the skies.]

Afterword

Oppatranslations

We hope that you enjoyed the book and our translation. It had taken us far more time than we had thought it would to finish this, but we are proud of the result. And worry not, work on book 3 is underway.

You can reach us at oppatranslations@gmail.com

[1] [신 파주]{New Paju} - A military city created to defend Seoul. The context is, this region is under threat by North Korea and is always on alert for an invasion from the North. Meaning this is how the Iron Blood Knights felt this village was like (sharing borders with Demon Realm).

[2] Three Strategies of Huang Shigong - In China, there are collections of works referred to as "the Seven Military Classics". Sun Tsu's art of war is a part of this collection. Two of the contributors in these seven lists are from the Three Kingdoms era, including 'Methods of Sima Yi', and 'Three Strategies of Huang Shigong' attributed to Zhuge Liang. Huang Shigong actually means "Duke of Yellow Rock". The Strategy reads as follows:

1) A leader must be both benevolent and awe-inspiring, according to what is appropriate.

2) Act according to the actual circumstances. Avoid responses which are based on imagination, memories of the past, or habits acquired in other circumstances. You must rely only on observation and perception and be willing to modify plans at any time.

3) Employ only the capable. This requires an accurate insight into others.

[3] Empty Fort Strategy - One of China's 36 stratagems (an informal oral tradition of loosely collected strategies), of which the strategies are often attributed to Sun Tsu or Zhuge Liang, but neither are actually real authors. They're just used as examples to exemplify a certain use of the strategy.

Empty Fort typically is a way to lure enemies in as a form of deception. Zhuge Liang opened the gates to his castle, had no soldiers or generals defend the wall, and had people sweep the open gatehouse as he drank tea and played music for the approaching army. Because Zhuge Liang had never gambled or did anything risky in the past, Sima Yi believed this was a trap of some sort and retreated, but in truth, Zhuge Liang had not even a thousand men defending this supply base. He remarks, this is not a strategy he could ever repeat in the future.

475

[4] Jeotgal - Jeotgal is a type of korean preserved food made with aquatic creatures (fish or oysters etc). Typically, the food would be salted, but that's where the commonalities end. Some Jeotgal are made into powder, others are made into wet paste. Some add spices where others only use salt. Although it could be eaten as is, it's also often used as flavorant to other foods, most famous being shrimp Jeotgal being used in many kimchi recipes.

[5] Izime - Japanese word describing a group picking on one person. A 'group vs individual' bullying.

[6] Hikikomori – Reclusive adolescents or adults who withdraw from social life, often seeking extreme degrees of isolation and confinement.

[7] Heel - In professional wrestling, a heel is a wrestler who is villainous or a "bad guy", who is booked (scripted) to be in the position of being an antagonist.

Printed in Great Britain
by Amazon

11358985R00284